I,
Joseph
of
Arimathea

I, JOSEPH OF ARIMATHEA

A Story of Jesus, His Resurrection, and the Aftermath

A DOCUMENTED HISTORICAL NOVEL

✠

FRANK C. TRIBBE

Blue Dolphin Publishing

Copyright © 2000 Frank C. Tribbe

Published by Blue Dolphin Publishing, Inc.
P.O. Box 8, Nevada City, CA 95959
Orders: 1-800-643-0765
Web: www.bluedolphinpublishing.com

ISBN: 978-1-57733-061-5 paperback
ISBN: 978-1-57733-321-0 e-book

Library of Congress Cataloging-in-Publication Data

Tribbe, Frank C.
    I, Joseph of Arimathea : a story of Jesus, His Resurrection, and the
aftermath / Frank C. Tribbe.
       p. cm.
    Includes bibliographical references.
    ISBN 1-57733-061-7
    1. Joseph, of Arimathea, Saint–Fiction. 2. Bible. N.T.–History of
Biblical events–Fiction. 3. Christian saints–England–Glastonbury–
Fiction. 4. Great Britain–Church history–To 449–Fiction. 5. Glastonbury
(England)–Fiction. 6. Jesus Christ–Fiction. I. Title.

PS3570.R452 I12
813'.54–dc21

                                                                99-058806

Printed in the United States of America

10   9   8   7   6   5   4   3   2

Fiction is not necessarily different from truth—it is different from fact.

But there are also many other things which Jesus did; were every one of them to be written, I suppose that the world itself could not contain the books that would be written.

—John 21:25

Arnold Toynbee wrote: "Plato taught me, by example, not to be ashamed of using my imagination as well as my intellect. He taught me, when, in a mental voyage, I found myself at the upper limit of the atmosphere accessible to the Reason, not to hesitate to let my imagination carry me on up into the stratosphere on the wings of myth."

If scholars today are fragmenting the Gospel and are making the Faith in Christ an interesting literary or historical problem, is it then blameworthy if somebody wants to give Faith a new life by religious creativity?... Perhaps some unknown authors will create something new about Jesus.... The time of myths is not ended, and perhaps in the future people will be filled with a new Jesus vision.

—Per Beskow, *Strange Tales About Jesus,* Fortress, 1983

✠

Table of Contents

✠

Foreword

ANYONE FAMILIAR WITH the Gospel accounts of Jesus will find great edification in this "rest of the story." The events in the tomb on the first Easter morning, the experiences of the three Marys and of those who met Jesus on the road to Emmaus, the thoughts of "doubting" Thomas: all are recorded here in plausible and finely detailed reconstructions.

Nearly the entire narrative has been founded on Biblical and extra-Biblical historical documents. The author has taken the stance that the so-called apocryphal New Testament texts may contain factual information about familiar New Testament personages. Some of these texts are, after all, nearly as old as the Bible, deriving as they do from the 2nd - 4th centuries. Whatever the reasons for their exclusion from the canon of the New Testament by the early Church Fathers, they do nevertheless represent the knowledge or misconceptions of literate 2nd - 4th century people. That there is much to be gained from the author's use of these documents is evident from the astounding *richesse* of biographical data found in the present book.

The extensive role attributed to Joseph of Arimathea in the period after the crucifixion of Jesus of Nazareth flows out of one of these apocrypha, the Gospel of Nicodemus, datable to the 4th century. Joseph's official position permitted him to approach Pilate and make all arrangements for the disposal of Jesus' body, for which he provided burial linens and tomb. The Gospel accounts of Easter weekend themselves point to his activity while the other disciples retreated in fear. On the face of what we have, therefore, there is a presumption of truth in the extensive reportage of Joseph's life in the apocryphon of Nicodemus. Or are we to believe that Joseph "came out of the closet" as to his Jesus-leanings suddenly and decisively, as the Gospel narratives imply, and then just as suddenly returned to business-as-usual?

As a second major structural element of the narrative, the book describes the survival and earliest history of a mysterious object still thought to be the most precious relic of Jesus: the shroud which wrapped his dead body and which was marked with his actual "photographic" image. The shroud's non-Biblical but entirely likely survival must, of course, be imaginatively recreated. The author does this, basing his account on the best scholarship and historical records pertaining to the Shroud of Turin, a subject on which he is a working expert. The Turin Shroud was, perhaps, the primary impetus behind Tribbe's engaging novel.

At least two other major plot strands are interwoven by Tribbe: the "lost years" of Jesus before he entered upon his public ministry (interpreted here as spent under the tutelage of his "uncle" Joseph) and the thesis that Joseph of Arimathea was the "Apostle of Britain," introducing Christianity to the West before ever it reached Rome. While certain authors propose the latter theory quite seriously, along with the notion that the Druidic Celts of Britain were originally the Ten Lost Tribes of Israel, Joseph's role should be enjoyed as good historical fiction, though floated upon a thin bed of fact.

The reader should also be aware that Joseph as an entrepreneur in tin has no basis in any ancient record. The Latin epithet *decurio,* sometimes used to describe him, simply means he was a member of the ten-man town council in Arimathea or something like a sergeant in the army. His relationship to Jesus as great-uncle cannot be based on a Talmudic passage, since the Old Testament Talmud could hardly be expected to address the question of Jesus' immediate ancestry.

The author displays an amazing grasp of the accoutrements of daily life in the first century. His thorough descriptions of travel in Roman times, with the details of preparation, navigation, geographical places and their modern equivalents, and prevailing winds, is a case in point. He presents accurate or plausible reconstructions of the Judaeo-Roman "postal system," coinage, weights and measures, business practices, languages, reckoning of time, literacy and education, and above all, ancient metallurgy. His saga conveys the reader from the Tigris to the Thames, encompassing the entire Roman world. By means of truly impressive scholarly research, Frank Tribbe transports the reader vividly into the ambience of Tiberius, Claudius, Nero, Peter and Paul, and of Jesus himself.

Daniel C. Scavone

Dr. Scavone is professor emeritus of ancient history at the University of Southern Indiana, is the author of *The Shroud of Turin* (Greenhaven Press, 1989) and numerous professional papers on the subject of the Shroud of Turin.

For the past decade, many active in Shroud research have considered Dr. Scavone to be the premier Shroud historian. I have used his findings in several situations in this volume. However, in one or two instances my extrapolation from his facts has resulted in projected activities and conclusions different from his.

—the Author

✝

Preface

W̲HAT DO I MEAN by labeling this a "documented historical novel"? It is much more than a story partially based on fact. All significant events and theses contained herein are Biblically and historically factual, and are supported by reference notes and citation of sources. Whenever significant events are uncertain, the best professional opinion is cited, and usually followed. All major characters and most minor ones are historically real.

I provide a fictional elaboration of Biblical events without altering them or contradicting Bible statements and, of course, many minor events and all conversations are fictional. However, all of the geographic, natural and physical background, the peoples and their practices, ideas and social attitudes of the times are as accurate as present-day specialized knowledge can make them. Because this is a novel, I have paraphrased passages of the Scriptures rather than quote any particular Bible version.

The idea, and to a degree the style, of Professor Paul L. Maier in writing his historical novels, *Pontius Pilate* and *Flames of Rome* (already classics in the field), have served me as pattern to emulate. Additionally, I have followed the lead of that giant (both as preacher and author), Harry Emerson Fosdick, who, in his landmark biography, *The Man from Nazareth* (Harper & Brothers, 1949), so wisely observed the risk of presenting an "interpreted Jesus" as the Gospels have done, and the near-impossibility of attempting to "leap into the self-consciousness of Jesus,... and to recover the uninterpreted personality"—even if he were *only* a genius. Invaluable as modern contributions have been, Fosdick underscores the dilemma of attempting to harmonize diverse interpretations of Jesus, for

example, "between Ernest Renan's sentimentalist, Bouck White's social
revolutionist, Bruce Barton's expert in salesmanship, Schweitzer's apoca-
lypticist, Thomas N. Carver's economist, Binet-Sangle's paranoiac, and
Middleton Murray's man of genius."

What is far closer to the possible and less subjective, Fosdick concluded,
is an indirect approach of viewing Jesus through the eyes of his contem-
poraries, friendly and hostile—What were the customary ways of feeling
and thinking, the biases, the convictions, the prejudices, the personal and
social needs of, for instance, the Herodians, the Zealots, the Sadducees,
the Essenes, the Bet Hillel Pharisees, the Bet Shammai Pharisees, Temple
functionaries and flunkies, merchants, shepherds, tradesmen, fishermen,
tax collectors, lepers, harlots, beggars, women, disciples, Roman officials,
soldiers? Those attitudes and viewpoints are significantly available to us,
and I will attempt, to a major extent, to utilize them; nevertheless, in the
setting of a novel, Jesus will of necessity respond in conversation as the
Jesus I have "interpreted."

Joseph of Arimathea may have been one of the more important
personages during the beginnings of Christianity. But, because the New
Testament says very little about Joseph, and secular history nothing at
all, most people assume that we know nothing more of him. This is far
from the truth. Archaeology and apocryphal writings tell us a fair amount
about Joseph, but we are unsure how reliable they are. However, it is in
Christian tradition and legend that we find such a richness about this
scion of Arimathean stock that it is an embarrassment to the historian
and a handicap to the novelist. Trying to be both, in this volume, I have
been greatly frustrated. Joseph was a real and important and well-known
person, both within Jesus' movement, "The Way," and in the secular world
of government and business.

Moreover, the probable full story of the Holy Shroud, which we know
today as the Shroud of Turin, is so strongly implied by historical traces and
by apocryphal documents of the early Church that the composite drama
almost tells itself. Those strong historical, scientific and religious inferences justify belief that this Shroud—this image-marked linen—is indeed
the very cloth in which Jesus of Galilee was wrapped in the tomb—and
this, despite the *apparent* conclusions that emerged from the badly-flawed
carbon-dating exercise of 1988 (see last Appendix). Nevertheless, such
implications and inferences do not compel acceptance of belief in the
Shroud, and *clearly* science cannot and will never *prove* this to have been the
Shroud of Jesus—a small leap of faith will always be necessary. Yet, some
two dozen kinds of scientific and historical data are fully consistent with
that conclusion (see my book, *Portrait of Jesus?*, 1983).

Records of the life of Jesus, of the first half-century of Christianity, and of the story of the Holy Shroud, together present us a series of not-quite-connected events and situations. To bridge or fill-in the gaps, to clarify the background and ambiguities and uncertainties, and to trace movements may never be possible based on hard data. And so, I will tell the story as it may have been, completely consistent with the Bible and history—but I will tell it as a novel, so that I can make those connections and clarify the ambiguities and uncertainties. I will trace the Shroud's movements and those of certain Christians, and hope to do so plausibly.

The key situations, especially from A.D. 33 to 83, that need elucidation, are these:

(1) The Bible tells us that a cloth was purchased, was used to wrap Jesus' body, was probably seen Easter morning by Peter and John, but was not taken by them; nor was the discovery of images on it nor the saving of it remarked upon thereafter. Nevertheless, the Shroud of Turin exists today, and its images are totally consistent with every facet of the passion of Jesus, and the best efforts of skeptical scientists cannot suggest a natural or man-made explanation for the making of the images nor for its many scientific enigmas.

(2) The city-state of Edessa, 180 miles northeast of Syrian Antioch, in the empire of Parthia, beyond the reach of Roman and Sanhedrin authority, was closely linked with Christianity for nine hundred years (ca. A.D. 33 to 944) by its possession of "The Face"—to which Christian pilgrims were drawn from all over the Mediterranean world. Church historian, Eusebius, reported as fact (but was it a legend?) the Edessan king's relationship with Jesus and the beginnings of Christianity there, weeks after the Resurrection; unknown Christian writers in Egypt and artists in the Sinai knew some of this Face of Jesus as a powerful healing relic; some modern historians identify it as the folded Shroud.

(3) Joseph of Arimathea, previously a secret disciple, apocryphally linked as a relative of Mary, mother of Jesus, did act as family representative to receive Jesus' body and bury it in his own tomb. For such action he presumably was imprisoned by the Sanhedrin but miraculously escaped and fled the country. As a businessman/importer for many years, legend links him to the tin mines of Cornwall, England, which was the Near East's principal source of tin, vital for the making of bronze. There, he presumably lived out his life in exile.

(4) Claudius, the Roman emperor (A.D. 41-54), ordered the invasion of Britain in A.D. 43; a few modern and ancient writers suggest that one of his motives may have been to exterminate Christianity. He briefly took field command of his armies shortly after they invaded England. Later,

through treachery, they captured King Caradoc (whom the Romans called Caractacus) and his family. Some of them lived out their lives as hostages in Rome, but Caradoc was permitted to address (and charm) the Roman Senate, and he was then given a palace and a huge estate in Rome, where the family lived with honor and complete freedom. Even though they were Christians, Claudius then arranged three marriages for the family members with his own and other prominent Roman families. That home was the Roman center of Christianity when Paul and Peter later arrived, and lived there. Linus, Caradoc's son, was made Bishop of Rome, about A.D. 66; he was invested by Paul after Peter's death..

(5) The best and latest Church history has no direct evidence of the very beginnings of Christianity in Rome. It did reach Rome in the early forties, but is connected to no known missionary, disciple or apostle until the early sixties when Peter and Paul arrived.

Was Joseph of Arimathea really so important in early Christianity and so much involved? Someone was! No one of Jesus' family or disciples questioned the propriety of Joseph's action in burying Jesus—nor did Pilate nor the Sanhedrin. Someone or some family or some company brought Cornwall tin from Britain to the Near East in the first century, and much earlier. Somehow Christianity got a foothold in England very early, especially among the ruling families and religious leaders—and clearly, those British hostages became Christian leaders in Rome. Joseph could have been that catalyst—why not?

The story of the burial shroud of Jesus of Galilee following his Resurrection, as recounted in the following pages, is a chronology some historians accept as possible—this author considers it probable.

To tell this story comprehensively, I present a blend of the historical strand, the Biblical strand, the apocryphal strand, and a fictional strand, to provide a composite story. This is the way it may have been. Each reader will have to decide for himself just how plausible is this telling of the story.

Frank C. Tribbe,
Valley of the Shenandoah, Virginia

✠

Acknowledgments

MY DEEP APPRECIATION for advice and assistance on research of a most complex sort goes to Geoffrey Ashe, Barbara Bunce, James H. Charlesworth, Sister Mary Fidelia Chmiel, Noel Currer-Briggs, Albert R. Dreisbach, Jr., Martin Ebon, Sister Mary Germaine (Findlay), Norma L. Goodrich, Kenneth Thurston Hurst, Paul L. Maier, Rex Morgan, Michael Perry, Leslie Price, Daniel C. Scavone, Ed Schaffer, Robert L. Sherfy, and Nick Whitmer.

And for the encouragement that kept me persisting, my heartfelt thanks go to my late wife Audre, to Alva, Bill, Alice and Tom, and above all, to my present wife, Florence.

The Jewish Homeland

artwork by Mary Lu Lewis

Jerusalem, ca. A.D. *33*

1. Antonia Fortress (res. of Pilate)
2. The Temple
3. Res., Joseph of Arimathea
4. Res., Nicodemus
5. Palace, Caiaphas
6. Palace of Herod
7. Palace of the Tombs
8. Golgotha

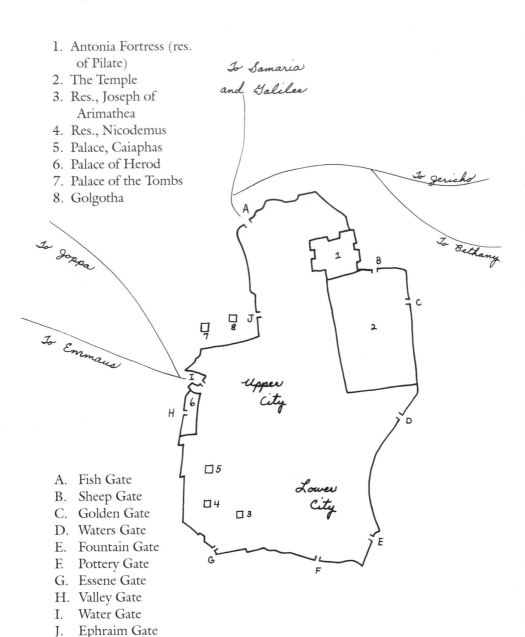

A. Fish Gate
B. Sheep Gate
C. Golden Gate
D. Waters Gate
E. Fountain Gate
F. Pottery Gate
G. Essene Gate
H. Valley Gate
I. Water Gate
J. Ephraim Gate

artwork by Mary Lu Lewis

Eastern Mediterranean and Near East

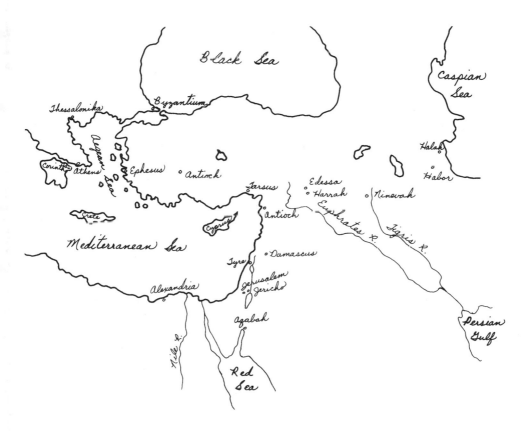

artwork by Mary Lu Lewis

The Routes to Britain

artwork by Mary Lu Lewis

Metal Ore in Ancient Britain

Tribal Britain, A.D. 1 to 50

artwork by Mary Lu Lewis

City Map of Edessa

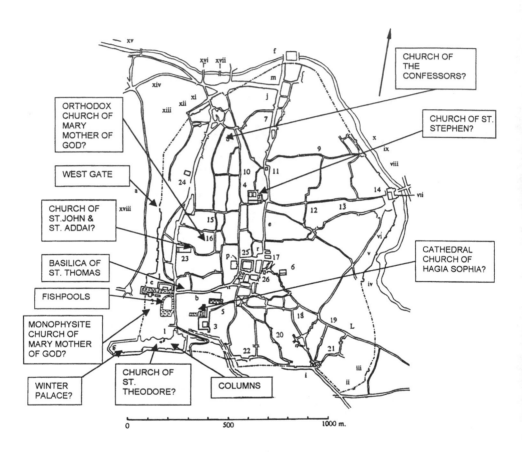

CHURCH OF THE CONFESSORS?

CHURCH OF ST. STEPHEN?

ORTHODOX CHURCH OF MARY MOTHER OF GOD?

WEST GATE

CHURCH OF ST. JOHN & ST. ADDAI?

CATHEDRAL CHURCH OF HAGIA SOPHIA?

BASILICA OF ST. THOMAS

FISHPOOLS

MONOPHYSITE CHURCH OF MARY MOTHER OF GOD?

WINTER PALACE?

CHURCH OF ST. THEODORE?

COLUMNS

0   500   1000 m.

City map of Edessa, Parthia, mid-first century A.D., based on data of J.B. Segal *(Edessa, The Blessed City)*; courtesy of Ian Wilson.

Shows eight Christian churches, and the famous West Gate, above which the hidden Shroud was found in A.D. 525 after the disastrous flood of the River Daisan. The Shroud of Jesus (Shroud of Turin?), sometimes known as the Mandylion or Face of Edessa or "achiropoietos" (not made by human hands), was reportedly kept in the Hagia Sophia from A.D. 33 to 57.

Part I

Resurrection and the Shroud

SIMON BAR JONAH: the fisherman-brother of Andrew. Andrew brought Simon to meet Jesus, who later renamed Simon, as Peter (Disciple).

MATTHEW (*also called* **Matthew-Levi**): a former Roman tax-collector in Capernaum, who became one of the Twelve disciples of Jesus. His parents, Mary-Heli and Cleopas-Alphaeus, may have moved from Capernaum to Emmaus at about the time their wayward sons became followers of The Way.

JAMES *(brother of Matthew)* was probably called "The Less" because of his short stature; he may have been an active Zealot before his call to serve with Jesus' Twelve. Matthew and James were first cousins of Jesus.

JUDAS BAR SIMON *(sometimes called* **Iscariot**): one of the Twelve, and ultimate betrayer of Jesus. Apocryphal records suggest his father was brother to the High Priest, Caiaphas; he may have had political employment and lived in Tiberias on the shore of Lake Galilee, where Herod's summer palace was located.

JOHN BAR ZEBEDEE: brother of James and Disciple of Jesus. The brothers were called "sons of thunder" by Jesus, possibly because of their volatile tempers and bombastic natures. They were cousins of Jesus twice-removed (their mother and Jesus' mother were first cousins).

JAMES BAR ZEBEDEE: one of the Twelve; sometimes called James the Greater, probably because of his size. Both were fishermen who worked for their father's fishing fleet operation, on Galilee.

MARY, *widow of Simeon,* was mother of young Mark who later became an Evangelist and was sometimes called John Mark. The family probably came from the island of Cyprus. Her brothers were Aristobulus and Barnabus.

PONTIUS PILATE: Roman governor of Judea. He was subordinate to the Legate of Syria in Antioch. He had been a Tribune of the Praetorian Guard in Rome; his ancestral family, known as the Pontii with its seat at Caudium (formerly, Samnium), were of noble blood but were demoted to the Equestrian Order after losing their last battle with Rome. His wife, Claudia Procula, was stepdaughter of Emperor Tiberius.

MARY OF MAGDALA *(also called* **Mary Magdalene**): youngest sister of Lazarus of Bethany; she had lived for a period at the palace and extensive property in the town of Magdala on the shore of Lake Galilee, which premises she had inherited at the death of their father.

MARY-HELI: youngest sister of Mary (mother of Jesus) and wife of Cleopas Alphaeus, who was half-brother of Joseph bar Jacob (who married Mary). When they moved from Capernaum to Emmaus to care for Cleopas' widowed father, Heli, Mary was often identified by the name, Mary Heli. Mary Heli and Cleopas were parents of Disciples Matthew and James the Less, and of Mary Cleopas, and Symeon.

LAZARUS BAR JOSIAH: brother of Martha and Mary, resided in-Bethany, where Jesus often stayed when in Judea.

CAIAPHAS: High Priest and son-in-law of Annas, the former High Priest.

CHAPTER TWO:

MARTHA BAT JOSIAH: sister of Lazarus and of Mary of Magdala; oldest child of Rachel and Josiah, residing in Bethany.

SALOME: widow of Zebedee, fishing fleet operator of Capernaum; their sons, James and John, were of the Twelve disciples.

CHAPTER THREE:

JESUS OF GALILEE: born in Bethlehem, raised in Nazareth, resided in Capernaum during his ministry. His teachings of The Way came to be known as Christianity.

MARY BAT JOACHIM: daughter of Joachim and Anna, wife of Joseph bar Jacob, and mother of Jesus.

JAMES, SIMON and JUDE: brothers of Jesus; another brother was Joses.

CHAPTER FOUR:

HOSEA: (fictional) a servant of Joseph of Arimathea.

JOHN BAR ZECHARIAH: John the Baptist. Elizabeth, his mother, was first cousin of Mary, Jesus' mother.

CHAPTER FIVE:

CLEOPAS: one of the Seventy disciples of Jesus. He was sometimes called Cleopas-Alphaeus, though *both* names are Hellenizations of the same Hebrew name, Halphai. This oddity may stem from the fact that his father was named Heli—a probable Greek name. His mother, Timna, of Jewish blood, married Heli after the death of her first husband, Jacob, with whom she had had six sons, the third being Joseph who married Mary bat Joachim, mother of Jesus.

CHAPTER SIX:

THADDAEUS OF PANEAS: one of the Seventy disciples; (fictionally conscripted as) an employee of Joseph of Arimathea.

ANNAS: the former High Priest. Although deposed by Pilate in favor of his son-in-law, Caiaphas, he obviously was still honored much like having a title of High Priest Emeritus. Prior to the advent of Roman rule, the office of High Priest had passed at death to eldest surviving son.

KING ABGAR V: of Edessa, capital city of Osroene, the westernmost province (satrap) of Parthia. Abgar's title was "Toparch." He was born 13 B.C., and ruled 4 B.C. to A.D. 7 and A.D. 13 to 50.

HAGGAI: (fictional) Jewish historian.

ANANIAS: Edessan diplomat.

MIRIAM: (fictional) wife of Thaddaeus.

TOBIAS BAR TOBIAS: host of Thaddaeus in Edessa, according to Church historian, Eusebius; (fictionally conscripted as) representative of Joseph of Arimathea.

CHAPTER SEVEN:

THOMAS: of the Twelve. He was raised in Galilee, though his original and later home probably was in Lydda of Judea. After the Resurrection, Thomas became responsible on behalf of the Twelve for the missionary effort in countries of the East, including Parthia, Babylonia, Armenia, Persia and India.

BARNABUS (Nathaniel bar-Nabus): A disciple of the Seventy; born in Cana of Galilee but living on the island of Cyprus.

STEPHEN: one of the Seventy, and one of the first deacons of The Way. He was born in Caesarea and raised in Tiberias of Galilee.

CHAPTER EIGHT:

FLAVIUS RUBRIUS: (fictional) deputy governor of Judea, under Pontius Pilate.

ELIAS BAR JACOB: (fictional) an artist and employee of Joseph of Arimathea.

CHAPTER NINE:

SAMSON: (fictional) servant of Nicodemus.

GAMALIEL: grandson of the illustrious Hillel, who had established the (to be) enduring branch of Pharisaic Judaism. Gamaliel was a chief priest and the only one to whom the Great Sanhedrin had given the title of Rabban (only six other persons were later given this title). Apocryphal accounts indicate the possibility he could have been a secret follower of Jesus.

SIRACH: a chief priest of the Great Sanhedrin and husband of Seraphia, who was a follower of Jesus; she was a cousin of John the Baptist.

REUBEN: (fictional) servant of Joseph of Arimathea.

RACHEL: (fictional) servant of Joseph of Arimathea.

RUFUS RUBICUS: (fictional) a Roman soldier stationed at the Antonia fort in Jerusalem, and who has a Jewish mother; he is a cousin of Rachel.

CHAPTER TEN:

ZACCHAEUS: a rich tax collector in Jericho who had become a follower of Jesus.

PETRONIUS: a Roman centurion and secret follower of Jesus, according to apocryphal sources.

SILVANUS: probably a Roman soldier or official, but secretly a follower of Jesus, and became one of the Seventy. He later became a missionary for The Way.

PHILIP: one of the Seventy, who was known as "the evangelist."

CHAPTER ELEVEN:

SAUL OF TARSUS: an exceptionally pious Pharisee who, as an agent of both Caiaphas and Pilate, was beginning a career of harassing followers of The Way.

CHAPTER TWELVE: (none)

CHAPTER THIRTEEN:

AGGAI: first secretary and robe-maker to King Abgar V of Edessa.

Joseph of Arimathea stained-glass window in English Church.
Courtesy of Goheen Antiques.

CHAPTER ONE

✠

Resurrection!

A.D. 33

IT WAS MOSTLY A MATTER OF INSTINCT, I suppose. A wealthy man soon learns not to be wasteful, else he won't be wealthy very long. So, whatever my unconscious reasons, **I, Joseph of Arimathea,** took the Shroud instinctively and without hesitation. After all, less than two days previously I had paid fifty silver shekels for that cloth—a very high price, that Nicodemus had chided me for paying, but I wanted only the very best burial shroud for our Master, and had no time to haggle over the purchase. And the Disciples were going to leave it in the tomb!

I should be fair and say that they were very confused that morning, and with good reason. They also were young, of course. Andrew, son of Jonah (brother of Simon whom they were calling Peter), and Matthew the tax collector, were barely in their mid-thirties. Most of the rest were in their late twenties, and with very little worldly knowledge—not only because Galilean life had given them very little sophistication, but also due to the fact that they had been cloistered much of the past five years while accompanying the Master. Judas, who was about of an age with Jesus, was the only cool head among them, and now he, too, was gone.

It was fear, as well as confusion, that caused them to run from the tomb. A fear born of several causes. Of course, we were all awakened in the gray dawn before sun-up by the terrible clap and roar of sustained thunder, and by the simultaneous tremor of earthquake. I don't know why, but in the instant of awakening I thought of the Master in my tomb. Several of us apparently had the same thought, because, from our separate lodgings, we converged on the tomb. It was nearly full daylight, though sunrise and the day's beginning were still an hour away.

We were all hurrying, but at age forty-nine I was not trying to race with the younger men. Even from a distance of fifty paces we could see that the guards were gone and that the tomb's entrance yawned black and without obstruction. As I approached more closely, I stopped with shock upon seeing the massive stone door lying more than ten cubits* in front of the opening! This was no act of grave-robbers, or even as a result of the earthquake's vibration. That round stone door is wider than I am tall, and considerably more than a hand-span thick; it had sat on edge in its deep channel, snugly against the tomb opening and carefully wedged in position so that it could not roll in its channel. It had taken proper tools and four of my strongest men to put it in place when I acquired the tomb.

Fear of the returning guards, I am sure, had also motivated the disciples, Simon Peter and "the beloved disciple," to stay no more than a minute or two inside the tomb. Desertion from their post would be punished by death if the Temple guard captain arrived before the guards mustered courage enough to return.

But once the Disciples left the tomb area, doubtless running for the dubious sanctuary of the home of Mary, young Mark's mother and widow of Simeon, I entered by myself. In only the few moments it took for a dozen breaths, I could see that fear of the unknown—perhaps even the unknowable—was the powerful fear that doubtless had gripped their hearts as they ran.

Don't misunderstand me—I was not calm and unperturbed myself, as my eyes adjusted to the murky light inside the tomb. But I intended to stay until I could take it all in. Not that there was so much to see. As approaching evening had signalled the beginning of Sabbath two days previously, Nicodemus and I had been careful to pick up every unused item we had brought with us, and had left the floor of the tomb neat and clean. The floor was still that way; it didn't take much time nor light to assure myself on that point.

Before we left the tomb after burying Jesus two evenings ago, we had assisted my two servants who rolled the stone door into the closed

---

*About 15 feet, computing one cubit as 18 inches. Measurements taken by archaeologists of first century A.D. structures (in modern Israel) indicate a "standard" cubit of 17.58 inches. However, length of a cubit varied at different places and for different purposes; the so-called Assyrian cubit was known as "the cubit of the market place," and measured about 21.6 inches. Thus, Joseph would doubtless have purchased a shroud 2 by 8 cubits, since the Shroud of Turin today, measures 43 by 171 inches (see Ian Dickinson's article in Sources, January 1990, Saint Louis Priory, Missouri).

position, wedging it carefully with tapered blocks driven into place with a heavy hammer. The two Temple guards, already arrived, stood at a respectful distance, but carefully watched as we secured the door. Then Pilate's representative moved up to seal the tomb's door, as ordered by Pilate, and promptly left the area, as did we.

Then, as Nicodemus and I had walked toward our respective Jerusalem residences, we noticed that the two Galilean women walked some distance ahead of us, after having stood at the edge of the garden of the tombs to see where we would put Him (these were Mary of Magdala, sister of Lazarus,[1] and Mary Heli, wife of Cleopas Alphaeus, who were parents of Matthew and James and of young Joses).

Now, as I moved slowly this fateful morning, I looked from every angle at the spectacle before me on the stone bench where the Master had lain. Obviously, the Disciples had not touched a thing. What could possibly have happened? The upper half of the long shroud that had wrapped his body, under and over, was still exactly as we had left it.[2] All along each side of the shroud sat the bags of extra spices that Nicodemus had brought—only a hand-span distance from one bag to the next. But clearly, the body was gone! The cocoon had collapsed!

Not that the shroud was totally flat—there was a stiffness in the heavy cloth, and his feet seemed still to be under the cloth. I touched it there, and the protuberance of cloth subsided. The position of the body was almost fully outlined by the oozings of blood that had soaked entirely through the cloth in places, and were readily visible with the morning light from the east that came in the tomb's doorway.

But the sight that had me shivering, even though hints of the day's forthcoming heat were already being felt, was doubtless the sight that had caused the Disciples to flee. It was the place where his head had lain. The shroud there looked exactly as we had left it—as if his head was still under the shroud! Such a thought was foolish, of course, because the rest of the shroud was flat against the stone bench; and as soon as I thought it, I realized the explanation. We had folded the *sudarion*, the jaw-band, from a large square of linen, until it was a band no more than two fingers wide; this we slipped under his chin and knotted tightly on top of his head to hold the mouth closed, as religious rules prescribed. That loop of cloth was stiff enough to hold the shroud in position, even though the head was gone.

I pressed firmly at that point and the cloth collapsed. I started, and took a sudden mouthful of air in an involuntary gasp, almost exclaiming aloud as I stepped back in surprise. There was still a lump there from the bulk of the *sudarion,* and also from the bundle of *keiriai* cloths I had placed at his head; these were strips of cloth that we would have used to make a final tie at ankles and wrists, and to hold the shroud snugly to the body at two or three points. These final steps we never got to take, as matters turned out. Nor did we get to make our final farewells to him, and worse still, I suddenly realized, we would never again have the Master's presence, his wit, his provocative intellect to spice and sweeten our gatherings.

My head reeled at the magnitude of this resurrection event that my mind still couldn't take in! I staggered slightly with dizziness and reached out to the damp, limestone wall of the tomb to steady myself. The light-headedness passed but my mind still whirled with confusion. The shroud had not been removed, but Jesus' body had dissolved while inside it.[3] He had known he would die and had willingly permitted his own execution. He had said, "Death will not hold me"; but we didn't understand. How could we? We couldn't have expected an occurrence like this! He had said that we are all spirits and would survive death; we accepted his statement, but this was *too* much! We believed he was truly a real part of God, and special to God—but that belief didn't really help me handle a happening of this nature and magnitude. No wonder Peter and the other disciple ran! They were intelligent men, but intelligence didn't help in this situation.

Thoughts continued to race through my mind, even though I remained in the tomb but a brief time. I was confused as I had never been before. Even though Jesus had said he would rise from the dead, I was numbed by the fact that he just wasn't there! He had brought Lazarus back from the dead, but it wasn't like this. I had buried a number of my relatives in other tombs, and I had opened the tombs later as our Law permitted, to verify that all was correct—but there was always a body there!

Once I fully knew what had happened—that the Master's body had to-tally dissolved and dematerialized, and in its spirit form had passed through the cloth without disturbing the burial clothes—I realized also that I did not care to be present when the guards returned.

This was the point at which my instinct took over. The shroud—already doubled (half had been beneath and half over the body)—I quickly folded in two, then in four, and then crosswise, brushing the bags of spice aside as I did so. I picked up this bundle containing all of the burial clothes, and then hesitated—the odor of the preservative spices, myrrh and aloes,[4] came strongly to my nostrils, reminding me that these were used burial clothes and were religiously unclean. But in the next instant I was struck by the intimacy of these clothes—the last to touch Jesus' wounded body, and now even that body was gone!

Then my emotions overcame me briefly as I hugged the shroud to my breast and buried my face in it. In these three days of intense grief I had not cried, but now the tears flowed and the shroud soaked them up. The spasm of grief passed quickly and, as I put the bundle under my cloak, with fresh resolve I left the tomb, turned just for a brief look at the black maw of the tomb's opening, and headed away from the city, for I had no desire to meet the guards.*

I was sure that I knew the neighborhood better than did the guards and soldiers, and I went quickly along little-used paths from the northern to eastern suburbs of the City, that would take me to the Bethany home of my kinsman, Eleazer—whose Hebrew name was known to the Greeks as Lazarus. This I did to avoid my townhouse in the City, until I could decide what to do with the Shroud of Jesus.

Leaving the garden of tombs, unreasoning fear threatened to grip me and my instinct was to break into a run along this deserted pathway, but my intellect was sufficiently in operation so that I knew a brisk walking pace would be less likely to attract attention.

Of course, even though the taking of the burial clothes was an act of instinct, I was fully aware that I was violating a taboo of Jewish law by touching, much less saving, used burial clothes, because they are inherently "unclean." But I realized as well that the actions of Nicodemus and myself, two afternoons ago, in burying Jesus in the way we did, probably violated several rules of Jewish law.[5] At that moment these were but half-formed thoughts—I hadn't really thought it all through —but the simple fact was that the events of these past four days, from his arrest onward, caused me to radically and permanently change my personal religious stance.

For perhaps five years, I had felt committed to "The Way" as taught by my great-nephew, Jesus, but I had assumed that it could be harmonized with conventional Judaism—now it was clear that such harmony was not possible because it would not be accepted by the Great Sanhedrin, and that I must turn my back on conventional Judaism.

✠　✠　✠

Months later, I learned it was being said in Jerusalem that I was arrested and imprisoned the evening of Jesus' crucifixion, on orders of the Sanhedrin. This, of course, was not true. Even scheming Caiaphas, the high priest, did not know his own mind that soon after the event, nor did his father-in-law, Annas, the former High Priest, have the wit to instruct him.

---

*The facts concerning the shroud of Jesus are adapted from, or are consistent with, those reported in the factual book, *Portrait of Jesus? The Illustrated Story of the Shroud of Turin*, by Frank C. Tribbe, Stein & Day, 1983.

It was, in fact, a month and a half later, the evening of the Sabbath following Pentecost, when I was seized by the Temple police and placed in a cell without windows. (Of course, my sudden departure from the country upon my escape gave Caiaphas the opportunity to quietly start several rumors about me, serving his own best interests. Nearly at the end of my life, I learned that one rumor had it that I was in the Jerusalem prison for thirty-six years!—a very great exaggeration, I assure you.)[7]

But much happened during the days following Jesus' resurrection of which I must speak first.[8] Also, my life in my earlier years will bear recounting as relevant to the years to come.

Chapter Notes:

1. The Mary of Bethany, Mary of Magdala, and Mary the sinner were all one person. A year or so after her conversion, she became a part of Jesus' retinue, and resumed permanent residence at Bethany. These facts and conclusions were accepted by Tertullian, Ambrose, Jerome, Augustine, Gregory, Venerable Bede, Rhabanus, Odo, Bernard, and Thomas Aquinas; concurrence of modern authorities comes from: *Lives of the Saints*, Vol. VII, p. 308, H. T. Thurston, S.J., editor, Kennedy Pub., New York, 1931; *The Coming of the Saints* by J. W. Taylor, Methuen, London, 1906; *The Early Church* by Gladys Taylor, Covenant Publishing, London, 1969, 1987; *Dedicated Disciples* by Henry W. Stough, Artisan Sales, Thousand Oaks, Calif., 1987.

2. Jews of the first century did not bind or mummify by winding the burial cloth around the body (*Jewish Burial Customs* by Joseph Marino, private pub., St. Louis, Mo.: Priory 1987).

3. The proper translation from the Greek of John 20: 6-7 is that Jesus "withdrew from the grave clothes without disturbing their arrangement" Paul L. Maier, *First Easter*, Harper & Row, New York, 1973. To the same effect is the report by John A. T. Robinson contained in *Face to Face with the Turin Shroud*, ed. by P. Jennings, Mahew-McCrimmon, London, 1978.

4. Pharisaic protocol required immediate burial of a corpse; aromatic anointing was permissible but not actions to preserve the body. Because time would not allow a burial ceremony before Sunday morning (after the Sabbath, which was from Friday evening until Saturday evening), Joseph and Nicodemus obviously chose to violate that "law" and used preservatives, myrrh and aloes, to prevent decomposition in that climate.

5. By burying Jesus Friday afternoon Joseph made himself ritually unable to join in the Passover celebration because of contact with the dead body.

6. Mary, the mother of Jesus, was the daughter of Joseph's older brother, thus he was her uncle and the great-uncle of Jesus, according to: L. S. Lewis in *St. Joseph of Arimathea at Glastonbury*, Jas. Clarke, Cambridge, England, 1922; Sheldon Emry, quoting the Talmud, in *Paul and Joseph of Arimathea*; C. C. Dobson in *Did Our Lord Visit Britain As They Say in Cornwall and Somerset?* Avalon Press, Glastonbury, England, 1936, 1949; G. F. Jowett in *Drama of the Lost Disciples*, Covenant Publications, London, 1975;

and H.W. Stough in *Dedicated Disciples,* Artisan Sales, Thousand Oaks, Calif., 1987; Harleian Library, London, 38-59 f., 1936.

7. Several apocryphal and medieval writings state that Joseph of Arimathea was arrested and imprisoned by the Sanhedrin, but they do not agree as to when it happened—the day of the crucifixion, the day of the resurrection, or several weeks later—nor do they agree as to how long he was incarcerated—a few hours, a few days, or thirty-six years. See the "Gospel of Nicodemus," in M. R. James' *The Apocryphal New Testament,* Oxford Univ. Press, England, 1924; C. T. Tischendorf's *Evangelia Apocrypha,* Lipsiae, Avenarius et Mendelssohn, 1953; John of Glastonbury's *The Cronica;* and additions to Tischendorf, *Narratio Josephi, Vindicta Salvatoris.*

8. The Canadian firm, Kolbe's Publications Inc. (2464 Forest, Sherbrooke, Quebec, Canada, J1K-1R4) published English editions (1989-90) of the writings by and about Italian visionary Maria Valtorta (four volumes titled *Poem of the Man-God* and a one-volume condensed version titled *The Diary of Jesus*). Her visions of the passion of Jesus mentioned four points which I had made based solely on logic and imagination, where the Bible, legends, apocrypha and scholarly speculation provided no details: (1) Joseph of Arimathea was the one to save the Shroud on Easter morning; (2) a simple sheet had been used as a carrying-cloth from cross to tomb; (3) the burial clothes were taken by Joseph to Lazarus' home for temporary safekeeping; (4) Joseph and Lazarus were the first to see the image on the Shroud.

CHAPTER TWO

✠

He Is Risen Indeed!

A.D. 33

I'M SURE NO ONE WOULD HAVE RECOGNIZED the bundle of linen cloth as used burial shroud, but to me it seemed very valuable, and so I kept it well hidden under my voluminous cloak.

The garden of tombs where we had buried Jesus adjoins Gareb Hill, a small elevation also known as Golgotha, where crucifixions are held; both were just beyond the wall of the City. The garden of tombs was merely a moderately narrow defile flanked by walls of rock rising two or three times a man's height; it had once been a quarry from which stone was cut for construction in Jerusalem. Into these stone walls tombs had been cut to serve families that could afford them. Going out of the garden, away from the City, it was less than a half-hour's brisk walk to the Bethany palace and farm of Lazarus. I walked rather fast, both from excitement and a feeling of urgency, but my mind was not on the walk. Of course, I was sorrowful (and on a deeper level, jubilant), but more than anything I was somewhat dazed, and perhaps foolishly I kept going over and over in my mind what I had seen in the tomb, unable to really take it in.

The sun was well up and in my face by the time I arrived, and with the shroud hugged against me I was perspiring freely. Nevertheless, I am sure it was more a matter of nerves than either heat or exercise that brought the heavy perspiration—nor would I have considered opening my cloak and risk a chance encounter with another early traveller which could reveal the precious burden I carried.

Fortunately, Lazarus was outdoors and near the gate when I arrived, and so I was able to ask for the use of a room for a few days without giving any explanation. He was dressed in mourning clothes and obviously was unaware of Jesus' resurrection. As he was walking me to my usual guest room, I told him that I would quickly bathe my face and put on a fresh robe which I had left there on a I previous occasion, and wished to meet in the great hall as quickly as possible with him, his sisters and with all followers of The Way who were on the premises at the moment—that I had important news.

During the last few minutes as I trod the dusty path and then the Bethany roadway, my mind had cleared somewhat and turned to more practical thoughts—what would I tell Lazarus?—how explain the bringing of the shroud? Should I share my news with the entire household or only a select few? Had I better wait to find out what story Peter would tell? Would Nicodemus and the other Judean disciples know what really had happened? Would the Galilean Twelve?—and where were they? With Judas dead, Peter and John in flight, that left nine unaccounted for—had they fled Jerusalem? Would I be able to tell anyone that I had the soiled shroud?—surely not the Galileans! Maybe I should destroy it and be safe. I didn't really need advice—I knew the Law—knew that the shroud from a crucified criminal was religiously unclean. No, what I needed was an emotional sharing, not a legal opinion. Thinking in this fashion, I knew what I would do—I would quietly put the shroud in the chest in the large cupboard of the guest room I normally used in Lazarus' home, and then would privately discuss it with him tomorrow. With that issue provisionally resolved, I could see clearly that I should share all of my experience of the morning (except the taking of the shroud) with all followers of The Way that were on the premises when I arrived. Circumstances would dictate any future sharing of information. Thus, when I arrived at the gate and saw Lazarus, I had no hesitation.

When I reached the great hall I was met by Lazarus and Martha, and about a dozen others whom I recognized as mostly his hired servants—since he had long ago ceased to use slaves or bound servitors. These were all open, friendly faces that I saw, fellow seekers on The Way with whom spiritual sharing had become a way of life; they looked expectantly at me with signs of solemnity and sorrow in their faces, and yet with looks of hope and curiosity, as they waited to hear me.

It was hard to put into a few words in a hurry my tremendous news—that Jesus' physical body had disappeared without disturbing the burial shroud; that the heavy stone door had been "blown" by a supernatural force some five paces from the tomb's opening; that the Temple guards had apparently been frightened from their post that morning; that Peter and his companion had briefly observed and then run in terror—probably to the home of Mary, Mark's mother.

I spoke as fast as I could, but doubtless used three times the number of words necessary. When I stopped for breath, I realized for the first time that Mary, their sister, was not present. "But where's Mary?" I asked in astonishment. Martha patiently explained that in my excitement I had obviously forgotten the arrangements for the formal anointing and completion of Jesus' burial—that I was to bring two servants to the tomb to roll the door, and was to induce the guards to permit the breaking of Pilate's seal. Of course, I had completely forgotten! Even had our burial activities been completed, the Law permitted examination of the body on the third day after entombment.

Martha continued to explain that her sister was to meet Jesus' mother, with Salome and others who had been preparing ointments and other materials for the formal anointing; and that they were to carry these items to the tomb, where they were to also meet Peter and others who would conduct the anointing and burial on behalf of The Twelve. Lazarus added that by now his sister would certainly know of the discoveries I had described and would surely return home shortly.

At this point, I remembered to inquire whether the bombastic storm and the earthquake had been an early morning occurrence in Bethany that day; I was assured that such had happened, had caused no damage, but had caused each member of the household to think immediately of Jesus in the tomb.

No one left the great hall, and I was pelted from all sides with questions, and the faces now showed excitement instead of sorrow. I tried my best to satisfy the questioners—about half of their questions merely required a repetition of the story I had already told; the other half sought answers I didn't have. Before we realized it noonday had arrived but Mary had not. We started the noon meal without her, and just as we had begun to express concern because of her absence, she arrived more out of breath and impatient to tell her story than I had been.

After several false starts and many interruptions she finally was able to recite occurrences in the garden of tombs that were just as spectacular as my story had been. Apparently, very shortly after the disciples ran from the garden toward the City and I thereafter hurried away in the opposite direction, the two Marys, with Salome and some servants arrived. They were surprised to find neither disciples, nor me, present; next they discovered the guards gone and the tomb door missing. And then they saw a young man dressed in white sitting in the tomb, whom they have since decided was an angel.

At this point, Mary tried to tell us the story of all three women. But obviously, each did not see and hear the same as the other two—also, the excitement and confusion had not helped. For more than three hours thereafter at the home of Mark's mother, they, as well as Peter, each told his version over and over. My best reconstruction of Mary's story as told to us is as follows:

The two Marys and Salome with their serving women and materials reached the garden of tombs about half an hour after the disciples ran from it. The sun was just appearing on the horizon but the shadows in the garden were still nearly as deep as I had seen them at the time of Peter's hurried departure. The women slowed their steps as they had expected to find us men on hand. They were commenting on their inability to move the door, when Mary, whose eyes had been searching the area as they walked, suddenly exclaimed, "But there is no door!"

All hurried forward and recognized the truth of her statement. "Do we dare go in?" asked Salome with a tremble in her voice.

"We *must* do so," insisted Mary. Jesus' mother had said not a word.

It was a small tomb, four steps below the outer court, and they didn't actually go in, because, just as they reached the entrance, by stooping slightly they each could clearly see a young man in simple raiment that was so white it glowed like a light. He was sitting on the stone bench along the tomb's right side.

I had required this burial bench to be formed by cutting an enlargement of three sides of the tomb, waist-high above the entrance pit which was five cubits on a side with headroom for a tall man. Two narrow interment chambers, which in Hebrew are called *kohk*, were cut into the left wall, and we would have put Jesus' body into one of them after the anointing was complete.

Nicodemus had chided me for acquiring a tomb when I could expect to live another twenty-five years, and for taking it in Jerusalem where gossip would say I did it to impress posterity. In fact, in our family many of my male peers have already died so that I am now responsible for quite a large number of people. Also, there are so many competent employees in our business that I hope to retire in less than ten years and move from Arimathea to Jerusalem where I would devote myself more fully to affairs of the Great Sanhedrin.

The *kohkim*-style, rolling-stone tomb[1] had been newly cut when I bought it a few months ago, and it would be my responsibility to enlarge it and finish it appropriately, which I had planned to do in time. Now, I think I shall never use it again, nor permit any others to do so; technicalities of Law would preclude it anyway, I suppose.[2]

The women knew this radiant young man was not one of Jesus' followers and was not a Temple guard, and were about to turn and run when the young man spoke.

"Be not afraid," he said. "You will not find Jesus here, for he has risen; you can see that I now sit where his body once lay.

"Tell his disciples," he continued, "that he is risen but will appear to them in his spirit body, and will give them his parting instructions."

CHAPTER NOTES:

1. This type of tomb, available only to the very wealthy, was closed by a flat, round stone, sitting on edge, that was rolled in a channel or trough, which might be either level or sloped toward the point of closure. The low doorway led into a "pit" some six to eight feet square and about three feet below the "bench" which ran around three sides, and upon which the body was placed for the anointing and burial ceremony. Beyond the bench on those three sides, were cut narrow chambers six or seven feet deep back into the rock; each of these chambers was called a *kohk,* and into them the bodies would be slid, head-first (lying on the back and wrapped lengthwise by a shroud), after completion of the burial ceremony. In recent years, many tombs of this type have been found and excavated in Israel and Jordan, dating from the first half of the First Century A.D. (See the ESSJ Report of 9-14-86 by Dr. E. L. Nitowski—Sister Damian of the Cross—Carmelite Monastery, Salt Lake City; also her article, "The Tomb of Christ from Archaeological Sources," *Shroud Spectrum Int'n'l,* No. 17, 1985; and her doctoral dissertation, "Reconstructing the Tomb of Christ from Archaeological and Literary Sources," University of Notre Dame, 1979.)

2. Pharisaic rules prohibited use of a "family tomb" for the burying of a criminal, and so any further use of Joseph's tomb would have been illegal.

CHAPTER THREE

✛

The Resurrection Image

A.D. 33

T O THIS POINT the stories of the women were in substantial agreement, with the exception of a possible second heavenly messenger and a possible guard present—neither of which seems likely. We listeners were absorbing her words in rapt silence.

As Mary's story continues, it appears probable that the other two moved slowly ahead toward the garden's entrance while Mary lingered weeping near the tomb. As she turned to leave, she saw standing nearby another man, strange appearing, though natural looking and not luminous like the messenger in the tomb, and who spoke, saying, "Woman, why do you weep?"

Thinking him to be a workman, she asked where her Lord had been taken.

Then he said, "Mary of Magdala!" This had always been Jesus' term of endearment for Lazarus' younger sister, ever since she had had her spiritual rebirth at Jesus' feet and he had become a regular visitor to her palatial Magdala home on the shore of Lake Galilee.

Hearing her name thus spoken in familiar tones, she knew the voice and suddenly, as if her eyes were wiped clear, she recognized Jesus.

With an exclamation of joy, she reached out to embrace him, but he stopped her with an upraised palm, saying that his spirit body was too recently released to be touched, but that she would do so in a few days. Sobbing with joy she fell near his feet until her emotion was spent.

Jesus' mother's story is different, but very well could be consistent with the above narrations: She was unaware that Mary had lingered at the tomb and, with eyes cast downward, did not realize that Salome's more youthful stride had taken her many paces nearer the garden entrance. Mary, the mother, heard a slight sound and lifted her eyes to see her son standing within arm's reach and smiling at her with great love and compassion in his eyes.

Though not frightened, she was frozen with disbelief until he began to speak: "My mother, I hope that you will be able in time to forgive my many acts that must have seemed callous and unloving. My acts respecting you may have reflected poor judgment, but believe me, mother dear," Jesus continued, "I was strongly impressed by Jehovah, our Heavenly Father, that my mission to the world must take precedence over personal feelings.

"Remember also," she heard from his lips, as she looked hopefully into his loving eyes, "'that I tried many times to explain my mission to you and my brothers—but you and James, as I read your hearts, could not open your minds to me since you so greatly feared the harm that might come to the family because of me—and, of course, you were right to have these fears. Only my youngest brother, Jude, and later Simon,[1] were open to my teachings, and it was with great joy that I welcomed them into The Twelve—also, I predict they will have a great and good effect on the world as they assist in spreading my gospel. For dear brother James, I have reserved a special and vitally important role in the propagation of my message, and I will speak with him on these matters very shortly."

With these words from Jesus, Mary straightened from her sorrow and a radiant joy shone through her tears as her love and pride were beamed to the man standing before her. "My son, my son!" her voice was strong and happily vibrant, "I am so grateful that you speak to me thus, giving me yet another chance to accept your gospel—which I now do with all my heart!

"When you come to the presence of the Heavenly Father," she continued, "say that I pray he will give me a very long earth-life so that I can make amends for refusing to listen with my heart—because I listened only with my ears and mind.

"If I am given sufficient years," she implored wistfully, "I will tell all people—and especially the leaders of your mission—how fully I support you—and will support them even after I die! And, of course, there was nothing in your conduct that I need to forgive."

Lapsing into silence, his mother heard Jesus say, "Selah, Selah; so be it!" as he reduced the visibility of his spirit body, so that it seemed to melt into the atmosphere.

Salome, widow of Zebedee and mother of James and John, was unable fully to comprehend that she had seen and heard an angel in the tomb, but she felt compelled to accept the fact that Jesus was risen, and that the incidents surrounding his resurrection must have been truly spectacular. She was just a little frightened and looked neither right nor left as she moved toward the garden entrance. Finally her steps slowed and she looked around just as the two Marys caught up with her. Later, as she listened to their accounts in the home of Mary, the mother of young Mark, she could verify the experience of neither Mary as to their sight and conversations with Jesus. She was silent and fully awed by what she had seen and heard.

After our noontime discussions with Mary I went to my room in an attempt to collect my thoughts on the morning's activities with their awesome implications. Suddenly I remembered Jesus' shroud, and thought of the blood stains on it. Considering that those stains might not be fully dried, I took the shroud from the sandalwood chest (with its top tastefully decorated with inlaid figures in ivory), kept in the tall cupboard made of the fragrant cedar of Lebanon, and proceeded to spread it (with the "inside" surface up) across my bed and three other couches, because of its great size (since half its length was spread under the body and the other half brought over the head to cover the front of the body, the cloth had to be longer than twice the height of the corpse).

After getting the shroud thus spread out, I examined it closely and found the blood stains to be totally dry—the body of Jesus must not have bled very long after we buried it late on the afternoon before the sabbath. In the back of my mind I knew that the Temple authorities were sure to claim the disciples had stolen Jesus' body from the tomb—and might even claim he had not died on the cross, that he had revived in the tomb and walked away. And so, I was excited all over again by the nature of these blood stains. Examining them carefully it was clear that these stains were pristine and perfect. That would answer the critics!

As everyone knows, when you place a cloth against a bleeding wound, and then lift it off, one of two results will obtain: if the blood was still moist, removal of the cloth would smear the stain on the cloth; if the blood was dry it would have formed a crust into the weave of the cloth and the crust would be broken when the cloth was removed from the body. But neither had happened! The stains on the cloth were neither smeared nor broken—they were perfect! The only possible explanation was a total dematerialization of the body inside the shroud—which was also the conclusion I was forced to make that morning by my discoveries in the tomb—it had to have been a supernatural, spiritual resurrection event![2] This shroud was perfect evidence to give the lie to Temple critics. It was certainly more valuable and important than I could ever have dreamed.

I took a couple of steps backward for a broader view of the blood stains, and could hardly suppress a shout of exultation, for the stains presented a *complete* record of Jesus' passion! His body front and back—from the crown of his head to his feet—from the predawn torture in Pilate's courtyard to the nighttime draining of blood from the major wounds after we closed the tomb—it was all there!

Blood was still oozing from the major wounds after we had wiped the body reasonably clean. But the blood stains I now see on the cloth also include the record of *all* the breaks in his flesh that came throughout that long day of torture, from considerably before day began at sun-up until we took him from the cross in late afternoon. Each was so clear and so accurate—how could this be?

Trembling with excitement, I began checking the realistic and accurate story told by these blood stains. All over the head, and especially noticeable on the forehead, were the flows of blood from the punctures inflicted by the miter-crown of thorns. The facial injuries to eyebrows, nose, cheekbones and mouth, as had been cruelly inflicted by stones, clubs and falls, were graphically to be seen. On the back in particular, the metal-tipped Roman *flagra* with which he had been scourged, left marks of its several dozen tears in the flesh. A huge puddle of blood surrounded the lance-thrust[3] in his side. Down each forearm from the spikes in his wrists were rivulets of blood reflecting the six hours he hung on the cross. Again, the puddles of blood at his wrists and feet had resulted from the spikes through them. What a fantastic pictorial record—no human artist could have drawn it!

I hurried across the room and threw back the drapes of the ceiling-high windows, now unshuttered, to let in the full, brilliant light of the mid-day sun—I had to be sure I was not being fooled by my imagination. I turned with the brilliance of the sun at my back and began to walk quickly to the shroud. Some three or four paces from it I stopped short, and thought I would faint. Even after all the excitement of this day, there was no way I could have been prepared for the fantastic sight before me. There on the shroud was the image of Jesus' body, as accurate as if painted by a great Greek artist! Not only were the blood stains accurate and descriptive, but now they were seen as markings on a complete body, front and back, just as Jesus' body had touched the Shroud. He had saved his greatest miracle for the last—in his tomb!

Attempting to view it from every angle, I moved around the room— and almost fainted again when the body image vanished as I moved several

Face of Jesus based on the Shroud of Turin.
This painting is considered by experts to be the most accurate in existence;
it was painted in 1935 by Ariel Agemian, artist and linguist,
a scholarly Armenian educated in Venice by the Mechitarist monks.
Photograph courtesy of the Confaternity of Precious Blood.

paces back from the shroud. Then I discovered with a great sigh of relief that there was pure magic in this image: when I got to within two paces of the cloth the image disappeared, and when I got farther away than about five or six paces the image disappeared; but in that medium distance it was as real as if the Master still lay there—beard and all. Yet the blood stains did not fade in and out with distance; they remained perfectly visible at any distance.

By examining the cloth closely I was able to satisfy myself that the blood was real, because by scraping it with my thumbnail (at a remote and less important point on the cloth) the dried blood would flake-off into my hand just as any dried blood on any cloth would do. Yet, when I tried similarly to find traces of the body image (at places where I knew it to be, even though I could not see it when close enough to touch), there was not the faintest indication of paint or any marking substance such as I had seen Grecian artists use. I even wet a piece of rough towel and scrubbed vigorously on spots where I knew the body image to be, but no stain or other residue came off on my clean towel, nor did the body image disappear or lessen due to my scrubbing.

My excitement now knew no bounds. *I* seemed twice my actual height. I felt to be walking on air and wondered if I would bump the ceiling. My breath was coming fast and my blood seemed to be racing through my body (if blood can move at all!). Initially, I had been applying my intellect to this remarkable relic, but now I was soaring spiritually and almost out of touch with my senses and my mind. I'm a pragmatic businessman and an Elder of the Sanhedrin, even an advisor to the Roman legate in Antioch, and have always assumed that I am continuously in control of myself. But this is too much!—it's fabulously strong stuff! I have been accepting and believing Jesus' teachings of the supernatural, but this is not an abstraction, and I'm just swept off my mental feet!—even faith and knowledge leave me without true comprehension.

Finally, a sobering thought entered my consciousness—what if my mind was diabolically possessed, or was suddenly sickened by some unsuspected malady? Maybe all of my observations about Jesus' shroud were fallacious imaginings of a mind out of touch with reality—maybe this shroud had on it only a few random and meaningless blood stains and nothing else. I had to find out.

CHAPTER NOTES:

1. "He came to his hometown and began to teach ... they were astounded and said... 'Is not his mother called Mary? And are not his brothers James and Joseph and Simon and Judas? And are not all his sisters with us?'" (Matthew 13: 54-56, NRSV)

2. Professor Paul L. Maier states that a proper translation from the Greek (for John 20: 6-7) is that Jesus "withdrew from the graveclothes without disturbing their arrangement." *(First Easter,* Harper & Row, 1973)

3. John 19: 34 states that "one of the soldiers pierced his side with a lance" (Jerusalem Bible, 1966); other versions (KJV: RSV: NIV) say, "spear." Matthew, Mark and Luke do not report the incident. Scientific studies of the Shroud of Turin are quite precise as to the side wound of the Man of the Shroud. Stevenson and Habermas *(Verdict on the Shroud,* Servant Pubs., 1981, p. 119) report: "The wound inflicted in the side of the man in the Shroud measures 1-3/4 inches by 7/16 inch. This opening exactly corresponds to the size of the tip of the *lancia,* a Roman spear with a long, thin, leaf-shaped head." Endnote: "...the Gospel of John states that it was the same weapon (Greek, *lonche)* which a Roman soldier thrust into Jesus' side...."

Ian Wilson *(The Shroud of Turin,* Doubleday, 1978, pp. 33-34) confirms the just-quoted measurement of the wound, which he calls elliptical, and says will fit only the Roman *lancea,* being the same word and weapon used by John in the Greek *(lonche).* He points out that the Roman spears were throwing weapons, while the lance was for continuous use and would have been standard issue for garrison troops, to be carried in a sheath. Giulio Ricci *(The Holy Shroud,* Roman Center for Shroud Studies, 1981, pp. 192-197) properly refers to the thrust as the *coup de grace,* and measures the Shroud wound as 1.58 inches long without noting its width; Ricci uses both terms, lance-thrust and spear-thrust. "Spear" would seem to be a less accurate translation of the New Testament Greek and inconsistent with both the Shroud data and modern historical knowledge of Roman military matters; "lance" would seem to be preferred.

THE WOMEN

At the Cross

Mt.: many women from Galilee, looking from afar, including Mary Magdalene, Mary Heli, mother of James and Joseph, and Mary Salome, mother of the sons of Zebedee.

Mk.: women looking from afar, including Mary Magdalene, Mary Heli the mother of James the Younger and Joses, and Salome.

Lk.: women from Galilee, at a distance.

Jn.: His mother, his mother's sister, Salome, Mary Heli, wife of Cleopas, and Mary Magdalene.

Watching at the Tomb Friday evening

Mt.: Mary Heli, mother of James and Joseph, and Mary Magdalene.

Mk.: Mary Heli, mother of Joses, and Mary Magdalene.

Lk.: women from Galilee.

Jn.: ——

Easter morning at the Tomb

Mt.: Mary Magdalene and the "other Mary" (Mary Heli, mother of James and Joseph).

Mk.: Mary Magdalene, Mary Heli, mother of James, Mary Salome (mother of James and John Z.).

Lk.: Mary Magdalene, Joanna (wife of Chuza, chief steward to Herod), Mary Heli, mother of James, and other women.

Jn.: Mary Magdalene.

✠

We Discuss the Image

A.D. 33

S UITING ACTION TO THAT THOUGHT I rushed into the great hall of the house in search of Lazarus, and found him sitting in a secluded corner lost in reverie. I touched his shoulder lightly and he looked up with a wan smile. Motioning to him, he arose and followed my quick retreat to my room. Just after securing the doorway I faced Lazarus to block most of the room from his view and said: "My dear kinsman, at this moment I am almost out of my mind, as well as out of my body, with euphoria and rapture, but I beg you to be patient and let me do all of the talking for a few minutes."

I then proceeded to tell Lazarus how I had gotten this shroud before daybreak, and brought it here; and I began to lead him by the arm all about the room, up to the shroud and away from it, all of the time describing and explaining my discoveries and my conjectures of the past half-hour. Then I sat quietly as he moved around, testing for himself all that I had shown and told him. Finally, he turned to me with tears streaming down his cheeks, with a brilliance in his eyes I had never seen before, and began speaking in low tones, but with his emotions barely under control: "Dear, dear Joseph! Yes! Everything you found on this cloth is true and beyond question. We thought my return to full and robust physical life after four days, or was it four eons (!)—in the heavenly planes was the greatest miracle, but it stands deep in the shade of this event. This is truly beyond comprehension. He just withdrew from the grave clothes without disturbing their arrangement.

"What perfect proof of his divinity!" Lazarus continued. "How else explain what we see except to say this was no mere man. Only the *Christos* power could have made a piece of evidence such as this—the body was dissolved into nothingness and, as it passed through the cloth, the full account of the Passion was pictorially recorded, in the blink of an eye perhaps. I'm sure that not even the passing of Elijah or Enoch,[1, 2] nor of any other since the beginning of the world has been so spectacular nor so convicting in its evidential quality. The body and the blood images on this cloth are not approximately natural and proper, they are exactly so! And, over-all, there is a mystical quality of this body image that defies even description, much less explanation! I'm so glad we can't fully explain or understand it!"

I was much relieved to have his corroboration, but in that moment I knew that the enormity of our discovery also had created some tremendous problems for us. I was about to speak along these lines when Lazarus interrupted my thoughts with a question: "Joseph, why do you suppose the eyes look so large; that is a little inconsistent with the naturalness I was speaking of."

"I had not noticed it, but you are right," I responded, "but I think I know the answer. To hold his eyelids closed as Law requires, I placed on them two Pontius Pilate leptons that I had with me, which doubtless accounts for the illusion you have noted."

"I'm sure that Pharisaic technicalities would not have greatly concerned you at that moment," commented Lazarus, "but if a priest had been formally officiating, would not the Roman coins with pagan images and bearing an augur's lituus have been forbidden for such a purpose?"

"You are right that I wouldn't have been concerned," I responded, "but I did raise the question rhetorically and somewhat facetiously. However, as you know, Nicodemus is without peer in knowledge of the Law, save only our knowledgeable dear brother Gamaliel—and Nicodemus promptly responded that the Pilate coins were perfectly permissible for this use—he explained, for comparison, that the shekel of Tyre is currently minted in Jerusalem under authority of Rome for the express purpose of use as Temple payments, and yet it carries the head of the Tyrian god, Melqarth, sometimes called Heracles—and contrariwise, the Roman denarius of Tiberius is not acceptable at the Temple, but the reason is that it is only 80 percent silver while the shekel of Tyre is 90 percent."

"Amazing!" roared Lazarus with a great laugh, "which just goes to show you the value of having a lawyer at your elbow if you want to operate in an area that would appear to ordinary humans as violating the law."

When a more serious look finally appeared on his face, I changed the subject by saying, "Lazarus, I am beginning now to be concerned about what we will do with this most powerful and meaningful relic. What do you think?"

Lazarus pondered my question for several moments before he said: "Yes, you are right to be concerned. I am beginning to sense several problems. Most obvious, of course, is protecting it from our enemies of the Sanhedrin, who will very likely make some search for it even without realizing how much they can be threatened by the message of this shroud. Also, you and I clearly realize that many of our number, even probably most of the Galilean disciples of The Twelve, and of the Seventy, may adhere so strongly to Jewish law that they would object to keeping an 'unclean' item of used burial linen and especially a cloth on which appears the image of a man. What is your suggestion, Joseph?"

"In one respect we are on the horns of a dilemma as to Jewish taboos," I replied; "in addition to the two you mention, there is the more serious one against an image of the Divine, which some would consider an idol; some of his strongest followers believe in Jesus' divinity and yet might object to an image of him because of the taboo!

"I'm afraid that many of our people of The Way still are infected with the Pharisaic piety of which you often speak, and who, if they learned of this shroud and the images on it, might report its existence to the Sanhedrin," I continued. "Accordingly, I feel very strongly on two points—one, that we must keep knowledge of the shroud to an absolute minimum of persons, and also that we should get it out of Judea for safekeeping. This is just too important a relic and one which may ultimately be vital to future propagation of the gospel of The Way, for us to chance either intentional or accidental disclosure to the Temple authorities.

"Moreover," I mused aloud, "I had intended to stay here with you for a few days until the furor of the last four days dies down a bit. But in the light of these discoveries and this conversation, I think I must leave immediately for Arimathea to find out what possibilities are available to us, and to learn the present intentions of Caiaphas and his friends. Is my servant, Hosea, still here on the premises, that I might send him into the City on this latter question?"

Lazarus assured me that Hosea could be sent to me right away, and added: "I also believe it is very important to learn of Caiaphas' attitudes and intentions. You and I may be subjects of his renewed ire. Which leads me to suggest that we take at least one of the Galileans into our confidence, so that wherever we and the shroud are, the people of The Way in Judea will know about it."

I agreed.

The importance of the Shroud of Jesus as a spiritual relic of the highest quality and significance, may take a little time to soak into one's consciousness, but ultimately it *cannot* be overemphasized!

Its full meaning has the effect of relegating to insignificance all the prior questions about Jesus and his ministry. Most of us who have been close to him realize the existence of these many questions—questions which will doubtless live on as long as the earth stands: Was there anything totally unique about his birth? Was Joseph bar Jacob his physical father? As a youth did he have superphysical powers or perceptions? In basic essence, was his spirit or soul different from the rest of us? At what point did the God-stuff invest and totally consume him, making him spiritually different from you and me—at birth?—at his dedication in the Temple?—at his baptism by John bar Zechariah?*

Was his message and his theology totally unique, or did he borrow from various religious sources? Was he truly the Jewish messiah, whatever that was? Did he contrive some of his conduct to give the appearance of fulfilling prophecy? Could he or should he have avoided the cross? Did God really predestine that death for him? Why the hiatus from his physical death on the cross two afternoons ago until his resurrection from my tomb, presumably just this morning? Why the total destruction of his body?

I have been asking myself some of these questions for the past ten years and before his crucifixion, and have found no satisfying answers to them, in spite of my kinship with him and my closeness to his ministry for several significant periods.

But I will ask myself these questions no more! Having seen this Shroud, examined it closely at varying distances and in a strong light, and pondered and meditated on it most seriously, those questions all fade into absolute unimportance. I am an educated and worldly-wise man, as well as a devout man, and I know beyond all doubt that before the presence of this Shroud I stand in frightening awe of the powerful handiwork of the great creator-God. In no small particular can I explain the striking image and markings on this Shroud, but at the same time I accept it unreservedly as the image of the person and passion of our Lord Jesus, given us

---

*Throughout the book I will use *bar*, meaning "son of" in Aramaic, the colloquial language of the area, rather than *ben* as used in Hebrew, the formal language.

through the inexplicable wisdom and power of our God. Maybe Jesus was the Jewish messiah for which we have waited—maybe not. His ministry and his miracles may not have been greater than by prophets of old. But those questions no longer are important. The Messiah, or "Christos" as the Greeks put it, can hardly be someone more favored of God than was Jesus of Nazareth whose surviving Spirit has so remarkably pictured him and his passion on the burial shroud in the moment of the Resurrection.

Above all else, I feel committed now to somehow preserve this awesome relic, which I know must at least quicken the faith of believers in the future—perhaps millennia in the future.

The shroud's message seems universal—but there is another message just for the Jews, and that is the message of the reality of spiritual life after physical death. Our brothers, the Sadducees, have not believed this at all. Even we Pharisees have given such theology little more than lip-service. Perhaps only our estranged brothers, the Essenes, really believe it. But when one observes the witness of Jesus' Holy Shroud, there no longer is room for doubt. Jesus *told* us of everlasting life, but his burial shroud gives us proof positive far beyond a *telling* by any speaker.

Our religious heritage as contained in our Holy Scriptures teaches us very little with certainty in this regard. And so, apart from us few professional religionists that work in the Temple, in the synagogues and in our Jewish government, our people of the rank and file of this nation give very little thought to the possibility of everlasting life. Even more is this true of our brothers outside our homeland, the Jews of the diaspora[3] as a result mostly of our military losses and foreign bondages; and with these must also be grouped our cousins in neighboring nations—in Moab, Samaria, Perea, Edom, Nabatae and Idumea, especially. Outside Judah and Galilee, our rabbis believe little and speak less of such matters as our enduring souls. Once the powerful witness of Jesus' Shroud becomes known, that foolish blindness can no longer persist—both the power of God and the reality of life hereafter will have to be acknowledged.[4]

CHAPTER NOTES:

1. Elijah was a prophet of the Jewish people in centuries past, who ascended into the heavens without dying. Enoch was a Jewish patriarch who walked with God, and God took him (without physical death).

2. See the scientific paper of this author, "Enigmas of the Shroud of Turin," pp. 39-49, SINDON No. 33 (December 1984), Centro Internazionalle della Sindone, Turin, Italy, listing twenty-one enigmas of the Shroud images which the STURP members find scientifically inexplicable.

3. Sometimes called "the dispersion"—embraced all of the Jews outside of the homeland who had migrated to other countries but maintained their religious faith in major
respects.

4. Critics who do not accept the Shroud of Turin as a probable first-century artifact,
may consider it inappropriate in a work claimed as a documented historical novel, that
I describe Jesus' resurrection shroud as if bearing the marks of the cloth made famous
at Turin. Support for my action can be sketched as follows: (a) In every particular that
we know concerning burial shrouds and ceremonies of the people of Jerusalem during
the first half of the first century A.D., the Shroud of Turin fits (see my book, *Portrait of
Jesus?* Stein & Day, 1983). (b) In every particular that we know concerning Roman
crucifixions of that period in the Near East, the Shroud of Turin fits (see *A Doctor at
Calvary.* Pierre Barbet, Doubleday, 1950). (c) In every particular we know from the
Bible concerning the torture, crucifixion, burial and resurrection of Jesus, the Shroud
of Turin fits. (d) History records that, beginning just weeks after Jesus' resurrection and
continuing for nine hundred years, there was in the Parthian city of Edessa a mysterious
"Face" which as a Christian relic attracted pilgrims from all over the Roman world—
which Face, historians now equate with the folded Shroud of Turin (see *The Shroud of
Turin,* Ian Wilson, Doubleday, 1978). (e) Art critics and historians now recognize that
throughout the Christian world—especially in the eastern areas—beginning in the first
century, many faces in art purporting to be of Jesus, are now matched *precisely* to the
face on the Shroud of Turin; a wave of new art of that face stemmed from Emperor
Justinian's sixth century "rediscovery" of the Face in Edessa, and his honor of it in the
Monastery of St. Catherine in the Sinai; one art depiction of it there clearly shows a
full burial shroud, not just a face (see *Portrait of Jesus?* and *The Shroud of Turin,* ibid.).
(f) Data from Constantinople in the years 944 to 1204 indicate clearly that the Face
of Edessa was what we now call the Shroud of Turin, folded to show only the face of
the image on the shroud (Daniel C. Scavone: *The Shroud of Turin,* Greenhaven Press,
1989; and "The Shroud of Turin in Constantinople—The Documentary Evidence,"
Byzantinishce Zeitschrift, October 1988). (g) By various interpretations of European
history vis-a-vis the Crusades, there is every certainty that the Face of Edessa was the
full Shroud of Constantinople (that hung full length in the Church during the Spring
of 1204), and that it survived, and is the Shroud of Turin today (see Wilson, ibid.;
Scavone, ibid.; Noel Currer-Briggs, *The Shroud and the Grail,* St. Martin's Press, 1987).
(h) In 1988, laboratories in Switzerland, England, and the United States were given
samples of the Shroud of Turin cloth for carbon-dating and they reported that the linen
was made from flax grown in about A.D. 1325. Shroud research scientists protested
immediately that the procedures used were badly flawed. Subsequently, Dr. Leoncio
Garza-Valdes and associates at the University of Texas tested the Shroud and have
reported that a natural microbe, the "isodiametric," which is often found on ancient
cloth and is definitely on the Shroud of Turin, exudes a gel known as *lichenothelia varnish*
which is high in carbon content; thus, every century the Shroud of Turin gets *younger*
by present carbon-dating techniques and no currently available method can overcome
this contamination, which skews the laboratory dating.

✠

On the Road to Emmaus

A.D. 33

As I waited for Hosea to come to me, I carefully refolded Jesus' shroud, ready to put it away, pending decision as to our ultimate disposal of it. I had just made the final fold and the shroud was in my lap when, from the doorway, Hosea asked, "May I come in, Master Joseph? And may I continue to eat my tardy lunch?"

As I answered in the affirmative, I quickly covered the shroud with the towel which I had earlier been using to rough-up and test a part of the body image. Not that I wouldn't trust Hosea with this secret. He had been with our family since before my birth, and I would literally trust him with my life. However, the difficulties he might encounter on the errand I was about to send him were unpredictable, and I preferred that he not have the problem of keeping a secret should his inquiries produce hostility in the Temple environs.

Hosea sat near me on a couch as he held on his knees a small serving platter on which lay the bone of a leg of lamb, from which he began to trim the last fragments of meat, using a sharp kitchen knife of good Damascus steel. Being a committed follower of The Way of Jesus, he was well aware of my current Sanhedrin problems with Caiaphas' Sadducee clique and the ultra-conservative Pharisees. Accordingly, I got right to the point, telling him that by putting Jesus' body in my tomb, plus his subsequent resurrection, my situation at the Temple may have worsened. I explained that Caiaphas might be planning action against me, including possible arrest, and that I might even have to consider leaving the country. I knew that Hosea had at least two relatives who were servants in Caiaphas' household, and I reminded him of the clerk in Caiaphas' office who was a secret follower of The Way.

I asked Hosea not to go near my townhouse, which might be watched by Temple guards, but to go directly and seek out those we could trust to learn if possible of Caiaphas' intentions toward me. I explained that as soon as he obtained all the information he could, he was to return to Bethany, and if I were not present to report his information to Lazarus.

Hosea was watching me closely as I concluded these instructions—too closely, in fact, because his knife hit a piece of gristle near the end of the bone and flew out of his hand. The knife looped gracefully in the air and we both were too stunned to act until it landed point-first on the inside of his left wrist. The point of the knife embedded in the bone of his forearm, and stood quivering there. It doubtless severed a major blood vessel because strong spurts of blood began to come from the wound on both sides of the knife. Belatedly, I jerked the knife out of the wound and quickly folded my towel and wrapped it around Hosea's wrist.

Finally he spoke in a quavering voice: "Master Joseph, the pain is great and I feel about to faint."

I knew that the blood he had lost was doubtless the cause of his faintness, and my eyes misted-over with concern for this faithful servitor whom I loved like an older brother. I tightened the towel and squeezed it against his wrist; at the same time I circled his shoulders with my other arm and bid him lay his head on my lap. As he did so I held his wounded wrist straight into the air in hope of reducing the surges of blood from the wound.

Just a few moments later Hosea opened his eyes and partly turned his head, saying, "Master, I suddenly feel perfectly well. I certainly am no longer faint, and think I can sit up."

I had misgivings, but his eyes showed no pain or fear or malaise, and so I assisted him as he sat upright. "Master," he said with some awe, "I truly feel that my wrist no longer bleeds—will you unwrap the towel?"

Again, his request did not seem sensible, but very slowly and carefully I unwrapped the towel and expected to examine the edge of the wound. But I couldn't find the wound! Finally, I had the towel completely off his arm. I saw nothing but a few dribbles and smears of blood, but no wound! I wiped his arm completely clean and we both examined the spot where we knew the knife had entered his wrist. There was not the slightest mark!

"Master! You have healed me just as the Lord Jesus healed!" he exclaimed.

Then, looking at the folded shroud in my lap, I knew what must have happened. Just as the woman with the issue of blood was healed by touching Jesus' robe while he wore it, now my servant was healed by touching Jesus' shroud through which his spirit essence had passed in the resurrection. Hosea's head had lain on the shroud and the elbow of his injured arm had rested on it.[1]

I was sure that I had not done the healing—I had not even had a thought or composed a prayer for his healing, but I decided to let him think as he chose rather than explain what was going through my mind. It was past mid-afternoon and we both had much to do, so I said a brief prayer of thanks for his healing and bid him start into the City. Checking the shroud carefully to be sure none of Hosea's blood had fallen on it, I put it away in the cupboard's chest.

Shortly thereafter I privately bid Lazarus farewell, telling him of Hosea's errand, and that I would return after a brief visit to Arimathea. It was late afternoon and I had much thinking and planning to do as I circled the City before picking up the lower road to Arimathea and Joppa. Actually, there are parallel roads to Arimathea and Joppa, and I took the southernmost one which passes through Emmaus; I never rode into the crowds of Jerusalem during festival periods, such as Passover, but always stabled my mule with my good friend Cleopas, one of the Seventy, who lived in Emmaus.

I walked as fast as I comfortably could, expecting to sup that evening in Emmaus, and would probably ride much of the night thereafter to reach Arimathea as soon as possible. My mind was in part occupied with thoughts of the remarkable healing of Hosea's wound, and of what this dimension of the shroud might portend for the future. Would it, in addition to all else, be an instrumentality for miraculous healings in the years and even centuries to come? What a spectacular outreach of Jesus' continuing ministry!—just another reason we must act with the greatest care and foresight to safeguard the shroud and to provide usefully for its future. And again, the question of limited secrecy arises. For the moment, Lazarus is the only one with whom I can share these questions and wonderings when I return to his home, probably on the morrow—and I haven't as yet even told him of Hosea's healing!

After circling outside the northern section of the City wall, on the pathway that led west and slightly north of Jerusalem, I joined the Emmaus-Joppa road, still lost in my thoughts, when someone hailed me, "Brother Joseph! May I walk with you?"

Looking up, I saw that Cleopas was a few steps away, smiling at me. He had been at the home of Mary, mother of Mark, and had heard the stories of the women and of Peter. Naturally, he was most anxious to hear the story of my experience at the tomb, and I began to recount it to him.

I had barely started a fresh telling of my story when a stranger suddenly appeared between us, showing obvious great interest in what I was saying. I say the stranger "appeared" because we had noticed no one close by on the road—just all at once he was there. Cleopas and I each gave him a close look, but did not remember having seen him before. He did seem oddly familiar to me, although I would not have been able to identify the familiarity. In fact, for some reason his face did not seem precise-featured and clear—it was as if he was walking in a mist or fog. I remarked on this thought in my mind but dismissed the notion, explaining to myself that we were walking into the westward-lowering sun, whose brightness was handicapping my vision.

Principally, though, the stranger's extreme eagerness to hear my story doubtless distracted me from thinking more fully about his identity. And his seeming ignorance of either the crucifixion or the resurrection of Jesus shocked Cleopas, who commented: "You must be the only visitor in Jerusalem who has not heard of the happenings of this weekend!"

"What happenings?" he asked.

Cleopas seemed to think this a good opportunity to practice on a stranger a telling of the Good News of Jesus' gospel and of The Way which he had inaugurated. He explained: "In recent years, we have been blessed in this country by the ministry of Jesus from Galilee, who has been a mighty prophet, a great teacher and the most powerful healer we have known in our lifetimes, but the chief priests of the Temple feared and were jealous of him, and they managed to induce the Roman authorities to crucify him two days ago, but today he rose from the dead through the sealed door of his tomb."

"But how do you know that?" asked the stranger.

To which Cleopas replied, "Why, some of our women saw him and talked to him, after finding a heavenly messenger presiding over the opened tomb."

For more than an hour we walked slowly on, and we found that the stranger himself was a powerful teacher and he proceeded to interpret for us the scriptures concerning Moses and the prophets. Also, he recalled for us all of the prophecies concerning the Messiah, and explained them to us. Cleopas and I were engrossed and intrigued by the profound explanations of Scripture given us by the stranger, our steps lagging to a complete stop from time to time as we became excitedly involved in his teachings.

When we found ourselves at Emmaus, we urged the stranger to stop there and eat with us so he could meet our brethren of The Way who lived there. He agreed to do so, and while we were at the table he took the bread, blessed and broke it. As he did this we immediately recognized that it was Jesus, but as we reached to embrace him he immediately vanished.

Cleopas arose from the table, saying he must go quickly to tell the disciples in Jerusalem. Whereupon, after lingering a short while for discussions with the brethren, I decided to continue my journey home to Arimathea, even though I would consume much of the night in doing so. I took my mule from Cleopas' stable and bid the brethren good-night, as I mounted the mule and turned my face toward Arimathea.

As I rode, I mused on the fantastic experience of the afternoon, and tried to make sense of it. I remembered Jesus' torture and crucifixion and burial of two days ago—of how badly his body had been brutalized and of how certain I was of his death. And I recalled the aftermath of the resurrection just this morning—the appearance of the shroud envelope in which his body must have dissolved and through which his soul must have flown—and then, the appearance of the image and blood stains on the shroud. Yet, how to rationalize those scenes with this afternoon, as Cleopas and I walked slowly and conversed extensively with Jesus all the way to Emmaus without recognizing him?

There was nothing special or unusual about his appearance as we walked in broad daylight and looked into his eyes less than an arm's length away—his body seemed solid, but it could not have been his physical body for there was no sign at all of the injuries of his passion—his face was no longer savaged as I last saw it in the tomb before covering it with the face-cloth—lacerated, bloody and swollen. And especially, it could not have been his physical body, for had he not melted into the atmosphere as we reached to embrace him there at Cleopas' table?

This morning at Lazarus' home, I felt that the enigmas of Jesus' resurrection were beyond my mental grasp—but now, what could I say, how explain, this spirit body in which he could live fully, but could dissolve it in the wink of an eye? All is possible with God—Yea, verily!

CHAPTER NOTE:

1. Through the centuries, healings seem to have occurred through or in the presence of the Shroud of Turin; see Tribbe: *Portrait of Jesus?* pp. 185-193.

CHAPTER SIX

✠

The Edessa Connection

A.D. 33

WHEN I REACHED MY HOME IN ARIMATHEA it was already the sixth hour of the night and only six hours more until sun-up, but I had much to do and so before retiring I arranged to be awakened at my usual time in the morning. I had sketched many tentative plans for myself as I rode on from Emmaus, and upon arising I was pleased to find that Thaddaeus was in my office, where he worked much of the time. I sent for him to come see me privately in my home, as we always shared our intimate thoughts about The Way. Thaddaeus was one of The Seventy,[1] and I had been happy to permit him to take off as much time from work as he wished in order to follow Jesus and listen to his teachings whenever Jesus was in Samaria and Judea, and nearby areas. He, and his father before him, had been effective and trusted employees of our firm. His family came from the old city of Paneas, where he was born; in earlier years we had called it Hemorrhissa, but the Greeks called it Paneas, and then Philip the Tetrarch made it his capital (after the death of his father, Herod the Great) and renamed it Caesarea Philippi in honor of Rome and himself. As usual, city names can be very confusing in our land.

Thaddaeus entered my study and embraced me warmly. "Is it true, Brother Joseph," he asked with a rush, "that Jesus is alive again after you buried him three days ago? Will he resume his ministry soon? Late yesterday afternoon we began receiving strange stories from the brethren in Jerusalem." This 28-year-old favorite of mine spoke at top speed and with the exuberance of a very vital young man.

"You ask much in one breath." I replied to him with a broad smile. "Now make yourself comfortable on the couch and be patient for I have much to tell you and to discuss with you. What you and I will say to each other today may amount to the most important conversation we have ever had."

Not having seen Thaddaeus since the day before the crucifixion, I decided first to give him a detailed account, insofar as I knew it, of the last twenty-four hours of Jesus' life, of the part played by Nicodemus and myself on the afternoon of the crucifixion, and of yesterday's experiences involving the two disciples, myself, the two Marys and Salome, Lazarus, the shroud with its mystical markings, Hosea, Cleopas and the "stranger" on the road to Emmaus. Thaddaeus was totally enthralled by this telling—going from climax to climax—and his exclamations of pain and suffering, surprise, joy and excitement, showed he was fully absorbing the story.

"Also, let me respond just briefly to the two questions you first asked me," I said. "It was the teaching of Jesus, which you know I accept completely, that the true essence of all mankind—of himself as well as each of us—is *spirit,* which never dies; that the death of the physical body is no real tragedy, for the spirit lives on without interruption. That transition happened for Jesus-the-Man at mid-afternoon of the crucifixion day. What happened at the tomb yesterday morning was much different; there, a resurrection event embracing the full *Christos* power, marked the inside of the shroud with his mirror-image, consumed the body, and blew the boulder from the doorway. It was undoubtedly an event unique in this world, for none such has ever been recorded for us before.

"That event," I continued, "was a demonstration of God's power and of the high status of Jesus the Messiah/Christ—but that event did not alter the spirit of Jesus-the-Man, which was released from the physical body at death. And, if those statements seem contradictory and confusing for you, they will always be so, to some extent, for me also. The Spirit-body of Jesus was shown to a few of us yesterday, and during the appearance to Mary of Magdala it was implied that he would later appear to more of the disciples. But it was not a physical body; he controlled his appearances so that neither Mary nor Cleopas nor I recognized him—though his mother did; also, for all four of us, he disappeared instantly by dissolving into the air. This was not his physical body, and therefore his physical ministry will not resume. His ministry will now have to be carried on by us who remain; he tried to tell us this in recent months.

"Maybe at this point," I added, "you are beginning to see that there are many very serious problems that I must resolve right away."

"Yes," he agreed, with seriousness replacing excitement in his face, "and certainly the safety of the shroud is the most important concern, but the palace of Lazarus should be a safe place for some time."

"Under different circumstances that might be true," I replied, "but you will recall that when Annas and Caiaphas heard that Lazarus had been raised by Jesus after four days in the tomb they were furious, and vowed to kill both Lazarus and Jesus. Because of Jesus' resurrection I feel sure Caiaphas will now find an excuse to kill Lazarus as well. Caiaphas cannot permit Lazarus to be living proof that Jesus had more spiritual power than he. All of that was aggravated further by Jesus' action last week when he attacked the money-changers and blood-sacrifice salesmen in the Temple. Revenues for the High Priest from those two activities and from the Temple tax are vital to Caiaphas' power and his opulent style of living.

"Similarly," I continued, "it seems inevitable that Caiaphas will soon plot my ouster from the Sanhedrin, my arrest and my death. I have sent Hosea into the City to inquire in these regards, but I must make my plans on the assumption that my departure from the country, perhaps never to return, is essential if I am to keep my freedom."

Thaddaeus was thoughtfully nodding his head in agreement and he mused aloud, "I *do* hope you are going to give me opportunity to participate in your plans, as I see that the problems are urgent as well as important."

"You certainly do figure prominently in my plans," I responded; "in fact, your role, if you agree to take it, is crucial to protection of the shroud of Jesus and the long-range success of The Way, as I see it. You will re-member that soon after your father's death I took you on a trip with me to the Parthian city of Edessa, lying some 180 miles north and east from Syrian Antioch, and there you met the King of Edessa, Abgar V. Edessa, known in their Syriac language as Urhai, is the capital of Osroene, Parthia's westernmost province, or satrapy.

"You will also remember that Lazarus, and just a few of us in this area, were privy to a very strange correspondence Jesus had earlier this month with King Abgar," I went on. "When the historian, Haggai, recently returned from a visit to Edessa in the company of the Edessan diplomat, Ananias, they stopped for a few days of rest here in my house, and asked how they might reach the healer, Jesus, because they had a letter for him from King Abgar. I sent you to escort them to the home of Lazarus in Bethany where Jesus was then staying. To refresh your memory, here are copies of that correspondence, which Lazarus was able to provide at my request just before I left his residence yesterday afternoon":

Abgar Ukkama [the Black],[2] to Jesus the Good Physician, who has appeared in the land of Jerusalem,

My Lord, peace:

I have heard concerning you and your healings that you do not heal with drugs or roots; it is rather by your word that you give sight to the blind, cause the lame to walk, cleanse the lepers, and cause the deaf to hear; by your word you expel unclean spirits and demons, and cure those in pain. You even raise the dead. So, when I heard of the great wonders which you do, I concluded that either you are God and that you have come down from heaven to achieve these things, or that you do these things because you are the son of God. Because of this and since I reverence you, I now write begging that you come and heal me of my grievous illnesses, of swollen joints and leprosy.

Furthermore, I have heard that the Jews murmur against you and wish to do you harm. My city is quite small, but it is highly esteemed, and there is space in it where both of us might live in peace.

To that request, Jesus dictated the following reply which Ananias wrote down and took to Abgar:

From Jesus of Galilee, To Abgar V, King of Edessa:

Blessed are you with your faith in me, although you have not seen me. Indeed, it has been written concerning me that those who have seen me will not believe in me, but those who have not seen will have faith and life. With regard to what you have written me, that I should come to you, it is necessary for me to return to my Father in heaven who sent me. But when I have ascended to Him I will send one of my disciples to you who will cure your illnesses and bring life to you and those with you.

As for your city, may it be blessed and may no enemy ever again rule over it.[3]

As he finished reading and looked up, Thaddaeus' eyes sparkled, and he almost shouted, "The shroud! The shroud of Jesus! If it could heal Hosea without either of you expecting, it, the shroud can heal Abgar!—and that would put it safely outside the Roman Empire and the reach of the Sanhedrin."

"You've read my mind," was my smiling response. "And not only that, it seems to me that Jesus knew how things were going to turn out—else why would he tell Abgar that he would 'send' a disciple and not do it? Now is when our serious planning must begin. How would you and your lovely wife, Miriam, like to move permanently to Edessa and take charge of my office there?"

"Why, it sounds too good to be true. I really liked King Abgar, you know neither Miriam nor I has a close relative left. But what about Tobias bar Tobias?—he has worked faithfully for you for many years."

"He has indeed, but the report I received from him by the caravan last month begs me to find a replacement for him because of his age and ill health. I've been worrying over that action ever since. Not that I don't have several good men I could send there, but I want to be absolutely certain that his replacement provides Tobias bar Tobias with an appropriate retirement income from the profits of the business. Some managers might skimp on that retirement pay to make the office reports look better; I wouldn't worry on that score with you there, Brother Thaddaeus."

"I can hardly wait to tell Miriam," he responded with a beaming smile.

"Yes, you will have to do so," I agreed, "because I may want you to start in three or four days. But you must caution her that she cannot mention the shroud to anyone, even to the servants you will take along. You see, we have a very special problem of secrecy that concerns our brothers, the followers of The Way. Although Jesus has made it clear that we are to take his Gospel to all nations, for some generations yet we Jews may be the backbone of his church. He also made it clear that much of "the law" that has been imposed on us by our scribes and priests is at least outmoded if it ever had spiritual value, but such a religious philosophy will not be understood or easily accepted by many Jewish followers of The Way. And I feel that taboos about unclean burial clothes and about images, especially of a man such as Jesus, which images some people would want to worship as an idol, are taboos too powerful for us to risk at this time. So, the shroud must be a secret relic for a while."

"I understand and agree with what you say, Brother Joseph," responded Thaddaeus, "and we can trust Miriam's discretion. Also, I am sure that the Galilean disciples, who are the ones likely to be leaders of The Way, are also ones who are so conservative that the taboos you mention will probably govern them. I doubt they will even want at this time to share the Good News with gentiles."

"True," I responded. "And that is the reason I want us to go to Bethany at once to discuss with Lazarus the problem of whom we will take into our confidence. He presently has custody of the shroud and is safekeeping it in his palace, is the acknowledged leader of the Judean disciples of The Way, and also was doubtless the man closer to Master Jesus on a personal basis than any other."

CHAPTER NOTES:

1. "The Seventy" is mentioned in Luke 10: 1-12 and 17. Jesus initially appointed them to go ahead as an advance party in the areas where he would come to preach. After the Resurrection they were the active missionary/preachers, while the Twelve seemed to take on a more supervisory role. Those of the Seventy who appear in this story are Cleopas, Thaddaeus, Barnabus, Stephen, Silvanus, Philip (the Evangelist), and Aristobulus. A complete list of the Seventy is only found in apocryphal sources and is probably not fully reliable. Chapters 12 and 13 of Eusebius' *History of the Church* discusses activity of the Seventy.

2. Abgar presumably was called Ukkama, "the black," because his malady was known as *black leprosy* (see Wilson: *The Shroud of Turin,* p. 237).

3. The text of these letters is reported in *The History of the Church* by Eusebius, ca. A.D. 325.

CHAPTER SEVEN

✠

We Make Plans for the Shroud Image

A.D. 33

By MID-MORNING Thaddaeus and I set out on the Jerusalem road at as fast a pace as our mules would take us and, as I had done the previous day, we circled the City instead of traversing it. The noonday meal had begun by the time we reached Lazarus' home in Bethany, but Martha quickly had food brought for us while Lazarus pulled couches to the table.

As soon as conventional politeness would permit, I told Lazarus we needed to have a further conversation with him in my bed-chamber. When the doorway was secured, Lazarus said that he hoped I was not expecting word from Hosea already, as he had not yet returned from Jerusalem.

"No, dear Lazarus," I replied "urgent as Hosea's errand was—and it could be vital to my life—it is nothing like as important as the matter of handling the shroud which we must now discuss, and that we briefly mentioned yesterday."

Lazarus showed no surprise because of my extreme statements, for he knew me well, and he merely relaxed on a couch and waited expectantly. "Our concern relates to Jesus' shroud and the images put on it by his resurrection," I began, "and I must abjectly apologize for not taking the time yesterday to discuss with you the expanded situation that developed as I was briefing Hosea."

"My revered Joseph," responded Lazarus, "you never need apologize to me; I was well aware that yesterday you had momentous problems on your mind that arose from the spectacular events in the garden of tombs and discovery of the markings on the shroud, and which were heightened in some way as you talked with Hosea. And I knew that you would discuss them with me when you conveniently could do so. Trouble yourself no more on my behalf—just explain the problems and tell me what I can do."

Of course, I relaxed at his words and began carefully to recite the story of the unexpected and instantaneous healing of Hosea's wound. I concluded by saying, "Not even Hosea suspects the channel of his healing, and only we three in this room have knowledge of the story of the shroud of Jesus. Let me now spread it out so Thaddaeus can see for himself."

Taking the shroud from the chest in my cupboard, I noted that my hands were shaking noticeably with my awareness of the power and importance of this relic, and I accepted the help of Thaddaeus and Lazarus in spreading it out on the couches. Then, we fully opened the window drapes to give us maximum light. I next repeated parts of my story for Thaddaeus as I pointed out to him the various features of these markings that I had found, and explained my speculations and the conclusions I had reached in my own mind.

Thaddaeus was obviously awestruck and had few questions. Finally, he observed: "You spoke of the mystical quality of the body image, and now I can realize that it defies description. Yes, even though the blood stains involve mysteries that cannot be explained, still they are real blood, as clear as any blood stains, and visible to us at any distance. But the body image—how ghostly—how heavenly!"

"Help me fold and put the shroud away," I requested of Thaddaeus, "for now we must make some difficult decisions of what to do with this cloth and who to tell about it."

As we settled down again I resumed the discussion by saying to Lazarus, "Perhaps the biggest problem of what to do with the shroud, seems to Thaddaeus and me to be solvable."

I then referred to the correspondence between Abgar and Jesus, of which I had requested copies from him yesterday.

"Aha!" interrupted Lazarus, "I now see the devious plot developing in your fine Pharisaic mind." He grinned, for he frequently joked with me about my service on the Sanhedrin. "The shroud clearly has miraculous healing powers embedded in it or available through it, just as the woman with the issue of blood found to be true of the cloak Jesus was wearing. Abgar received Jesus' promise of a healing, to be delivered by a disciple, and here stands disciple Thaddaeus—or should I say floats?—for I perceive

him to be so excited that his feet hardly touch the floor. Am I correct? It
is a beautiful plan. It is perfect!"

"We all laughed, and I acknowledged that indeed this was the way of
our present thinking,

"You know," continued Lazarus, with a far-off look of reminiscence
in his eyes, "this reminds me of the interesting conversation that occurred
here, when Abgar's emissary, Ananias, was brought to this house by Haggai
and Thaddaeus, to present Abgar's petition to Jesus. Of course, impracti-
cal as the specific request was—with Jesus' thoughts then on Golgotha—I
knew he would never insult the diplomat nor flatly reject a plea for help—
so, I was most curious to see how he would respond. Jesus, with that characteristic twinkle in his eye, obviously was not going to quickly respond,
but was going to keep Ananias, Haggai and myself guessing a while as to
what his response would be.

"He began to paraphrase and summarize for us from the Scriptures
concerning the chronicles of our great kings, and specifically of the years
when our northern kingdom was beholden to the kings of Syria, then
known as the land of Aram, who intermittently harassed our cities with
their armies (and which kingdom of Aram in those years, of course, embraced the present satrapy of Edessa).

"I began to see the point of his story when he mentioned that the commander of all the Syrian armies, a man of great valor and highly respected
by his king, was suffering from the ravages of leprosy. He told of the young
slave maiden, Naomi, carried off from Israel by a Syrian army to be a servant to the wife of this great general, and who confidently told her mistress
that the prophet, Elisha, residing in Jericho could heal the general. Upon
learning of this, the general went with a troop of horses and chariots, all
the way from Damascus to Jericho, to the house of Elisha.

"Jesus was then smiling broadly, as he recounted that Elisha would
not come out of his house but instructed the general that if he wished to
be healed he should retrace his steps, less than an hour's journey down
the mountain slope, and dip himself seven times in the River Jordan. To
the general this was an insult, and in a fury he stepped into his chariot to
return to Damascus. However, as they neared the River, his aides urged
him that the instruction was so simple, why not try it? His anger having
subsided somewhat, the general agreed, and went down into the River,
and after submerging seven times, indeed his flesh and skin were as healthy
as that of a child.

"'Now,' said Jesus to Ananias, 'I perceive that your illustrious monarch
knew this story, and told you to tell me that he would come to the Jordan
or would do anything I asked, if I would heal him.'

"Ananias was aghast," continued Lazarus, "his mouth had dropped open and he stammered, almost speechless, before he was finally able to acknowledge that Abgar had read to him, Ananias, the story of Elisha's healing of General Naaman,[1] and had said those very words to him. Ananias explained that a few months ago, as he returned from a mission to Egypt for Abgar, he stopped over briefly in Jerusalem, and that he listened to Jesus' teaching and saw him healing—that he saw him heal lepers completely and instantly just by his mere touch.

"Jesus then said to him, 'I am impressed that you believed what you saw, that your King believed what you told him, and that he knew our beloved Scriptures well enough to find the story of Naaman which happened three-quarters of a millennium ago, and I regret that I am not free to go to him; nor would I wish to humble him by compelling him to travel in his present condition. Tell him to be of good cheer, that his troubles will soon be resolved. If you will serve briefly as my scribe, I will dictate my reply to your King.' And that was how the letter, whose copy you have seen, came to be written."

Both stimulated and awed as I listened to Lazarus' account, I was silent for a few minutes after he finished, and then I continued with our plans.

I explained that I had to replace my present office manager in Edessa and that Thaddaeus and his wife, Miriam, had agreed to make Edessa their permanent home, so that the Shroud of Jesus could in this fashion be given a safe repository outside the Roman Empire and beyond the reach of the Sanhedrin. Also, that it was my thought that Thaddaeus might leave here with the shroud on the morrow or the following day, and that he and Miriam could leave a day or so later for Edessa.

"This plan seems eminently practical and desirable from the standpoint of our problem," was the way Lazarus summarized it for us. "Now, we must carefully consider whom we should consult and advise about this plan. As you may know, for some months Jesus and the Galilean disciples have discussed missionary assignments for the Seventy and missionary responsibilities for the Twelve; these assignments and responsibilities are presently firm and final in only a few cases, but for the Empire of Parthia, which includes Edessa's little country of Osroene, it seems almost certain that Thomas will have responsibility on behalf of the Twelve."

Turning to me, Lazarus asked, "Thomas has been almost a neighbor of yours for years, has he not?"

"Yes, certainly," I replied; "his home in Lydda of Judea is very close to Arimathea, and both as boys and men we have had a long and pleasant friendship. He has spent many nights at my home. And I see your point, Lazarus, and I agree that we must include Thomas in our consultation.

Also, I have no concern at all as to his trustworthiness. Some people criticize his doubts and hesitancy at times, but Thomas merely wants reasons for his beliefs and actions—yet, once he has them, he is as tough and fearless as anyone."

"So, this brings us to a single question," said Lazarus: "What Galilean shall we select? At this time in their spiritual development, I fear no Galilean of the Twelve can be trusted to agree with us about the shroud and then resist the criticism of his peers."

"I agree," I replied, "and your latter point is the crucial one—the attitude of his friends. However, we don't necessarily have to have one of the Twelve. Barnabas is a man of spiritual stature who has strength as well. I would like so much to have him with us, but fear we must pass him over; he is a native of Cana, near Jesus' village of Nazareth, but having spent most of his adult life on Cyprus I feel he may not be in Judea or Galilee enough during the coming months and years to present our views to the leaders of The Way when the time seems right to publicly disclose the existence of the fabulous shroud of Jesus with its enigmatic images. Of course, I'm assuming that it's likely neither of us will be here."

Thaddaeus had been quietly listening to this long conversation between Lazarus and me, but at this point he asked, "What about Stephen?"

We both smiled at this surprising but logical suggestion. Stephen was equally prominent and of spiritual stature when compared with Barnabas, and was not only strong but was often aggressive and fearless in presenting his views. The Galileans certainly considered him one their own, for he had been raised in Tiberias although born in Caesarea. His Jewish parents came from the Greek city of Ephesus and his father had been a life-long civil employee of the Romans. Although a Hellenist who could be expected to support our views, he was so fully approved by the Twelve that it is now a foregone conclusion that he will be one of the first deacons to be chosen when the Twelve get over the shock of the crucifixion and begin to take care of organizational problems.

Seeing agreement in my face, Lazarus spoke for us all: "Excellent! I know I can reach both Stephen and Thomas through the home of Mary, mother of Mark. Let us plan a further meeting as soon this afternoon as they can get here. I would like them to see the shroud while there is still good daylight, if possible."

CHAPTER NOTE:

1. Naomi was a Jewish maiden who was carried as a slave into Aram (Syria) in antiquity. Elisha was a Jewish prophet of the same period. Naaman was a high general of the armies of Aram (of the same period) who was a leper.

CHAPTER EIGHT

✠

A Casket Will Present a Face

A.D. 33

*F*ORTUNATELY, Thomas and Stephen arrived within the hour. In the meantime, Lazarus and I were each engaged in mental planning and personal thoughts, but every once in a while I noticed Thaddaeus pacing like a worried old man—he obviously was anxious for action and was made nervous by waiting, though his face showed pleasure and excitement.

I was especially pleased that we were resolving our problems so quickly—it was now just past noon of the second day of the week, and the events of yesterday morning at Jesus' open tomb were still but a few hours behind us. Moving with this speed it seemed unlikely that we would meet official interference from Caiaphas, as we would have Thaddaeus on his way before the week's end. Thaddaeus had left appropriate packing instructions that morning in Arimathea, and I had arranged for a Phoenician ship under a captain I trusted implicitly. Of course, in many ways it would have been simpler to pack a string of burros and join a northbound caravan, but it would have made Thaddaeus and his precious cargo vulnerable to Caiaphas and Herod for several days—a risk I was not willing to take. By ship, he would leave Joppa and not touch land until reaching Seleucia Pieria, the port of Syrian Antioch, where he would buy pack animals for the overland trip to Edessa. Two-thirds of their trip would be on the Great Sea, which would be very pleasant in this spring-time of the year—during the month of Nisan, which some knew as Abib.

With a minimum of ceremony, after greeting Thomas and Stephen, we conducted them to my bed-chamber. I told them that we three had a secret concerning Jesus that we were going to share with them, and I asked that they pledge to keep it a secret from all others for at least a week, and hopefully for such further time of months or years as their own judgment should dictate.

Thomas quickly replied, "Brother Joseph, you have never served me ill in my entire life, and if our friendship is not worth a week of silence then it is worth nothing at all! Of course, I agree."

Stephen did not hesitate to add, "I agree, also."

So, I proceeded to explain what had happened with me the previous morning at the tomb, what I had discovered on the shroud when I examined it, and how Hosea had received an instantaneous healing by touching the shroud. At this point, Lazarus and I moved briskly and eagerly, like schoolboys with something to show in class, and carefully removed the shroud from its chest and spread it across several couches, while Thaddaeus opened the window drapes to give us maximum light. I then went over its features slowly so that they could see for themselves the wonders, the clarity and the enigmas of this so holy cloth.

Thomas and Stephen had said nothing at all while my explanations and their examinations were in progress. Finally, when they, and I, were satisfied that they were fully informed, they stood staring at the shroud in almost disbelief for several moments more, and then said, almost in unison, "Surely, this was the Christ, the Son of God!"

We refolded the shroud and put it away, and I then told Thomas and Stephen of the assignment with the shroud which Thaddaeus would begin in a day or two. Lazarus also brought out for their examination the correspondence between Abgar and Jesus which only Thomas had known about, but even he had not seen.

After further silence, Thomas spoke again: "It is an excellent plan to involve Thaddaeus and King Abgar in this fashion. I agree completely with the plan. I also agree fully with your decision as to secrecy. This is too important a relic for it to be prematurely made public. As for me, I will go to my grave in silence on this subject if that seems the appropriate stance, as our fortunes unfold."

After a further silence, he said, "In truth, this was a miracle greater than all those performed in his lifetime added together!"

"I am greatly honored," was Stephen's comment "but do not really know why I am included in this august group. I also agree this is a perfect plan, and I will guard the secret with my very life, if need be. Having been raised as a Galilean, I must say that you have been kind and generous with my Galilean brothers of The Way, in your evaluation of their probable reactions to this shroud. With the exception of Barnabus, if he can be called Galilean, no other one from that region would be able *today* to appreciate the enlightenment that awaits him on the threads of this cloth, when able to put aside the blindfolds of priest-made taboos. I am sure that the Holy Spirit which Jesus promised will change most of them in time, but until that happens you are right that this relic with its earth-shaking message must not be jeopardized.

"Each of us has his own path as we progress upon The Way," he continued; "dear Thomas, here, with his inquiring mind and impeccable logic leaps far ahead of we plodders; and it is no wonder that of all our company Jesus expressed a personal love for only Lazarus, whose meditative and mystical insights took him soaring to spiritual heights that only Jesus understood; yet who is to say but what our fundamentalist Galilean brethren might win the most souls, since they will be understood by the multitudes of like mind. Yes, it is a good plan."

"Stephen belittles himself," interposed Lazarus. "A plodder he may be in some respects, but Jesus was the only other man so effective in public debate with the scribes and chief priests. When you hear, as I have, with what audacity Stephen attacks these Temple stooges to their faces you must have admiration for him."

Thomas held up his hand at this point, to get our attention, with as serious a look on his face as I have ever seen. "Friends and brethren," he began, "I would like to make a brief speech and then make a few suggestions. I think I have been listening to everything said by each of you—I hope I have—but I have been thinking too:

"Why did God, or his Christos facet incarnate in Jesus, decide to have the resurrection event yesterday morning in that tomb? The body of Jesus was already dead, for two days, and his spirit had completed its transition into the afterlife. The destruction of the physical body is really going to be a handicap to The Way. We would be better off if the body were available as proof that Jesus had died. We didn't need the boulder blown from the doorway—we could have rolled it.

"It seems to me that the only possible reason for the resurrection was to mark the images on the shroud," he continued. "The marked shroud is necessary to give us proof without question that Jesus—though a man— was not a *mere* man. That as Messiah, or Christos, he was God-man and more God than we are—that he was special in God's sight and highly favored of God.

"That's the end of my speech," he said, smiling, "but here are some further thoughts: I suggest that we all go over to the home of Mary, mother of Mark, where the brethren are gathered and have Peter conduct a formal ceremony of consecration for Thaddaeus; we can do this without mentioning the shroud, in view of his imminent departure, the nature of his assignment by Joseph, and the large Jewish community in Edessa. I will recommend it to Peter. I think there is no doubt I will be given responsibility for Parthia, Persia and Armenia and countries to the east, since I've had some experience there and no one else wants them. Accordingly, I will definitely plan to leave for Edessa in a couple of months and stay with Thaddaeus as long as necessary to see that his ministry is well established."

We all expressed pleasure at these suggestions, and then he continued: "In Jerusalem, we learned from Cleopas how he and you, Joseph, met with the Lord Jesus on the road to Emmaus, but perhaps you have not yet learned from Lazarus of the occurrence last night at the home of Mary, mother of Mark. At about noon yesterday, after hearing all of the stories from the garden of tombs, I left her home to take care of some pressing business in Jericho that I had neglected, and returned about noon today to learn that I had missed a most spectacular visit from Jesus at supper last night when ten of our number were there.

"Now, I *do* accept his resurrection and the record of this fabulous shroud, even though I can't explain, it," he went on, "and I do not mean to doubt your honesty and sincerity, dear Joseph, nor of the others, but his appearances—that are solid, and are not solid—are something I am not willing to believe until I have the experience myself. I hope you are not offended by my doubts—I think Peter was! Jesus seemed to imply another evening visit at that house in the near future, so I am going to spend every evening there for a while."

We all laughed with Thomas about his doubts—for which he was well known—but in all seriousness I assured him that I might be doubting just as much as he if the experience had not come to me on the road to Emmaus.

"Those are most helpful suggestions and comments, Thomas," said Lazarus, "but I have the feeling you have not finished—was there more?"

"In fact there is," he responded, "but I just haven't completely thought it through; maybe you all can help. There will be several customs posts Thaddaeus must pass through and to minimize the risk of close examination it will be useful if we can have a semi-official document to keep the officious ones at these posts from being too nosy. Flavius Rubrius is second in command to Pontius Pilate and he secretly is a follower of The 'Way. He has been in Jerusalem for a few days and I believe he is to depart for their headquarters in Caesarea at about noontime tomorrow. I think if I see him in the morning I can induce him, without explanation, to provide a transmittal document that will appear to be covering a gift from Flavius to King Abgar, relating to a diplomatic mission from Tiberius Caesar to Artaban the Parthian Emperor, of which mission Flavius was a part last year. The Emperor forced them to stop in Edessa and negotiate from there; he would not let the mission come to his capital, Ctesiphon, and thus gave a small insult to Caesar, but Abgar was most cordial to Flavius and the other Romans."

We all expressed happy agreement with this proposal, and then Stephen interjected: "It is fairly common in every nation and region to find Jews serving as customs officers. If one of them noticed the blood which has soaked through the cloth in several places, and then suspected this was a used burial shroud, I can see that Thaddaeus still might have a small up-roar on his hands. The taboo against images is much less likely to spark an emotional outburst, so why not fold the shroud so that only the bloodied face is shown and fix it firmly into a ceremonial and decorative casket, deep enough only to accommodate the thickness of the folded cloth and with a hinged cover to protect the face. Thus, the document from Flavius (cover-ing transmittal of a gift from a Roman official to a foreign king) would, in most instances, preclude even a lifting of the cover."[1]

"A beautiful and practical idea," responded Thomas, with a gracious nod that was almost a bow, to Stephen, "and thus it will also be possible for Thaddaeus to delay disclosure in Edessa of the image's true nature as a burial shroud until the climate is right. For you can be sure that if we add large numbers of the Edessan Jews to our movement, they will soon be telling relatives in Jerusalem of everything new in Edessa."

From Thaddaeus' beaming face I knew he had a thought he could not much longer hold back, so I smiled and said, "Yes, Thaddaeus?"

"Brother Joseph," he almost shouted, "since Elias bar Jacob in your art shop returned from his months of training in both Armenia and Macedo-nia, he does the most beautiful inlay work with ivory, pearl, copper, silver and gold in the precious hardwoods you import from the Arabian coast. I am sure he could make a shallow casket with decorative lid that would be a most fitting repository for the Shroud of Jesus—and you know he would work day and night, gladly."

"You are right, of course," I replied, "and I know that Elias will safely protect our secret."

"Dear friends," interposed Lazarus, "it is already mid-afternoon—a messenger from Nicodemus is in the atrium, wishing to take brother Joseph from us for a few hours—also, I must ensure that Martha will provide us an evening meal before we go to Thaddaeus' consecration service."

"Before you both go," interrupted Stephen, "let me say just briefly: You all know that I have tried to put my Scribes School training to good use for our ministry by recording all of Jesus' sayings and discourses that I could during the past two years, in hopes that when a knowledgable and skilled writer is ready to tell the full story of Jesus, he can use these Sayings to embellish his telling. I have been worrying about possible destruction of the Sayings by an enemy of The Way, and have made a complete extra copy which is now at the home of Mary, mother of Mark. Don't you all think it would be wise for Thaddaeus to take this copy with him to Edessa for safekeeping and the future use of writers?"

All agreed enthusiastically with this suggestion, and I was beginning to feel that the threats inherent in the machinations of Caiaphas and his associates might force us to spread the gospel of The Way farther and faster and with more sincerity of effort than if we were warmly accepted into Judaism and became complaisant at home.

Indeed, I was being tempted to even consider Jesus' crucifixion might give us more persuasion to others, more opportunity to spread the gospel, and more zeal and devotion to the propagation of our beliefs. And it was this marvelous and provocative Shroud with it images of Jesus and his passion that began to open my mind to what Jesus had probably been trying to tell me after his descent from the mountain-top experience that the Twelve were beginning to call the Mount of Transfiguration.

CHAPTER NOTE:

1. From A.D. 33 to 944 a Christian relic in Edessa attracted pilgrims from all over Christendom; it was known as "The Face" or "The Image of Edessa" and, although history does not explain its origin and legends are varied and implausible on the point, it was assumed by all to be the "true likeness" of Jesus. It had two descriptive Greek names: *tetradiplon* which means "doubled in four" (*Writings of the Ante-Nicene Fathers*)— see Note XIV-16 of Wilson in *The Shroud of Turin; acheiropoietos* which means "not made by human hands."

CHAPTER NINE

✛

Easter Morning and the Guards

A.D. 33

HURRYING THROUGH THE GREAT HALL TO THE ATRIUM I found Nicodemus' huge servant, Samson, waiting for me. Born of the tribe of Dan, his parents must have known when they named him that he would be a large man, and he is immense, being a full head taller then any others of us who think ourselves tall.

Smiling broadly, he greeted me warmly and said, "Master Nicodemus bids me urge you to come to his home for supper this evening, as he will have the honorable Gamaliel, Sirach and others of The Way who will wish to listen to your special news. He knows that you rightly may be reluctant to walk the streets of Jerusalem unescorted, and I will see that no harm befalls you. I will gladly wait for you here until later in the day, if you wish."

"Dear Samson," I replied, cocking my head back to look him in the eyes, "I am highly pleased to have you as my escort and will certainly have no fear with you at my side. Let me advise Lazarus, and I will go with you right away, so that I can stop off for an hour or so at my townhouse before we continue on to Nicodemus' home."

Whereupon I sought out Lazarus and explained that I would be supping with Nicodemus and others, and would meet him later at the home of Mark's mother for the consecration ceremony for Thaddaeus. Bidding a brief good-bye to Thaddaeus, Thomas and Stephen, I set out with Samson for my own home. I wanted to be sure to take care of any household matters needing attention, and if time remained wished to be able to spend an hour in prayer and meditation, and in collecting my thoughts, as the expression goes.

Small talk from the ever-happy and garrulous Samson gave me all the gossip from Nicodemus' household and, before we hardly knew it, we had arrived at my premises, where I introduced Samson to the kitchen staff, knowing that he always was in the mood for food.

Shortly thereafter, as I mused, lost in my thoughts, while sitting in my study, Reuben—who runs the household in Hosea's absence—approached and softly said, "Master Joseph, may we speak with you?"

Looking up, I saw that Rachel, our very competent housekeeper, was with him. "Yes, certainly," I replied, though I suppose my welcoming smile was a bit wan. "How can I help you both?"

"Rachel tells me something that you might find important," replied Reuben, "and I have asked her to share it with you. You may recall that she has a cousin, Rufus Rubicus, who is a Roman by virtue of birth in Ephesus, though his mother, Martha bat Solomon* is Rachel's aunt. Rufus presently serves as one of Pilate's guards stationed in the Antonia fort adjoining the Temple. Rachel was just talking to him, when he stopped by for a bite of the tasty food in your kitchens, as he does when he gets homesick for his mother's cooking."

I laughed at the thought of the temptation of our Jewish food for the Roman soldier. "I remember meeting your cousin, Rachel, and a fine looking young man he is. What has he had to tell you?"

"Master Joseph," she replied, "rumors in the Antonia were that Pilate's wife, Claudia Procula,[1] urged the governor to be sure his seal on your tomb, where Jesus lay, be not broken and the tomb entered. Whether that be true or not, orders came from Pilate to the Antonia that a soldier be dispatched to the tomb to examine the seal and remain there on duty. My cousin Rufus was ordered for that duty. He tells of such an awesome happening while in the garden of the tombs yesterday morning that I asked him if he would tell it to you. He said he would. If it is important, I would not wish to trust my memory for the telling of it."

"Thank you so much, Rachel, for bringing this news," I responded. "When would Rufus be available to talk to me?"

"He just went down the street to a nearby shop," she replied, "and said he would stop here before returning to the Antonia for duty."

---

*"Bat" means "daughter of" in Aramaic.

"I think I hear him in the atrium, now," Reuben broke in to say. "Shall I fetch him?"

"Yes, please do," I said, "and Rachel, you are free to stay if you desire, but I well remember Rufus and shall welcome his visit." She excused herself and was just leaving the room as Reuben brought the soldier to me; she gave her cousin a smiling nod as she went through the doorway toward the rear of the house.

"Rufus Rubicus!" I greeted him. "Welcome to our home. I am pleased to see you again, and Rachel tells me you have interesting and perhaps important news for me regarding the tomb where we buried Jesus the Galilean."

"Yes, honorable Joseph," he replied. "I think you will find my report to be important. I would not have mentioned the matter in this house or elsewhere, but for the claim that Jesus is risen from the tomb. And I ask that you accept what I say in confidence, as I would not want my officers or Governor Pilate to know of this occurrence as an account told by me—I have certainly made no official report of it."

"I quite understand, and will respect your confidence, Rufus," I said. "Also, for whatever interest it may have for you, I can say from personal knowledge that Jesus' body had stiffened in death when we buried him, and yet I walked from here to Emmaus with him yesterday afternoon."

"As Rachel may have told you, we think the Governor's wife had urged his action, but, whether she did or not, we received his order two evenings ago, when your Master Jesus had been in the grave slightly more than a day," said Rufus. "As you know, it was I who put Pilate's seal on the door of the tomb, as you completed the burial in the late afternoon of the previous day. Accordingly, they waited for me to come on duty to carry out this special order. Your day begins at sunset, but the Roman day begins at midnight, so that is when I was sent forth and told to stay at the tomb until relieved."

"It must not be more than a fifteen minute walk through the Ephraim Gate from the Antonia to the garden of the tombs," I commented.

"That is just about right," he responded, "and I found everything in order—two Temple guards had a small fire going and were well awake; also, the seal was properly in place and had not been tampered with.

"And so," he continued with a smile, "I found a comfortable rock to sit on some ten Roman-paces* from the door of the tomb and prepared for a long vigil. Everything was peaceful for about five hours or a little more, as the two guards stayed by their fire and took turns sleeping."

---

*About fifty feet (the Roman-pace was two steps, or about five feet).

"Was it permissible," I wanted to know, "for them to sleep on duty in that fashion—by turns?"

"I don't know their regulations," Rufus responded, "but it's quite customary for them to do so. In any event, one of them was sound asleep and the other barely awake when, shortly after the Roman fifth hour, a violent thunder storm with heavy rain began and the jolt of a moderate earthquake accompanied it. I was adjusting my hood against the rain and had my eyes on the tomb when, without a sound, that heavy stone door seemed blown from the opening and gracefully flew some three Roman-paces; it landed very close to the guards, scattering their fire quite a distance. The guards were untouched, but I've never seen anyone leave a spot so quickly and run as fast as they. I'm sure they were out of the garden before a person could say 'Julius Caesar'."

"It must have been frightening for you, too, was it not?" I asked.

"Strangely, it was not," he replied. "I'd say I was more stunned than anything. But what happened next was the most amazing. I say, 'next,' but really there was no time interval. The door had no sooner sailed from the tomb, than I saw the whole tomb area, inside and out, as a ball of brilliant light. At first it seemed an iridescent blue, and then pure white. For a few moments the brightness hurt my eyes and I had to squint them almost closed. After perhaps two or three minutes, altogether, the light dimmed rapidly and then all was dark."

"Did you see any figure in or emerging from the tomb?" I asked.

"No, there was nothing—no shape of any sort," was Rufus' response.

"What did you do then, Rufus?" I wanted to know.

"After a bit, I cautiously approached the tomb and tried to look inside," he said, "but it was too dark and I could see nothing, because the full moon had already set, even though the eastern sky was beginning to show a white horizon—perhaps the brilliance of that ball of light had partially blinded me for a bit. Not knowing what story the guards would tell, I decided to look for them. Somewhat by instinct, I went first to the guardhouse and barracks which are located near the Council House at the southwest corner of the Temple. Sure enough, they were there, still trembling and without the nerve to awaken the captain of the guard."

"I dare say they were glad to see you," I observed.

"They certainly were," agreed Rufus "and when they found that I supported their story and would face their captain with them, they mustered nerve enough to wake him. Of course, they had left the garden of the tombs too quickly and without a backward glance, so they were unaware of the ball of light, and I certainly didn't volunteer that information."

"Was the captain of the guard hard to convince?" I wanted to know.

"Not especially, after he learned that I supported the story told by his men," Rufus replied, "but I feel the guards would have been in trouble but for me."

"And that was the end of that, was it Rufus?" I asked.

"Oh, no," he replied. "The captain asked me to accompany the three of them to the palace of Caiaphas to tell our story again, and to receive instructions. He seemed to sense that this was too important for him to hush it up."

"And what did Caiaphas have to say about all of that, Rufus?" I asked somewhat eagerly.

"Well, he didn't see us; at least he didn't see the two guards and me," Rufus replied. "The captain talked to some of the chief priests, and then the guards and I told our story to three of them. I think there was then a brief, private meeting of the chief priests and elders who were available. In any event, after a half-hour of waiting, the captain brought the same chief priests to us, who said: 'Here is one hundred silver shekels for each of you, and you must tell anyone who asks, that Jesus' disciples came by night and stole his body while you slept; if this comes to Governor Pilate's ears, we will satisfy him and keep you out of trouble.'"

"So, you took the money, did you?" I asked.

"Yes," he replied. "I knew if I told my office a different story, it would go to Pilate, who might choose to believe the priests—so, I just reported that the seal was already broken and the door removed when I arrived, and that what the guards *claimed* of a previous theft while they slept was all that I knew. I said that I accompanied them to their guardhouse and thereafter to Caiaphas' palace, in order to be able to give an 'official version' to my officer."[2]

"So, Rufus," I asked, "who knows this true and complete report?"

"Only Rachel, Reuben, and you, honorable Joseph," he replied. "And I will tell no other."

"Your news is very important and helpful, Rufus," I said, "and I thank you from the bottom of my heart. Good-day, dear Rufus."

This was momentous news, and once Rufus had gone I began to tingle all over. I must certainly share it with Lazarus at the first opportunity, and with Nicodemus and Gamaliel later this afternoon.

One small point in Rufus' report was personally gratifying to me, and that was his statement of watching as the stone door was seemingly "blown" from the tomb entrance and landed about five Roman-paces away—just where I had seen it perhaps a half-hour later. Peter and his companion, quite properly, convinced the two Marys and Salome that it had been an angel they saw in the tomb—but then went on to *assume* that the angel must have "rolled" the stone door from the tomb entrance. On the contrary, I was satisfied that the Christ-power, in the moment of resurrection, had done three things: had imprinted the incredible picture of Jesus' body on the Shroud, had consumed his physical body (probably transmuting it into spiritual energy), and had blown the stone door from the opening; Rufus' observations confirmed the latter point for me. Moreover, had an angel "rolled" the door, it would have stayed in its channel alongside the opening.

CHAPTER NOTES:

1. Claudia Procula, wife of the Roman governor, Pontius Pilate, was possibly related by marriage to the emperor, Tiberius Caesar, as reported by unverifiable legends which suggest she was an illegitimate daughter, perhaps grown and married at the time her mother became the third wife of Tiberius. Apocryphal accounts suggest that she had dreams about the trials and passion of Jesus, and was impressed by some of her dreams to the point of attempting to influence her husband in the handling of Jesus' case. Though her name is not certain, it is verified as Claudia Procula by the *Dictionary of the Bible,* Vol. III (J. Hastings, editor, Scribners, 1900), by the *Catholic Encyclopedia,* Vol. 12, Robt. Appleton Co., 1911, and by the *Cyclopedia of Bible ... Literature* (McClintock and Strong, editors, Harper, 1879). In any event, she was venerated as a saint by the Greek Orthodox Church; October 27 is the day dedicated to her. That veneration is attested by (1) Sophronios Eustratiades, *Hagiologion tes Orthodoxou Ekklesias* (probably Athens in the 1950s), a dictionary of the saints of the Orthodox Church; (2) Hippolyte Delehaye, editor, *Synaxarium Ecclesiae Constantinoplitanae (Propylaeum ad Acta Sanctorum Novembris),* Brussels, 1902. The latter is the definitive modern edition of the synaxarium (a collection of lives of the saints) used by the Patriarchate of Constantinople in Byzantine times. In both of these references she is identified as "Prokla," equivalent of the Latin, Procula. Similarly, in *The Apocryphal New Testament* (translated by M. R. James, Clarendon Press, Oxford), an appendix to The Acts of Pilate, called "The Letter of Pilate to Herod," refers to my wife, Procula." Additionally, she was venerated as a saint by the Abyssinian Coptic Church, which assigned June 25 as her feast day, as reported in the *Catholic Encyclopedia,* Vol. 12, citing as authority the writings of Origen (Hom., in Mat., XXXV), Tertullian and Justin Martyr, and listing her name as Claudia Procula. Also, see the similar views of novelist Roger B. Lloyd in *Private Letters of Luke,* Channel Publishers, 1958.

2. An apocryphal account states that guards at Jesus' tomb came to the Sanhedrin and told of seeing the Resurrection; they were given money to say Jesus' disciples stole the body by night *(Gospel of Nicodemus).*

CHAPTER TEN

✠

The Judean Disciples Meet

A.D. 33

THE AFTERNOON WAS NEARLY SPENT, and I was too excited to meditate further, so I sent for Samson, and we set out for the brief walk to the home of Nicodemus.

The narrow streets were quite crowded here in the Lower City, but everyone seemed intent, each on his own affairs, and paid no attention to us. I felt self-conscious anyway, because I was so excited and exhilarated that I thought it must surely show in my face!

Although it was still a few minutes before the supper hour, I assumed, from a quick glance around, that all the guests were present, and they seemed nearly to inundate me with embraces and welcomes. In addition to Nicodemus, Gamaliel and Sirach of the Sanhedrin, I was greeted by Zacchaeus and Barnabus, and was told that our Roman friends, Petronius and Silvanus were on duty, while Philip—one of The Seventy, called "the evangelist"—was with the Galileans at the home of Mary, mother of Mark.[1]

The crucifixion and burial of Jesus had already been described to the others by Nicodemus, as well as the excursion he and I had made to Pilate, to buy supplies, and to importune our servants to bring items to assist in the burial.

Knowing that I would have to watch myself to avoid mentioning anything about the Shroud, I thought my story would make more sense if

I told it in the order of its happening. Accordingly, I started with my most recent news, the story of the soldier, Rufus, about the blowing of the stone door from the tomb and the tremendous ball of light. I concluded it by saying, "I don't care how widely you tell the story of the parts played by Caiaphas, the chief priests and the Temple guards, but please be careful that no one knows we got the complete story from Rufus—the involvement of Pilate and his soldiers should not be mentioned at all by us; I gave Rufus my word on this point."

All said, in effect, "Have no fear, we will forget totally that Pilate and his soldiers were involved at all."

Mischievously, Nicodemus said, "Your soldier friend—I don't even remember; what was his name?"

I then told them of the happenings a few minutes later at the tomb—of the actions of Peter and the "beloved," as I observed them, and as they told it in the home of Mark's mother—and then, of my entrance into the tomb, what I observed and of the protuberances at head and foot of the cloth, which collapsed when I touched them.

With a twinkle in his eye, Nicodemus commented: "I wasn't listening very closely, but I'm sure you didn't touch the unclean burial cloth that was covered with blood, else you would have to start all over again with the purification process."

"Lawyers!" exploded Sirach, and everyone smiled.

Predictably, Gamaliel next made a short speech: "Dear, revered, brother Joseph, we have already heard Nicodemus' version of the crucifixion and burial, and I wouldn't ask you to repeat what would doubtless be the same account, but you know that these happenings will provoke controversy both within and outside The Way for a very long time. So, please be patient and humor us—I would like your reasons why you know Master Jesus was dead when you and Nicodemus buried him."

I knew I would have to answer this same question for a much more skeptical audience, the Galileans, later this evening, but I briefly listed my reasons: the officer's *coup-de-grace* through the heart; the large amount of blood lost from the many wounds throughout the day; the advanced rigor of death; the secured shroud through which his spirit body had to pass, but which proved to me that the physical body had dissolved within it.

Gamaliel responded: "Excellent! And our lawyer friend here was not nearly so cogent and logical." All laughed, and Nicodemus the loudest and longest.

Then I described the stories of the three women at the tomb, as I had reconstructed them from the somewhat disjointed account we had received from Mary of Magdala over a two-hour period of discussion in Bethany.

Sirach observed: "I am impressed that his appearance to each of the Marys was somewhat different, and yet their stories dovetail, as you have presented them."

Next, I described the experience of Cleopas and myself, walking all the way to Emmaus with the stranger, who turned out to be Jesus. "This," I concluded, "had to be a materialization by his spirit body. This was not the physical body because he vanished instantly while we talked with him at the table in Emmaus. Nor was it a heavenly apparition, as James bar Zebedee had described, when Moses and Elias appeared on Mount Tabor, because he could see through them."

That mountain-top experience, which the Disciples were calling the "'mount of transfiguration," is one which I shall describe in detail later in this account, and which my present audience in Nicodemus' home had heard of but superficially. Accordingly, I then elaborated with the discussions I had had with James bar Zebedee and Jesus about that so-mystical happening, and which may very well have been the deciding point for Jesus in submitting to the cross.

"Again, a beautiful presentation and analysis of these events, brother Joseph," said Gamaliel, "and, very helpful."

"Also," Nicodemus put in, with a frown on his forehead, "I find in your account of the 'mount of transfiguration' happening, a possible explanation for a point that has puzzled me for a long time—and that is Jesus' reasons for selecting the Galilean Twelve that he did. I am convinced that he had specific reasons for every deliberate thing that he did, and I could see important qualities emerging in the characters of the others as he trained them from month to month—but those two hotheads, James and John, and Peter with nothing but bone between his ears, those three choices always baffled me.

"Now, the words of Jesus that you report may explain it," he continued; "calling them his 'spiritual power support' begins to make sense to me. He had to have his wits about him and be acting intellectually, so he needed their spiritual power to help Moses and Elias with their appearances. Jesus always talked to us of spiritual power in prayer, meditation and healing—maybe I'm slow, but I'm beginning to see what he meant and to see the value to him in Peter, James and John."

"Even now," added Gamaliel, "Jesus may not be finished with those three—or with any of us for that matter. I do sense a strength in Peter that may yet work wonders for The Way. He still has weaknesses, to which we may have paid too much attention, but I think he also has courage."

"I also must comment on Peter," I interjected. "I was told by young Mark that during the Last Supper, Jesus seemed rather to belittle Peter when he told him that before the predawn crow of the cock Peter would deny his association with Jesus. As we heard by the gossip from Pilate's courtyard on the morning of the crucifixion, he probably did just that, out of possible fear for his own skin, but I must say in his defense that he was the only one of the Twelve who was there at all in the late night and early morning hours—all the other Galileans had fled and hid themselves. That took courage on Peter's part, even though he may have been trying also to avoid a similar fate by his denials."

Barnabas held up his hand with a smile, for his softer voice could not always compete with the rest of us, and said: "I think Sirach made a very important point a few moments ago when he commented on the different experiences of the two Marys. Then we have dear Joseph's account of the long walk to Emmaus with Jesus talking much of the way, and yet recognition did not come until but a moment before he dissolved into the air at the dining table.

"And again," he continued, "last night at the home of Mary (mother of Mark) when he came through stone walls or locked doors to stand in the midst of the Ten, talk to them at length, offer his wounds to be touched, and then melt into the air. I must agree with our revered Joseph that this was full control of a *spirit*_body—God-power, I would say!"

Zacchaeus was smiling from ear to ear, and so Nicodemus said to him, "Even short people are permitted to speak in this house. Climb upon that chair and give us your views."

"There is no need," he responded. "I may be short, but I have big ears and am fully enjoying myself. I do echo Barnabas' comments; his thoughts bring a ring of truth in my heart."

"One final bit of information," I said—and told them of the expected report from Hosea about Caiaphas' plans against Lazarus and myself. "I'll discuss this matter with you all more fully in the coming days. I would not-want any action of advocacy on my behalf that would jeopardize yourselves, but do keep your ears open and keep me informed of developments that come to your attention.

"Brothers," I continued, "we could talk all night, and another time we will, but I am due right now at the house of Mary where Peter will consecrate Thaddaeus, whom I am sending on permanent assignment to Edessa. So, regretfully, I must leave."

All bid me good-night.

CHAPTER NOTES:

1. Neither a formal nor cohesive group, the key Judean disciples of Jesus probably included Lazarus, Joseph of Arimathea, Simon the Leper, Nicodemus, Zacchaeus, Sirach, Gamaliel, Petronius the centurion, Philip the evangelist, Barnabus, Stephen, and Silvanus the lawyer (the number twelve is coincidental, not contrived).

The Galilean Twelve are not as certain as is usually assumed; more certain than their names is the fact that six of them were probably related to Jesus:

Matt. 10:2	Mark 3:14	Luke 6:13	Acts 1: 13
1. Andrew bar Jonah	do.	do.	do.
2. Simon bar Jonah (Peter)	do.	do.	do.
3. John bar Zebedee*	do.	do	do.
4. James bar Zebedee* (the Great)	do.	do.	do.
5. Philip	do.	do.	do.
6. Nathaniel bar Tolmai (Bartholomew)	do.	do.	do.
7. Thomas	do.	do.	do.
8. Matthew bar Alphaeus**	do.	do.	do.
9. James bar Alphaeus** (the Less)	do.	do.	do.
10. Lebbaeus bar Thaddaeus	Thaddaeus	Judas bro. of James	do.***
11. Simon the Zealot***	Simon the Canaanite	do.	do.
12. Judas (Iscariot)	do.	do.	Matthias

---

*Second cousin of Jesus
**First cousin of Jesus
***Probably brothers of Jesus

Numerous scholars have suggested that one or more of The Twelve were relatives of Jesus; these included: Jos. Gaer in *Lore of the New Testament,* Little-Brown, Boston, 1952; W. S. McBirnie in *The Search for the Twelve Apostles,* Tyndale, Wheaton, 1973; D. I. Lanslot in *The Primitive Church,* Tan, Rockford, Ill., 1926, 1980; C. B. Ruffin in *The Twelve,* Our Sunday Visitor, Huntington, Ind., 1984; Wm Barclay in *The Master's Men,* SCM Press, London, 1960; S.G.F. Brandon in *The Trial of Jesus of Nazareth,* Stein & Day, N. Y., 1979; G. Cornfeld in *The Historical Jesus,* Macmillan, N. Y., 1982.

The first five were fishermen, and Nos. 10 and 11 were probably carpenters; Matthew was a tax collector, and Judas Iscariot was likely an employee of Herod at Tiberias. No. 10, a brother of Jesus, was usually known as Jude.

CHAPTER ELEVEN

✠

The Shroud of Jesus
Leaves Jerusalem

A.D. 33

ERHAPS TWO HOURS AFTER SUNDOWN and the new day's beginning, my "escort" Samson and I set out for the nearby home of Mary, mother of Mark. I knew that Lazarus, Thaddaeus, Thomas and Stephen would not leave Bethany until there was total darkness, since Lazarus would not care to tempt his enemies by walking into Jerusalem in broad daylight. And neither would I, without protection.

Just before we left, Nicodemus insisted that Samson stay with me and accompany us on our return to Lazarus' palace after the meeting. It was a comforting thought. Samson and I arrived almost exactly as did the four from Bethany, who had had a very much longer walk.

All of the Eleven were now present and a prayer service was planned for a slightly later hour, but before Thomas could explain the reason for the presence of myself, Lazarus and Thaddaeus, the ten Galileans immediately converged on me, saying, as one voice: "Joseph! Joseph! Was Jesus truly dead when you buried him?"

I had anticipated the question, but not the urgency of it. After all, I had spent more than two hours with Jesus on the road to Emmaus and at the table there, and he had certainly been a very solid-appearing and live person. So his presence in this room last night would clearly raise that question—did he really die on the cross?—especially since most of them were too frightened to be present at the cross. I think John bar Zebedee may have been the only one of the Twelve that was there, and I can't say I say I saw him.

Very carefully, then, I explained each item: the lance thrust through the heart administered professionally by the officer in charge of the crucifixion, and the large volume of blood lost through that and other wounds; the considerable passage of time while I went for Pilate's consent and he sent a messenger to verify the death—and while Nicodemus and I procured shroud, spices and other necessary items, and gave instructions to our servants; when we and the soldiers extracted the spikes and removed the body we found it frozen as if it were metal, in the usual rigor of death—this was the most impressive fact because the neck and upper back were bowed forward, the arms were extended, and the left leg was bent considerably at the knee so that that foot could be nailed over the right one. And finally, I explained that the shroud, anchored by bags of spices, had not been removed from the body—that the physical body had dissolved within it!

"Yes, he was truly dead!" I concluded—and they sighed. Inwardly, I sighed, too, with relief, because they did not ask me what had happened to the shroud! Of course, we all knew that the Temple guards had moved back to the tomb and had taken charge of the premises shortly after the resurrection became known, and they were still there.

Thomas then promptly consulted Simon Peter, recommending a formal consecration service for Thaddaeus, in order that he would be able, more properly, to lead an effort among the Jews of Edessa, telling them of Jesus' gospel.

Peter quickly agreed, saying, "It will give us something positive and specific to focus on. We were floundering and frightened, and I the worst of all. But the Master's appearance here last night has revived our spirits and our courage, so we need now to have something meaningful to do, even though Jesus told us that this was to be a time of prayerful waiting."

Accordingly, Peter called on the group to listen, as he told them what we were about to do. Then, addressing his words to Thaddaeus, he explained the true meaning of the gospel of Jesus, and warned him of the problems and temptations he would likely encounter. He talked eloquently for the best part of an hour, and then asked Thaddaeus to sit on a stool in the center of the room and instructed the Ten to kneel in a circle around him and Thaddaeus. He suggested that the rest of us might want to kneel outside the circle and support their efforts prayerfully.

Peter then lay both of his hands on the head of Thaddaeus and, looking to the ceiling of the room, with eyes wide open, he began to pray to the spirit of the Lord Jesus. It was a beautiful and lengthy prayer which was mostly a paean of thanks for all of the specific things Jesus had done for us and the opportunities he had put in our way, without condition—thankfulness that he received us as we were, warts and all. Finally, Peter held up the name and: the life of Thaddaeus, extolling his efforts and his virtues and asking that Jesus anoint Thaddaeus with spiritual power and wisdom to better serve in The Way. We all echoed Peter's "Amen" and rose from our knees.

✛   ✛   ✛

Considering all that was before us, Lazarus, Thaddaeus and I, with Samson striding purposefully beside us, left rather promptly to spend the night at Lazarus' palace. We had the streets to ourselves now—an hour into the second watch—and were soon at Lazarus' gate where Samson bid us good-night. In Lazarus' absence Hosea had arrived, brimming with news, and so we all went to my bed-chamber to hear what he had to report.

Hosea's news was somber all right, for from several sources it was clear that Caiaphas was carefully building cases against both Lazarus and myself. For several reasons there would be no risk taken by Caiaphas through the usual developing of formal charges before a proper court, or of involving the oft-burned Pilate. Rather, it was now certain that Caiaphas, guided by his father-in-law, Annas, was compelling the support of a large number of specifically-identified persons of the rabble, who were always in abundance around the Temple, to serve as "executioners" when the time was right.

At the same time, a group of lawyers and scribes were diligently at work developing pseudo-charges and fallacious arguments calculated to impress the rabble and the Caiaphas-clique within the Sanhedrin—meanwhile the reactions of the rabble were being carefully orchestrated in advance. In this fashion, public, but informal, charges would "spontaneously" set off the rabble, who would "take matters into their own hands" and hustle the victim outside the walls for a quick and fatal stoning.

Although this would be an illegal execution by not having Pilate's advance approval, Caiaphas could avoid responsibility (as could Pilate!) by saying that the Sanhedrin was merely "considering" charges, and had not yet reached any conclusion—that the rabble had heard rumors and acted on their own.

We didn't yet know who the key lawyer was, but Caiaphas' lackey, Saul of Tarsus, was enlisting, training and would orchestrate the rabble. This operation was far better planned than were the charges against Jesus, since in his case Annas' blackmail of Pilate with threats of disclosures to Caesar (with at least a color of substance and truth) had been enough to convince Pilate and make him a willing dupe of Caiaphas. In Jesus' case, Pilate had been able to find enough "possibilities" and "suggestions" of sedition, or of collusion therein, to avoid Caesar's wrath. Also, we could be sure that in the cases of Lazarus and myself the timing would be handled so that we would be dead before any of our friends could intervene.

The report of Hosea, supported also by the preliminary report on inquiries initiated by Lazarus, indicated that probably several weeks of grace could be counted on, as the lawyers and scribes were having difficulty fabricating charges that would not be transparently false. This was crucial for Caiaphas, since to all important Jews both Lazarus and I represented wealth, position and respectability, as well as much genuine friendship and many obligations to us.

Also, even though Caiaphas and the Sanhedrin could technically escape fault, it would be necessary that the charges they were "considering" against us have some substance to preclude any local reprisals against Caiaphas, as well as further embarrassment of Pilate in Rome—in which event, Pilate or his successor would need a scapegoat and the result most likely would be the sudden dismissal of Caiaphas if not his imprisonment—thus, truly double jeopardy for him.

☩   ☩   ☩

After thanking Hosea for his valuable efforts, we excused him so that he could be shown to a bed-chamber for the night—he would return to my townhouse in Jerusalem on the morrow.

Thaddaeus went quickly to bed, but Lazarus and I talked on into the night, considering what steps we would take, and what our timing would be. With so many arrangements to make, we both expected to take risks by staying on in Judea as long as possible. It seemed clear that I, as a business-man, was more vulnerable to insidious attacks, but ultimately, because of my international commercial connections and service to the Empire, my life was probably not in as great jeopardy. I was sure that Pontius Pilate, for many favors rendered, and his superior, the Legate of Syria in Antioch, because of my boni-fides established in Rome, would protect me from physical harm, but both would insist that I leave the area if I did not have the good sense to do so on my own initiative within a reasonable time.

The situation of Lazarus was much different. He doubtless had more personal wealth than I, but it was made up mostly of lands and improvements on them, and of investments with bankers both in nearby cities and abroad. Disposition of lands without suffering a major loss would be a difficult and time-consuming maneuver, and the shifting of funds to foreign bankers was always fraught with a degree of political risk, as well as the depreciation to be expected in transferring from one monetary system or currency to another.

Lazarus did have an effective hold on Annas and Caiaphas and others of power in the Sanhedrin (as does my friend, Nicodemus) through extensive loans that permitted them an opulent life-style to which they had become accustomed and would hold onto "till the death." Thus, through the brokering of certain loans, Lazarus would now begin to place financial power in hands Caiaphas could not reach, and which could ensure catastrophe for the high priest even beyond Lazarus' death—and, of course, it would be arranged that knowledge of such transfers would come promptly to Caiaphas' attention.

The more difficult problem for Lazarus would be disposition of the palace and extensive estate in Bethany, and of Mary's very considerable and valuable property in Magdala which had come to her, at their father's death, at such an early age that she had been pulled to the gutter by the exhilaration of being on her own and accountable to no one. But for intervention by the Master Jesus, her life would be beyond saving by now—if indeed she would still be alive.

As soon as it was full daylight the next morning, Thaddaeus and I mounted our fast mules and he took the shroud, innocuously bundled, on his lap. Accompanied by a guard provided by four of Lazarus' strongest men, well armed, we set out around Jerusalem again, and on by the shortest (the northern) road toward Arimathea.

At the first opportunity, when we had the road to ourselves, Thaddaeus rode close to me and said he wanted to describe his experience during the consecration ceremony. First, he asked whether Jesus had appeared during the ceremony, and I assured him Jesus had not. "Well," he said, "it was the most profound spiritual experience of my life, and totally different from the thrill and the awe in seeing the Shroud. How long did it last, anyhow?"

I told him that Simon Peter's instructions to him, much like a sermon, had consumed nearly an hour; that the prayer of consecration might have taken a half-hour.

"This is about what I have since assumed," he said, "but from the time Peter placed his hands on my head I think I heard no more than a dozen words, and yet the time that elapsed seemed like several hours. I immediately saw Jesus floating before me, smiling and natural, although I thought

I had closed my eyes when Peter started to pray. Jesus nodded to me and I went with him—floating away with him. I don't remember seeing his lips move, but he seemed to be speaking to my mind. I tried for hours last night, as I lay sleepless in bed, to recall some of the things he told me, but I could not. Yet, I am sure these were some of the greatest truths in the world, and I wonder if I will ever recapture them.

"He took me to what seemed to be heavenly realms," he continued, "and I remember that there was beauty beyond description. I am certain that he assured me of his love, and that he would always be with me, that with him I would accomplish much. I don't remember him leaving me, but I next was aware of Peter's voice—he seemed to be talking to Jesus about me. His hands were burning hot and I was sure he was searing the skin and flesh off my head. I seemed to be shaking so violently from head to foot that I was sure I would fall off the stool. Then I heard everyone say, 'Amen,' and I carefully opened my eyes, and found myself bathed in perspiration. What does it mean? Was I out of my head?"

"No, you were certainly not out of your head," I replied. "You were having a very wonderful mystical experience—a privilege that comes rarely and not to everyone. Maybe in the years to come parts of that experience or its meaning will come back to you—maybe not. But you can always be thankful you had it. I would predict that you will find you have more spiritual power now than ever seemed likely for you. Wait and see."

✛

Fabrication
of the Shroud's Casket

A.D. 33

*B*ACK IN ARIMATHEA, I ensured that the ship was ready to receive our travellers on the morrow. Miriam and servants had made good progress, their possessions being efficiently packaged to accommodate individual burros from Antioch onward, and many such bundles had already been stowed aboard the vessel.

Relieved that such progress was being made, we then went to the workshop of Elias bar Jacob, which was housed in a building on the grounds of my home, taking the shroud with us, surreptitiously we hoped. Explaining to Elias the reason for total secrecy on this project, which secrecy might have to continue for his lifetime, we described and showed him the shroud of Jesus with its stains and images which, though enigmatic, thundered its truth to anyone "with eyes to see," as Jesus would have put it. We told Elias of the casket we had in mind, and the reason for it.

When Elias had taken it all in, tears began to stream down his face. And when he could control himself, he beamed upon me and said: "Oh, Lord Joseph, may you be blessed forever for giving me this opportunity to create the receptacle for such a relic. Yes, I have the materials and will make a rich but suitable casket. I will make it so strong and so beautiful that it will last a millennium."

"But Elias," I cautioned, "it is nearly noonday and we will want it by this time tomorrow so Thaddaeus can take it aboard yonder vessel on his journey to Edessa. Will you be able to do this work and finish it so soon?"

"Have no fear. It will be ready," he replied.

✛ ✛ ✛

The following noontime I saw Thaddaeus and Miriam and their servants and possessions safely off on the sturdy Phoenician vessel.

In good time, an impressive document had arrived from Thomas, that had been signed by the deputy governor, Flavius Rubrius. It was quite clear that he had done much more than sign it; the wording and style showed careful structure of the document to impress and even frighten any customs inspector who might be curious. The document was pointed and emphatic in declaring that the enclosed package was both an intimate, personal one, and moreover, was in response to a diplomatic obligation of high governmental importance. Under such circumstances, I could hardly visualize a customs officer audacious enough to ask for an opening of the waterproof wrappings under diplomatic seals that protected the casket.

And most specially, a beautifully decorated casket had been presented us by Elias bar Jacob, with red-rimmed eyes—inside it the Shroud had been cleverly mounted. The efforts of Elias in creating the casket truly resulted in a work of art to be cherished and appreciated by many future generations. Although quite light in weight, it also was strongly made and would survive for many years if necessary. It was fabricated of several beautiful and aromatic spice-woods I did not recognize, which were precisely inlaid in colorful patterns, and the paper-thin lining was of our famous cedar of Lebanon whose distinctive red color gave a warm setting for the Shroud, while the aroma was not only pleasant but was said to ward off predatory vermin that might otherwise feast on the cloth.

All corners of the casket were stoutly bound with our best bronze, while the hinges and latch for the lid were made of Corinthian brass which has such a rich color that it is often mistaken for gold. The latch was Elias' special pride, for into it was devised a hidden mechanism that served to securely lock the casket until the owner with knowledge of its secret pressed successively in certain spots to release the catch.

The lid of the casket was beautiful beyond description, and I regretted that Lazarus and Stephen could not have the pleasure of seeing it—Thomas, of course, would do so upon his projected stay with Thaddaeus in Edessa. The simple but lovely design in the center of the lid featured the large Greek letters Alpha and Omega, fashioned by inlay with mother-of-pearl from Galilee—one of its major items of export. Of course, to followers of The Way the cryptic message of these letters would bring immediate visions of Jesus, who liked to refer to himself thus, as The Beginning and The End.

The other key decorative feature on the lid, inlaid with turquoise from The Sinai—in the area remembered for the activities of Moses—were the words, God Is Love, in sixteen languages around the perimeter of the lid. A more appropriate setting for Jesus' Shroud would be hard to imagine!— truly, Elias had done a superb job from every standpoint, and in such a short time!

While Thaddaeus and I marvelled at the beauty and workmanship of the casket, and thanked Elias profusely as we embraced him, he became seriously apologetic because he had wanted to make a decorative cloth-of-gold overlay that would be sewed in place to cover the Shroud, with a hole in the center to show the Face of the image. He explained: "That wide expanse of unmarked and unadorned linen should be appropriately covered to enhance the mystique and beauty of the Face, and cloth-of-gold with a simple pattern would be just right, but I've none on hand."

His distress was largely appeased, however, when Thaddaeus said: "Have no concern at all, dear Elias. One of my first projects in Edessa shall be to find a superlative worker in rich fabrics to make such a cloth-of-gold overlay for the Shroud."[1]

Received also that morning, was the precious copy of the Sayings and Discourses of Jesus that had been recorded and compiled by Stephen. Although I had but a brief while that morning in which to examine this carefully executed Scroll, I was greatly impressed on several counts. For one thing, I was quite surprised by the length of it; I knew that Stephen was reported by several sources to be very professional and competent as a scribe, but I was not prepared to see how extensive had been his efforts in capturing, the words of Master Jesus. There had been literally dozens of his major discourses here recorded in addition to the numerous pithy and provocative shorter sayings.[2]

Of course, I couldn't resist the temptation to read a few of the longer discourses, because I had heard only one or two of them myself, but had heard the excited comments about others of them. To have this opportunity of reading such a careful and accurate transcript of these discourses seemed a rare privilege—and what grandeur and deep perception was to be found in Jesus' words!—how they moved me!

I couldn't help reflecting on how they might move readers long into the future who would only have a written record from which to know

Jesus. Yet, in one way, I couldn't imagine they would get any the less from these great lessons, for I sensed that Jesus himself would doubtless stand at the shoulder of the mind of any truly dedicated seeker for the wisdom of Jesus. And hadn't he often commented with words such as: "Blessed is he who has not known me and yet seeks and understands, for his glory shall be greater than all those who walked with me and understood not."

How I hoped a competent writer would be found who could do justice to Jesus' life and then have these priceless recordings to quote from.[3] And finally, I was impressed by Stephen's technical excellence as a scribe, for he had not only caught the essence of Jesus' philosophy, but the tell-tale expressions that were uniquely Jesus, the wry humor and biting sarcasm, the beauty of metaphor, were all there in exquisitely accurate detail, as I had often heard them. Such were the "signature" of Jesus, but not one scribe in a thousand would have captured those details so well as had Stephen.

It hardly seemed possible that it was only the fourth day of the week, because so much had happened and we had accomplished so much. It was one of the things I had learned from Jesus, that when the time is right and the course of action is right, circumstances will fall into place without strain. The ease with which all had been accomplished made me feel it *was* right. Not that I didn't feel qualms and concerns. Many of us were making decisions that would drastically affect the rest of our lives.

I wasn't really concerned about myself—though to an extent, perhaps, I was living in a fool's paradise with such a confident and complacent attitude; as matters turned out, there were certainly some anxious moments ahead for me personally. Mostly though, I was thinking of family and friends and my good associates in our trading and manufacturing organization. What choices might various ones make and how would they fare without me in Arimathea? Many conversations would be necessary before I could begin to firm-up plans for myself.

We certainly could not have asked for better weather for this coast-wise run to Antioch. The Great Sea was placid as a farm-pond. Its long swells, only a cubit high, come in to shore at long, lazy intervals—this was nothing like the tempestuous waves I had always seen on the Ocean Sea (as called by the Romans) whenever I sailed beyond the Pillars of Heracles,[4] taking the water route to the Tin Islands. Modest winds from the west would permit our Phoenician captain to use his sails to advantage by tacking northward along the shore.

I watched the little ship slip over the horizon, and then I slowly turned to trudge up from the quay to the hills above and to home. Looking back from this height, I could see the beauty of the water's color—light green near the shore where the sun's rays seemed to penetrate to the limestone out-croppings, and a very dark blue farther out where the deeps masked the mystery below the surface of the Sea.

Weariness seemed to descend on me, and I thought I would possibly sleep for a week. I *was* satisfied. In the last conversation that morning with Thaddaeus, he had promised to write me promptly after his arrival but to make no mention of the Shroud or anything that would compromise its safety. We agreed that when I was safely out of the reach of our enemies and had a safe address he could write to me, using the Roman courier system for the most part, he would then feel free to tell me in detail of his situation and the story of the Holy Shroud.[5]

As I walked through the gateway to the garden surrounding my home, I made a mental note to talk at length with Nicodemus and Gamaliel, but I couldn't bring myself to consider sharing our Shroud secret with them at this time.

CHAPTER NOTES:

1. Such a cloth-of-gold overlay, leaving only the Face exposed, probably was a part of the actual relic which later came to be known as the "Shroud of Turin"—see Wilson—*The Shroud of Turin,* pp. 98, 100, 120, op. 179, and Tribbe—*Portrait of Jesus?* pp. 46, 47, 248.

2. This fictional scroll of "Sayings and Discourses of Jesus" as recorded by Stephen correlates with Bible scholars' assumption that such a document did exist, and they call it the "Q" document.

3. In the notes following Chapter 32 I will indicate that I find convincing and satisfying the proposals of Dr. Schoneberg J. Setzer concerning authorship of the Gospel of John—that the narrative of same was written by Lazarus, who was in fact the "beloved disciple," and that the second "hand" was that of John of Bethphage (disciple to Lazarus) who added the references to an unnamed "beloved Disciple," and gave *his* name, John, to the Gospel, with Lazarus' consent.

In 1996 the volume *Eyewitness to Jesus* by C. P. Thiede and M. D'Ancona (Doubleday) was released. Thiede, a specialist in the study of papyrus writings, now firmly dates three small fragments, known as the Magdalen (College) Papyrus, to no later than A.D. 50 to 60, and certifies them as from the Gospel of Matthew and as written by the Disciple Matthew. A comparable fragment—from a common origin—is kept in Spain and is known as the Codex of Barcelona. Thiede suggests that Matthew wrote not long after the Crucifixion.

Thiede says Matthew was more than a Tax Collector; the Greek word, "telones," implies that he was in charge of a Customs Station at a major border crossing (Capernaum on Via Maris). He would have had both professional qualifications and financial resources, be fluent in Greek as well as Aramaic.

Thiede suggests that Mark 9:1 ("Truly, I say to you, there are some standing here who will not taste death before they see that the kingdom of God has come with power.") does *not* refer to Jesus' "second coming," but is a reference to the "transfiguration of Jesus" which occurred six days later (and also reported in 2 Peter 1:16-18).

New Testament writers: Lazarus, Matthew, Luke and Tychicus were probably professionally competent as writers. The earliest significant effort was undoubtedly the narrative portion of the Gospel of John as written by Lazarus. The earliest rough notes may have been by the unknown writer of the "Q" document, and possibly by Mark. Careful research was likely done by Luke. The first formal release of a complete NT document probably was the Gospel of Matthew. Formal release of the Gospel of Mark was rather certainly in A.D. 70, as he attempted to distance Christians from the Jews in the wake of the destruction of Jerusalem and Judea; *Mark* was distributed early enough to reach Qumran before A.D. 73. *Luke* was in the first group of Christian codices (later than scrolls). *Mark* probably had the most bias and guesswork on the part of the writer.

Other than the four writers first mentioned above, all other NT writers doubtless relied to a lesser or greater degree on an amanuenses who, in the First Century often composed entire letters and documents on the basis of mere notes of instruction. With reference to Paul in such regard, see 1 Cor. 16:21; Gal. 6:11; Col. 4:18; 2 Thes. 3:17; Phil. 19. Shorthand, called *tachygraphos,* was virtually a compulsory skill for a trained scribe of the First Century Palestine, and Levi-Matthew may well have been quite capable of taking down the Sermon on the Mount verbatim.

4. The Pillars of Heracles we know today as the Straits of Gibralter.

5. The mystic, Anne Catherine Emmerich, was an Augustinian nun of Westphalia, Germany (1774-1824), who had repeated vivid visions of the passion of Jesus, of which she dictated descriptions to her amanuensis, Clemens Brentano. Of the burial and burial cloth of Jesus she recorded the following: "I have seen many things connected with the subsequent history of this holy winding-sheet, but I cannot recall them in their precise order. After the Resurrection it, along with the other linens, came into the possession of Jesus' friends. Once I saw a man carrying it off with him under his arm when he was starting on a journey. I saw it a second time in the hands of the Jews, and I saw it long in veneration among the Christians of different places.... I have seen the original, somewhat damaged, somewhat torn, held in veneration by some non-Catholic Christians of Asia. I have forgotten the name of the city, but it is situated in a large country near the home of The Three Kings." *(The Life of Jesus Christ and Biblical Revelations* from the visions of the Ven. Anne Catherine Emmerich, Tan Books and Publishers, 1979; pp. 337-339, Vol. 4)

✠

King Abgar is Healed by the "Face"

A.D. 33

*I*T WAS JUST OVER THREE WEEKS since the departure of Thaddaeus and Miriam from Joppa, when his most welcome letter, via Roman post, arrived. I was very nervous and could hardly wait to break the seals and read:

> From your Servant, Thaddaeus, now of Edessa;
> To My Lord, Joseph, of Arimathea;
> Greetings and grateful thanks from Miriam and me, and from King Abgar, and may the blessing of Jesus the Christ be with you.
>
> The special package, transmitted by the courtesy of Flavius Rubrius, was duly displayed after my arrival here, and the results were more spectacular than we could have imagined. I shall describe the circumstances more fully in a future letter. The transmittal document accomplished everything in the way of courtesy that could have been hoped for—I say, courtesy, but maybe I should say, awe, on the part of the officials concerned.
>
> May I say also that King Abgar, who is now in vigorous good health, has made us welcome beyond our expectations, and is urging that my first order of business be a series of discourses to acquaint all citizens of his kingdom with the good news of The Way as taught by Jesus the Galilean.*

---

*Abgar ordered the public's attendance, according to Church historian, Eusebius (Chap. 13).

King Abgar, and Aggai, his first secretary of the kingdom, both insisted on the second day after my arrival that I baptize them into the fellowship of The Way, which I was pleased to do.

Our trip from Joppa to Edessa was uneventful, pleasant and reasonably swift. Miriam had never before been on the Great Sea, and she enjoyed the experience immensely. She asks that I describe to you her beautiful time on the morning of our second day at Sea: The Captain provided Miriam with a roll of padded cloth, so that she could comfortably stand in the extreme prow of the ship, leaning on the thus-padded gunwale. The sun was brilliant in the clear air, and she stared down into the water ahead of the boat, on that stretch of the Sea that the prow would reach in another moment. Soon she realized that no two waves or swells are ever exactly the same. The Sea was so calm and still that there were no whitecaps. Then she could see that even the tiniest wave casts a shadow from the bright sun, and all those shadows, from so many very small wavelets, looked like a huge piece of lace floating on the water. She called to me to see this so, so beautiful sight. The water itself had such a very deep blue color that it was nearly purple—I don't believe the great Greek painters have ever caught the beauty of the Sea's color on their canvas. Miriam says this is so, "particularly, because of the water's partial transparency which gives a certain inimitable hue to its color."

After our noon departure, we sailed the balance of that day and three more, arriving at Seleucia Pieria a little after sundown. Because of problems with shoal water on the River Orontes, we anchored in the small harbor at its mouth until morning, and with the first light proceeded up river by sail and oars, reaching Antioch in little more than an hour.

Your Antioch agent had received your urgent message, had purchased for us an adequate string of pack animals, and arranged for us to join a very well organized caravan leaving two days later, whose first stop would be Edessa. After a couple of hours spent in checking the arrangements, and in purchasing a few supplies, Miriam and I spent most of our two days of waiting by walking the wide avenues of Antioch and enjoying the beauty of the city.[1]

It has been fourteen years since, as a boy, I passed briefly through this city with you on the way to Edessa, so I remember little from that trip about Antioch. The buildings of the Roman government on the river's island, called merely, The Insula, are most impressive, as you know; those in Caesarea and Jerusalem cannot compare. Miriam most greatly enjoyed strolling along the great colonnades that flank Via Caesarea, cutting through the center of the city from one side to the other and ending at Mount Silpius, hard by the hills at the city's edge, where stands the Roman castle-fortress. Along the colonnades were such a variety of sales shops and workshops offering products and services beyond imagination, that Miriam refused to hurry and we consumed more than three hours traversing that one avenue.

We discovered that late afternoons and early evenings provided a special exhibition for us, just by watching from the banks as many beautifully canopied and lighted pleasure barges slowly plied the Orontes, while Romans and wealthy merchants relaxed and cooled themselves on the barges as breezes blew up from the Sea.

Our caravan started before sun-up, and very fortunately your agent had us placed fairly near the head of the column, so that we were not unduly troubled by dust where the road traversed raw dirt. By late afternoon we reached the foothills of the mountains and stopped f or the night.

Our progress the next five days was much less, but still quite gratifying; the road wound back and forth, but the passes were low and the animals were not unduly fatigued. We crossed the mighty River Euphrates just before sundown on the fifth day, and within sight of the river a stone marker told us we were leaving the Roman Empire and entering Parthia, whose capital, Ctesiphon,[2] was many leagues to the east on the banks of the River Tigris.

On the last day we had a full, but easy journey, traversing the thirty miles from the River into Edessa. Tobias bar Tobias[3] met us at the city's edge where the caravan would split up, and new movements, both eastern and western, would originate. His employees joined our servants in managing the animals and packs, while we went directly to our new home that Tobias had selected for us.

Although somewhat weary, I spent several hours that night discussing business and our various problems with Tobias. His health indeed has deteriorated badly, but I believe that by staying in his comfortable home, without the need for movement to the office, to your warehouses, and all over the city, he may be able to live several more useful years without significant discomfort. His principal problem, of course, is his weight, which is at least twice what his physician believes proper, but no medication or practical regimen has been effective.

Tobias is not a gluttonous eater, but eats with laudable restraint, no more than is necessary to maintain his strength. I feel that I, your business, and Tobias, all will fare best if he continues active in the business as advisor and I regularly consult with him at his home and have the benefit of his long experience here. Also, such an arrangement will permit me to take fullest advantage of the many business friendships that he has established over the years, for I am satisfied that he is highly regarded in this city.

Tobias had learned of Jesus' death just three days before my arrival, and did not know of the resurrection and the spirit-body appearances of

Jesus until I reviewed all the happenings with him the following morning. After exhaustively providing him with all my knowledge on this subject as we had planned, I brought out the special relic that will be kept for followers of The Way in Edessa. With a minimum of explanation, and making reference to that correspondence we had read, I said that I wished to show this relic to King Abgar at his earliest convenience.

Accordingly, an audience with the King was arranged for late that afternoon at the King's palace, to which Tobias accompanied me. As preliminary, I was introduced to the First Secretary, Aggai, who was most cordial in his welcome, and who seemed to look upon Tobias with the warmth of good friendship. Aggai explained to me that the King's disability and weakness would preclude his movement—that he had been assisted onto his throne where he would have to remain until assisted from it—that most of his joints, especially those of his legs, were enormously swollen and stiffened to rigidity, and that he could speak barely above a whisper because his malady had invaded the throat area around his voice-box.[4]

With these words of caution, we were led to the throne room, where huge bronze doors, chased with a variety of alloys and engraved exquisitely, were barring our way. I promised myself a future opportunity to carefully examine this beautiful metalwork, since the skills in metallurgy you taught me made these works of art especially impressive. The doorkeepers swung open the doors and Aggai led us three paces into the rich and ornate throne-room, which again, I later realized, was impressively enhanced by every facet of metal-artists' work, including a high ceiling of fretted copper in a maze of entwining forms and figures. There, Tobias and I dropped to our knees while Aggai introduced me as—"Thaddaeus, new agent of the revered merchant, Joseph of Arimathea, and spiritual representative of the late lamented Jesus the Galilean."

Abgar bid us rise and me to approach the throne and speak, and so I stepped to the middle of the room and spoke thus: "Oh, mighty and illustrious King, I bring you blessings, best wishes and felicitations from my master, Joseph of Arimathea, and from others who are followers of The Way. You have just recently learned of the horrible death of our Messiah, the Lord Jesus of Galilee, which death he prophesied of himself. I have much to tell you concerning the events surrounding his demise, when you can spare the time to listen. In accordance with his promise by letter to you, I have come to show you a special relic, left by his grace as a blessing to you and to all others forever who will believe in him and his gospel message. It is intended that we will build a shrine with reliquary here in your blessed city to shelter this relic, that all followers of The Way may come here from all nations to be blessed by it. Here, I show you the relic of his passion, his death, and his resurrection to fullness of spirit."

So saying, I lifted up the casket I had been carrying under my arm, and swung wide the lid that Elias had fashioned, so that the King might see the relic.

A few short moments elapsed in silence as Abgar stared from his throne at the relic I held up facing him (some three or four paces away).

Then, with a wild and loud shout of, "Hallelujah," he leaped from his throne and raced across the floor to me, where he fell on his knees and reached up for the casket, which I then let him hold.[5] He gently kissed it, and then, through his tears, looked quizzically at me and asked, "But, where did it go?"

I smiled reassuringly to him, took the casket and stepped back three paces.

Seeing the reappearance of the relic, he smiled hugely as with the greatest pleasure, and commented with great feeling and reverence: "Of course! It is most appropriate that one not approach too closely. One must keep a respectful distance from so holy a relic."[6]

For a short space of time we were all four jabbering at once like a group of foolish children. As we ran out of breath and recaptured our manners, Abgar insisted that we all come at once to his private dining room where we would have a proper feast and would talk as fellow followers of The Way.

Needless to say, except for interruptions by many questions, I did most of the talking, on into the late evening, telling all I could of the Master Jesus. I will write more of Abgar, another time.

The few hours that I could spare before leaving Arimathea had been highly profitable as, following your suggestion, I took special instruction in the Syriac language spoken here. But, as you know, Syriac is merely a dialect of our own Aramaic, and so all educated persons and almost everyone else hereabouts understands both spoken and written Aramaic.

Considering the care that Thaddaeus had taken to avoid describing the relic, or identifying it as a burial shroud, or telling how it had come to be made, I felt that he had done a masterful job in describing the events in Abgar's palace. Consequently, I lost no time in getting to Bethany to share my news with Lazarus, and slightly later with Thomas and Stephen.

CHAPTER NOTES:

1. Antioch was surpassed in size and splendor in the Empire only by Rome and Alexandria.

2. Ctesiphon is just a ruin today, on the left bank of the Tigris near Baghdad, its successor.

3. Tobias bar Tobias is recorded as the Edessan host of Thaddaeus (see Eusebius: *The History of the Church,* Ch. 13).

4. He suffered from rheumatoid arthritis and black leprosy (see p. 237 of Wilson: *The Shroud of Turin*).

5. In Eusebius, *The History of the Church,* Thaddaeus' arrival in Edessa and the healing of Abgar is recorded as the year of Christ's ascension (Ch. 13). Eusebius reports that Thaddaeus laid hands on Abgar in the name of Jesus the Christ and "Abgar was instantly cured." Oddly, however, Eusebius states that when Thaddaeus was presented to Abgar "...at the moment of his entry a wonderful vision appeared to Abgar on the face of Thaddaeus. On seeing it Abgar bowed low before the apostle, and astonishment seized all the bystanders; for they had not seen the vision, which appeared to Abgar alone."

But legends and apocryphal writings state that it was the Holy Face of Edessa—the face of Jesus—which Thaddaeus had brought with him, that was the instrument of the healing—and I have chosen to follow that tradition. One of the reasons for my choice is the subsequent circumstance: The "Face" (the Shroud) was apparently sealed in a chamber over the West Gate of the city from A.D. 57 to 525; when a flood in 525 damaged the city wall and disclosed the relic, faces of Jesus copied from it soon began to appear all over Christendom, and Dr. Alan Whanger at Duke University (among others) has demonstrated the identity of those copies; three such faces now repose among the art and relics of the Monastery of St. Catherine, Mount Sinai, Egypt, one of which is a painting commissioned by Emperor Justinian I and executed between A.D. 527 and 565 (see third color photo following p. 128, *Portrait of Jesus?* by Tribbe), showing Abgar and Thaddaeus with the Holy Face on a cloth between them. Eusebius was writing three hundred years after the event (ca. A.D. 325) and one wonders if he chose to ignore the legends and ascribe a conventional healing, especially since the Holy Face was then missing—bricked-up in the chamber over the Gate.

The Shroud of Turin (Italy), bearing the mystical image and blood stains of a crucified man (by many now accepted to be the shroud of Jesus) has been publicly and continuously known in western Europe since 1357. Recent scholarship, based on archaeological, historical and scientific data, now concludes that it travelled from Jerusalem to Edessa (Parthia) folded into a frame or shallow casket with only the face visible; that it remained there until 944, known as The Face of Edessa, when it was moved by the army of the Emperor to Constantinople and became known as the Mandylion; that it became known as a full shroud with a full image of a man on it during its stay in Constantinople, until 1204 when the City was over-run and sacked and the image disappeared. Today's scientists cannot explain how it could have been made and, in effect, give credence to the claim of the ancients that it was "not made by human hands" (see Ian Wilson, *Shroud of Turin, and* Frank C. Tribbe, *Portrait of Jesus?*). Researchers are now validating early legends whose obscure meanings were earlier mistranslated, and finding their Shroud image references to be valid (e.g., see Linda Cooper's "The Old French Life of Saint Alexis and the Shroud of Turin," *Modern Philology,* August, 1986). Many items of ancient art depicting Jesus' face and crucified body have now been validated as *exact* copies of the Shroud face by Dr. Whanger through his technique of superimposition using polarized transparencies—including items from Roman catacombs of the late first century, Byzantine coins and icons, church art from Russia and Athens to western France, and even medieval drawings in England identified with the Knights Templar.

Apocryphal background for the Edessa connection is found in part in three books: the (Greek) *Acts of Thaddaeus,* the (Syriac) *Doctrine of Addai,* and the *Epistles of Christ and Abgar.*

In 1988, Church authorities in Turin permitted three laboratories to take small pieces of the Shroud cloth for carbon-dating. In their report, released in Turin on October 13, 1988, the laboratories concluded that the cloth was of early 14th century origin. Shroud researchers promptly condemned the report as badly flawed and erroneous. See "Is the Shroud of Turin a Fraud?" by Frank C. Tribbe, *Journal of Religion and Psychical Research, April 1989.*

6. The phenomena described in Chapters 3 and 4 is again noted in Abgar's experience—that the body-image on the burial cloth will disappear if one approaches too close. This is one of more than two dozen scientific enigmas of the Shroud of Turin: the image is only visible in the optimum viewing range of about six feet to fifteen feet—closer or farther, the image disappears.

PART II

My Early Years
and My Family

THE CHARACTERS
IN ORDER OF THEIR APPEARANCE

CHAPTER FOURTEEN:

Rebecca: wife of Josephus of Arimathea; mother of Joachim, Joseph and Enygeus.

Enygeus: sister of Joseph of Arimathea, who married Hebron and was the mother of twelve sons and one daughter.

Josephus: wealthy trader/manufacturer of Joppa/Arimathea; Elder of the Great Sanhedrin; married to Rebecca; father of Joseph, Enygeus and Joachim.

Hannah: (fictional) a servant in the household of Josephus of Arimathea.

Johanan: (fictional) brother of Josephus of Arimathea, and partner in their trading and manufacturing enterprise.

CHAPTER FIFTEEN:

Eliud: married Ismeria; lived in the Galilean capital of Sepphoris; father of Anna, Eliud, Maraha, Bianca, and Sobe.

Joachim: brother of Joseph of Arimathea; married to Tabitha, who died childless; married to Anna (daughter of Eliud), and their children were Mary (mother of Jesus), Esau, Salome, Judith and Mary-Heli.

Anna: daughter of Eliud and Ismeria; married Joachim.

Esau, Salome, Judith: the other children of Joachim and Anna.

Tabitha: first wife of Joachim.

Joseph bar Jacob: the third son of Jacob and Timna; he married Mary bat Joachim.

Jacob: son of Matthan (sometimes called Matthat); married Timna, with whom he had six sons, the third being Joseph.

Timna: after Jacob's death, married Heli, with whom she had the son, Cleopas-Alphaeus.

Mary-Cleopas: second child of Cleopas-Alphaeus and Mary-Heli; married Cleopas of Caesarea Philippi.

Symeon: son of Cleopas-Alphaeus and Mary-Heli; became bishop of Jerusalem after the death of James.

Eliud: son of Eliud and Ismeria; died, a youth.

Maraha: daughter of Eliud and Ismeria; never married.

Bianca: daughter of Eliud and Ismeria; married to Emerentia; their daughters were Elizabeth aid Leah.

Elizabeth: daughter of Bianca and Emerentia; married the priest, Zacharias; their son, John, became known as The Baptizer.

Leah: daughter of Bianca and Emerentia; married David; their daughter, Seraphia, married Sirach.

Seraphia: an open follower of Jesus; married to Sirach.

Sirach: a secret follower of Jesus; member of the Sanhedrin.

Sobe: fourth daughter of Eliud and Ismeria; married Solomon, and their daughter, Mary-Salome, married Zebedee.

Zebedee: fishing fleet operator on Galilee; partner of Simon/Peter and Andrew, sons of Jonah.

CHAPTER SIXTEEN: (none)

CHAPTER SEVENTEEN:

Aaron: (fictional) employee of Joseph's family business in Arimathea.

Ali Sylleus: (fictional) owner of Damascus metal-works.

CHAPTER EIGHTEEN:

Elyap: fiancée and later, wife, of Joseph of Arimathea.
Jarius: elder brother of Elyap
Hiram bar Abram: (fictional) Phoenician shipmaster of Tyre.

CHAPTER NINETEEN: (none)

CHAPTER TWENTY:

Cymric: (fictional) leader of a family group of Cornwall tin miners.
Rachel: mother of Martha, Lazarus and Mary.
Josiah: father of Martha, Lazarus and Mary.
Tobias of Jerusalem: (fictional) young brother of Josiah.
Anna bat Joseph: daughter of Joseph of Arimathea and Elyap.
Josephes: son of Joseph of Arimathea and Elyap.

CHAPTER TWENTY-ONE:

Salome bat Joachim: younger sister of Mary, mother of Jesus.

CHAPTER TWENTY-TWO: (none)

The Armorial Bearings attributed to
JOSEPH OF ARIMATHEA

Purported Coat-of-Arms of Joseph of Arimathea,
displayed in a church at T. Woodcock, Somerset, England.
(Goheen Antiques)

CHAPTER FOURTEEN

✠

With My Father and in School

9 - 3 B. C.

THE YEAR OF MY NINETEENTH BIRTHDAY spanned both the greatest opportunity and gratification, as well as the greatest tragedy, of my young life. But the full meaning of that year can be understood only upon a recounting of the significant events of my younger years.

When I was seven, my mother, Rebecca, died as she gave birth to my sister, Enygeus. My father, Josephus, never remarried. By the time I was nineteen, I could barely remember my mother. I was raised partly by one after another of my many female relatives who lived from time to time in our spacious home in Arimathea. Mostly, I was raised by our wonderful servant, Hannah.

And yet, in a manner of speaking, I wasn't raised by these loving women at all. Because, from the death of my mother, my father and I were inseparable whenever we both were at home. Of course once or twice a year he would be gone for several weeks on a business trip. Most of the travelling, however, was done by his younger brother, Johanan, who was a partner in the business. Also, my education required my absence from home for extended periods, but even when attending classes or other duties in Jerusalem, I always spent the Sabbath at home.

Workers in our offices in Arimathea and Jerusalem, in the Joppa ware-houses, and in the foundries and factories in Arimathea always kidded us, saying that I was my father's shadow. We both enjoyed that good-natured ribbing, because never were a father and son closer than we. And it was not just a superficial relationship that we had; from my earliest years my father discussed his business affairs with me in detail, just as if he wanted my advice—and he never failed to listen seriously to any comments I made.

Arimathea is also known as Ramalleh (or Ram Allah or Ramtha) to our Edomite "cousins" who were descended from Esau, while we Judeans were descended from Jacob, called Israel.* Many Edomites live in Ari-mathea, which is just four miles from the moderately good port of Joppa that serves both Judah and Edom—although Edom, to the southeast, is now mostly known by the name of its conquerors, the Nabateans. For one who takes pride in his hometown, Arimathea is always mentioned as the home of the famous Samuel,** prophet and king-maker of our nation, our location being at the western border of the "Hill Country of Ephriam," where Samuel was born.[1]

Though perhaps not as fertile and lush as Galilee, this area abounds in natural beauty. Typically, the evergreen *sycomore* trees, with their clusters of fig-like fruit which are edible but not of wonderful flavor, are found in Ari-mathea and in profusion in this hill country from here to Emmaus—how-ever, they are mostly in private gardens since they are not self-propagating and must be raised from shoots carefully nurtured and planted.

Names are a great problem among us Jews, especially if we wish to identify a person—or even oneself. Take me: can you imagine how useless it would be to identify myself as Joseph bar (son of) Josephus—for the latter is merely a variant of the former. And can you imagine how many thousand Josephs there are in Judea, Samaria and Galilee? Even by identi-fying myself as Joseph of Arimathea, I haven't solved very much, because in earlier years our town was known as Ramathaim—and besides, it is so small and little known that for many acquaintances to mention Arimathea raises more questions than it answers!

As our nation has grown, this problem has been compounded by our old custom of naming a son for a recent ancestor (and a daughter, as well). Fortunately, we are beginning to break away from this practice, and the *diaspora* has resulted in many of our brothers in foreign countries follow-ing local practices in naming offspring—that is, they use a never-changing

---

*Esau and Jacob were sons of the patriarch, Abraham, of the Jews.
**Samuel was a prophet in antiquity of the nation of Israel.

family name, or surname,* to which a birth-name, or given name, is added—and then, when they return here to live or visit, their examples are sometimes followed in Judea. Of course, the foreign practices often bring their own confusion, because one must sort out and attempt to identify Hebrew, Greek and Roman spellings and pronunciation for any particular name. The result, as might be expected, is that persons often are known by more than one name, or only by a descriptive word or their occupation—which probably is how names started after all! And so, as is not surprising, it is becoming commonplace for men, and sometimes women, to use double-names for distinction's sake, although that is not a part of our Jewish tradition.

Arimathea is also on the Roman high road, named Via Maris, "The Way of the Sea," that connects by a side spur to Jerusalem, runs northward to Nazareth, Tiberias, Capernaum, Caesarea Philippi, Damascus, Hamath and Antioch; and by a southern leg, takes one to Egypt. North of Damascus it branches eastward to Babylon. It is the route of the ages-old camel caravan trails.

Arimathea is the choice of all who can afford to live here, in preference to the port area which can be miserably hot much of the year. Here in the hills we have the view of the Great Sea, plus its cooling breezes which are rarely felt at sea-level.

Just two centuries ago, during the time of the Maccabean Revolt, and for centuries previously, Samaria was much larger than today,[2] including much of our southern coastline for some fifteen miles inland. The port of Joppa and my town of Arimathea were both Samaritan. The port was at one time totally destroyed by Judas Maccabeus. His successor, Jonathan Maccabeus was a better politician, and by alliances and bluffing he played the Greeks, Seleucids, Syrians and Romans against one another. Then, finally, the Syrian king, Demetrius II, delivered Arimathea and Joppa to Jonathan as a toparchy and he became the ruler-in-fact of Judea, and extended *its* boundaries both eastward and westward.

Arimathea has been Judean ever since, but one may ask, "was our house in fact Samaritan by blood?" I can only say that as a boy I heard my grandfather many times declaim emphatically that our bloodline was pure, directly from King David.

---

* The Bible's use of the word "surname" is largely meaningless, as anything added was more likely a nickname, even though it was used to avoid confusion (Note: Mark 3:16, "And Simon he surnamed Peter," and Mark 3:17, ". . . and John the brother of James; and he surnamed them Boanerges, which is, the sons of thunder.")—surname does not mean family name as used in the Bible.

However, because for many centuries we were politically Samaritan, I had been taught from childhood to love and respect all Samaritans, realizing that they were at worst half-cousins because Jews of the ten northern tribes of Israel, some seven centuries earlier, had been forced to intermarry with their conquerors, the Assyrians, as well as subservient foreigners—whether they were of the families carried into captivity or the families that stayed in Israel—now Samaria.

As I grew older and thought more for myself, I could never understand the arrogance of many citizens of Jerusalem who despised the Samaritans for this enforced dilution of the bloodline—for had not many thousands of Judeans done the same thing *voluntarily,* from David and Solomon[3] to the lowest, by marrying Idumeans, Nabateans, Ammonites, Moabites and Edomites—half-cousins all?—as well as Egyptians, Babylonians, and Phoenicians (Canaanites?).

Because I was seven when my mother died, I should have been starting in one of the Temple schools in Jerusalem at that time. But my father did not want to chance the effect of a double trauma, and for six months I hardly left his side from morning till night—and it was his continuous conversations with me, involving me in his work during this period, that set the tone for our relationship. Upon reflection, I realize that my father lived his business, and nothing else, all his waking hours six days a week—so he knew nothing else to talk about to me. But in his love and his wisdom, he knew that I must not have the risk of loneliness or premature introspection. Listening to my father those years gave me an exhaustively thorough understanding of our family business in international trade and manufacturing. It also gave me so intimate an understanding of my father that I soon realized how fully he lived his religion in his business relations. This was, for a growing boy, a perfect object lesson of how to succeed in business. Moreover, this experience and these observations soon developed in me a great admiration and a great love for my father.

Because we talked of my schooling off and on during that six months, school was but a natural step that did not bother me at all when the time to start finally arrived. My gentle mule carried me safely to Jerusalem the first of each week, and back each weekend. The figures and records of my father's business gave me a background and an incentive, so that I soon became a leading student with a minimum of special effort.

At the age of twelve my studies began to take on a more serious aspect. My mornings were spent in the Scribes' School, where I learned the best styles of writing with various materials—such as the vellum made from the best quality of fine-grained lambskin, the beautiful Egyptian papyrus made from their tall grassy sedge, and the so very thin rice-paper imported from the Far East. Although I conversed easily in the Greek and Latin languages necessary in the business world, I must now learn to read and write in these languages, as well as in our colloquial language of Aramaic,[4] and our formal language of Hebrew in which the Law of the Jews is beginning to be written. This latter language, according to some of our scholars, is actually the native tongue of this land, and in earlier centuries it was called the Canaanite tongue.

In the afternoons I began attendance in the School of Law where we learned that living under the Ten Commandments also must include a thorough knowledge of the six hundred and thirteen laws of interpretation of the Commandments. Every Jewish male must learn a skill by which he can earn a living, so I would certainly expect to learn my father's business in addition to the education I was getting at school. However, it was my firm intention to be fully involved in that business just as my father was and to learn the special skill of metallurgy. The vocation of lawyer, scribe or priest held no interest for me; although I could easily qualify for any one of them in time, I would follow in my father's footsteps and hope merely to succeed to his Sanhedrin seat as an Elder. I might possibly be more active in that role than he chose to be, but I would still be primarily a businessman.

We schoolboys came mostly from patrician or wealthy families, and in consequence of our closeness in living quarters and in classrooms it was inevitable that we would make lasting friendships. Though he was three years my junior, in Scribes' School I developed a genuine fondness for young Nicodemus; his father was a banker and money-lender of considerable stature, who chose to remain domiciled in his native town of Jericho. Nicodemus looked upon me as his model in every way, somewhat to my embarrassment at times.

Similarly, after I had been in the School of Law for a while I found myself emulating the mannerisms and style of a brilliant upperclassman by the name of Gamaliel, and we soon became the closest of friends. I had occasionally to tussle with my conscience when tempted to ignore Nicodemus so that I could spend more time in the company of Gamaliel, but fortunately Gamaliel's maturity helped me to see the necessary balance, and his generosity found ways to always include Nicodemus in our extracurricular activity; thus, we three developed into an inseparable triumvirate. Gamaliel's interests clearly ran in the direction of priestly studies, and even at this age he was discerning enough to know that he preferred the Pharisaic School of Hillel, his grandfather, which had been established some fifteen years previously. Nicodemus, on the other hand, had firmly made up his mind to be a Temple lawyer, but in no sense would he ever be considered a demagogue.

CHAPTER NOTES:

1. The town of Arimathea was doubtless in the hill country of Ephriam, lying roughly westward from Jerusalem; it *may* have been known as Ramalleh or a variant thereof, but many of the better historians and geographers refuse to speculate as to its specific location, which might have been somewhat south of west or north of west from Jerusalem. Both the *Moody Bible Atlas* and the *Oxford Bible Atlas* locate Arimathea as 23 miles northwest of Jerusalem and 16 miles east of Joppa, but provide no citation or explanation for their judgment. This writer has chosen to be influenced more by the *Zondervan New International Dictionary* which locates Arimathea as 20 miles northwest of Jerusalem and 6 miles southeast of Antipatris (Aphek), and by G. F. Jowett in *The Drama of the Lost Disciples* who describes Arimathea as "on the caravan route from Nazareth to Jerusalem." More specifically, Map 13 in *Harper's Bible Commentary* (Harper & Row, 1988; copyright by The Society of Biblical Literature) shows Arimathea (with a question mark) at the approximate location I am using. But, I would place Arimathea at least five miles west of the point shown on that map, on the brow of a hill overlooking the Plain of Sharon and the port and city of Joppa—and thus less than five miles from Joppa; it would be adjacent to the ages-old Via Maris, the "Way of the Sea." The precise location I am using is shown on Plate 258 (p. 163) of the *Macmillan Bible Atlas*, New York, 1977.

2. Samaria's capital city, also named Samaria, was built some thirty-two miles north of Jerusalem about 880 B.C. by Omri, the sixth king of Israel and father of King Ahab who was better known to posterity. The city was built on a hill called the 'Watch Mountain."

3. David, and his son Solomon, were the second and third kings, respectively, of the combined kingdom of Judea-Israel.

4. Aramaic, at and before the time of Jesus, was the common language of the whole Near East, from India to Ethionia (see *The Jews in the Greek Age* by E. J. Bickerman, Harvard University Press, 1988).

CHAPTER FIFTEEN

✠

My Extended Family; A Visit to Athens

2 – 1 B.C.

THESE WERE IDYLLIC, HAPPY YEARS because I was eager to learn and was very comfortable with my classmates and instructors. Nor did I enjoy my weekends in Arimathea any the less, because they were family times that nearly always included as house-guests a sprinkling of both close and distant relatives. Usually they were interesting in their own right, and at the same time could be depended on to tell us fascinating accounts of other family members.

One of my great favorites as a house-guest was old Eliud of Sepphoris, the capital of Galilee, who only visited us twice during my youth because of his age, but his conversations so intrigued me that I always dropped in on him for a talk whenever I was in Galilee, and continued to do so until his death. He would talk about the many interesting people in our families, about the history of our nation, and always had the most colorful ways of explaining the mysteries of our Scriptures; especially, I enjoyed hearing him discourse from his limitless knowledge of the scrolls and practices of our communal-living, monastic-like brothers, the Essenes.

Our people are renowned for the importance we attach to our sons, but no one could have been more proud than was old Eliud of his four daughters. Their families, in turn, were so complex and so fascinating

that I would ask Eliud, each time I was with him, to name his family for
me again—never, as a youth, could I remember them all and keep them
straight. He would laugh heartily at this standard request from me, and
then he would start out with obvious pleasure:

"Well, its just a small family, you know—Ismeria and I had only four
daughters, Anna, Maraha, Bianca, and Sobe, and a son, Eliud, who died
in his youth.

"Anna became the second wife of Joachim, your brother—how much
older than you is he?"

"Twenty-four years older," I interjected.

"Yes, that's about what I thought," he continued, "and I believe his
first wife, Tabitha, had died childless."

He raised his eyebrows, questioningly, and I nodded agreement.

"Anna and Joachim, of course, live in the Valley of Zabulon, just
southwest of Nazareth," he went on, "and to them were born Mary, now
the mother of Jesus, and Mary-Heli who married Cleopas Alphaeus. Their
other children were Esau, Salome, and Judith."

At this point I would usually interrupt him to ask, "Why two Marys?"

He would grin happily and ask, "Does it confuse you? I thought the
confusion of Jewish names was only supposed to confound our enemies!
Well, it's really very simple: When your brother's first wife, Tabitha, was on
her deathbed she urged Joachim to marry again, and asked him to promise
that his first daughter would be named, Mary, for Tabitha's mother, Mary.

"Of course, he promised, and the first-born of Anna was a girl, and
they duly named her, Mary," he continued. "She, who later became the
mother of Jesus, was from childhood a very introspective and solemn child,
and the ebullient Anna used to chide Joachim by saying she had carried
and birthed the child just for Tabitha, and that someday she wanted to
bear her *own* Mary. And so it was, that twelve years later when she bore
her last child, a girl, she insisted on naming her, Mary. Then, *this* Mary,
wed Cleopas Alphaeus—half-brother of the *first* Mary's husband, Joseph
bar Jacob—who lived in Emmaus with his widowed father, Heli, so we
all began to call her Mary-Heli. We must suppose it was inevitable then
that she named her second child, Mary, who later married a Cleopas from
Caesarea Philippi, so *she* has been known as Mary-Cleopas."

And I would interrupt to say, "And to add to the confusion, Master
Eliud, *both* Cleopas and Alphaeus are Hellenizations of the same Hebrew
name, Halphai!"

"So true, so true!" he would respond, and we would both laugh until
tears ran down his cheeks.

"The other children of Mary-Heli and Cleopas Alphaeus," he continued, "were Matthew and James the Less (so-called because of his diminutive size), both of whom were called to be part of the Twelve of Lord Jesus; and then, Symeon.

"Those four are all first cousins of Jesus, are they not?" I interjected.

"Yes; correct," he agreed. "And then, back to my daughters: Maraha, as you know, has always been sickly, and has never married, but what a cook she is! Next is Bianca, who married Emerentia, and their daughter, Elizabeth, married the priest, Zacharias, and their son was John" (who came to be called The Baptizer).

"Since Mary and Elizabeth are first cousins, Jesus and John must be cousins-twice-removed," I observed.

He nodded assent, and resumed: "Bianca's other daughter, Leah, married David, and their daughter, Seraphia, married Sirach (who was named to the Great Sanhedrin about the same time I was).

"Then, our fourth daughter, Sobe, married Solomon, and their daughter, Mary-Salome, married Zebedee, fishing fleet operator of Capernaum, and their sons were James and John."

"Who also were cousins-twice-removed of Jesus and both became his Disciples," I finished for him.

"Yes; you remembered. See how simple a family tree!" he replied with a huge smile.*

I was not the only young person who enjoyed listening to Eliud. Somewhat later, Jesus often visited him since Sepphoris was only four or five miles northwest of Nazareth. Similarly, John bar Zacharias liked to visit with Eliud, but his interest was more limited, because John was so fascinated by the piety and asceticism of the Essene practices, and his life seemed bent in that direction right from these days of his youth.

While we were young, Essene theology seemed exciting to many of us, largely because it was roundly condemned by the Tempe lawyers, and by most of the rabbis who took notice of them. Eliud explained that the Essenes had their own Torah, or law, and did not recognize Rabbinic Judaism as established at the Jerusalem Temple. In later years I could see that Jesus had adopted a few of the basic Essene doctrines as being truer to the Mosaic code than was normative Judaism.

However, the Essenes held to a more strict insistence on ritual purity than did the Pharisees and were more intolerant of those who disagreed

---

*An appendix provides a probable genealogy chart for the interrelated families of this story.

with them; in these respects Jesus, in his later ministry, reacted strongly against the Essenes and often ridiculed them with sarcasm. He once commented, "Beware the leaven of the Herodians," but was referring to the Essenes by playing on the gutter-nickname, "Herodians," that was colloquially given to the Essenes because it was said that Herod was a protector of the Essenes. Obviously, this was before John bar Zacharias, preaching from his Essene base, infuriated Herod and brought on his own execution.

Another time Jesus told his audience, "You have heard it said, 'Hate thine enemy,'" but of course, there is no such writing from traditional Judaism, yet in the Qumran community's Manual of Discipline, the oath of allegiance for new converts who join the "Sons of Light" (the Essenes) requires them "to hate for all eternity the Sons of Darkness"—meaning everyone except themselves. Naturally, Jesus' doctrine of love was as far to the opposite extreme as one could get.

I probably did not make as much use, as did Jesus, of the knowledge imparted by old Eliud, but I certainly enjoyed sitting at his knee.

The four years from my fifteenth to nineteenth birthdays were extremely exciting ones for me. My days, of formal attendance in the Temple schools were substantially over, though I occasionally was there for a few weeks at a time to receive special instruction, such as the learning of esoteric languages that my father wisely explained would be useful in my worldwide travels that were now beginning. He recognized that carefully planned travel was educational in and of itself, and I will never forget the weeks I spent with him in Athens during the summer of my sixteenth year; there I was able to climb to the lovely ruins of the Acropolis, attend sessions of courtroom trials, quietly listen from the gallery as the law-makers sat in public session, and lose myself completely while reading in their great libraries.

Athens has seemed like a fabled city forever. Five hundred years—a half-millennium ago—the great lyric poet Pindar, though he was from Thebes, wrote an ode about Athens, calling it the "Shining violet-crowned, song-famed bulwark of Greece." And one could wax lyrical just to view the setting of the city as it lies on a smallish plain, looking westward over the small harbor and its town onto an arm of the Aegean Sea, and somewhat protected on the east by the arc of three low mountains—Parnes, Pentelicon, and Hymettus. A part of the city is the fabulous height known as Acropolis, with its temple ruins; I had a bit of knowledge of the art and architecture of the Sacred Rock, but I found that the vision of its temples in antiquity must be experienced on a personal and emotional level, not with a head full of dates and dimensions. Each time I looked at the Acropolis it touched my heart in a different way, especially because its mood and color changed with the time of day.

One of the reasons for the visit to Athens with my father was to arrange for me to study in centers of metallurgy in nearby cities. Farther north, into Macedonia, and just west of Thessalonica, is the city of Berea, which has a large community of our brothers of the diaspora, and is well-renowned for its metallurgists and craftsmen. As a consequence, it was agreed that I would come to Berea in the early Fall for three months as an apprentice workman under the guidance of one of the owners of a large operation of alloying, forging, casting, fabricating, and finishing metal products. Also, I knew that not too far from Athens was the fabled city of Corinth, whose bronze was said to be almost as beautiful as gold.

In addition, almost due east from Athens, across the Aegean Sea, is the Greek city of Ephesus which is renowned as the city of silversmiths.. It is located in a shallow basin where the Meander and Cayster Rivers meet just before emptying into the Aegean Sea three miles away; shallow-draft vessels can come up the Cayster to dock in the city. Thirty miles to the south, the fine harbor of Miletus accommodates the larger vessels, and is connected by a stone-paved Roman road to Ephesus.

The evenings after these cultural explorations in Athens found me a veritable chatter-box, while my father listened patiently with occasional words of explanation and elaboration. Nevertheless, in spite of these recognized cultural values, it was clear that my father considered travel and cultural pursuits to be secondary to my education in the business itself. My Uncle Johanan was involved mostly in buying and selling abroad and thus did most of the travelling for the firm. My father was clearly the business manager and knew intimately every facet of our far-flung operations. But he showed me early in life the importance of his plan for me—which was to become a true expert in the technical side of the business, metallurgy. He showed me the advantage of having a better product than our competitors, saying that it was only on this basis that we had a right to succeed. Although our technicians and their supervisors were competent and loyal, few of them could be called brilliant, although many were very thoughtful and innovative.

Father expected me to soon begin to share control with him, and ultimately to be his successor as business head of the firm, but it was his belief that new ideas, better products and new products were vital to us if we were to continue our supremacy in business and with international advantages. Consequently, as I began to phase out of and complete my studies in the Temple schools, I started to involve myself more deeply and extensively in the foundry and metal-working shops of the business, and with our gifted artists. Soon I was able to work effectively alongside our better-skilled workers and learn from them not only how, but why, each facet of metal development, design of product and crafting of each item was done.

CHAPTER SIXTEEN

✠

Metallurgy and Visits to Aqaba and Petra

1 B.C.

*I*ONCE ASKED MY FATHER, "Who invented bronze?"

And his reply was: "There must have been a beginning, but bronze seems to have come to us from antiquity. It is a wonderful metal made from plentiful copper and very scarce tin, blended together, in proportions of about ninety to ten percent for standard bronze. It is a great resource because the strength of the metal is complemented by the ease of fabrication."

"Is there no other metal that is comparable?" I asked.

"Well, we are just now beginning to see and to find uses for a variant that is called 'brass' and which the Celts call 'brace,' that seems to have been developed only a few years before your birth—I'm not sure if it was developed in Rome, but they have taken credit for it. It is combined from copper and a mineral by the name of 'zinc'—in proportions, I am told, of 83 to 17 percent, and sometimes tin, not to exceed two percent, is added."

"Are we making or using any of it, father?" I wanted to know.

"Not yet," he replied. "Our firm is exploring the availability of zinc, which we think is also found in Britannia where we get our tin—if we can get it there, we will be experimenting with it soon."

"Considering our success with bronze, why should we bother with brass," I asked.

"It seems to have some very valuable characteristics," he responded. "We understand that brass is less liable to corrosion around sea air and sea water. Also, I have learned that it can be hammered or beaten more easily than bronze, and can be rolled paper-thin and then used as a substitute for the so-costly gold-leaf."

"But the artists in our shops really like to work in bronze, don't they?" I asked.

"Oh, there's no question it is a favorite with them," he replied, "because it can be gilded, silvered, inlaid, encrusted, enameled, and engraved. Also, the 'bronzing' of wood or of other metal objects can be achieved by use of bronze powder mixed with lacquer."

He had earlier explained to me that, fortunately, copper is close at hand and not costly. Among the oldest and richest copper mines known to us are those on the nearby island of Cyprus, and my family has had close working relationships for many years with the owners of those mines. There is also much copper available from the kingdoms of Oman that our merchants have dealt with since King Solomon's negotiations with the Queen of Sheba; those shipments come easily to us through the Gulf of Aqaba, the northeastern arm of the Red Sea.

During that discussion, I had said: "But, father, the copper we receive is of good quality and comes to us in blocks. This is not the way the miners find it, surely?"

"Not at all," was his smiling response, always pleased when he could interest me enough to think and to ask questions. "Although pure veins are occasionally found, it most often is found mixed with various kinds of rock or other minerals which must be separated from the copper."

"That's what you call 'smelting,' isn't it?" I asked.

"Correct," he responded, "and now the mining communities have been taught this process so that we need to transport only the pure metal."

"Did we have to import the ore and smelt it ourselves, in olden times?" I asked.

"I'm sure that was true, but it was some centuries ago," he replied. "At the head of the Gulf of Aqaba* are remnants of the old cities of Elath and Ezion-Geber, and nearby Timna, where legend tells us Solomon smelted copper ore that was mined nearby in the Wadi Arabah, and possibly had also been brought from Oman. The wooded hills of Edom, just to the east, served him as a convenient source of the necessary charcoal to develop the extremely high temperatures essential for smelting. Though less easily obtained, there also seems to be plentiful copper in the Sinai. Of course,

---

*At the southern tip of modern Negev, Israel.

there are other major sources of copper in Iberia and Dalmatia, but Rome is not disposed to share them with us."

In order that I would understand the basics of copper smelting, later that summer my father took me to study it in a primitive setting, by a brief trip to the southern end of the Wadi Arabah and, slightly north where the South Timna Wadi joins it. We spent three days in this area, examining closely the mines, slag heaps and the remains of the copper smelters, presumably left by Solomon's workers. Pieces were identifiable as granite mortars and pestles, and hammers, with which the ore was crushed.

My father explained: "An open charcoal heap burned in a shallow cavity in the ground, and the smelting charge of crushed ore was dispersed onto the fire. If the ore had been finely ground, the pellets of pure copper would fall through the slag to the bottom of the smelting heap. A key factor in such a primitive operation was the requirement of a strong force of air to adequately raise the temperature of the burning charcoal. Most of the year there are strong and continuous winds that blow steadily down the Arabah from the north, and could be channeled into the fire; this would obviate the need for hand-operated bellows—the latter would obviously be inadequate for a sizeable smelting operation. Often lime or crushed limerock would be added to the 'charge' to aid in separating the copper, since it created a fluid slag by a fluxing process."

In the winter months, near the end of our Jewish year, the weather in this arid part of our land would be a bit more pleasant—at least the heat would be more tolerable—but my father explained that in this late Summer season we would experience the very strong north-wind, and could thus appreciate one of the unique features of the area that made it ideal for a smelting operation.

"This area, with its remains of the mining/smelting operations of long ago makes a good classroom for me," I observed, "but why doesn't anyone mine and smelt here anymore?"

"Simply because the copper here in the Arabah contains so much sulfur and other impurities that no one, either in antiquity or later, has been able to bring good quality copper from this site," he explained.

I greatly enjoyed this brief outing with my father. The area from the Wadi Arabah westward to the Great Sea, and from Judea all the way south to the Gulf of Aqaba, is mostly wasteland and much of it is as sandy as true desert. Nevertheless, there are low hilltops and locations of wet-weather springs that have been cultivated off and on over the centuries from antiquity, by using reservoirs, impounding dams and terraces, flumes and canals, to utilize every drop of the sparse rainfall.

This part of our country is in some ways harsh, and in others, beautiful. To the southwest we can clearly see the historic and mysterious mountains of the Sinai where Moses met with God; some parts of that hulking massif are of weathered sandstone, in hues from dun to rose, and other towering peaks of granite seem to have been impervious to the weather's rigor. The nearer hills of Edom, to the east, are wooded but sparsely now, raw and colorless usually, but the setting sun from Egypt finds colors in these old hills we didn't know were there. *

In every direction, but especially east and north from the Gulf, we see weird and almost life-like shapes where the soft rock has been carved by the winds of the ages. Even though the temperature is searingly hot, the air, we found, is always dry.

The atmosphere here is so thin and clear at night that the stars seem close enough to touch just with the aid of a ladder. The sunrises and sunsets in this semi-desert are truly things with souls, and the violence of their color is incredible, splattering the sky, clouds and mountains with a surging beauty. They are truly marvellous sights, but my rhetoric is really not poetic enough to do them justice. I am partial to the sunsets because I don't have to get up early to see them!

"Father," I asked, on the morning of the third day as we were preparing to start for home, "could we return by way of the great wadi, instead of northwestward to the Sea?"

"Why, yes," he replied "our mules are strong and our water supply is adequate. We can easily follow the old caravan route which some call the "Kings Highway"; it will take us east of the Salt Sea,* past Petra and through Perea, where we can cross the Jordan to Jericho and Jerusalem."

"And can we stop at Petra?" I asked, excitedly. "I've always wished to see it."

He smiled, and nodded. "We should reach there well before nightfall."

We had spent the night in the Timna Valley which is part of a vast crater-like depression, and frequently, as we travelled northward we could see ruins of buildings from ages past, and even an ancient Egyptian temple. Some of the wind-sculptures we passed were so smooth and shapely that they seemed man-made. One feature, nearly a hundred cubits high, father said was called "King Solomon's Pillars."

Later in the afternoon we saw some granite formations several times that high.

About mid-day we stopped at a cool, clear spring; my father said, "The Edomites call this, 'Ein Netafim,' because it's always sweet and pure. And

---

*The Dead Sea.

see, back just a little way are gazelle tracks in the hard clay that may have been made years ago."

Just beyond the spring we followed a wadi to the east with high, red walls on each side. The hills soon got higher and more rugged, and then well before sun-down, we reached Petra, the ancient Nabataean city. The red sandstone has been cut deep by water and wind in ages past, and in more recent centuries men have built the city by cutting buildings into the rock walls. It's military worth is great because the city can be reached only through a narrow defile where one can often touch both walls at the same time.

Temples, amphitheaters, altars and tombs have been cut into the walls of Petra, as well as the buildings of government and residences for the people. The fronts of many of the buildings are quite ornate and very impressive, with Greek and Roman columns and sculpture decorating them—all of living rock.

The following morning we visited in several public buildings and climbed the steps and sloping pathways up the cliffs which encompassed the city, before departing mid-morning, for Jericho.

The mysterious Nabataeans, a bedouin people from Arabia who are descendants of Ishmael,* came suddenly out of the desert to the southeast some century and a half ago and took the kingdom of Edom (established by Essau), making Petra their capital, and no army has seriously threatened it since. When the people of Judea were conquered and carried off to Babylon some six centuries ago, the Edomites took over much of the land, especially to the east and south, and it became known as Idumea—Herod the Great being Idumean. Then, when the Nabataeans later took over, there was little conquest—they merely intermarried and absorbed the Edomites. The present ruler is Aretas IV.

This mountainous area is known as the Selah. Petra is just east of the Arabah depression, exactly parallel with Kadesh-Barnea to the west, and some thirty miles south of the Salt Sea. The entrance to Petra is within sight of the Kings Highway, if one knows where to look. Of course, the name Edom means "red," doubtless taking its name from the crimson sandstone cliffs just west of Petra's entrance.

The city's entrance (running west to east) is a narrow gorge called "the Siq," which is a mile and a quarter long and from seven to twenty cubits wide.** Since the walls of the Siq are not straight up, one rarely can see the sky while traversing this entrance passage with walls one hundred cubits

---

*Son of Abraham and Hagar.
**Ten to thirty feet.

high.* Inside, the walls widen and stand some eight hundred cubits apart on the average,** and this canyon in effect makes Petra a walled city, and extends about three-quarters of a mile in length.

The canyon's craggy rock walls are red, pink, white, brown and violet, and are honeycombed with natural caves; these caves have been enlarged and shaped as buildings and fancy facades have been carved onto the fronts of many of them. The Nabataeans cut catchment channels to feed water to their cisterns from the nearby Wadi Musa during the torrential winter rains, so that the city never has a water problem.

---

*One hundred and fifty feet.
**Four hundred yards.

✠

I Learn Metal-working in Damascus

1 B.C.

*I*HAD BY NO MEANS FINISHED TALKING, to anyone who would listen, about my exciting trip of nearly three months that Fall, studying with the metallurgists and craftsmen in Beria of Macedonia, with a three-day stop to watch the Corinthians cast their "golden" bronze, and a six days' sojourn to observe the beautiful work of the Ephesian silversmiths.

Corinth, the capital of Achaia, was a fascinating city in its own right, but I was especially intrigued by the activity along the *diolkos,* and I spent each evening of my three days there—until dark—watching the traffic of ships on dry land! I suppose the *diolkos* always has and always will be important to commerce because the Aegean is such a stormy sea; from early fall 'till late spring few sea captains risk an east-west crossing and even in mid-summer, if the Etesians are blowing, sailing is impossible. For these reasons many ships avoid threading through the islands along the Achaian southern coast and save time as well by using Corinth's two gulfs, the Saronic on the east and the Corinthian on the west; thus, ships have only the three-mile-wide isthmus to cross at the edge of Corinth city, and the stone-paved roadway, called *diolkos,* begins and ends under the water; the cradle-like trucks can be positioned under the ship while still in the water, and are then rolled quickly across the isthmus to the opposite gulf. With this accommodation, ships to and from the Asian port of Myra or the island port of Rhodes in the east and Rome's southeast port of Brundisium have a short and swift run. I heard talk in Corinth that some day Roman engineers would cut a ship canal from gulf to gulf, but this seems unlikely because a mountain of solid rock would have to be pierced.[1]

⊹ ⊹ ⊹

Although the casting and forging of iron and the working of steel products in our shops at Arimathea would always be minor in extent, father knew that a well-rounded education in metals would be essential for me. Accordingly, that Winter I took the second extended trip by myself, to Damascus for a three-month apprenticeship in the iron and steel works of Sylleus and Brothers, who had been closely associated with our firm for a number of years.

Since one of the early races to settle in Syria had been the semitic Amorites from Arabia, Aramaic and its derivative, Syriac, would be the languages spoken most often in Damascus and I would have no language barrier to worry about.

In the months before my trip to Damascus I had tried very hard to learn our own processes and the right questions to ask in Damascus. I spent many hours in our Arimathea foundry, observing and asking questions of our foundry supervisor, Aaron.

One day I asked: "Aaron, why do we use bronze for most everything we make?"

"That's easy," he replied with a smile. "Bronze is ideal and best for all our customers' needs. It is perfect for handles, hinges and latches, for plowshares, for decorative but sturdy chains, for the strengthening of wooden members and structures where iron would be too heavy and cumbersome and steel far too expensive. On the other hand, many of the builder's tools we import, already finished, in Damascus steel, since we are sales agents for our associated Syrian firms.

"Householders, too," he continued, "find bronze to be the superior metal for the many utensils and cutlery, for implements and handles, for tools, candlesticks, mirrors, frames for wall-hangings, and appurtenances needful in one's buildings and gardens for the care and maintenance of one's premises.

"Why mirrors, Aaron?" I asked.

"Because we can make a thin sheet of bronze that we can grind to a smooth surface, and then, with gritty paste we can polish and buff to a high gloss that reflects your face as hardly any other metal will do," he replied.

"We make a lot of small items, I notice, which have little practical value," was my statement, asking a question.

He grinned, and said, "Oh, yes, and on most of *them* we make our highest profits."

"Of course," he continued, "candelabra, bells, and a wide variety of ecclesiastical ornaments are in demand for the Temple and the synagogues, while government authorities need coins, medals and other symbols of office."

On another occasion I asked Aaron to tell me about some of our products for use by the farmers.

"It's a shame, of course," he replied, "that so few of them can afford our metal products, for we can make their jobs much easier."

"For instance?" I asked.

"Well, peasants' carts sometimes have no metal parts, but usually the ends of the axles are covered by a steel sleeve and the wheel will have an iron hub revolving on the metal of the axle," he explained. "However, farmers and householders who can afford it come to us for special bronze hubs. These we make by adding ten to thirty percent of lead to our bronze in the molten state, and pour this bronze-alloy into molds for the wheel-hubs. The lead, a very soft mineral, comes to us mostly from Persia—sometimes by camel caravan but more often by ship from the River Tigris through the Persian Gulf and the open sea to the Red Sea and our Gulf of Acaba. This bronze-lead alloy is very easy for us to cut and work with—when molten it flows readily into every crevice of the mold."

"That must be very important for anything that has a moving part," I observed.

"You are so right," he responded. "As craftsmen have become proficient in making useful items with moving parts, they need our bronze-lead alloy as bushings and bearings to seat the moving parts, since this alloy has the property of minimum friction and will not seize to moving parts as copper would, especially when tallow or other lubricant is applied from time to time."

My father was not interested in manufacturing swords and other instruments of war—though there was much profit to be made in such activity—and as a consequence we had a very comfortable and friendly relationship with the steel makers of Damascus. They realized that our firm would never be a competitor in the manufacture of military supplies, and they respected the integrity of my father and uncle, so did not hesitate to engage in cooperative projects and even to share some of their secrets for the making of quality iron and steel.

In Damascus, iron and steel products were mostly wrought and forged to their final form—that is, shaped by heating, hammering while hot, and quenching in water; fine edges could thereafter be ground and honed on the swords, adzes, spears, axes, and the like. For the most part, steel was too hard and therefore not suited to our needs in Judea—we could, in fact, more often use the basic iron rather than steel. But iron was often too soft to be durable and our favorite metal was bronze—and occasionally, the rather new metal, brass.

As the son of our senior partner, I could easily have devoted my time in the executive offices of Ali Sylleus and learned technical details in a scholarly fashion. But it had been agreed before I left Arimathea that I would learn by doing the basic tasks alongside the workers. Initially, I worked with the strong-backed men who fed the iron-ore from nearby mines into the heavy smelting crucibles that could handle up to one hundred pounds of material at a time; they then drained off the molten iron into rough molds to make iron blocks for easy handling. In a few days I moved on to work in the foundry where molds of special sand were formed around wooden patterns carved by the artists; when the patterns were removed to leave sculptured holes in the molds, the iron blocks were remelted, and the molten iron was carefully poured into the molds and forced to cool slowly to make the desirable, grey cast-iron that was not brittle, but very practical and soft enough to be worked with tools.

Of course, most of the products cast by Sylleus were fairly plain items, and the patterns were easily made by carpenters and other craftsmen. However, I was permitted to work one week in the art department where many beautiful things were cast from a variety of molten metals. In Arimathea, we occasionally cast decorative pieces for the homes of the wealthy and sometimes for the Temple, but since our religious laws forbid the making of an image of a living thing, the scope of our artwork was somewhat limited.

Here in Syria, Sylleus and his competitors felt no such restraint and artists from Persia and Greece were employed to make patterns from which beautiful statues would be created. In order to cast anything so detailed and delicate they used the "lost wax" process which we used but little in Arimathea, so I observed carefully and asked many questions. The pattern could be made entirely of wax, with a clay casing, and vents provided for gas to escape and the wax to run off. For hollow pieces they might use a clay center held by pins. Sometimes they would use a layer of wax over the clay pattern or model, covered by an additional layer of clay. The mold was placed briefly in an oven, and then the metal was poured.

Ali Sylleus came in this shop while I was watching.

"It seems so easy, when you know how," I observed to him. "Are there no hazards or pitfalls of which to beware?"

"To be sure!" his smile seemed ear to ear. "Never pour the metal until you are sure every bit of the wax has run out. Else the mold will be blown to pieces and everyone nearby will be badly burned by the liquid metal."

"So, that's why the mold goes into the oven first?" I asked.

"Right. And the drain-hole for the wax must be positioned exactly, so that none of the wax is trapped inside. Then, after the mold is removed from the oven, *that* hole is plugged and an upper hole is used to receive the molten metal. You understand?" asked Ali.

I assured him that I did.

During my second month in Damascus I worked in the wrought-iron shops where I learned first-hand the skills of forging. As a beginner, I was given a huge steel-headed mallet and taught to beat in harmony with a partner upon a heated piece of iron while the forger, using tongs, turned it this way and that, and with grunts and motions indicated to the two beaters where the blows were to be struck. Whenever the metal cooled it was returned to the bed of charcoal, burning under a bellows-forced draft, until it was cherry-red again and ready for our further beating. Needless to say, most of the iron beaters were huge, ebony-black Nubians, twice my size, and I certainly had no problem of insomnia at nightfall. After a week of that effort, I was permitted gradually to serve as forger of simple pieces where great precision was not required.

Much of the steel-making process, during which impurities were removed and alloys (such as carbon) were added while heated in their special crucibles, still was a closely guarded secret, so that most of my third month involved training in the fashioning of steel products—not the converting of iron into steel. In any event, this would be the stage at which our shops in Arimathea would get involved with the raw steel we purchased from Sylleus in Damascus.

I became really excited on occasions when I watched certain of the steel-working processes, not especially because of the great skill employed, though it was sometimes spectacular, but because I could see how our shops could utilize those techniques in other metals and products, such as in our specialized bronze work.

Of course, the decorating of metal products has long been a high skill and art of these Damascus workers. One technique which I watched them use, especially on the blades of their most expensive swords, involved the cutting of fine channels in the steel, to carry out a particular artistic design; this was done just before the last hardening stage, and into this channel would be laid a gold wire. The burr caused by the cutting of the channel was worked down to hold the gold wire in place. The final hardening was then accomplished with the result that even the grinding which puts a cutting edge on the blade does not remove the inlaid threads of gold.

I could see how readily we, in Arimathea, could use *silver* wires to inlay our bronze and brass items with beautiful designs. Similarly, I could see adaptations we could make of another wonderful Sylleus process, whereby a decorative bronze handle of a knife was *cast onto* the steel blade previously forged; this joining of the two metals was possible because an alloy of bismuth had been added to the molten bronze, thus permitting effective adhesion of the molten bronze to the cold steel blade.[2]

Before ending my interesting and highly educational stay in Damascus I was having a final conversation with Ali, and he said to me:

"My young friend, I have had reports of you every day of your time with us, and all have been highly favorable; I have concluded, among other things, that you are fully as morally responsible as I know your father to be. If there is any question you wish to ask about our operation—*any question*—I will be pleased to answer it."

"Sir," I replied, "I know you have secret procedures in the making of your famous steel, but I have no desire to know of them. However, during my first weeks here I noticed that the men who fed the iron-ore or copper-ore into the smelting crucibles, would stop every half-hour or so to take a swallow or two of thick liquid that was kept warm over a candle. What was the purpose—since it surely could not cool their hot bodies?"

His wide smile exploded into a roar of laughter, and as he sobered, he responded: "Of course, it appears to make no sense, but we know it to be a matter of life and death, though we can't explain it. The fumes that come from the molten metal, especially the copper, seem to be harmful. Centuries ago, metal refinery workers had a very short life—an average of ten years in such work; but someone discovered that melted goat's butter fully combats that danger—although it puts a little padding around the middle"—he concluded, with a smile, as he pointed to his own generous abdomen.

"Is an observer of the process at risk, then," I asked.

"Not from a discrete distance, I think," he replied, "but when one of us needs to get closer, we always soak a cloth in water and cover the lower part of the face—to breathe through. Carelessness in such regard can cause severe nausea and vomiting."[3]

CHAPTER NOTES:

1. In A.D. 67, Emperor Nero began such a canal, using six thousand Jewish prisoners captured during the Revolt in Judea the previous year, but had to abandon the effort. French engineers finally accomplished the task in 1881-93. See "Corinth in Paul's Time—What Can Archaeology Tell Us?" *Biblical Archaeology Review,* May-June 1988, XV-3.

2. The use of bismuth for this purpose has been found in the artifacts of the pre-Incas at Machu Picchu, Peru.

3. Metallurgists from earliest times drank melted butter (or some analogous substance) to absorb the poisonous fumes thrown off when refining ore (p. 36, *The Mystic Symbol,* by Henriette Vertz, Global Books, Gaithersburg, Maryland, 1986).

CHAPTER EIGHTEEN

✠

My Betrothal

A.D. 1

DURING THE YEAR I WAS SIXTEEN, I began to sense the stirrings of romantic feelings. And it was very easy to know why—for on each occasion it happened in the presence of the lovely Elyap, to whom I was introduced by my close friend, Nicodemus.

Since our early classroom days, Nicodemus and I visited for a week or more in each other's home several times a year. His parents' home in Jericho was an especially pleasant place in the winter months because of its mild climate and the invigorating warm springs which abound there. Jericho is more than three thousand feet below Jerusalem and one thousand feet below the level of the Great Sea, and thus it is sheltered from winter winds. King Herod and many prominent persons have chosen it for the location of their winter palaces.

All of the palaces have their own private pools, and Nicodemus continually invited in friends who did not have the advantage of such arrangements. These included Elyap and her older brother, Jarius, a craftsman for whom she kept house; they lived in a more modest dwelling on the outskirts of Jericho.

The three occasions that year when we had the pleasure of each other's company in Nicodemus' home, convinced me that I wanted to look no further for a wife. And so, at the time of my seventeenth birthday, in the month of Nisan,* my father arranged with Jarius for the betrothal of Elyap and me, with our wedding to follow in the Fall.

---

*Nisan, the first month of the Jewish year, approximately coincides with April.

114

In the meantime, one of the great adventures of my life occurred that Spring and Summer. Shortly after return from my sojourn in Damascus, my father announced that he would take me on an extended trip to the Tin Islands that the Phoenicians call by the Greek name, Cassiterides—a part of the northern area the Romans have named Britannia.* We were to leave about the middle of the following month, Iyar, and be gone for about three and a half months. This summer period was usually ideal for trips on the Great Sea,** and we would be going, to its western extremity and then beyond the Gates of Heracles (as named by the Greeks) and onto the Western Sea, which the Romans call the Ocean Sea. At that point we would turn northward along the coasts of Iberia,*** sometimes called Hispania, and past the land of Transalpine Gaul.****

As I have explained, copper was rather plentiful and close at hand for us. However, it is too soft for practical purposes, and it is therefore essential that we have tin to make bronze, and occasionally lead, as well as zinc for making brass. And so, several decades earlier, my father and his father before him had sought for adequate sources of tin and the other metals. Of course, we are told that there is tin in the mountains northeastward from the shore of that dark sea the Greeks call the Euxine (black), but not even the Romans are able to utilize that source because they have not yet "civilized" the area.

Reaching far back in time, we are told that ancient Greece fought a war with Troy over access to the tin mines beyond the mountains north of Macedonia; that access was later taken over by the Romans. Also, some tin is to be found in Iberia which, naturally, the Romans are not sharing. As a consequence, my forebears, with the assistance of their seafaring friends among the Phoenicians, were finally able to establish a plentiful supply of tin in the "tin islands"[1] of that far northern land. By taking our own exports of olives, olive oil, linen end jewelry, my family has been able to establish our firm as buyers and sometimes partners of the Celtic mine-owners there.

Consequently, I spent most of the next six weeks pestering my patient father with questions.

"Father." I asked, "is this long sea voyage the only way to get to the Tin Islands?"

"By no means," was his reply, "but when the summer weather is good, it is the fastest and most comfortable way to go. If it were either earlier or later we might consider it prudent to avoid the Western Sea by going to

---

*England.
**Mediterranean Sea.
***Spain and Portugal.
****France.

Massalia,* the central southern port of Transalpine Gaul. From there we would have several choices by shallow-draft boats on rivers running from the north and northwest, and debouching into the Great Sea near Massalia; from the headwaters of these rivers, by very short portages—where the boats are portaged to other rivers running north or west, by using wooden rollers to move them overland—ultimately, we would thus reach the narrow body of water the Romans call Fretum Gallicum,** which separates the northern coast of Gaul from the southern coast of Britannia. That Channel is often covered with fog but, when clear, one can actually see across it."

"But, Father" I asked, "is it not possible to go all the way by land, at least to the channel above northern Gaul?"

"Yes," he replied with a smile, "if you wouldn't mind spending several months on the back of a mule. The Roman post-roads carry mail and official messages to every part of the Empire, and are also available to other travelers as well."

I grinned, because he knew I didn't care that much for mule-back riding. "Some of them are very good roads, though, are they not, Father?" I observed.

"The Romans truly are great engineers," he replied. "Their roads run to Rome from every corner of the empire, and they run as straight as possible, often necessitating steep slopes. Many of their roads are engineering marvels, built to last a millennium. A trench is dug so that a base four to five feet deep can be provided; the base is built of large, and then small, stones, covered by rammed gravel. Often, the paving of the surface is then accomplished with good quality concrete, or by the laying of large paving stones a foot^2 thick and one-and-a-half feet square. Mountain roads may be only five to six feet wide, but main roads and those across better terrain are usually fifteen to twenty feet wide. Stone and concrete bridges cross most of the streams, and lime-mortar is mixed with silica whenever it is necessary for the concrete to set under water."

"I should say they are great engineers," I responded, with awe in my voice. "I have seen some of those roads north from Damascus, and also crossing Macedonia, but I didn't realize what a marvel of construction is involved.

"Father, when we leave the port of Joppa," I continued, "will we sail straight for the Pillars of Heracles?"

---

*Marseilles, France.
**The English Channel.

"Not at all," was his smiling response. "Our Phoenician captain, Hiram bar Abram of Tyre, like the most competent of the Phoenician ship-masters, is up in years, and he didn't live a long, time at his trade by taking unnecessary chances. We will rarely be out of sight of land all the way to the Tin Islands."

"Won't that make for a much longer trip, though?" was my obvious question.

"Quite to the contrary, the winds will favor us most all the way," was his response; "the prevailing north wind, here in the eastern basin of the Great Sea, will permit us to make very good speed with the shores of the desert lands of Egypt, Cyrenaica, Tripolitania, and Mauretania on our left hand as we sail westward."

I thought I would never be able to wait those few weeks, but in fact, the time flew by, and Hiram's huge ship, a *gaulos* named "Astarte," pulled in along the quay of our harbor one morning shortly after sunrise, using its twenty oars after the sails had been quickly furled.

"Father, look," I exclaimed, "how low it sits in the water and we haven't yet begun to load our goods."

He laughed, and said, "Yes, it's low. They load it with stone as ballast, because a light ship is hard to control and steer when it rides too high. You see, our trading goods of olives, olive oil, linen and jewelry are not very heavy, and neither is the Phoenician glassware and purple cloth that Hiram has brought at my instruction, so we need that ballast. The only items of weight are a few shovel-blades, picks and hammer-heads of Damascus steel, and some iron tools, all of which I am taking for the miners."

"We won't need the ballast, though, once we load the tin mad other metals in Britannia, will we, Father?" I commented, rather lamely.

He grinned in acknowledgment, as we started down to the port to greet Hiram and his crew. As we walked, I said, "Father, why are we taking Phoenician glassware for trading in Britanicus when we could take Judean glassware?"

"Their glassware is exquisite," he replied, "and also it is unique. The sandy Phoenician shore has just the right proportion of chalky ore which, when fused with pure sand, forms a clear, white-hot, liquid glass they pour into the many delicate molds of the master glassmakers. We have glass, yes, but nothing to compare with the Phoenician quality."

That afternoon, while Father conferred with Hiram over business matters, I sat in our garden and composed my first letter to the lovely Elyap, my betrothed. It is not often, in our land, that fathers consult with sons over the choice of a bride, and maybe that was a part of the reason I was so overjoyed in my betrothal. I wrote her as follows:

My dearest One: It is with mixed feelings that I set out tomorrow for Britannia (I repeat the admonition that our destination must be a secret). It is certainly the most exciting trip of my life until now, and perhaps one of the most important I shall ever take. But I leave with reluctance, knowing that our twice monthly visits (alternating Jericho and Arimathea) will not spice and sweeten my life until I return in early Fall. Several of my friends have married in the past three or four years, but all were parentally arranged marriages, and no peer of mine has evinced the joy I feel—there must be a connection, and I will always be grateful to my father—but from the first time we met I knew the real meaning of romantic love, which 'till then I knew only from reading—I never saw it in friends and acquaintances. The whole time we are gone on this trip, I will remember what I saw in the deeps of your eyes, when my eyes devoured your lovely face at our last meeting. I will think of you often every day—do remember me, my Sweet.

That morning, without delay, our warehousemen had begun moving our merchandise, and carefully stowed it below decks, plus all the other provisions, ready for us to sail at first light on the following day. We went on board with all of our personal belongings while it was still dark that morning, when the eastern sky was showing just a rim of light. By the time ships and other objects in the harbor were clearly visible, ten crewmen were straddling a bench near the gunwale on each side, the mooring lines were cast off, and the twenty oars hit the water in unison to send us quickly past the jetty and breakwater into the open Sea. Rapidly then, the oars were shipped and the huge square sail was set.

"Well, young Joseph," said Captain Hiram, whose bare feet had given no warning as he stepped to my side, "how do you think you will like sailing for a month?"

"I'll love every moment of it, Captain," was my smiling reply.

"The ship is in excellent condition, I have a veteran crew, and the weather should be good, so I'll have quite a bit of spare time," he advised me; "if you want to ask questions don't hesitate. Your father and I have sailed many times together, so he and I won't need to talk."

"Thank you," I replied, "and if I may start now, I'd like you to educate me by bragging a little about Phoenicia. I know you are a people of great ship-building skill and are great mariners. What else would you say?"

Hiram smiled broadly and said: "You may not know it, but we are the original Canaanites. When your General Joshua began pushing us westward from the Jordan/Salt Sea basin in brilliant military moves complemented by aggressive colonization, we were compressed along the coast of the Great Sea, and ended as a confederation of city-states, of which Tyre and Sidon are now chief, both having been built on islands, though we have since expanded onto the mainland.

"Phoenicia technically lost its independence to the great empires of the East, but under the Persians, Phoenicia was a semi-autonomous satrapy. Three centuries and a half ago, shortly after his defeat of Darius III, king of Persia, Alexander the Great of Macedonia took the port-cities of Phoenicia. However, Alexander merely replaced Persian satraps with Grecian or local satraps and left the rest of the local governments intact.

"With the rise of Roman power, a different attitude eliminated local autonomy. Early on—a little over a century ago—Rome moved eastward and gradually annexed the entire Hellenistic East with the defeat of the Grecian Seleucids (the generals who succeeded Alexander), and then moved inexorably through Syria, Phoenicia and Judea under the armies of Pompey. Julius Caesar defeated Pompey, and was assassinated shortly thereafter, but the pattern had been set, and Phoenicia like the rest of the East began to lose its individual identity as a nation.

"Upon the death of Julius Caesar, the Parthians and their allies invaded Syria, and Judea for a brief time, but then withdrew beyond the Euphrates River. Herod the Great fled to the bastion of Petra, just east of the Salt Sea until the Parthians were safely away.

"Nevertheless, from antiquity, under whatever name (and the Egyptians once called us Ptolemais), our reputation as ship-builders/seamen/navigators has been supreme regardless of name or conqueror. Moreover, I am proud that important traders such as your father and his father before him have always chartered our ships, even when Egyptian or Grecian shipping has been available at a lower fee. Of course, far enough back we're probably related," he said with a smile.

"As perhaps you know," he continued, "the word Phoenicia is a Greek word, meaning 'purple,' because of the world-famous purple dye which we make from our *murex* shellfish. Our architects and stonemasons were so great that your King Solomon begged my namesake, King Hiram, to come build for him the Temple in Jerusalem. Of course, you must know that our craftsmen and jewelry-makers and ivory-carvers are the world's greatest, but did you know that we invented the alphabet which was subsequently taken over by the Greeks and given to the world?"

"I shouldn't have asked," I said, laughing, "but I'm very glad you have told me. Maybe you will also tell me the ports at which we will stop?"

"Fair enough," he said. "We'll not bother to stop at Alexandria, but will go straight west to Cyrene, the capital of Cyrenaica, and we should be there easily in five or six days."

"Then I won't get to see the famed Pharos Light of Alexandria?" I asked somewhat wistfully, as I'm sure my disappointment was showing.

He laughed. "I promise you'll see it. I'll wake you myself if necessary, because we will pass it on our second night —close enough to give you a good view. Do you know how it is built?"

"No, really I don't," was my response.

"Sitting on a tiny island at the outer edge of the harbor, the Pharos completely covers the island," he explained. "It is square at the bottom but the upper structure is circular, six hundred feet high from the water, and constructed entirely of white stone. On its top is a giant mirror before which a fire is kept burning from sunset to sunrise, the beacon thus is visible to sailors more than thirty-five miles at sea and guides them right to the harbor. Even though we will not go in to Alexandria's harbor, as we pass the Pharos we will be able to check our position by its strong light."

"I suppose the sun, when it is shining, tells you the direction we are going, but how about at night or when the sun is hidden," I asked.

"At night we call it 'celestial navigation' because we guide by the 'southing stars' and by the north-pointing stars. And, come in here to the pilot house," he said, taking my arm.

There, he pointed to an open cask of water in which floated a wooden disc with concentric circles marked on it. From the center of the floating disc stood an upright peg. "If the sun shines," he explained, "we observe the shadow of the peg at noon, and then from my charts I can tell our location. Every Phoenician ship's captain carries a mariner's chart that has been compiled from the careful reports of mariners' observations recorded over the centuries."*

"And why are our hull and sails totally black," I asked next.

"Mostly because it's always been done, I suppose," he replied. "You see, before Rome made the seas safe, we had to fight for our lives and our cargo on every voyage, and black made us harder to see—and perfect for night fighting. Of course, a trading vessel, a *gaulos*[3] like this, is not prepared to fight. Also, space below the deck is used mostly for cargo, so we have only oarlocks in the gunwales, above deck, and therefore are doubly vulnerable."

"I notice that we are steered by the double-sweeps, aft, and that we carry stone anchors, fore and aft, made much like a pyramid with a hole in the top, but to me the most unusual feature of this ship is its mast," I said.

---

*The good sailing season on the Mediterranean for craft of the first century was from May 27 to September 14, and the outside limits were March 10 to November 10. Even though some vital shipping went on in the winter it was definitely hazardous. Visibility due to mist and fog was as much of a problem as storms in the winter months.

"Why is it not straight upright, as is usual? This mast is slanted backward."

"Great as Phoenician ship-builders can properly claim to be," he explained, "this is a feature which a century or so ago we borrowed from the Egyptians. The purpose is so that we can safely carry a very much larger sail than any other vessel with a conventional, straight-up mast. Slanted, it makes a much more efficient use of the wind and gives us great power for propelling larger ships and heavier cargoes, and for withstanding ocean waves—which you have yet to see! Of course, as you can observe for yourself when you go below, the slanted mast requires a heavier socket made of our famous cedar timber into at the point where the mast is stepped into the keel."

"That is surely fascinating, Captain," I said. "Now, you told me that our first stop would be Cyrene; where do we go from there?"

"The next stop will be Lepcis Magna,* on the coast of Tripolitania," he replied, "and from there we will go due north to Syracuse on the large island of Sicily. I haven't yet decided if we'll stop at Caesarea Mauretania** in Mauretania, or go directly from Syracuse to Gades,*** just beyond the Pillars of Heracles

"At the moment you must excuse me while I attend to a navigational problem," he concluded.

CHAPTER NOTES:

1. In those years, the Bristol Channel coast of Cornwall England, was a marshland dotted with many islands, some of which were man-made.

2. The Romans brought the "foot" measurement into general use; it was slightly longer than one-half of the "cubit" which was the standard in the Near East. Similarly, they established the "mile" as 1,000 paces, or about 420 feet shorter than today's mile.

3. Named in an earlier century, the word means "tub"; however, by the first century A.D. the merchant vessel would have been more sleek-appearing, especially those designed for ocean travel.

---

*Tripoli.
**Algiers.
*** Cadiz, Spain.

CHAPTER NINETEEN

✠

To Britain,
Via the Mediterranean
and Atlantic

A.D. 1

PASSING THE PHAROS LIGHT was everything I had expected, and much more. It was only the third hour after sunset on the second day out of Joppa when we were due north from the light, so Captain Hiram had not needed to awaken me to see the Light. The Captain's confident statement that we were nearly thirty-five miles from it was quite a shock to me, for its beacon was so strong that I would have guessed the distance at no more than five miles. So fascinating was the sight that I stayed on deck, watching from the port gunwale for two hours until its brilliance began to fade.

Our stop in Cyrene was for little more than an hour, while our casks were refilled with fresh water, and a few fresh food items were procured at a dockside market.

As we waited for the shore-party to return I asked the Captain: "Your charts of the Sea make the diagonal from here to Syracuse seem the more practical. Why, instead, do we sail on westward to Lepcis Magna and then nearly north to Syracuse?"

"There really may be no reason in fact," he acknowledged "but its a sound precaution. The inner harbor at Lepcis Magna is one of the best on our entire route and, although the steady level of our bilge, below, shows no likelihood of leaks, on so long a voyage it is prudent to have a look at the outside of our hull before we venture onto the Western Sea. So, one extra day of travel time and a day in dry-dock makes certain that we will stay afloat all the way."

The inner harbor at Lepcis Magna was like a very small, though longish, lake lying parallel to the Sea, and with a small mouth to the east where it joined the outer harbor. Docks and quays around the inner harbor were very busy, but a dry-dock was available for us. Everyone debarked while oxen plodding in a tight circle winched our vessel up the slick skids until the keel and rudders were fully clear. While inspection and maintenance proceeded, I limbered my muscles by a walk to the top of the narrow, low ridge which separated the inner harbor from the Sea.

So sound and well maintained was the "Astarte" that in less than a half-day the job was done and she was again afloat and ready to resume the voyage. The small city was mostly hidden by the shoreline ridge, and by sunset little could be seen of the low-lying coast at our stern.

As we watched the colored clouds and Sea that beautified the scene for more than an hour, I asked my father: "The captain explained to me the desirability of our stop in Lepcis Magna, but why, Father, do we go out of our way to stop at Syracuse?"

"It's another of our precautionary practices," he said. "Some twenty-two years ago a very great man died at his home just a few miles northwest of Syracuse. His name was Diodorus, and the Romans called him Diodorus Siculus, which merely means Diodorus of Sicily. The Romans called him a historian, and indeed he was that, for about thirty years ago he published a world history in forty volumes, written in Greek. But we, your grandfather and I, knew him more as a geographer, a cartographer and a collector of valuable information. His beautiful maps show Sea currents, as well as prevailing winds at various times of the year for all known bodies of water. He collected information from us and from other traders and sea-captains about locations and travel routes for various products all over the world."

"So, I can guess that his operation still continues," was my observation.

"Quite true," responded my father. "Diodorus' son, Palermos, who is about my age, had worked with his father and continues the collection of valuable information. In fact, I believe, is even more reliable than his father, whose views, many thought, were too greatly colored by his admiration of Roman rule and by his love of Stoic philosophy. However, in fairness, I must say that such bias on the part of Diodorus never seemed to adversely affect his information gathering, his geography and cartography pursuits—even if his histories were colored thereby."

"Will we stop over long at the establishment of Diodorus?" I asked.

"We should lose less than a day, and we will have come very little out of our way, because the African headland is actually north of Syracuse where we round the point on which Utica and Carthage have been rebuilt," he replied.

"But we won't stop there, either?" I asked.

"No. Since Rome destroyed and then rebuilt those Phoenician cities, there is no reason for a Phoenician ship-master to make that area a port of call," was his response. "We'll sail right on to Gades, just beyond the Pillars of Heracles."

"And the Diodorus establishment, Father, is it far from Syracuse?" I wanted to know.

"No," he answered. "Just north of Syracusa, as the Romans call it, is a sheltered Gulf, about half-way to Catania, where we'll anchor near the shore, and a shallow-draft boat will take us up the Simeto River a few miles to the Diodorus studios, within sight of the volcanic Mount Etna. Diodorus was born in the nearby town of Agyrium, the son of a prosperous farmer, Apollonius."

"Did Diodorus call our destination, 'Cassiterides,' the Tin Islands?" I then asked.

"He mentioned that Greek name, because he wrote in Greek, but he preferred to call them, 'Belerion,' which may have been a Celtic name," my father replied.

Our stop at the Diodorus studios was just as my father had anticipated it would be. I was surprised and impressed by the tremendous library of books and scrolls, and by the huge maps that hung on the walls, as well as by the staff of six or seven studious young men. Our captain purchased additional maps with important weather data. It had been but two years since my father had made this trip, so there was very little new information for us, and in no more than an hour we were finished and on our way back to our ship.

In just about twenty days out of Joppa we began to approach the Pillars of Heracles. I was first aware of our approach when the high coastline on both sides of us began to encroach and narrow our passage. On the right, there loomed before us a massive and majestic mountain, shaped like a huge pylon, that was actually an island near the shore, rising sheer almost to a point where it pierced the sky.* Although our sail was full and our speed

---

*Gibralter.

was very good, I soon noticed the groaning of our ship as it seemed to be moving beneath our feet.

Captain Hiram noticed the concern on my face and motioned me to him, smiling.

"We're beginning to feel the Western Sea! She's trying to rush in through this narrow slot, pushed by her own tide," he explained. "If the new Diodorus charts are correct for this time of the year, within the hour the tide should change and suck us out through the Pillars of Heracles."

I was not too comforted by his descriptive words and it was several days before the idea of tides began to make sense to me. Looking at the shore, I could see that we were still moving westward at a good speed, and the movement of the turbulent waters did seem to slow us for an hour and then to move with us instead of against us. Now our speed picked up noticeably, and as the cloud-darkened sky hid the sunset we rushed through the famous Pillars and into the open Sea, with land falling quickly away on both sides. Soon, our helmsman steered us nearly on a northward course and we raced along with the dark headland close on our right.

Sleeping that night was more difficult, as our ship seemed to roll from side to side as well as to pitch forward and aft like an angry donkey. This was nothing like the smooth passage we had had on the Great Sea. Actually, I was hard-pressed to find a way to wedge myself so that I would not roll out of the bunk altogether.

Shortly after noon the following day we came into the beautiful land-locked harbor for the city of Gades, and tied-up at quayside of a very busy, bustling seaport. The Phoenicians had founded this city more than a half-millennium ago, and named it Gadir; then their colony, Carthage, took it and ruled for three centuries—but two hundred years ago it was taken by Rome and named Gades. At that time the tin mines of the interior were lost to the Near East countries, and the Phoenicians pioneered the availability of tin from the Cassiterides in the far north.

Again, our stop was brief as we needed only fresh water and food-stuffs, before setting a course westward into the lowering sun, bucking this strange phenomena, "the tide," which now came at us head-on, while in addition the waves seemed rolling at us five and six feet high—which contrasted with the mild waves of no more than a foot high on the Great Sea. I own I was a little frightened, but excitement for two days had fatigued me and I slept in spite of the wild movement of the ship that night.

Late the next afternoon we headed due north along a rugged and mountainous coast just a few miles on our starboard side. This course now gave us the full effect of the waves into whose troughs we wallowed a full half of our time.

"I'm glad you stay near the shore," I told Captain Hiram the next day; "I feel safer!"

"I'm sure you do," he replied, "but that's not the reason we do it. If we were a mere fifty miles at Sea we would find a 'river'* running southward in the Sea and it would almost eliminate our headway."

"There's just one amazement after another," I said, "but if that river continues to flow that way a few weeks hence, I suppose we'll let the current carry us back."

"Exactly so," he replied with a large smile. "I think you would make a good seaman, should you ever get tired of being a merchant."

⊹   ⊹   ⊹

In just over a week on our northward course, I awoke one morning and went on deck to find no land in sight, and a low bank of clouds sitting right on the water. For the last three days we had been steering a more easterly course across the mouth of a huge bay with land just barely visible in the distance. But now, there was no land at all.

"Where are we, Captain Hiram?" I asked as he approached me.

"Master Joseph, we are almost there! Tonight or tomorrow morning, depending on visibility, will see us into the big estuary** that runs eastward into Britannia," he told me. "Right now we are crossing the great Channel that separates the north coast of Gaul from the south coast of Britannia. Through that channel there is often much cold air moving which creates this blanket of fog, obscuring everything."

"And, Meare Island, our destination, is in that large estuary, is it not,?" I asked.

"Yes, along its marshy southern shore is a small estuary running southward on which I shall anchor while you and your father go by small boat and by cart southward to the tin mines.

"Will we have to bring the tin overland to you, then?" I asked.

"The chances are that many ingots of tin will be awaiting us at Meare, and I will be removing our stone ballast and will replace it with the bars of tin, while you and your father are at the mines," he replied.

"What will you do with the ballast?" I asked; "just dump it in the water?"

"No, my friend," he said with a smile. "I make profit both ways. These people will gladly pay me for the stone, which they will use as foundations

---

*The "Gulf Stream."
**Bristol Channel.

for buildings and for the loading-quays they must build and continuously repair. You see, this area for miles around Meare Island is a huge swamp and many of the islands are under water at high tide; also, the ground is very spongy so that filling is constantly required. They bring many timbers down from the forests for that purpose, but our stone is even better—it won't rot."

✠ ✠ ✠

My sight of Meare Island was just one more surprise, for the houses were all small and the walls were made of reeds plastered with clay, which they called a "wattle" construction. The floors of the houses were crossed timbers, sometimes five or six layers deep, as they had settled into the muck; when they stabilized, a floor of stone or clay would be laid on the timbers; the center of the house had a fire chamber positioned under a hole in the middle of the thatched roof so the smoke could escape.

The following morning after our arrival my father arranged for a small boat to take us southward across the marsh, dotted with hundreds of islands, to the beginning of slightly higher and more solid ground. There a cart pulled by a bullock took us on the roughest ride of my life! Because of the marshy ground, a roadway—which, oddly, they called a Trackway—had been built by laying timbers side-by-side cross-wise of the road, and adding more timbers whenever a section sank into the muck. No mule or even camel provided so rough a ride, jarring our spines as the wheels bumped continually along the Trackway.

"Father, is there no other way to the tin mines." I asked at a rare smooth stretch of high ground.

"Yes," he replied. "We can go to Ictis Island on Brittannia's southern shore, on the Great Channel, but the Channel waters are so tempestuous and unpredictable, and the anchorage there less protected, so we use that approach only when Spring and Fall visits are too dangerous by way of the Ocean Sea. Then, we cross Gaul by river and make a quick run across the Channel to Ictis."

"I guess that coming the way we did, with Captain Hiram's large ship, we can carry more tin than if we had crossed Gaul by way of the rivers," I observed.

"Indeed, so!" he replied. "We carry more than twice the amount of metal this way. In any event, the tin fields lie about equidistant from the north and south shores of this large peninsula of Britannia."

"And seeing the marsh and its hundreds of islands," I added, "I can now understand the name, 'Tin Islands.'"[1]

CHAPTER NOTE:

1 About 600 B.C., Ezekiel noted that tin was an article of commerce in the markets of Tyre. In about 440 B.C., Herodotus wrote that that tin in Tyre came from the Isles of the Cassiterides—which word merely means "tin" in Greek. However, all classical geographers thereafter identified the location as the Scilly Isles off Cornwall or as Cornwall itself.—Barbara Tuchman, *Bible and Sword,* N. Y., Univ. Press, 1956.

✠

CHAPTER TWENTY

In the Tin Fields of Britain

A.D. 1

*T*HE WEATHER-BEATEN LEADER of the tin miners seemed genuinely pleased to see my father again, and was obviously trying to make me welcome, although I couldn't quite understand the words of his Celtic tongue.

"I feel I *almost* know what he is saying, Father," I said with some astonishment.

"It's my belief that the Celtic tongue and our own Hebrew may have a relationship in the distant past," my father replied. "I feel sure you will find it easy to pick up a working knowledge of their language in a few days."

Only a few years older than I, the Celt was a bandy-legged and grizzled appearing man of short stature and quick movements, and clearly had considerable strength in his husky arms, shoulders and back. He moved spryly around the mining operation explaining various matters to my father with expressive gestures, and I listened closely trying to pick up the meaning of his words. The mining operation was located in and adjacent to a small but fast-running stream which was coming down a slope from slightly higher elevations covered with gray rock formations, very rough and broken by many fractures.

"Father, I didn't expect the tin fields to be so close to the outcropping of bedrock," I observed. "Do they have to dig through the rock to get to the tin?"

"Not very much," he replied. "Most of the mining here is what we call 'streaming,' since they work right in the stream or divert it, and use the moving water to help separate the tin ore, the cassiterite, from the dross. The stream has washed much of the tin out of the crevices and fissures in the rock formations higher up and often is now in layers lower in the stream bed. Also, they occasionally find crevices in the stream banks that are filled with tin which they break open and pick out. Sometimes these crevices filled with tin will in fact lead to a lode, or large deposit of tin, deeper in the rock—reaching it is hard work, breaking through the solid rock, but well-worth the effort."

"Can they always tell whether crevice tin will lead them down to a 'lode,' as you call it?" I asked.

"By no means," he responded with a smile. "But old Cymric, the leader of this family operation, and his youngest son, Llane, both have a curious spiritual ability of walking with a forked stick* extended so that it will point for them to the large deposits of tin underground. Perhaps our own Moses, ages ago, used this ability to find underground streams of water."

"I see that they are able to carefully wash out lumps, pebbles and grains of the blackened tin ore from the bed and banks of this stream, but is that the only way they can get the ore?" I wanted to know.

"It's the easiest and most common method in these tin fields," he replied. "But sometimes when they find large quantities of the gray rock** with many, many fissures solid with tin, they will take lumps of the rock and work them by pounding, crushing and grinding so the tin ore can be washed out. However, the stream tin is usually so pure it can be taken directly to their smelting operation."

At this point Cymric walked up to us, smiling from ear to ear, and was holding out to my father a thin ingot of tin.

"Did he say, 'Listen,' Father?" I asked, trying, to understand this strange tongue.

"He did indeed," was my father's pleased response. "So, listen!" he said, grasping each end of the ingot and bending it slightly in the middle.

From the metal came a high keening noise, much like the wail of a small child.

---

*Dowsing.
**Granite.

"This is the way you can know quality tin," exclaimed my father. "If it 'cries' it's the very best, with no impurities at all. I know of no other tin that has the cry of the Cassiterite from Britannia. Of course, the commercial-size ingots that we'll carry back to Judea are too thick to test by bending." And he handed the thin ingot back to Cymric with an approving comment.

"Father," I said, "you have bank credits in Rome and other cities. Why do you not use Letters of Credit here as you do in Greece and Asia, or coins as you do in other places?"

"The people of Britannia have no trust in, or use for, coins and Letters of Credit, though hopefully they will change in time," he replied. "They do business only by barter of things they can use. The jewelry and glassware we brought is of no interest to them either, but Captain Hiram will trade those items for staple foodstuffs in Meare, which we can use along with our olives, olive oil and linen in paying for our tin."

"Are we the only traders that come here for tin?" I asked.

"By no means," he replied.. "For at least three centuries traders have come here from Greece, Phoenicia, Carthage, Maretania, Syracuse and Massalia, as well as other Greek and Phoenician colonies in the western basin of the Great Sea—but by way of the open Sea, they come mostly in Phoenician ships."

As we walked around the tin-streaming operation I noticed one pit where ore was being brought up by bucket. "How deep will they go in such pits?" I asked.

"Rarely more than twenty-five to thirty feet," my father replied. "Cribbing with timbers is not too practical in following a meandering fissure, and they might otherwise risk a cave-in."

As we watched the nearby smelting operation, set up in a large basin cut in the live rock, I observed that it was very similar to smelting I had seen in Syria and Judea. "But, Father," I asked, "what are the black blocks they are burning, filling the air with such a strange, exotic scent."

"It is a local product found as surface layers in large areas of the bogs that abound in the lower reaches here," he answered. "I suspect that it is vegetation that has lain there for millennia but doesn't quite rot because of the weather conditions. They cut it out in blocks and got a very hot fire from it.* Often the tin grounds are under this material."

We watched the molten tin being poured into molds that had been carefully cut into the rock. "Father," I said, "what strange shapes most of the ingots have!"

---

*Peat.

"Yes, they are unusual," he replied, "but for good reason. The weight of the tin and the roughness of the road would quickly beat their carts to pieces, so they carry the ingots to the trading stations and ports on special saddles worn by horses and mules—they call them split-saddles and, as you'll see in a moment, ingots are balanced on each side of the animal and leather straps securely hold the odd-shaped ingots."

"Water seems crucial to the tinning operation, Father," I commented, "so it is fortunate that there are many small streams all over the peninsula, even though there are no great heights, except for the few conical-shaped hills I see, mostly farther east."

"The hills are called 'tors,'" he replied, "and we'll climb one while we're here when there's a real clear day. As for water, yes, it's essential to tin streaming, but there are problems with it, too. Fall and winter rains (mid-fall through the winter) and excessive tides all may bring flooding to these low-placed operations, and sometime an excessively dry summer season will cut a stream's flow. So, ingenuity, patience and toughness are essential parts of a tin streamer's character."

The weeks of our stay in Meare and the tin fields passed in rapid succession. Father and I went by small boat to a trading station eastward up the large estuary and made the purchase of a number of ingots of lead and a few of zinc, which came from mines in the hills to the north. The following day Captain Hiram's crew rowed there with the tide, loaded the lead ingots, and rowed back to our anchorage as the tide flowed outward. The crew were laughing about that short trip, for several of them had had no previous experience with tides and they could hardly believe how easily the ship rowed with the tide's support, both ways!

An island was farther east across the marsh, whose name, Father said, might mean either Island of Glass or Island of Apples—and maybe with a sense of humor they may have intended both, for at high tide or during a flood it might seem to sit on a sheet of glass, and in addition, at the base of the tor, which rose from the middle of the island, was an orchard of trees producing a fruit, called "apples."

Arriving at this tor on a clear day, Father and I spent nearly an hour in leisurely climbing to its summit. It is laced by paths spiraling to the top. An old man in Meare had told us that some religious leaders claimed the pathways represented a secret maze. From, the summit we indeed could see a tremendous distance—the hills to the north where the lead mines were located—the huge estuary opening westward to the Sea with a large island far out near it mouth—and other smaller tors to the southwest and southeast.

"Father," I said, "If I ever were to live in Britannia, I think I'd like to live at the foot of this great tor."*

"A lovely spot," he agreed.

When we had loaded all of our tin and a few other products we had purchased, plus fresh water and foodstuffs, we set off for home one day in late summer. We sailed as much to the west as we could, considering the promontories of the land or large island lying to our starboard,** and late on the second day the ship hit a "bump" as if we were on wheels going over a knee-high obstruction!

Captain Hiram laughed uproariously when he saw the surprise and fear in my face. "It's all right, Master Joseph," he said, still laughing. "We just climbed up the river bank!"

A short while later he ordered the helm put over to head southward in this fantastic ocean current; he explained that rivers on land run below their banks, unless at flood, but that this "river" in the ocean sea was in fact from one to six feet above the surrounding ocean, and so we felt a distinct "bump" when we hit the side of it head-on.[1]

Because it was a bit later in the season than we had planned for our return, Hiram said we would row most of the daylight hours from here to Gades, to supplement sail and current. It would be easy rowing for the crew and would make up several days' time. The return trip did seem very much shorter, and after Gades we stopped only at Lepcis Magna before reaching Joppa.

✠　✠　✠

And so, mid-way through my seventeenth year, Elyap and I were married at my home in Arimathea, and I seemed to be living in a dream-world for several weeks thereafter. I had been sure that I was in love with my betrothed, but I had not realized how happy marriage would make me.

The ceremonies were attended for several days by a few friends and many members of both our families. Elyap was a year younger than I, and in addition to her brother, Jarius, she had a sister Rachel, considerably older than Elyap, who was married to Josiah and lived in Bethany. Their children, Martha and Lazarus, age five and four, respectively, thus became my nice and nephew by marriage. Josiah had a brother, Tobias, just two years older than I, who was already associated with my father and uncle in

---

*Glastonbury/Avalon; the apples of Britain and Europe were largely unknown in the Near East.
**Ireland

our family business, and the following year he was to become the head of the Jerusalem office of the business, to concentrate his efforts on the finding of new markets for our products, both at home and abroad.

Though Rachel was destined to live only another five years, dying as she gave birth to Mary, my closeness to the family of Rachel and Josiah began at once with my marriage to Elyap. Lazarus was three years younger than Jesus and thirteen years younger than I, but, as the years passed, circumstances and a natural affection between the three of us resulted in a closeness that exceeded usual family ties.

Between the times of our betrothal and our marriage, my father had a new wing constructed onto our home in Arimathea, so that Elyap and I had a place of our own in which to begin our marriage. (In the following five years our children, Anna and Josephes were born to bless us and I cannot imagine a happier family than were we.)

Elyap soon began to take charge of the running of our sprawling home, to the great pleasure of all concerned; and above all others, my father seemed so happy with Elyap's presence that friends and relatives began to say to him, "Who is the new bridegroom around here, anyway?" His sorrow at my mother's death had been totally concealed, because of his feeling of responsibility to me, but now he seemed able to release his inner self and enjoy living more fully.

CHAPTER NOTES:

1. The "Gulf Stream," after having originated in the Gulf of Mexico, bears several names for its various sections; it runs up the U. S. east coast and eastward across the North Atlantic, and then its main thrust moves southward along Ireland, France, Spain and Portugal. As it passes the Straits of Gibralter (Pillars of Heracles) it takes the name of Canary Current, before swinging westward as the Equatorial Current to-the Caribbean Sea, where it rejoins its source and turns northward again as the Florida Current. This complete loop, or circle, is known to nautical specialists as a "gyre" (from the Greek, *gyros*—meaning a circle as described by a moving body).

The Gulf Stream is a current of warm water, whose banks and bottom are the colder adjoining waters; its noticeable contrasting color is indigo—a deep, violet-blue—which has caused some to call it "the Blue God." The segment known as the Florida Current is about twenty-four miles wide and one hundred fathoms deep. The Gulf Stream averages a speed of four miles an hour that is added to a Stream-borne vessel's normal speed in the nearby slack water. Seamen refer to the adjoining cold water as a "wall" and the speed and warmth of the Gulf Stream current causes it to bulge slightly above the level of the adjoining waters, the difference being quite noticeable to small craft. See *The Gulf Stream* by William H. MacLeish (Houghton Mifflin, 1989, and *To the Ends of the Earth* by I. M. Franck and D. M. Brownstone (Facts on File Publications, 1984).

At places along the Florida coast, the Gulf Stream is no more than a half-mile from shore, so that its distinctive darker color and its "bulge" of three to four feet above the adjacent ocean make it clearly visible from shore, especially from any slight elevation. One special phenomenon is interesting and relevant—on occasion, when there is a strong "land-breeze" (blowing from west to east) in contrast to the usual sea-breeze, the wind will cause a "surf" to break against the landward side of the Gulf Stream and these high-splashing white breakers are easily visible from shore; Florida natives call this the Galloping Gulf Stream.

CHAPTER TWENTY-ONE

✠

My Early Years in the Family Business

A.D. 2 - 4

*I*DID VERY LITTLE TRAVELING during my eighteenth and nineteenth years. Instead I devoted myself to the offices and shops of our family business. Tobias, Josiah's brother, became a full partner, in charge of the Jerusalem office and responsible for all sales and the developing of new markets for our products at home and abroad. My Uncle Johanan continued to be the travelling-trader, bringing in raw materials and scarce products from abroad in exchange for our exports, some of which we manufactured.

While my father, as senior partner, coordinated the entire operation, during these two years he, in effect, separated himself from the development and manufacture of products which became my sole area of interest. Of course, he was always available to consult with me and provide invaluable advice from his experience, but in every practical respect I was on my own to innovate, experiment, initiate and expand our manufacturing operation, and to utilize my new knowledge in metallurgy and product creation.

I was fully aware of my limitations, and carefully brought in new employees who had skills superior to my own and who could soon be given intermediate authority. I was in correspondence with our friend, Ali Sylleus in Damascus, who agreed to release to me one of his best workmen, a Jew of the diaspora who, for family reasons was anxious to return to Judea; this expert, I was sure could add much to our abilities in alloying and casting new metals, as well as improving the forging techniques for the making of our industrial and agricultural products. Also, I found a similarly situated employee of my erstwhile host/employer in Berea, Macedonia, who was quite willing to come to Arimathea to take charge of our expanding shop in the creation and manufacturing of jewelry and decorative household products. Additionally, I was hopeful that in a few months we would find skilled workers that would come to us from the metal-working operations I had visited in Corinth and Ephesus.

I was especially interested in the alloying of new metals and was anxious to begin experiments with the zinc we had obtained in Britannia, in view of the information my father had given me of its use in making this new alloy, brass. If, as he had been told, brass had a high resistance to corrosion around sea air and sea water, this would be a tremendous boon to ship-masters. I could readily visualize a very sizeable business in providing brass fittings in place of other metal for the many Phoenician ship-builders and ship-masters with whom we had dealings. Of course, we did not know how pure were the zinc ingots we had obtained, nor how accurate were the proportions my father had been given for making brass. Above all, we would need to do considerable testing to learn the other properties of brass—its tensile strength, its brittleness, it wearing capacity—before we could be sure of precise uses to which it could properly and safely be put. All of which gave me an excitement of anticipation and an eagerness for action.

The weeks sped into months which rolled inexorably into years, and I couldn't have been happier. My challenging work, my close relationship with my father, and my idyllic home-life, altogether made me feel a joy of living so that my feet were hardly touching the ground as I walked.

I had barely turned nineteen when our home was blessed by the arrival of our first-born, Anna. She, of course, became the center of our lives in a way that the business could never match. But I certainly felt that "my cup runneth over" when my father then announced that I was to become at once a full partner in the business.

Our only sadness in the first half of that year was the death of Elyap's sister, Rachel, in early summer, as she was giving birth to their third child, Mary, nine years after the birth of Lazarus. Her death left Josiah, Lazarus and ten-year-old Martha, completely devastated with grief. Elyap was at the time nursing two-month old Anna, and so could not get to Bethany to help Josiah.

✛   ✛   ✛

It was early Fall in my nineteenth year when a business opportunity for our firm came along that occupied my father and Uncle Johanan for the better part of a week. The firm I had worked for in Berea wrote, enclosing an inquiry which they recommended to us: a joint-venture had been created by the leading mercantile firms in Thessalonica, with the financial support of the city government, and they were interested in purchasing a large quantity of olive oil to relieve the shortage that resulted from a bad growing season. Our firm easily could fill the order but the serious question was what items of barter could profitably be accepted in exchange for our shipment.

Not surprisingly, a month passed before correspondence developed tentative arrangements; their proposals were acceptable as a general matter, but quantities and prices would depend upon quality, which would have to await actual examination of their product. Under these circumstances, it was decided that both my father and uncle should accompany the shipment of olive oil and complete the negotiations in Thessalonica.

By the time this stage had been reached it became essential, in view of the lateness of the season for shipping, to take the most readily available vessel. Given his choice, father would certainly have selected Captain Hiram and his "Astarte," but they were just then *en route* from Dalmatia to Alexandria and would not be able to reach Joppa for another ten to fourteen days. A reliable Phoenician ship-master and ship were in Caesarea and could sail at once and be ready to take on cargo in Joppa in two days—so that arrangement was made, and transportation of the olive oil was begun. In just over four days the shipment was loaded and the ship left port with my father and uncle aboard.

Shipping activity here in the eastern basin of the Great Sea would normally continue for another two to three weeks, and since we had agreed to take Spring delivery of their products, our ship would be returning empty, and thus seasonal weather should not be a factor.

In about two weeks I received, via Roman land post, a copy of the final contract, with a note from my father saying that they would be returning in due course, but might take a coastal vessel home from Tyre so that the cargo ship would not have to make the needless run from Tyre to Joppa to Tyre. Under these circumstances, I would have had no concern about their return, except that some three days before arrival of father's message a violent Fall storm passed through Joppa, apparently from the area of the traditionally tempestuous Aegean Sea.

Consequently, I waited with some trepidation for the return of my father and uncle. An additional week passed after arrival of the message, when the Roman post delivered to me another message, which was a very lengthy one from the owner of the cargo ship on which father and Uncle Johanan had sailed. The simple fact was that two days out of Thessalonica on their return, the storm had hit with little warning and capsized the ship. All hands and passengers were lost except for one seaman who had clung to the floating mast and was picked up by another ship and taken to Ephesus.

I went through the necessary motions of taking care of major business problems and family affairs for the next two weeks, but I could hardly tell you what I did. My sister, Enygeus, twelve years-old, was inconsolable, because our father had been her whole life—just as he had earlier been for me since her birth and our mother's death. I wrote immediately to my brother Joachim who, with his wife, Anna, live in the Valley of Zabulon, between Sepphoris and Caesarea, and asked if his daughter, Salome, now twenty-one, would be able to come stay with Enygeus for a few weeks. She did come within a week and was able not only to love my sister back to health, but also managed to run the household so perfectly that Elyap was relieved of much pressure and concern. Salome, childless and widowed at this time did, in fact, stay with us for more than three years, and trained Enygeus in the art of homemaking.

How can I describe the following months? My heart was so heavy and my loss so great that the love and consideration of my dear Elyap was all that kept me sane and functioning. The winter weather was mercifully mild and by the time my twentieth birthday arrived, I found that I could smile again.

The business operations seemed almost to run themselves because of the excellence of our employees, and the new technical staff from Damascus, Berea, Corinth and Ephesus were performing beyond expectation. With considerable personal regret I realized that I could no longer afford the luxury of devoting myself significantly—much less exclusively—to creative metallurgy and product development.

As a brash sixteen-year-old, I had suggested to Elyap's brother, Jarius, that as a craftsman he should consider coming to Arimathea to work for our firm. He let me know quite clearly that he was not interested—that he liked the climate of Jericho and that he preferred to be his own boss. As a "mature" twenty-year-old business executive, I approached him again with the proposal of near-autonomy as head of our metallurgy and products operation. I think that keeping house for himself for nearly three years may have been the deciding factor—in any event, he accepted. His decision solved my biggest problem for it freed me to devote at least part of my time to the travelling-trading role that had been my Uncle Johanan's.

Also that Spring, the Great Sanhedrin notified me that I had been elected to my father's seat as Elder. I have no doubt that I had Gamaliel to thank for that action—and thank him I would!

The final honor that Spring was an appointment by Gaius Caesar, the new Legate of Syria to serve on his permanent commission on business and trade. In some respects this action gave me a standing of high prestige with the Empire for the rest of my life, because I met with the commission every year without fail for the next thirty years. The appointment had been addressed to my name, identifying me as head of our firm. I have often wondered if the Legate thought he was appointing my father, and his scribe, having current information, had substituted my name as the present head of the firm. In any event, the appointment entitled me to the title, "Decurion," as a member of a provincial council or commission (in addition to its other meaning, "leader of ten men"); in dealing with Roman officials, this earned honor often stood me in good stead.

CHAPTER TWENTY-TWO

✠

Consecration of Jesus at the Temple

A.D. 6

*T*HE YEAR JESUS WAS TWELVE, he accompanied Mary and Joseph to the Temple in Jerusalem for the Passover feast days and for the special ceremonies relating to his maturity.

Because of his early interest in matters concerning Jewish religious Law, it was agreed that he should stay with me in my Jerusalem townhouse so I could take him with me to meetings of the Great Sanhedrin and other events from which the general public was excluded. Mary and Joseph preferred to stay in tents with their caravan group outside the City walls, so that it would be more convenient for visiting with relatives from other areas whom they had not seen for a year or more.

Jesus soon learned that Sanhedrin sessions could be (and usually were) dull and very boring, and that the most intellectual excitement was to be found on the Temple porches where visiting rabbis would hold forth on a great variety of subjects. Many of these were not only very learned in the Law, but were also quite clever in confounding or surprising their listeners who readily participated in dialogue with the rabbi. I permitted Jesus to spend his days in this fashion, on his own, since the Temple was a simple twenty-minute walk from my house.

After his second day of attending such sessions with various rabbis, Jesus inquired of me that evening:

141

"Uncle Joseph, would it be possible for me to stay here a few extra days after the caravan leaves for Nazareth?—wouldn't there be a safe way for you to send me back to Nazareth from Arimathea, later? It is so interesting, listening to the rabbis, and I think that in a few more days I will be bold enough to ask the rabbis some important questions."

I told Jesus that he wasn't deceiving his old Uncle—that he didn't lack courage—that I knew he was just waiting until he was completely sure of his position—at which point Jesus smiled in acknowledgment. I assured him that transportation home would be no problem and that I would be glad to obtain his parents' permission for his extra stay—and that I was sure his mother would routinely come by to see me before they left, and I would speak to her about it at that time.

It had not occurred to me to tag along with Jesus to listen in when he began to converse with the rabbis, as I had no doubt of his ability to give a proper account of himself, and with due courtesy. Consequently, it was nearly a week later during a pleasant evening with Nicodemus and Gamaliel that the former asked if I had listened to any of the colloquy between Jesus and the rabbis at the Temple. I admitted that I had not.

"You missed a rare treat," he said, "and I will recount for you as much as I heard."

"I noticed a rather large group around one visiting rabbi," he continued, "and thought he must be unusually eloquent, so I moved in closer to hear. Then it was I saw that Jesus bar Joseph was his questioner, and that the audience was more interested in the boy than in the rabbi.

"Jesus was speaking," Nicodemus went on, "'with a kind of shy passion, an outrage softened by courtesy'—as others have described it. His voice was low and almost trembling as he asked, 'But, reverend sir, why must the priests kill and sacrifice with fire the gentle lambs in order to satisfy God? He created the lambs as he did us—can their deaths really please him?'

"The rabbi was taken aback. He cleared his throat and looked furtively backward to see if Tempe officials were within earshot.

"'Abraham told us to do this, my son,' he replied. 'And Moses, in the Holy Books he inspired has added his own requirement. It is the law.' He was kindly, but firm.

"'Maybe there is no longer a reason for the Law,' Jesus persisted. 'David was not in favor of peace offerings of thousands of oxen and sheep, and the prophet Isaiah condemned the custom, did he not?' And then taking a deep breath, Jesus concluded, 'When God himself spoke through Hosea the prophet he said, "For I desired mercy, and not sacrifice, and the knowledge of God more than burnt offerings." Should we not listen to God, rather than Moses?' He obviously was shocked and embarrassed at his own words, and lamely added, 'I'm very sorry; I did not mean to offend you.' The rabbi smiled a bit wryly and softly said, 'You have not offended me, my son, and I doubt that you have offended God, either.'"

"I certainly wish I had been present," I said. "Though perhaps it is just as well I wasn't, for I might have caused a commotion by voicing my support for his words. I'm certainly proud to be his uncle. And did you hear this discussion, Gamaliel?"

"No," he replied, "I did not, but I greatly regret having missed it."

The week passed quickly both for Jesus and for me. I had Sanhedrin duties and private business matters that were pressing, and friends were always dropping in for an annual visit after their trip to the Temple. One of them mentioned in passing that the caravan to Nazareth and Sepphoris had left two days previously. With that news I suddenly realized that Mary had not come by for a farewell visit and that I was remiss in not getting her permission for Jesus' prolonged stay.

At this point I hurried over to the Temple to advise Jesus of my inadvertence, and arrived there only a few moments after Mary and Joseph themselves did so. They had finally missed Jesus—having assumed he was with the caravan but spending his time with some of his cousins. Just as I approached the group who was listening to Jesus and his (by then) favorite rabbi in an involved discussion, I saw the arrival of Mary and Joseph from another direction and heard her worry-filled voice as she admonished Jesus for his absence.

His naive response was: "Didn't you realize that I wish to be about the business of my heavenly Father?"—which further perplexed and distressed his mother.

As they left the Temple precincts I caught up with the three from Galilee and interrupted their talk to take the blame for Jesus' unexpected absence from the caravan. Mary was then doubly embarrassed, both for her intemperate public scolding of Jesus, and upon realization that had she not failed to pay me a farewell visit she would have been precluded any concern. I laughed and embraced her with protestations, and said that in any event, all's well that ends well.

It was only a few months later in the same year, that I received the sad news from Nazareth of Joseph's death at the age of sixty-eight. He had not complained of ill health—though Joseph was not the complaining sort—but the life of a woodworker and builder[1] is a physically hard and exhausting life, and Joseph had worked very long hours and travelled all over Galilee, mostly on foot, in his attempt to support his fairly large family.

As the nearest male relative I, of course, advised Mary promptly that I would not shirk my responsibility for support of her family. Also, I explained that as soon as her present involvements in Nazareth made it feasible, I would plan to move the family to Capernaum where I had several suitable residential properties. Knowing that both Jesus and James had had significant carpentry training from Joseph, I had in mind a Capernaum house that would not only accommodate their number, but also had facilities that could readily be converted into a shop and storage yard for the family business of woodworking.

Even more importantly, however, I immediately had the Temple records inscribed to show that thenceforth for life (barring Mary's possible re-marriage) I would stand in the place of husband and father as guardian for Mary and the children. This record was also duly inscribed at the synagogues in Nazareth and Capernaum.[2]

Although these steps were no more than my lawful responsibility, Mary was exceedingly grateful, and in the months that followed she and I became much closer than had ever before been possible, and routinely I came to know the children more intimately and to learn of her motherly concerns for each of them.

In the past there had been casual duty-visits by members of the Nazareth family to my Jerusalem townhouse on rare occasions, but now they all lived with me in Arimathea for several days at a time, two or three times a year. During these most enjoyable visits, Mary, of necessity, discussed the needs, and personal facets of character, of each of the children.

More of our discussions centered on Jesus, not only because of his growing responsibilities as eldest son, but because of the growth of his special personality that seemed more noticeable every month.

In this atmosphere of intimacy it was but natural that I ultimately raised the question—as gently as possible—about matters concerning Jesus' advent which had been discretely discussed by townspeople in both Bethlehem and Nazareth—though there had never been maliciousness in such talk, and it had largely died out in recent years, due primarily to the exemplary life led by both Joseph and Mary and the excellent behavior of all the children.

To my question, Mary quietly responded: "The events surrounding Jesus' conception, the months I carried him, and the time of his birth, were truly mystical and are still laden with mystery for me. They were private times when the love between Joseph and me was so great we could hardly contain ourselves, and they were very, very special times. There may someday be someone who will need to know these secrets of my heart—perhaps to serve some great purpose for God—though I can't now conceive of such.[3] I only know the time to speak is not now."

Of course, I could not ask further, in such a situation.

CHAPTER NOTES:

1. The reference to Joseph in Matthew 13:55 describes his work with the Greek word, "tecton," which means "builder," not carpenter.

2. The appointment of Joseph of Arimathea as guardian was routine for the male next of kin, as noted by several authorities; typically, see *The Drama of the Lost Disciples,* by G. F. Jowett, Covenant Publishing, London, 1975.

3. Some scholars have presumed that Luke may have had extensive discussions with Mary, as the source for many statements in his Gospel.

PART III

Jesus' Life, Ministry and Crucifixion

THE CHARACTERS IN
ORDER OF THEIR APPEARANCE

CHAPTER TWENTY-THREE: (none)

CHAPTER TWENTY-FOUR: (none)

CHAPTER TWENTY-FIVE: (none)

CHAPTER TWENTY-SIX:

Cornelius: Roman centurion, assigned to Caesarea; secret follower of The Way of Jesus.
Nathaniel bar Tholomew (Tolmai): one of the Twelve.
Simon: sometimes called the Zealot or the Canaanite; a brother of Jesus and one of the Twelve.
Jude: diminutive for Judas; sometimes called Lebbaeus or Thaddaeus; a brother of Jesus and one of the Twelve.

CHAPTER TWENTY-SEVEN:

Obadiah bar Samuel: (fictional) cousin (through Joseph) of Jesus; the surviving representative in Bethlehem of Joseph's family.

CHAPTER TWENTY-EIGHT:

Hebron of Caesarea Philippi: later known as Bron. Husband of Enygeus who was sister of Joseph of Arimathea.
Rebecca: (fictional) aunt of Hebron.

CHAPTER TWENTY-NINE: (none)

CHAPTER THIRTY: (none)

CHAPTER THIRTY-ONE: (none)

CHAPTER THIRTY-TWO:

Simon the Leper: in Bethany, a neighbor of Lazarus, who had been healed by Jesus.

CHAPTER THIRTY-THREE:

Mark bar Simeon (of Cyprus): and son of Mary, now widowed; Mary was sister of Aristobulus bar Nabus of Cyprus and Joseph bar Nabus (Barnabus). Mark was sometimes called John Mark and probably was author of the Gospel of Mark.

CHAPTER THIRTY-FOUR: (none)

CHAPTER THIRTY-FIVE: (none)

CHAPTER THIRTY-SIX: (none)

✠

CHAPTER TWENTY-THREE

The Friendship of Lazarus and Jesus

A.D. 14

*T*HE YEAR OF STUDY in the Temple school for priests, for which I sponsored my ward, Jesus, was perhaps one of the more crucial periods in his life. Although, at age twenty, he was one of the oldest in his class, this was the first opportunity for such education because James, just two years his junior, was only now able to competently manage the family business of woodworking.

One of the benefits to Jesus of this experience was the prerogative of being addressed as rabbi, in the sense of self-appointed teacher, even though he chose not to complete his studies and was not formally-consecrated as a priest. To be an *officially* recognized rabbi, our Law explicitly provides that, "An unmarried man may not be a teacher." He had been so eagerly studious as a youth that the guidance of the local priest in Nazareth had been adequate to make him fully knowledgeable in our scriptures, The Law, as well as beautifully accomplished as a scribe and an eloquent speaker in Aramaic, Hebrew, Latin and Greek.

Another major benefit of long-term consequence by attending the Temple school was the close association there with the seventeen-year-old lad, Lazarus of Bethany, who was my wife's nephew. One might not expect that, with three years difference in their ages, they would become particularly close with only the school experience in common. But from the very first moment they each sensed a spiritual kinship that seemed literally to grow day by day, and neither of them ever had a friend thereafter who would be so close. Occasionally, during the rest of his life, Jesus was wont to refer to Lazarus as "the one with whom I have the greatest spiritual love." And anytime he was in Judea, for the rest of his life, Jesus never failed to stop at the house of Lazarus for conversation and spiritual communion, if not for several days' visit.

From infancy, Lazarus had had a physical weakness that limited his activity and kept him much of the time in bed. And in spite of his father's wealth, no physician, from near or far, was able to relieve those debilitating symptoms. Nevertheless, except for Jesus, I have never known a person in our land who had the mental brilliance of Lazarus. Seemingly, as compensation for his physical short-comings, from the earliest age he drove himself long hours every day in his quest for knowledge, understanding and wisdom. Fortunately, on both sides of his family his uncles Jarius and Tobias were exceptional scholars, and they devoted much of their time to the education of Lazarus. As a result, when he was prematurely (for his age) admitted to the school for priests he was already superior to most of his instructors in the skills of reading, writing and speaking, and in the reasoning of the Law. Consequently, it was but natural that he and Jesus should notice and be attracted to each other.

They both had a restlessness of spirit that sought to question and even challenge many of the established traditions and the accepted interpretations of the Law. The sabbaths of that entire year were spent by Jesus at the Bethany home, where discussions with Lazarus and his uncles often continued far into the night. The sisters of Lazarus were less in evidence that year; because their mother, Rachel, had died giving birth to Mary, eighteen-year-old Martha had by now become the serious and competent mistress of the household; while Mary, at age eight, was still too shy to come closer than the doorways when these very serious discussions were in progress. Nevertheless, Jesus always took time each sabbath to let Mary show him some surprise or pleasure from her week, and it was obvious that the child idolized him.

Given the spiritual inquisitiveness of both Jesus and Lazarus as well as their reflective bent, it was no surprise that they decided, two years later, to spend a half year in residence with full commitment with the Essenes. This religious sect of our people originated some two centuries ago. It had developed a communal style of living with common ownership of property. The views of some Essene groups on ceremonial purity includes abstinence from conjugal relations, not only for the betrothed but for those duly married as well. They are scrupulous regarding cleanliness, bathe frequently and wear only white garments. They insist on religious purification by baptism and believe in immortality. They are extreme ascetics who often embrace full monasticism, and usually live in isolated communities. Warfare and any sort of violence is to them anathema. They engage in pastoral and agricultural activities and in the production of various handicrafts. Perhaps the greatest value Jesus and Lazarus derived from their stay with the Essenes was the learning of effective meditation as the very important companion to prayer. The meditation techniques he learned from the Essenes were used by Jesus constantly the rest of his life and were taught to his disciples.

The nearest Essene community was less than a day's journey from Bethany and upon arrival Jesus and Lazarus were promptly accepted as provisional members of the Order.

On the west bank of the Jordan, in the hills well south of the Jerusalem-Jericho road, the river flanks a wild and rocky area of hot springs and boiling geysers where deep fires of the earth seem to have broken through near the surface to make a very unstable earth's crust. One follows a rocky trail where even horsemen must walk and lead their mounts, since sudden bursts of steam from rocky crevices come frequently and without warning. It is one of the wildest and most desolate regions imaginable, once the Jordan River ends by pouring its fresh water into the Salt Sea. This Sea is very strange and is useless even for ablutions because its saltiness forces one to float mostly out of the water. The various mineral salts in the water have formed salty "toadstools" one to two cubits high and three to four cubits across along the shallow portions of the Sea and, much like stepping stones, occasionally extend quite a distance from the shore.

This area is known as the Wadi Qumran, and was home for the Essene settlement joined by Jesus and Lazarus; the community itself is called Asad Hasidim. In this section of rough land both cold and hot springs abound, and the sparse soil is of rich volcanic residue where vegetable production is adequate for the group's modest needs.

Individuals who have chosen to live in the wilds as hermits, as well as some of the smaller and more isolated groups, may differ on the question of bodily hygiene and cleanliness, but everything at Mesad Hasidim was spotlessly clean, yet with a sterile quality that Jesus and Lazarus noticed had somehow a coldness about it. The people here doubtless considered cleanliness next to godliness, as they bathed several times daily in the pools of warm water that are so highly charged with minerals it makes the skin tingle. Even the frugal morning meal comes after the ritual morning ablutions, and consists usually of dates, dark bread and goat's milk.

The most important and one of the largest activities of Mesad Hasidim was the operation of a scriptorum. Stone walls support a roof of palm-trunks, which had been covered with the plentiful rushes from the water's edge; the rushes had then been topped with a thick layer of wet clay. Once the hot sun baked the clay to pottery-hardness it was virtually indestructible. The well-lighted scriptorum had many windows, and was a very large room filled with heavy tables and benches where a large staff of scribes was copying religious documents with every technique known. This activity appealed instantly to Lazarus.

Much of the writing was done on conventional papyrus, the best quality of which was imported from Egypt. This plant, growing in stagnant Egyptian marshlands, is a reed whose center is a sticky pith. This is first cut into long, thin strips. To make a sheet of papyrus, these slices are placed side by side on a hard table, with their edges slightly overlapping. On top of this a second layer is put with the slices running at right angles to the first layer. As they dry under pressure, the two layers become welded together. Thereafter, the surface is polished with some type of rough stone until the papyrus becomes perfectly smooth. Scrolls are made of papyrus by pasting some twenty sheets together into a roll; they are rolled onto wooden rods with horizontal fibers on the inside, and the writing is usually done on this inside surface in narrow columns.

A poorer quality of papyrus is made by the Essenes from the rushes growing along the Jordan just before it reaches the Salt Sea, and using the Egyptian methods of manufacture.

The more popular material, parchment, is of limited supply since it comes almost entirely from the Asian city of Pergamum that specializes in producing thin sheets for writing, which are made from the skins of kids. Parchment and vellum, both made from skin, are now beginning to replace papyrus because they are sturdier. Leather of other kinds, which is thicker, is used for the copying of special documents that might be protectively framed and hung on a wall, or sewn together to form a continuous sheet that can be rolled. Many of these skins are tanned right in Mesad Hasidim, where they also make their own ink, usually from charcoal.

Some very tedious work is performed by craftsmen-scribes who carefully etch their letters on thin copper sheets which will be rolled like a scroll. Also at this time, papyrus sheets are beginning to be adapted into a codex, whereby a sheet is folded in the middle, making two leaves of four pages. Many of these sheets are then stacked upon one another and bound on the edge to fashion a book.

Although the Torah of Moses was the subject of some of the copying, the Essene's own scripture, called the Manual of Discipline, is carefully reproduced in great quantity by these copyists to serve the various other Essene communities, since it is the special Law by which they are governed. They also have religio-philosophical documents which guide their ascetic development of self-denial, proclaiming the vital characteristics of steadfast love as espoused by the Teacher of Righteousness whom they believe will come to them. These scriptures speak extensively about the forces of light and darkness that war for the good and evil natures of mankind.

Lazarus, because of his beautiful penmanship, was welcomed as a worker in the scriptorum, where he thereafter spent most of his six months among them. Jesus found time to read every manuscript available in the community library, but spent most of his time in lengthy discussions with the Essene elders. It was easy to see from his own later teachings that he accepted a number of their principles—such as agape love, a rite of baptism, the absence of animal sacrifice, a conviction about immortality, a preference for the solar calendar which caused the Passover meal of Pessach to fall a day earlier than the lunar calendar of normative Judaism, benevolence to strangers, and a rejection of all forms of violence.

However, although willing to learn from them, he by no means became an Essene, and did not hesitate later to condemn some of their beliefs. Hillel[1] and the more liberal of the Pharisees specifically found much foreign and anti-Jewish elements in the teachings and practices of the Essenes, even though the latter were said to be a branch of the Pharisees. Although he had then been dead little more than a decade, it was already being whispered that Hillel was a secret Essene; to those of us who had known him, this seems clearly in error and unfair.

Even the doctrine of brotherly love, as the Essenes state it, could not be accepted by Jesus because they related it only to their own members and had no love for the rest of the world. He once summarized: "For a religion to be worth having, it must be a religion to live by. But who could live by the religion of my cousin, John (the Essene)—or would want to."

✠　✠　✠

A.D. 19

Elyap and I have now been married for eighteen years, and the wonder to me is how our love for each other continues to grow year after year. We enjoy each other's company more all the time; we can talk on the most serious and important subjects, upon the most trivial and silly subjects, or upon the most personal and intimate of subjects—or we can sit in each other's presence and not talk at all, and enjoy each of these relationships fully.

Our family is different than most in this land, in that we encourage our womenfolk to accept education in languages and in our holy scriptures. Elyap had learned very little in these regards before our marriage, but she has been eager—with my encouragement and help—to remedy those deficiencies by learning language skills of reading, writing and speaking, and study skills as well—and she is a very good student, as it turns out. Although I must travel extensively in our business, I am always eager to get home to be with Elyap, and share our respective experiences while we were apart.

I had several times inquired whether Elyap would like to travel, but she seems to have no desire for the discomforts of travel or the meeting of strange people. Her real interests lie in her home and gardens and her children and others of our extended family. She did one time comment that my descriptions of the city of Athens, its institutions and people were appealing and that she might like to go there sometime. Consequently, when I found it necessary this summer to go there for a brief matter of business, I suggested that she might like to go along and spend a week or two there.

"That would be lovely!" she replied. "Will you be able to go sight-seeing with me?"

I assured her that I would—two days would suffice to attend to my business. The results were most delightful. We took in the Acropolis and all of the historic sites, but she was most interested in the Grecian art, especially their sculpture and painting. Not only did we see beautiful artwork in the markets, public squares and buildings, but also in the collections of art that are becoming quite common in Athens. Most exciting of all for Elyap was when I arranged for us to visit studios of some of the more prominent artists and watch them create their pieces—to sculpt and to paint, especially to paint.

Nearly two weeks passed before we left Athens, and I was immensely pleased by the thrill this visit gave Elyap.

CHAPTER NOTE:

1. Hillel was a Pharisee leader who died in A.D. 10; Gamaliel was his grandson. Hillel founded the Bet Hillel liberal school of Pharisaic teaching that has survived to this day; from 30 B.C. to A.D. 70 it was very subordinate to the conservative school of Bet Shammai, which latter did not survive the holocaust of A.D. 70.

CHAPTER TWENTY-FOUR

✠

The Travels of Jesus

A.D. 19/20

NOW THAT JAMES IS OLD ENOUGH TO LEAD as well as carry his share of the work, and especially as the younger brothers have begun to be helpful, Jesus more frequently asks Mary's consent to make extended visits to various places for study. Yet, whenever I happened to ask Mary of these special visits by Jesus, some of which I felt sure involved considerable travel, she acted embarrassed as if it was not a subject she should speak of, and made it clear that I should be asking him, not her. In fact, it was likely that she knew very little more than generalities about such activities.

Because of my extensive business interests, however, with some frequency I would be told of his presence in Damascus or Athens, in Alexandria and other centers where opportunities for learning could be found. Also, I was sure that occasionally he spent a week in the company of his cousin, John, at the large Essene community near Qumran.

In the late Fall of the year, on one of Jesus' infrequent visits to Arimathea, he chanced to mention that he was on his way back to Capernaum after a sojourn in Alexandria, Egypt.

"A very busy city, is it not?" I observed to him.

His shy response was, "I guess so, Uncle Joseph, but I really wasn't noticing the business world very much. In fact, most of my time I spent with the monks at several of the great monasteries that are in the hills near the city. The pace is rather slow there, reflection is the order of the day, and one is not aware of a busy city just a few miles away."

"I know there must have been one or more significant areas of learning that occupied you," I commented. "I know you well enough to be sure that you wouldn't have travelled that distance for just the opportunity of reflection."

He smiled broadly and his eyes sparkled with good humor. "You are right, of course," he replied. "Would you like to hear about one very interesting philosophy that I learned of while there?"

"Of course, I would," I replied.

"Well," he began, "one that I found especially intriguing was the ancient wisdom that the Romans call *Hermaica,* handed-down from the ancient Egyptian seer whom the Greeks and Romans name *Hermes Trismegistus,* but the Egyptians call Thoth, the same name as that of an Egyptian god. I found this wisdom very useful in understanding and evaluating mystics and true mysticism. I considered that Thoth/Hermes had dug out virtually the 'whole truth.' Let me show you a couple of provocative passages that I copied and brought back:

> God is hidden, yet most manifest. He is apprehensible by thought alone, yet we can see Him with our eyes. He is bodiless, and yet has many bodies, or rather, is embodied in all bodies. There is nothing that is not He, for all things that exist are even He. For this reason all names are names of Him, because all things come from Him, their one Father; and for this reason He has no name, because he is the Father of All.
>
> Wherewith shall I sing to Thee? Am I my own, or have I anything of my own? Am I other than Thou? Thou art whatsoever I am. Thou art whatsoever I do, and whatsoever I say. Thou art all things, and there is nothing beside Thee. Thou art all that has come into being, and All that has not come into being.

"Isn't that beautiful, and profound, and sensible? Religion must be so, don't you agree, Uncle?" he asked.

"Nephew, I couldn't agree more," I responded. "It's a shame our priests cannot put things so simply.

"Last year I told you of my friend, the great rabbi, Philo of Alexandria," I continued. "I hope you had the opportunity to visit him."

"Indeed, I did," Jesus responded with enthusiasm. "He is a most fascinating scholar, highly regarded in the community as you know; once I told him I was your nephew, he insisted that I stay with him, which I did for three days, and we talked almost without stopping. I was pleased to find so astute a scholar still in the vigorous prime of his life."

"Yes; he is only four years my senior, as I recall," I replied. "What did you learn from him?"

"Much, Uncle, much!" he responded with sparkling eyes. "I was amazed to find his grasp of Greek philosophy to be better than one can meet with in Athens itself! He is fully competent in the entire range of the Greek philosophical tradition, and acquainted with the texts firsthand. Plato is his 'idol,' so he is a convinced and ardent Platonist, and wishes to lead others into the embrace of philosophy as Plato taught it. But the importance of Philo, I believe, is his deep and devoted loyalty to Judaism and his conviction that our Jewish religion and Greek philosophy are compatible and that he can prove it. He did so to my satisfaction."

"I agree that it is exciting to listen to Philo, nephew," I observed; "he is of a wealthy, aristocratic Jewish family, so that his influence is truly felt. What do you think you learned from Philo that can be meaningful for daily life here in our homeland?"

Without hesitation, Jesus replied: "Philo, with his synthesis of Greek philosophy and Judaism, insists on a doctrine of eternal creation, which excites my mind. If God, *often using us,* is engaging continuously in creation, then miracles of healing must be within the laws of Moses!"*

"Yes, nephew, I would agree; and it *should* excite one's mind," I replied. "And was everything you learned in Alexandria to your liking?"

"By no means," he responded with a laugh. "One of the most ridiculous things I observed was the antics of a group known as the Therapeutae. They are hermits who, by flagellation and other foolishness done to afflict their bodies, believe that they are thereby strengthening their souls. I can't imagine anything more in error. They doubtless are a branch of the Gnostics."

"I guess it takes all kinds of people to make a world," I observed. "And by the way, your old Uncle hears a number of things about you once in a while, because I do get around. Earlier this year I was in Edessa, capital of Parthia's easternmost province, Osrhoene, to consult with my agent, Tobias bar Tobias, whose health is too poor to ask him to come to me. I had a double purpose, for I took fourteen-year-old Thaddaeus with me; his father had just died, leaving the boy an orphan, so I thought the diversion would be good for him. While there, several friends mentioned that you had been in the area, mostly outside the City, talking to scholars and reading endlessly in libraries. Tell me, what of interest did you learn there?"

---

* For a brief but comprehensive summary of the religious philosophy of Philo, see the treatise on "Philo of Alexandria" by Dr. Daniel C. Scavone in *Great Lives from History, Ancient and Medieval Series,* Vol. 4, Salem Press, Englewood Cliffs, N.J.

"Quite a bit, Uncle; quite a few things," he responded. "It's not only a caravan crossroads where many cultures meet, but is also rich in history. The Harran of our ancestor, Abraham, is just thirty miles south of Edessa, with little but cornfields in between, and as far as the eye can see in the flat area to the south. And in Edessa itself there is a fish-pool named for Abraham, Birket Ibrahim, while another pool, Birket Zulha, is named for Potiphar's wife, Zulaikha.[1] Just outside Edessa's southern wall is Bir Eyup, the Well of Job,[2] which in earlier centuries was called the Well of Jacob; also one quarter of the City is named for Job, Eyup Mahallesi.

"Satellite towns south and east from Edessa are also interesting" he continued. "Palmyra and Sumater Harabesi are oases to the south and southeast, respectively, while Hierapolis lies to the southwest. To the east is Adiabene where the ruling family has converted to Judaism, and the city of Nisibis which has such a large Jewish population that they have one of the largest Academies of our faith; I spent most of my time there talking to scholars and reading in the Academy's library."[3]

"I suppose it was religion rather than history, though, on which you spent most of your time," I interrupted him to say.

"Yes. True," he replied. "And what a hodgepodge of religions. In Edessa and most of the towns nearest it the people worship the stellar bodies as gods—mostly the sun god, 'Bel,' and the moon god, 'Sin.' Other stellar bodies which we know well they call 'Servant of Bel,' 'Greeting of Atha,' 'Nabu' and 'Bar Kalba'; farther east, in Mesopotamia, however, they tolerate many of these strange religions but insist on a single god-head—even saying that the stellar bodies may be a habitation of deities but only as agents of a *supreme* Deity."

"But there's nothing wrong with knowledge of the stars, is there?" I asked.

"By no means," he replied. "Our ancestor Jacob well-knew the qualities seemingly imparted to a person by his birth-star, and he forecast the lives of his twelve sons accordingly, as our scriptures tell us.[4] Another of the strange faiths, called Gnosticism, is led by one Valentinus, and seems to come from a mix of Oriental theism and Greek philosophy; they disavow the body and seek to safeguard the purity of the soul to the extent of avoiding all pollution and uncleanliness, including contact with birth and death, and abstain from eating animal meat."

"That sounds neither attractive nor practical," was my comment. "But did you find any religion that you felt you could learn from?"

"Yes. I was interested in some aspects of one called Zoroastrianism. During the exile in Babylon, our people were yearning to return home while at the same time trying to adjust to an alien culture. When Cyrus of Persia overthrew the Babylonians, he not only allowed Jews more freedom but made plans for their return to Jerusalem. This made our people more willing to assimilate much of the Persian culture, especially the Zoroastrian religion to which Cyrus subscribed. Believing the universe to be both a unity, forging toward perfection, while at the same time contending with the presence of evil, the Zoroastrians taught that the ensuing human struggle had to be faced boldly. The evil attribute-spirit they called Angra, Mainyu, the Lie, and later, Shaitin. They believed that upon death, the soul faced judgment. On the fourth day after death, the soul had to cross a bridge called Chinvat. The bridge connected this world with the unseen world. While the bridge expanded for the devout so they could enter into the House of Song, the bridge became razor-thin for the non-devout and plunged them into the pit of darkness below. This pit was guarded by the caretaker-creature called Shaitin, or as we know it today, Satan.

"As you know," he continued, "many Pharisees today espouse some of these concepts. The Zoroastrian religion provided a concept of God and the good, but also a very intense imagery of evil, death and hell. For the Zoroastrians, good exists but must constantly battle the evil because man is endowed with reason and free will. If he brings evil on himself, it is because he yields to the Deceiving Principle within him and strays away from the abode of his higher self. Behind the material universe and all spiritual existence is the creator, Ahura Mazda (light), the one supreme and only God., the spirit and guide for one's life."

"Well, nephew, I said, "I can't say I would be totally comfortable with that religion, but your recitation of its relation to our people does show how we may have strayed from our Torah."

"So true, and that was my purpose in studying it," he replied, along with Mithraism which grew out of it."

"You and I have each been to Athens and other important Grecian cities on the nearby islands and mainland, and we've talked at times of the Grecian philosophies," I said, "but have you found any interesting cultures between here and there, for instance in Asia, so-called by the Romans?"

"Two cities, at least, come to mind in that connection.," he replied; "Tarsus I found especially interesting because of its great university—and of course it has a large Jewish population. The Phoenician/Hellenistic/Roman mix of attitudes, beliefs, backgrounds and interests makes it a fascinating place to be and to study.

"But the really fabulous city in that area is Pergamum," he continued, "for its immense library rivals in importance and size the more famous one in Alexandria; the building of the library's collection—said to embrace a quarter-million books—was commenced by King Eumenes II some two centuries ago. Eumenes, as you know, was one of the successors of Alexander the Great, whose empire was initially divided between his four generals. The world's best parchment is made in Pergamum, and its citizens claim parchment was invented there. In addition to the library, I was interested especially in the Temple of Asclepias, erected in honor of the great medical center, Asclepium, where Galen and other great physicians developed the healing arts."

"Something I'm going to do next year might interest you," I observed. "You've heard me speak of my occasional trips to Britannia, where the Tin Islands provide us with metals essential to our business. I just returned from a brief trip there and I'm committed to go there twice next year. Our ship-master, Hiram bar Abram of Tyre, had a contract with the Roman Legate of Syria which necessitated his early return this summer. When we were within a few hours of sailing, the Celt, Cymric, leader of the tin miners with whom I deal, approached me to ask that we forge for him multiple copies of six or seven special mining tools that he had designed in his mind. With language limitations and a technology-gap I knew it would take at least two or three days to work out the details with him, to sketch designs and record measurements; and so I promised to come back as early as possible next Spring, work out the details with him, come back to Arimathea to fabricate the tools, then take them to him in late summer."

"And, Uncle,'" Jesus interrupted me to respond, "you will let me accompany you and stay in Britannia the two or three months you will be gone?—I hope," he added with a wistful look.

"Yes, that is what I have been thinking as we talked, today," I said. "The religionists of the Celtic people are known as Druids, and I thought you might find them worth studying."

Accordingly, it was agreed that day—and so, the very earliest date, a week before Nisan, the next Spring, I met Jesus in Caesarea, where we were permitted to board a fast Roman bireme *en route* to Tyre. It was a light ship, and with two sets of oars, one above the other on each side, we made very good time even though adverse winds precluded all but occasional use of her sails.

Once at Tyre, we found Captain Hiram ready to take us on a coast-hugging trip that should be fairly safe in spite of the earliness of the season.

From Tyre, we took a northerly course inside the island of Cyprus, landing briefly at Selencia on the Sicilian coast; from there, we sailed due west for a quick stop at Myra on the coast of Lycia; and then, inside the island of Rhodes, we raced across the mouth of the Aegean Sea and turned north along the western shore of Achaia, the Grecian isles, to stop finally at Nicopolis. From there it was an easy run into the mouth of the Sea of Adria and across it to the port of Brundisium. Here is the beginning of the of Via Appia, a concrete roadway that runs to Rome. I rented a chariot and driver who took us across to Neapolis* on the Sea of Tyrrhenum. Here we had to wait three days before getting passage on a ship bound for Massalia** on the southern shore of Gaul, at the mouth of the great Rhodanus River.***

Crossing Gaul from south to-north was slow but scenic along rivers full with Spring flood. Three-quarters of the way due north across Gaul brought us to the Rhodanus headwaters, then we walked for less than a day while they portaged the boat on rollers to the headwaters of a northwest-ward flowing stream. At last we arrived at the northern Channel[5] and found a small ship which would take us across to Ictis Island,**** only a day's run. Here there were horses belonging to Cymric; they had just brought ingots of tin to Ictis and we were able to ride two of them back to the site where he was streaming. Cymric greeted us with unabashed enthusiasm.

As matters developed, it was most useful for Jesus to be with me when I began to record the data for fabrication of the mining tools, because each of the tools would ultimately have to be fitted with wooden handles, and so his expertise in woodworking stood us in good stead, advising me how the metal parts could best be made. Nevertheless, it took us a full week to complete the task.

By cart and by boat we made our way northward across the peninsula from the tin-streaming grounds to Meare Island, where I had to wait only two days for a ship to take me to Gaul. I made arrangements there for Jesus to be accommodated for the two or three months until I returned. Seeing the great Tor nearby, he asked if we could climb it. We spent nearly all day on and around it and Jesus was thoroughly fascinated by the place.

As we got in our borrowed boat to row back to Meare he said: "Uncle Joseph, I'll stay in Meare a week or two to learn the language and to study the strange 'wattle' construction of their houses, and then I'll come back

---

*Naples
**Marseilles
***Rhone River
****St. Michael's Mount

here and build me a small house at the foot of the great Tor.* That's where you will find me when you return."

"Yours is an interesting decision," I told him. "On my first trip here with my father I told him if I ever were to live in Britannia, this is the spot where I would want to be."

Because Spring was now well advanced, the ship-master took me down the Ocean Sea along the west coast of Gaul to the huge estuary of the River Garonnus, flowing from the southeast. Here a river-boat took me up to its headwaters, portaged a short distance and then on to the gulf of the Great Sea, about a day's sail west of Massalia. From Massalia I was fortunate to get a ship going directly to Alexandria, and so home to Joppa for a much shorter trip than the way we had gone out.

With all of the tools made, Captain Hiram picked me up in late summer and we made good time through the Pillars of Heracles and up to Meare Island. I obtained transport and took the tools to Cymric while Hiram supervised loading of a shipment of tin that was awaiting us at Meare. Needless to say, Cymric was wildly ecstatic over the tools and the ease with which handles could be fitted to them, as well as the natural and efficient manner of their use.

I borrowed a boat the following day and rowed to the great Tor to find Jesus, and there he was, in a beautifully constructed wattle house that was as good if not superior to any to be found on Meare Island. I think he was quite proud of it and I certainly praised the job he had done.

"Why should you be surprised, Uncle Joseph?" he asked. "I am a carpenter."

Captain Hiram had loaded and re-provisioned in the past two days, I settled all my accounts that evening, and we sailed at daybreak on the third day to be sure of beating the Fall bad-weather.

Jesus was as fascinated as I had once been with the "river" in the middle of the Ocean Sea, but I don't think it frightened him as it had me. As we ran "downhill" to Gades and the Pillars, I tried to draw Jesus out as to his experience in Britannia, but he told me very little of what had transpired. He did say that he had been accepted as a novice in the Druidic religion, had been permitted to worship with them, and had been instructed in the tenets of their faith which he found to be, for the most part, quite ennobling and quite compatible with his own code of worship and beliefs in Judaism.

But for the most part, his experiences of the summer had been internal, and he was still introspective and not disposed to talk about it. Of course,

---

*Glastonbury

Joseph of Arimathea and Jesus at Glastonbury—
banner of the Pilton Church, Glastonbury.
Photograph courtesy of E. Raymond Capt

he strongly expressed his gratitude for the opportunity, and spoke glowingly of the beauty of the area and the kindness of the people.

The only meaningful comment he made as to his deeper experience was to say he had continuously communed in meditation with the Father-God, and felt he now understood the divine plan for his ministry, including details of its probable termination.

CHAPTER NOTES:

1. Potiphar, husband of Zulaikha, was a high official of Egypt during the time the Jewish hero, Joseph, was a slave in Egypt.

2. Job was a Jewish patriarch.

3. Where was Ur of the Chaldees and where was Haran?—and especially, where was the Land that Abraham was "promised"?—was it present-day Israel? These are questions Bible scholars and archaeologists have never satisfactorily and thoroughly answered. Kamal Salibi, a professor of history in American University, Beirut, in his book, *The Bible Came from Arabia* (Jonathan Cape, London, 1985), by using linguistic and geographical research, makes a very convincing case for the Red Sea coast of western Arabia (an area of about 360 by 120 miles) as the total sphere of activity of the Hebrews-Jews-Israelites of the Old Testament, up to about 400 B.C. when they began anew in Palestine after the return from Babylonian captivity, duplicating less than a dozen place-names for locations remembered in western Arabia—and then, in a few generations' time, forgot those Arabian beginnings.

Whether his proposals are valid does not change the fact that Edessa, Haran and the neighboring cities of Parthia in the First Century had large Jewish populations, and all people of the Near East *then assumed* this to have been Abraham's penultimate home—even if it should be true that he never left southwest Arabia.

4. Genesis 49:1-28.

5. The English Channel, often called "The Narrow Sea," was named *Fretum Gallicum* by the Romans.

✠

Jesus' Capernaum Study Group

A.D. 24

ALTHOUGH HE WAS TEN YEARS MY JUNIOR, I never felt an age difference when I was with Jesus. And that's not to say he was old for his age. He just seemed perfectly at ease with everyone regardless of age. Children found him fascinating and would hardly let him go anytime he gave them his attention. By the same token, the very elderly and the handicapped quickly sensed the special love and consideration he had for them; once he paid a single visit, the shut-ins always asked for his return, and never forgot him. Moreover, they usually insisted that their health and physical strength invariably was enhanced by his presence and they felt better thereafter.

Jesus was a focus of attention anytime he passed through a crowd. His slender and muscular body seemed to move with a slow majesty, and his face was quiet and serene, his beard and uncovered hair shone in the sun (or moonlight); and above his head and shoulders one sensed (or saw?) an iridescent radiance—seemingly glowing, though nebulous. He was far taller than the average male and was well-muscled and strong, but he seemed negligibly interested in physical pursuits, except to do the best job possible when a job had to be done.

Beyond all doubt, Jesus' mind was of tremendous calibre, unmatched in my experience. Regardless of the subject matter, it soon became obvious that he was an expert in everything. Jesus was a master carpenter, yet before his death Joseph was wont to say that he could hardly take credit for teaching the trade to his eldest son, because Jesus instinctively was able to do a better job than *he* could.

For example, if a customer wanted a new yoke for a team of oxen, Jesus always asked that the oxen be brought for examination. He would then measure each one carefully, would feel of certain muscles and make especial note of calluses, scars or defects; he then required that the oxen be returned for at least one "fitting" of the new yoke. Ultimately, if a finished yoke made by Jesus was compared with any other yoke, slight but clear differences in its shape would readily be found. He seemingly had the ability to sense exactly how the ox would work under the yoke, with the result that the curves of the timber would permit the ox to apply its strength most efficiently and with the least discomfort. Nor was such a result conjectural, for many owners swore that, working under a yoke made by Jesus, their oxen performed considerably more work and were definitely not as fatigued.

The hills and valleys, streams and Lake of Galilee, provided a wonderful area for development of a nature-loving boy such as Jesus. Galilee, so fertile and rich and extensively cultivated with fields of many grains, and flowers everywhere, is in sharp contrast with the barren landscape in much of Judea; in Judea there is a fertile coastal plain, but it is only lush around Jericho.

Even while still a boy, learning his craft in Nazareth under Joseph's tutelage, he was always fascinated by everything respecting the sea and was never happier than when taken for a day's outing to the Sea of Galilee. It was on these boyhood excursions that he first met and learned from the Galilean fishermen, many of whom later became his lifelong friends. And his carpentering skills quickly came into play, because he always wanted to know what put the greatest strain on the oars, pulleys, masts and other wooden fittings that he assisted Joseph in making for the boats. Whenever such an appliance was broken, Jesus insisted on seeing the broken piece, so that he could puzzle out the explanation and make a better replacement. In some instances his improvement might consist in shaping the piece to better follow the grain of the wood, and in others he would wait to obtain wood from a different tree that should be tougher in a particular use. And, especially, he was very ingenious in seasoning his own wood by using pressure to bend it while the timber was green and freshly sawn, so that contours of the finished piece would follow the grain without weakening it in the finishing process. Consequently, it can be no wonder that the fisherfolk around the Sea were later always willing to listen attentively to anything Jesus had to say.

Jesus neither disdained nor sought physical labor, but he always seemed more interested in those persons whose tasks were hardest. And his interests were wide-ranging. Whenever he had time to spare, he could be found visiting with a sheepherder, or a stone mason, or a fisherman; in those situations he was always ready to step in with a helping hand if needed.

But there could be no doubt that it was in the areas of mental challenge where he excelled and was most happily involved. Without shirking his duties at home or in the home-shop, Jesus eagerly looked for opportunities to broaden his knowledge and to tussle with unusual mental problems. For the seasons and the hours that he could be spared at home, Jesus, from his earliest years, absorbed like a sponge all that the local priest could teach him. Nor did he wait for assignments, but avidly read and reread every scroll that the synagogue had, committing innumerable long passages to memory. He did not have my good fortune respecting the opportunity to study at length in the Temple in Jerusalem, but in the few brief periods when such experience at the Temple came to him, he seemed to absorb so much learning so fast that no other novice was in his class at all, and before long, very few priests were.

By the time he was barely eighteen, the priests in Nazareth and Capernaum sighed and candidly told Jesus that there was no more he could be taught, either of writing skill or reading, or of wisdom from the scriptures, but that Jesus would always be welcome at the synagogue for conversation and for the use of its library of scrolls.

He was never one to talk much about himself, much as he liked to talk, whether his audience be one or a hundred. My niece, Mary, readily showed her pride in her first son in those days, but even throughout the period of his twenties she had seemed to sense that he was a private person, and she would speak little of his activities that went on outside the family circle. She was quite voluble though, as to his involvement with family matters, and would talk endlessly of his loving manner and of the things he did with them.

Because my business obligations were continuous and sometimes onerous, there were usually intervals of three and four years between my brief visits to my kinspeople in Nazareth, Sepphoris and Capernaum, and the possibility of them seeing me in Arimathea or Jerusalem was even more rare. But misfortune is in a way good fortune, sometimes. Early in my fortieth year it became necessary for me to undertake a very long business trip to seek out a new source for a vitally needed mineral. After a long ride by camel-back to the port of Aqaba, I embarked on a boat trip that eventually landed me on the coast of the Sabaean kingdom. If legend is reliable, this is the land with which our ancestor, Solomon, had a very profitable alliance.

I was determined to learn whether its mineral resources still existed and whether my varied interests could make them a tempting offer.

That venture was reasonably successful but the trip's duration exceeded expectations, and onset of their rainy season showed me the variety of unpleasantness that accompanies a tropical deluge when it appears never to quit. As a result, I arrived back in Arimathea very near to death, with a raging high fever. By the time my excellent physicians had the malady under control, my body was totally exhausted and I was little more than skin and bones. The physicians knew that I was most anxious to resume control of my affairs, so they told me in no uncertain terms that my health was so precarious I must have a period of complete relaxation and recuperation for six to eight weeks, out of reach of business affairs. It was this circumstance that decided me to make an extended visit with my kinspeople in Capernaum.

The time was most propitious from the standpoint of getting intimately reacquainted with my great-nephew, Jesus, for I found that he had largely ended his wanderings in search of knowledge, and seemed to be enjoying a quiet life in the little towns around Lake Galilee, especially in visits with Andrew, Simon, James and John, who lived just east of Capernaum on the Lake.

His brothers appeared satisfied that Jesus was not significantly involved in the family carpentry business, yet he was always most willing to assist in a heavy or difficult job. More than that, they recognized that no unusual or near-impossible problem could come to them but what Jesus could conceive a practical solution. As for his sisters and other female relatives, they obviously were eternally in love with him, and could not spoil him or wait upon him enough.

We had always known that Jesus could convey his knowledge to others with the greatest of ease, yet I had been in their home but a day or two when I discovered that he had developed another technique for honing his skill as a teacher. Each weekend as the Sabbath approached, a series of arrivals of young men produced a group that varied from a half-dozen to a dozen, who spent the Sabbath with us, being taught religious philosophies by Jesus, that evening and most of the following day. As the second evening approached, they would depart with negligible leave-taking in expectation of being home by midnight and ready for a work-day on the morrow. At least four of them came from towns on the Sea (Lake) of Galilee; these were the sons of Jonah and the sons of Zebedee who were fishermen. Of course, these and several others of the group were later to become his Galilean disciples.

I fell easily into this weekend pattern and probably enjoyed his discourses as much as any of the others, especially since my studies at the Temple in Jerusalem gave me considerably more background of preparation for these teachings than was enjoyed by any other of his students. Jesus was already embarked upon a theology calculated to shock his listeners enough to awaken their minds and bring gasps of surprise from them.

It was soon obvious that one of the major products of his years of study was his profound belief in the power of prayer. But he had nothing but disdain for public prayers as the church leaders practiced them. Often he would say, "They have their reward! They want only the adulation of the crowd, and that is the most that their prayers accomplish." He not only insisted that a silent prayer would accomplish as much as a public one, but explained that verbalizing accomplished only one thing anyway—it merely helped the pray-er to focus on the problem. His sense of humor often showed itself in sarcasm, and although these were friends whom he loved, he used the barb of sarcasm to drive his points home.

"If our Heavenly Father is as all-knowing as we say he is," he would begin, "won't he know your needs before you ask them?—won't he know the fullest dimensions of your needs even better than you do?—so you are just belittling God when you presume to tell him the problem, are you not?"

This was heady stuff, but it made eminent good sense, as even fishermen and tax-collectors knew. He was even more insistent that while praying they not hold in their minds a preconceived solution for the problem. "Why should you limit God?" he would say. "God can think of solutions to give you that are a hundred times more bountiful and desirable than you could ever dream of! Give God a chance to demonstrate his love for you."

"But, if we are not to tell him the problem, and are not to hold in our minds the desired solution," asked the puzzled Simon, "what are we to say and what thought are we to hold in our minds?"

"Ah, Simon!" he replied, "so near do you come to enlightenment, but you do not see that ultimate step. The answer is simple, is it not?" he would ask as he looked around the circle. Getting no response, he would say, "Say nothing! And empty your minds, completely! That is the ultimate prayer. Then will God speak to you! And this is the great secret of prayer that very few men know."

Simon, again, would stubbornly plunge ahead: "But, Master, how do we empty our minds? Whether I'm resting or whether I'm working, my mind is always whirling—thinking of my problems, thinking of my hopes and dreams, thinking maybe of stupid things, but always thinking. I know of no way to stop it or empty it!"

"Simon, Simon," Jesus would lovingly respond, "I never need have concern when you are with me, because you will always tell me what is needful. Yes, I must teach you how to empty your minds, for it is only in this fashion that God's still, small voice can give you guidance. In the time that is given us to be together, I will speak to you of the wisdom you now can accept. Beyond that, you will learn little by little as you listen, while God our Father speaks to you in meditation; he will always know exactly what you need and how much you can accept."

Thereafter, for several weekends in a row, he led us gently with guided meditations of many sorts that he had learned in his travels. These exercises had but one purpose, to focus our minds and then to still them. After each such exercise he would patiently question each of us in turn, to learn what our experience had been while our eyes were closed in the silence. He never was impatient or critical regardless of how many times it was obvious many of us had merely fallen asleep. "That, too, can have its value," he would say, "for haven't I read you of the patriarchs who were visited by an angel while they slept, and upon awakening had memory of a dream that included the visitation. In future lessons I will teach you also about the wonderful, heavenly world during sleep—much of which we mistakenly call 'dreams'."

Jesus' students were eager to learn, and often became excited and thrilled by the great truths he imparted. One evening, Andrew, the quiet one, expostulated: "But, Master, should not these great truths be told to the multitudes? We are all willing to walk the length and breadth of the land with you to tell your story to everyone."

"Everything in its season, Andrew," he replied. "My time is not yet come. When the harvest is ready, I will know. And I will come to each of you, saying merely, 'Follow me!'—and then you will know. That will be the time for action. And mark this well: You will be my disciples because I have chosen you—you did not choose me."

CHAPTER TWENTY-SIX

✠

Jewish Politics and Jesus

A.D. 25/29

*I*AM CONVINCED THAT THERE WAS TRUE HEALING in those powerful meditation sessions in which Jesus led us. At least there was, indirectly. My
mind and my spirit were revived and revitalized completely under his guidance, and I was totally convinced of the truth of his words, that "a healthy
mind and a happy spirit will make you a sound body without a conscious
thought on your part."

It certainly worked for me. In half the time my physicians had pre-
dicted, I was returned to health and anxious to return to work. However,
knowing that my physicians were always suspicious of my self-diagnoses,
I availed myself of the pleasure of the Galilee home for a full six weeks,
enjoying conversations and long walks in the hills with Jesus.

So healthy was I in mind and body upon my return, that in a few
short weeks I had my affairs under full control. In any event, so excellent
were the employees in my Jerusalem and Arimathea offices, the Arimathea
shops, and at my docking facilities in the port of Joppa, that I really had
no serious problems at all to face upon my return from Galilee.

However, the pleasure of Jesus' company and the excitement of his new
theology were such that I insisted before leaving that he promise to spend
a day or two with me at least twice a year in the future. In this fashion I
was able to keep informed on his activities and on the scintillating growth
of his religious concepts.

Nor was this a solitary liaison. Almost from his first visits I was able to
draw together a small group of like-minded persons with whom to share

171

the wealth of Jesus' thought. Initially, there was Nicodemus, now a professor of law and theology in the Temple school which we had both attended in our youth, and who now serves with me on the Sanhedrin. Also, at the first such meeting with Jesus at my Jerusalem townhouse was my kinsman Lazarus; so excited was he by these new teachings that by common consent we soon were having most of our meetings at his expansive suburban residence in Bethany whenever Jesus was in the City.

And, inevitably, of course, our beloved senior professor, Gamaliel, was drawn into our circle, for it was his influence more than anything else that had opened our minds to the potential of new teachings concerning our Faith. Repeatedly, we had all heard him say that if a new theology was not of God it would shrivel and die; but if it were of God, woe be unto the one who attempted to destroy it, or even to ignore it.

Another member of the Sanhedrin who soon joined us was Sirach, who quietly but firmly always supported the lead of Nicodemus and myself; he was married to Seraphia, great-grand-daughter of Eliud and Ismeria of Sepphoris, to whom I am distantly related by marriage, through my much-older brother, Joachim. We four Sanhedrin members did not openly acknowledge our allegiance to The Way of Jesus in the early years of his ministry, for obvious reasons.

For equally obvious reasons, two Romans who met with us whenever feasible did not disclose their participation. These were Petronius, a centurion on duty in Jerusalem who discovered Jesus' teachings while previously assigned in Capernaum. He was a close friend of Cornelius, another centurion, whose duty station was Caesarea, but who met with us if he happened to be in Jerusalem at the time of Jesus' visits to our area. One with a Roman name, Silvanus, had a Jewish mother and was a lawyer in Jerusalem; he was very successful in spite of—or possibly because of—this hybrid status, but dared not risk disclosing his association with us during Jesus' early ministry.

In addition to Lazarus, those of our group who openly followed Master Jesus included Zacchaeus, the Jericho banker who was a partner more often than a competitor of Nicodemus' banker-father there.* And of the younger men in our area, there were those of The Seventy: Thaddaeus, Barnabus and Stephen.

Shortly after Jesus sought baptism from his cousin John in the River Jordan, he called the Galilean Twelve to follow him as daily companions in the commencement of his formal ministry. However, their selection had been tacitly made during the prior three or four years; they knew who the

---

*Before his conversion, Zacchaeus had been a tax collector.

group would be, and each was eager to drop his work and follow Jesus. Consequently, I will begin now to refer to them as "the Twelve" even though their formal association was a short while in the future.

As a practical matter Jesus knew that the "cash crop" of consequence in Galilee was the fishing catch on the Sea of Galilee and that it was the key to the economy of the area. And so, it was not only in deference to the "fishermen five" but for broader reasons as well that when Jesus made his *call* to the Twelve to begin their life's work with him, he set the pattern of their ministry to embrace the summer half of the year when the fishing was poor and the climate was hospitable to outdoor living. Thus it was that the winter half of the year, the commercial fishing season in Galilee, provided Jesus with the extensive time he needed for solitude, retrospection, meditation and prayer—at the same time, he used the winter months for the extended visits to Judea which became such an important part of his ministry during its formal years.[1]

Apart from our problems of secrecy, the Judean disciples were never a close-knit single unit like the Twelve of Galilee for other reasons as well. Principally, we were men of property, and of business or professional involvement, who had extensive relationships which could not be left for extended weeks or months at a time—nor did Jesus ask that we leave all and follow him—that sort of following he already had with the Galilean Twelve. But the positions of us Judeans were useful in many ways to Jesus.

Except for a few of us—his Judean disciples—who were actually of an older generation, Jesus never had a close friend except Lazarus with whom he could freely discuss any subject, enjoy a simple intellectual conversation, or sharpen his sense of humor. The Galilean Twelve afforded him no such companionship and most had minimal formal education.; of these:

Matthew knew only the governmental world of taxation and had studied in Scribes School just long enough to qualify for appointment at Rome's tax office in Capernaum. Judas was both close-mouthed and morose; his attendance at the School of Law (for priests) was less than that of Jesus himself, but his contacts as an employee of Herod[2] at Tiberias, as well as from boyhood association with his uncle, the Chief Priest Caiaphas, had certainly taught him the political facts of life in our land. Similarly, Thomas was very intelligent but uneducated; he had attended the School of Law but briefly. Philip, the coachman and fisherman, was the only one to have finished a course of schooling—in the Temple's Scribes School. Nathaniel bar-Tholomew was a herdsman and James the Less a stonecutter; Simon and Jude were nominally carpenters; the other four were fishermen. Most had begun to work at their trades as soon as they were strong enough to throw a net or swing an adz. Moreover, James the Less had left home at age fourteen to join the Zealots, along with his cousin, Simon, then eighteen, who was Jesus' brother.

Of course, from age five to twelve, all males are required to attend basic classes in their local synagogue, where they are taught to read the Hebrew scriptures, to speak well our native Aramaic and Hebrew, and to speak and understand oral Greek ana Latin to a limited degree. Few are taught writing except to sign their names. Thus, intellectuals were in short supply among Jesus' Galilean friends. The result was a sensing, on my part, of loneliness in Jesus—and he certainly had the reputation as a loner and a dreamer, since he chose to spend much time alone when he could, along a stream, on the Lake, on a mountain-top.

The limited background of the Twelve of Galilee is worth mentioning here not only because they afforded Jesus no intellectual companionship, but it was unfortunate in one respect that he chose the Twelve from among his boyhood associates. On numerous occasions during his formal ministry Jesus engaged in legalistic arguments with lackeys (if not spokesmen) of the Temple hierarchy, which often turned on technical points that left the Galileans completely confused and misinterpreting what had been said. All the Law of our people is "religious law," through and through, nevertheless it applies to every business, practical, personal and intimate activity of every citizen—many of whom are too ill-informed and untutored in the Law's intricacies to be able to avoid numerous violations every day.

Nor is there uniformity. The Essene communities live mostly in a world apart, accepting nothing of the Law the Temple attempts to enforce. To compound the disciples' confusion, Jesus had a high regard for John the Baptizer, who was an Essene—at least by his own lights. Then there is the Herodian political party; in Samaria and Galilee, especially, it is comprised mostly of those who have employment or graft from Herod, and who live as Herod approves, rather than by the rules of the Sanhedrin. Next there are the Zealots—a movement which began in the Galilean hills two hundred years ago as the Maccabean revolt; they would undertake any violence[3] to embarrass or interfere with Roman rule, knowing that at the same time such activity undercuts the High Priest and, to a lesser extent, Herod.

Jesus was very basically a man of peace, though not an extreme pacifist, nor does he condemn the Zealots—in fact, his brother, Simon,[4] and his cousin, James the Less, have never left the Zealot movement, though they would spend most of their time with Jesus during his Galilean ministry. Moreover, in every respect except for military aggression, The Way espouses the same views as the Zealots—and in every respect except belief in Jesus' *return* as Messiah, the Zealots espouse the same views as do followers of The Way. Both stress the sovereignty of God, reverence for the Torah and the Temple; both have extreme repugnance for Roman rule, the pro-Roman sacerdotal aristocracy of the Temple, and generally for the Herodians and the Sadducees.

The Sadducees are a much smaller party than the Pharisees, but individually they are of wealthy and politically powerful families. They accept only the *written* Law, the Torah, and do not believe in an afterlife or a spirit world since such was not mentioned by Moses in the Torah; the writings of the Prophets they consider sacred but not of ruling consequence. They are definitely a worldly sect, influenced by Greek culture and their alliances with the Romans; they believe in freedom of will. They do not look for a messiah. Though few in number, they are in total control of the Great Sanhedrin and all Jewish life and institutions.

The lack of sophistication and education of the Galilean Twelve was most noticeable in connection with Jesus' many confrontations with the Pharisees. The Galilean disciples identified the Pharisees mainly with their notorious piety, their excessive concern with defilement by contact with anything or person that is not acceptably Jewish, and their insistence an strict observance of the Law, both written and oral. Under the oral Law the Pharisees presume to define what is "unclean" and therefore anathema, along with that which is non-Jewish; this strictness alienates the poor, who find strict observance almost impossible.

However, except possibly for Thomas and Judas, the disciples were unable to recognize any difference between those wearing the Pharisee "label." Jesus' short term of priestly study in the Temple school confirmed his choice to be a Pharisee, and quickly convinced him of the rightness of the Pharisee School of Bet Hillel, which he was sure would prevail in time. Yet, for more than fifty years now, the Hillel philosophy has been eclipsed by the competing Pharisee School of Bet Shammai[3] which, by alliance with the Sadducees, have total control of the Law.

Hillel's grandson, Gamaliel, is the present leader of the Bet Hillel, and is the only one to be accorded the exalted title of Rabban (meaning "our master") by the Sanhedrin, which makes him the chief presiding officer of the Sanhedrin for all but extraordinary proceedings. The Bet Hillel supports prayer for the sick on the sabbath, and stresses love, humility and salvation of all mankind; these precepts appealed deeply to Jesus. On the contrary, the Bet Shammai, although they agree with the Bet Hillel in belief of an afterlife, do not consider that a gentile can ever merit a place in the world to come; they endorse polygamy, incestuous marriage and easy divorce.

Because of the prominence and power of the Shammai Pharisees, it is always they who challenge Jesus in public and against whom he pours out his vituperation with exaggerated expletives; it is in fact against the Shammai that he rails when he condemned roundly: "You Pharisees, priests, lawyers and scribes." Nor are his disagreements and criticisms his alone; these are exactly the arguments of Bet Hillel spokesmen against the Bet Shammai, and often using precisely the same words as does Jesus.[3]

Unfortunately, this distinction is largely lost on the Galilean Twelve, and they too often see the words of Jesus as roundly condemning *all* Pharisees, the entire religious establishment, the religion itself, and the Jewish race—rather, his target is the Bet Shammai, the Sadducees and the hierarchy they control. Jesus is content to remain a Jew, and a Pharisee, and to embrace the Judaism of his ancestors as proclaimed by the Bet Hillel. He is not willing to accept the Temple hierarchy and their beliefs and actions. Moreover, he sees progress under the liberality of all Pharisees, since they are much less rigid than were the ultra-strict Hasidim of two centuries ago.

But, in summary, I must emphasize that I believe Jesus made no basic mistakes, and that is true as concerns his choice of the Twelve of Galilee. Unsophisticated and largely uneducated they may be, but so are the bulk of the world's population. They will carry his message to people who will understand them. He and the Father will empower them.

Chapter Notes:

1. Hershel Shanks, Editor of *Biblical Archaeological Review,* advised me that the expert on commercial fishing on the Sea of Galilee is Mendel Nun at Kibbutz Ein-Gev, Israel. Mr. Nun wrote me (July 1988) as follows: "The main commercial fishing season on the Sea of Galilee in ancient times was between November and May (before new species of fish were introduced). The other months were poor in fishing."

Mendel Nun has made the Kinneret (Sea of Galilee) his specialty, in all its aspects from archaeology to zoology, and is known as Israel's "Number One Kinneretologist." (See "The Galilee Boat" in *Biblical Archaeology Review,* Sept/Oct 1988, XIV-5.)

2. Herod Antipas was ruler as tetrarch for Rome in Galilee and in Perea.

3. See *Jesus the Pharisee* by Harvey Falk, Paulist Press, Mahwah, N. J., 1985, for the distinction between the Pharisees of the Bet Hillel and the Bet Shammai in Jesus' time; as for the Zealots, that author notes that they were associated with the Bet Shammai, by whom violence was not eschewed in pursuit of a desirable end. Especially, he notes that the charges of the Bet Hillel against the Bet Shammai were word-for-word the same as those made by Jesus.

4. The name, Simon the Zealot, as given in the Bible, implies that he was *still* a Zealot; if he had renounced Zealotry, it would have been an insult to continue using that descriptive name for him.

CHAPTER TWENTY-SEVEN

✠

Bethlehem at Jesus' Birth

A.D. 30

Aᴛᴛᴇʀ Pᴏɴᴛɪᴜꜱ Pɪʟᴀᴛᴇ ʜᴀᴅ ʙᴇᴇɴ ɪɴ ᴏꜰꜰɪᴄᴇ as governor of Judea for about four years, he and the high priest, Caiaphas, asked me to serve briefly on a special joint commission to survey certain problems arising from the aqueduct Pilate had built to bring water to Jerusalem from hold-ing pools near Bethlehem some six miles away. Two embarrassing aspects of the project had arisen. First, was faulty engineering by Pilate's crews, which resulted in several cave-ins as they tunneled beneath the town of Bethlehem, causing some minor property damage. The second concern (that would not involve my commission) was the "unexplained" disclosure to the populace of Jerusalem that in fact, under a secret agreement, the aqueduct had been financed with Temple funds;[1] Pilate stayed aloof as to this matter, because the *shekalim* fund, generated by the half-shekel Temple dues, was specifically for "the city's needs"—and who could deny that cure of the chronic water shortage was a real need of the city of Jerusalem?—besides, the Great Sanhedrin had approved the funding.

Knowing that I would have to be in Bethlehem for several days, I sent word to the surviving family of Jacob and Timna that I would like to stay with them. Of course, those two both had died before I was born, and Timna's second husband, Heli of Emmaus, was also long dead. I received a most hearty response from Obadiah bar Samuel—Samuel being the second son of Jacob.

I had never met Obadiah and his family but their welcome was as warm as if our relationship had been one of blood rather than by marriage.

177

I should explain that Jacob's third son was Joseph, who married my niece, Mary bat Joachim; Joseph and Mary being the parents of Jesus.

Obadiah was quite interested in my assignment, and in spite of Bethlehem's closeness to Jerusalem, they knew little of Temple politics and of the Roman rulers.

"What sort of fellow is Pilate?" he wanted to know.

I explained: "Pilate has a lot of good qualities and I get along with him well enough, especially since I serve on the permanent Empire Trade Commission for his boss, the Legate of Syria, but Pilate is a very inept administrator. He was a member of the Praetorian Guard in Rome, but that is no training for a governor. He is overly sensitive about his position, too, and expects much more subservience than we Jews give him."

"I see what you mean about him being an inept administrator," was Obadiah's response. "Bringing Caesar's graven standards into the Temple area was not very smart; he should have known the City would revolt, to a man."

"Yes, and he got his knuckles rapped by Tiberius* for it," was my comment.

"We just heard recently that Pilate is requiring Temple funds be used to pay for this aqueduct you are looking into," observed Obadiah; "isn't that rather high-handed?"

"Really, it isn't," I said and explained the propriety of it. "The mistake was in making a secret agreement, which Caiaphas certainly 'leaked' to the public himself, knowing that the people would then blame Pilate. Caiaphas' reasons for agreeing to the funding were politics and power; we of the Great Sanhedrin by consensus came to the same conclusion for reasons of public policy."

When our talk shifted to family matters, I mentioned that I had not known Obadiah's uncle Joseph until he was betrothed to my niece, Mary, but that I had come to respect him highly in the dozen years thereafter, even though I had not gotten to know him well.

"I have regretted that I was so busy in those years that our friendship remained rather superficial; I would have welcomed an opportunity for deep conversations, but he never felt he could leave his work to visit Arimathea, and I seemed also to be a committed workaholic," I commented. "His death at age 68 seemed so early, coming just after Jesus' consecration at the Temple—but you could see that he died of exhaustion, and no one ever worked harder at his job than did Joseph bar Jacob."

---

*Tiberius Caesar, the Roman emperor A.D. 14 to 37.

"Yes, he was my favorite uncle," said Obadiah. "He was a quiet type, but I liked to be around him even though he didn't talk much. He was perhaps the most devout member of our immediate family, and he just exuded love."

"How did it happen that he moved from Bethlehem to Nazareth?" I asked.

"It was simply a matter of economics, I guess," was his reply. "There were just too many carpenters in Bethlehem. My three youngest uncles were killed many years ago in a brief fighting with the forces of Nabataean king Aretas while they were in the service of Herod. My father, Samuel, and Joseph, and my oldest uncle, Malachi, worked together in our carpenter shop, but there was not enough to keep all three busy, plus the need we younger ones had to be gainfully employed."

"But Nazareth is even smaller than Bethlehem," I observed.

"True," he replied, "but with Herod's Galilean capital, Sepphoris, only five miles away, and his summer lake-front palace in Tiberias little more than twice that distance, Joseph felt sure he could keep busy—especially since the nearby shores of Lake Galilee would give him opportunity to satisfy a long-felt desire to get into boat building.

"And incidentally," he added, "it seemed strange to us that the Romans made people like Joseph return for the census from such a distance to be counted in their home towns."

"'Well, to the Romans this was not unreasonable," I replied. "In Egypt they have required the same thing[2] and the distances there are much greater and the roads not nearly as good. Under Roman law a property owner has to register for taxation in the district in which his land is situated, and I understood that Joseph did own some land near here."

"Technically, yes," replied Obadiah. "You see, when my Grandfather Jacob died he left his principal estate to the oldest son, my Uncle Malachi, and then a town-house to my father, Samuel, and finally a section of grazing land south of Bethlehem to Uncle Joseph—but the rents he got from it did little more than pay his taxes on the land. Incidentally, upon Malachi's death, without descendents surviving, the main estate passed to my father and on his death to me."

"As for Roman censuses." I added, "one has to understand the mentality of the late Emperor Augustus. He had been greatly concerned about the shrinking population in Rome, and had sought by various devices to raise the marriage and birth rates. Out of this concern came his decrees for the taking of several censuses. These enrollments also aided Rome by augmenting the tax rolls.

"Also, there was a special reason in this country, because Herod* had come into disfavor with Augustus just two years earlier and was consequently being treated as a subject prince rather than as a friend, and his semi-autonomy had ceased. You will recall that Herod was getting old and quite ill, and had much trouble with his sons who were struggling among themselves over succession to the throne. Finally, Herod executed his sons, Alexander and Aristobulus, so it was a logical time for Augustus to take a census and make an evaluation of Herod's domain before his imminent death.**

"And of course," I concluded, "provincial census-taking always lagged behind; the one that caused Joseph's trip had been decreed by Augustus two years earlier—in A.U.C. 746, by the Roman calendar."***

"Yes," responded Obadiah, "I remember the fuss made by Herod's flunkies, because it should have been taken two years earlier—a lot we cared!"[3]

"True," I agreed. "Herod was being pressured from Antioch by the acting legate, Publius Sulpicius Quirinius. There was no Legate for nearly a year and Quirinius, who had once been a Consul in Rome, was then in Syria as a military commander and served as acting-legate.[3]

"Obadiah." I added, "the law would have required *only* Joseph to make that trip to Bethlehem to register. Why do you suppose such a sensitive man as Joseph would bring, Mary on a five-day trip by donkey when she was so close to her time for birthing?"

"We wondered about that at the time," he replied, "but it was clear from the little they said to us that they *both* were resolute and determined on this point—Mary would definitely not have stayed behind in Nazareth."

"They told us that over-crowding by the arriving registrants left no public lodging for them, and that Jesus was born in a cave for animals behind the Inn. Why did they not stay at your house, here?" I asked.

"I am covered with shame that you should have to ask, and that I cannot make a sensible answer," said Obadiah, as his face flushed with embarrassment. "It is the only time I know of that my uncle Joseph ever did anything that could be criticized as offensive to another person. There was quite a bit of local comment about the birth event, and we heard of it

---

*Herod the Great, an Idumean who was Roman ruler, as King, 37-4 B.C., of the entire Jewish nation.
***Chronological Aspects of the Life of Christ* by Harold W. Hoehner, Grand Rapids, Zohdervan, 1977.
***A.U.C. (ab urbe condita) meant "from the founding of the city." a.u.c. 746 = 8 B.C.

before the noonday following Jesus' birth. My father and I hurried to the stable-cave, for we could hardly believe that it was *our* Joseph—but it was.

"We remonstrated with him, of course," he continued. "Joseph was clearly distressed for offending us, but the best explanation I can give—for he actually gave us none in a categoric manner—was that Mary's labor pains were already strong and frequent by the time they reached the Inn by the highway at nightfall, and any attempt to cross Bethlehem through the jostling crowds to our home on the far edge of town might have been disastrous. And yet, I felt there was something more. They seemed embarrassed and unwilling to tell us fully—though they willingly came with us at once, and permitted us to give them everything needful at our home."

"Birth in a stable-cave was almost like being out of doors," I observed; "was that not difficult for Mary and the baby?"

"Actually not, I believe," he replied. "The innkeeper's wife was a local midwife and she assisted in the birth and provided whatever was needed that they didn't have. Also, the weather was quite mild, as I recall, it being about the end of Nisan when the lambing season was well advanced."[4]

"The baby seemed healthy and in good condition, then?" I asked.

"He was a beautiful baby!" enthused Obadiah. "Bright appearing and active. He was perhaps a bit small—Joseph and Mary were definitely reticent, but I had the impression that she might not have carried the child quite to full term."[4]

"They stayed with you then, until they left for Egypt?" I asked.

"Yes, it was a bit more than a year before they left for Egypt, as I recall," he agreed. "And again, that was a very strange situation. Joseph obtained excellent employment in the construction of a palace on the edge of Bethlehem, just a few days after Jesus' birth, and he could have continued in that position for at least a number of months more. But again, they were unwilling to discuss their reasons with us—in fact, they seemed frightened!"

"Was there anything that they had to fear?" I wanted to know.

"Nothing that they could have known about," he replied. "But their departure was most fortuitous as things turned out, for it was only about a week later that a full Company of Herod's palace guards descended on Bethlehem before daybreak and burst in on every household in an orgy of killing, the likes of which we had never before known. And we never heard a satisfactory explanation—but what king ever explains? The result was the slaughter of about twenty-five babies—all males, and none more than two years old. It was horrible! We understood that the soldiers continued their slaughter in the out-lying region for several miles beyond Bethlehem, but I've no idea how many more babies they killed."

"Did you see them on their return from Egypt?" I asked.

"Yes, but very briefly," he replied. "Only overnight, as a matter of fact. Jesus had become such a lovable child, that all of our family urged them to stay—again, employment for Joseph would have been available. But all that seemed to interest Joseph was politics. He wanted to know everything we could tell him about the new Herod—Archelaus, that is.

"The next morning," he continued, "I asked Joseph how he had slept, but he only muttered something about a disturbing dream, and said they must leave at once for Nazareth. And they did."

"Well, even though you know little of those events, you know much more than I did," I acknowledged, "and I am much comforted to have these explanations."

"But you can tell me," said Obadiah, "what of the grown Jesus, now, and the exciting stories we hear of the preaching he is doing in Galilee and the north?"

I talked for the better part of an hour, telling him of my fairly limited contacts—at that time—with Jesus' ministry.

"But," I concluded, "Jesus is, I believe, a true mystic and a prophet[5] of whom we shall hear much more in the years ahead. His intellect I highly respect. He is certainly the most truly devout man I've ever known. Yet, his relationship to Jehovah seems more like that of a son to a father. He will leave his mark, I am sure."

CHAPTER NOTES:

1. See "Jewish Antiquities," p. 264. *Josephus—The Essential Writings* by Paul L. Maier, Kregel Publications, Grand Rapids, 1988.

2. See *Chronological Aspects of the Life of Christ,* by H. W. Hoehner, Zondervan, Grand Rapids, 1977, p. 15.

3. Of the several factors bearing upon the fixing of the year of Jesus' birth, all fit perfectly with the year 6 B.C. except for questions of the census and the fact that Publius Sulpicius Quirinius was not then Legate of Syria. But the above explanation seems to adapt those two factors; viz.: the census was ordered in 8 B.C.; it was taken in Herod's domain in 6 B.C.; HEROD died in 4 B.C.; Syria had no legate in 6 B.C., but it is a clear possibility that Quirinius could well have been Acting Legate or could, while on military duty in Syria, have been ordered by Rome to implement the census in Palestine, and thus fulfill the provisions of Luke 2:2. See J. Finegan, *Handbook of Biblical Chronology,* Princeton Univ. Press, Princeton, 1964; S.G.F. Brandon, *Trial of Jesus of Nazareth,* Stein & Day, N.Y., 1979; P. L. Maier, *First Christmas,* Harper & Row, N.Y., 1971; National Geographic Society, *Everyday Life in Bible Times,* Washington, D.C., 1967; *Jerusalem Bible,* Doubleday, N.Y., 1966—Notes, Luke 2:2. Whether the "star of Bethlehem" was truly a celestial body is impossible to know, or if it was continuously available as guide like the "pillar of cloud/fire" that guided the Israelites from Egypt. And perhaps we should

not totally ignore the arguments of Rev. Barry Downing in his book, *The Bible and Flying Saucers*, in these regards, to the effect that the phenomena was a UFO for both.

A large number of astronomers have devoted considerable effort to a determination of the time of Jesus' birth, based on the celestial data for the Star of Bethlehem. Of course, we cannot know with certainty the country of origin of the Magi, how soon they began their journey, how many months or years it took them, whether the "star" appeared more than once, which if any appearance coincided with Jesus' birth, nor whether they indeed went to Herod in Jerusalem as reported in Matthew or to his winter palace in Jericho; nevertheless, these scientists are in general agreement that the years 7 B.C. and 6 B.C. do fit the Biblical scenario. David Hughes, in *The Star of Bethlehem* (Pocket Books, 1979), concludes that the Star "was an actual physical object, explicable by scientific law"—the scientific explanation being the repeated conjunction of two or three stars (Jupiter, Saturn, and sometimes Mars) during those two years; similarly, see *Griffith Observer* of the Griffith Observatory, Los Angeles, which has carried articles on this question in their December issues of 1971, 1975, 1976, 1978 and 1980. Paul L. Maier in *First Christmas* notes that "Jupiter, Saturn and Mars were in conjunction in February 6 B.C., in the sign of Pisces (the fishes) ... in a tight triangle no more than two moon-diameters apart, on the western horizon as viewed from Persia/Babylonia." Moreover, despite its present-day "bad name" due to abuses and commercialization, and its bad name in ancient eras, there should be no doubt that astrology contains considerable reality and was so recognized by patriarchs of the Old Testament and leaders of New Testament times (see *Astrology in the Bible* by H. deCompton, Parkway Press, 1985; *The Glory of the Stars* by E. Raymond Capt, Artisan Sales, 1976; *What the Bible Says About Your Personality* by David O. Yates, Harper & Row, 1980). Using the technique of "rectification" that fixes anyone's time of birth by retroactive projection from major life events, a number of modern astrologers using computer-assisted calculation find that Jesus' birth date indeed must fall in the years 7 or 6 B.C. (7 B.C. is equivalent to the astronomical year -6). *Search for the Christmas Star* by Neil F. Michelsen and Maria Kay Simms (ACS Publications, 1988), and "A Christmas Fantasy" by Zipporah Dobyns in *The Mutable Dilemma*, 9/1, 1985, present several possibilities.

4. This author favors the season of Jesus' birth as being the Spring, probably late in the Jewish month of Nisan, equivalent to the middle or first half of April. Although unsure of the year, Bible scholar W. E. Filmer (among others) considers that Jesus was born in the Spring (see *J. of Theological Studies*, XVII, October 1966, pp. 283-298). Although the details concerning angels and shepherds as reported in Luke may be controversial, there must surely be significance in the words, "...shepherds out in the fields, keeping watch over their flocks by night" (Luke 2:8). Weather in the fields just south of Bethlehem would be raw and inclement (if not downright bad) during the winter months and the flocks of sheep and goats would be kept in pens or sheds without need for shepherds to be on nighttime duty. H. W. Hochner (*Chronological Aspects of the Life of Christ*) notes that in Judea the sheep were taken into enclosures from November to March, especially at night, because of the inclement weather. However, Spring was the lambing season, and then the presence of shepherds would be necessary because of nocturnal birthing and related problems with the young animals. Luke reports that the angel Gabriel visited Mary in the sixth month (Luke 1:26) and told her that she *will* conceive. The provincial people of Galilee and of Bethlehem with whom the author "Luke" may have talked would doubtless have reckoned months by the ecclesiastical calendar

(not the civil one), and thus, the sixth month would have been, Elul; counting both Elul and Nisan would make eight months; however, Nisan (called Abib in antiquity) was preceded by an intercalary (extra) month of 29 days every leap year. Christmas was not widely celebrated until the third century, and was celebrated first on January 6, then on March 25, and finally December 25 came into general observance by A.D. 394, probably to replace the pagan Feast of Saturnalia that celebrated the winter solstice.

5. Was Jesus either a priest or a prophet? The priests were committed to order; theirs was the job of providing continuity and of putting a recognizable face on life day-after-day; for authority, they always cited specific scripture. Prophets, on the other hand, measured the nation against the standard of the Reign of God and pressed for change; they cited a mystical communication from God ("thus saith the Lord"). Jesus claimed authority in himself ("but I say unto you")—but came closer to playing the role of prophet.

✠

CHAPTER TWENTY-EIGHT

In Caesarea Philippi with My Brother-in-law, Hebron

A.D. 7/8

*I*N THE YEAR THAT MY SISTER ENYGEUS BECAME SIXTEEN, she spent Passover week in our Jerusalem town-house with me and my beloved wife Elyap and other members of our family. Consequently, she was present when a cousin brought as a guest to our home for the evening meal a handsome young man from Caesarea Philippi, by the name of Hebron. Though only a couple of years younger than I, Hebron was the chief scribe to Herod Philip who reigned in Caesarea Philippi as Tetrarch of the Gaulanitis-Bashan-Abila area* east of the Jordan and north of Galilee.

Before the evening was very much advanced it became obvious to us all that Enygeus and Hebron were very much smitten with each other, and seemed very well matched and compatible. Consequently, it was not surprising that, before the week was out, Enygeus asked me to respond favorably to an expected overture from the family of Hebron—and so,

---

*Sometimes called Iturea and Trachonitis.

within a few weeks thereafter, they were betrothed and the following year were married at his home.

I was pleased to travel with Elyap to Caesarea Philippi as representatives of our family to see Enygeus happily married. I soon learned that Hebron was one of Philip's most trusted advisors, and so was much more than just chief scribe to the monarch. Also, it was quite obvious that Enygeus was very pleased with and proud of the new home which Hebron had had built for her—with assistance from Herod Philip, I believe. Their homesite was at the northern edge of the city in the foothills of the majestic, snow-capped Mount Hermon; looking westward, they were within sight of the headwaters of the River Jordan, and the easternmost of its four sources flowed just along the city's western border, while the ancient town of Dan still survived (barely) on the west bank of the River—and, spreading southward, as they looked over the tops of the city's new and beautiful buildings which supplemented the more modest structures of the previous Greek city, Paneas, was a sweeping view of the upper Jordan valley, before the River reached the Sea of Galilee.

At the urging of both Hebron and Enygeus, we stayed for another ten days after the week-long marriage celebration. As previously recounted, my niece, Salome, had come at the death of our father to comfort and be a foster parent to the orphaned Enygeus, who was then twelve; she stayed for three years, and when she departed a little more than a year ago, Enygeus transferred her affections to Elyap—because at age fifteen, Enygeus looked upon twenty-one-year-old Elyap as a grown and mature woman. This closeness and warmth between the two was the principal reason Hebron and Enygeus wished us to stay longer.

I knew Herod Philip to be the "best" of the three sons of Herod the Great, and he was usually deemed a man of generous mold and who sought justice in public affairs. After changing the name of his capital from Paneas to Caesarea Philippi, he beautified it markedly and added many impressive governmental buildings; later he changed the name of Bethsaida (in Ituria) to Julias, for a daughter of Augustus Caesar. Philip had married Salome, the daughter of Herodias, who was the second wife of his brother, Herod Antipas.

Hebron's high office boded well for the future of this handsome young couple, but when I commented on his good fortune, he replied: "Yes, Brother Joseph, indeed we have a fortunate arrangement here; however, working for a ruler who has the blood of the Herodians in him is neither truly a pleasure nor the sinecure it may seem to some. He has not killed wives nor sons as did his father, but he is certainly unpredictable, works me long hours, and has a mean side of his nature that one sees occasionally. If ever I have the opportunity for a different life, I am likely to take it."

✝ ✝ ✝

A.D. 28

Some twenty years later I chanced to stop off in Caesarea Philippi for a day and found that Hebron was just beginning to recover from a serious accident. He had been accompanying Herod Philip by chariot to one of his subject cities, and the chariot lost a wheel causing a crash in which he was injured. He very likely could have saved himself from harm, but he instantly seized Herod to protect him and cushioned Herod with his own body. Herod was clearly touched and appreciative of Hebron's action and had his own physician attend the treatment of Hebron's badly torn and bruised right shoulder and arm. The physician fashioned a sling for the arm and advised Herod that Hebron should rest and not start using his hand for writing for the next six months.

Upon the physician's advice and his own charitable feelings in the premises, Herod had urged Hebron to take an extended trip so that he could truly rest.

As Hebron recited this story to me in the presence of Enygeus, I responded, somewhat facetiously: "Why, I have just the solution for you, Hebron. I am leaving next week on one of my regular trips to Britannia to bring back a shipload of tin, and you could go along for the rest; we would be gone for three to four months."

Before he could reply, Enygeus responded enthusiastically: "Oh, Hebron, you must go! I know you would enjoy it, and you'd never rest around here with thirteen children underfoot."

Hebron grinned expansively and replied: "It does sound inviting. Brother Joseph, were you sincere in your suggestion?"

"Indeed I was," I replied, "and if you'll meet me in Arimathea two weeks from today, I'll be ready to escort you aboard Captain Hiram's ship, the *Astarte*. It will be a pleasure for me to have you on the trip, because Hiram and I have about exhausted all subjects of conversation that we have in common."

And so it was that fifteen days later Hebron embarked with me for Britanicus under beautiful early summer skies. Hebron had never sailed on the Great Sea, and, of course, barely knew of the Ocean Sea, so there were many special sights, sounds, smells and unique experiences for him, which he enjoyed to the fullest. During the weeks in Britannia he was constantly amazed by life in the island villages and by the streaming for tin when we went inland. Also, he was surprised and pleased to find how quickly he was able to converse extensively with the Britains, using a combination of their language and ours. He was especially pleased that they liked his name, though they insisted on shortening it to "Bron."

Hebron was not at all ready to embark for home when our business was finished and the tin all loaded.

"Brother Joseph!" he exclaimed, "I like this land and I love these people. Should the opportunity ever come to me, I would gladly live here for the rest of my life."

✢   ✢   ✢

A.D. 32

As often as convenient—at least every year or two—I managed to visit the growing family of Enygeus and Hebron, which had reached the happy number thirteen—with twelve sons and one daughter; Aaron, the eldest, now being age twenty-four.

Knowing of our relationship to Mary and her children, Hebron was most anxious on one of my visits to tell me of his experience with the healing ministry of my great-nephew, Jesus.

"Brother Joseph," he said, "the healing service of Rabbi Jesus to which I took my crippled Aunt Rebecca, was one of the most impressive religious moments of my life. Soon after Jesus and The Twelve came to our area, preaching and healing, I asked the disciple Nathaniel Bartholomew (bar-Tolmai)—to whom I am distantly related: 'Who can be brought to be healed by Jesus?'

"'Why, anyone,' he replied; 'bring anyone you wish who is in need of healing.'

"I had my Aunt Rebecca in mind," he continued, "because she had been handicapped and in great pain for several months with swollen and aching joints, which malady had especially made walking almost impossible for her."

"So, you took her, did you?" I asked, for encouragement.

"Yes, when I learned the following day that Jesus would again be healing in the afternoon along the bank of the Jordan just south of the city, my cousin and I managed, with some difficulty, to get this rather heavy lady onto the back of a donkey. The heat of the summer's day had passed, and the gentle beast picked his way slowly and carefully to the hillside scene, where a religious ceremony of sorts was taking place. Sick and crippled, handicapped and disturbed people were being brought to the healer Jesus, and I could see him briefly laying kindly hands on the distressed people and speaking a few soft words to each—the result seemed to be a healing—every time. There was a hush over the crowd, yet I sensed an excitement, and certainly felt an excitement myself."

"Had you not seen Jesus, previously?" I asked.

"No; this was my first sight of him," Hebron replied. "As we got closer to him, in the line of people seeking healing, I began to hear his soft voice. He refused no one and imposed no conditions. In some instances we could hear a gentle admonition: 'Go, and sin no more'; 'Go, and tell no one'; 'Go show yourself to the priest'; 'Your faith has made you whole'; 'Rise and walk.'

"As we got close to Jesus," Hebron continued, "I especially noticed his eyes—what kindness and compassion—what love, I saw in them. And his face—a mixture of gentleness and firmness—lines of mirth around the eyes and lines of sorrow around the mouth—paradoxes of beauty for a face so young. The timbre of his voice expressed so much love—how *deeply* he felt for each supplicant!

"Then it was our turn, and I led the donkey close to Jesus, and, as Nathaniel had instructed me, I asked: 'Lord Jesus, make this one whole, as you have promised.' He touched her lightly on head and shoulders, and his lips moved as he looked upward.

"'Selah, selah,' he then said in benediction.

"And I responded, 'Thank you, Master Jesus.' As we started to move away, my aunt turned to me and said: 'Hebron, give me your hand; I will get down, as I feel quite able to walk.'"

"And, could she?" I asked.

"Indeed, so," he replied. "She walked all the way home—a full mile—and has had vigorous, good health ever since."

✠

The Theology of Jesus

A.D. 32

I ALWAYS GREATLY ENJOYED THE RARE OCCASIONS when I could have an extended discussion of religious philosophy with my favorite great-nephew, Jesus. His ideas were not only exciting and revolutionary, but were always sensible and logical as well—this latter aspect of his views was not always fully appreciated by his Galilean disciples, who, with one or two exceptions, had little formal education to train their minds.

Jesus did more preaching in Galilee, across the Jordan, and in the north country than he did here in Judea, and so I rarely heard his formal discourses or sermons. But from the accounts that came to me it was clear that they differed little from his private teachings in at least one respect—and that was he did not hesitate to be controversial. He readily and clearly showed his disdain for many details of our interpretative law which he considered no longer had meaningful value, especially many of our dietary, health and holiness laws.

Typically, he would heal or otherwise help anyone in need without waiting for a religiously more propitious time, even though he violated a taboo of the Sabbath in doing so. He would eat with Samaritans or gentiles, or with tax-collecting publicans, those employees of the Romans who, though of Jewish blood, no longer followed our dietary laws respecting proscribed use of cooking-ware and serving dishes, and the like. Jesus commanded that we love one another. His test was, do the religious laws facilitate or obstruct our love?

He often would commence a discourse by shocking his audience with an audacious statement, phrased—"You have been taught of old, 'so-and-so,' but I say unto you, such-and-such"—with almost an opposite dictum. Of course, the scribes and lawyers in the audience would yell, "blasphemer!"—because their livelihood depended on the hundreds of "laws" which they had written to interpret earlier laws that interpreted the Ten Commandments. The whole fabric of the law was thus so complex that its re- interpretation by an "expert" was continually necessary.

Some of Jesus' novel extrapolations of scripture come readily to mind: He once told a crowd, "You have heard it said of old, 'you shall not kill,' but I say to you that whoever is angry with his brother shall be liable to judgment." Another time he said, "The law says that 'a woman caught in adultery shall be stoned,' but I say to you, let him who is without sin among you cast the first stone." Yet again he said, "You were told of old to 'honor those who speak well of you,' but I say to you, love your enemies." On these occasions the scribes, particularly, were furious because any interpretation of scripture was considered to be their province.

I came to realize that often Jesus spoke at more than one level in a given statement. And great as he was on symbolism, it was often a mistake to look only at the symbolic meaning. A few months ago when he told his audience that he would be the Sign of Jonah to this generation, some of The Way's deeper thinkers concluded that the general clamor for a "sign" had been taken by Jesus as a mere pretext, and that he *really* was pointing out that the Bet Shammai Pharisees, like Jonah, were angry and thought that God should punish sinners instead of relenting; especially, they thought, Jesus was very sensitive on behalf of those who sin unaware—since God had told Jonah that the people of Nineveh were "simple people who cannot tell their right hand from their left."

I'm sure Jesus had that in mind, but now I see that he also spoke on a pragmatic level of his three days, somewhat like Jonah, in the belly of the earth, because the Resurrection Image on his burial shroud is indeed a Sign from Heaven!—of a Son in whom God is well-pleased. Moreover, he was doubtless not unmindful of the fact that the native village of the prophet Jonah had been Gath-Hepher, very near to Jesus' first home in Nazareth.

From a political standpoint, especially in matters that concerned Rome, what Jesus meant was of little importance; what *was* important, was what the people thought he meant.

But it was technicalities that counted with the Sanhedrin, and reasons were of no moment. For instance, on occasion he encouraged his hungry disciples to pick and eat ripe grain and fruit as they passed it, even on the Sabbath. He would not do this promiscuously just to flaunt the law, but there were many times when he had taken his group on exhausting tours through desolate country, resulting in total lack of food for two and three days. In these situations, he felt that the serious nutritional needs of the men were more important than a technical rule.

And there can be no doubt that local priests and high priests alike were infuriated anytime he implied or even hinted that he might be a special person in God's eyes. As many claims of messiahship as we've heard just in our own lifetimes, you might think that the authorities would react more casually. But to small minds this seemed blasphemy and a threat to their power, though in the next breath the same ones would bemoan God's delay in sending the Messiah.

How would they recognize him and who would they accept as messiah, was a question Nicodemus or I often asked at meetings of the Sanhedrin, without receiving any attempt of reply—the response was only a stony silence during which hate was strong enough to be physically felt.

I've had few opportunities for private conversation with Jesus since he began his public ministry, teaching The Way. Particularly, I've heard only a few comments from his lips respecting messiahship. His critics ridicule such a thought, but perhaps if they didn't protest so much little would be heard on the subject. It's my impression that the disciples' claims on his behalf are largely reactions to the critics' ridicule. I'm not at all sure that Jesus has ever made a claim of messiahship on his own behalf, though he is clearly aware of the issue being bandied about.

It was barely a month before the end of his life that I had the occasion to ask Jesus bluntly, "But, are you the Messiah?"

To which query, he replied, "My revered Uncle Joseph, The Father has not yet told me of a certainty. I am still asking."

Of course, from our studies, both he and I realize that the belief in a messiah, a God-incarnate, a Deliverer, runs through all the religions of the world. Socrates called him the Divine One. Aristotle called him Deliverer. Plato called him Man of Gold. The Egyptians call him Horus. He is not only known and looked for throughout the world, but is to be of world-wide impact. Even our own Isaias wrote of him as a Light unto the Gentiles.

It's almost ludicrous in a way, because hardly a decade has passed during the last three centuries without the appearance of someone claiming to be messiah, and never before have the Temple authorities given them credence by showing irritation or anger at such claims. Criticism of Jesus on this matter is even more preposterous, in a way, since it is the usual popular assumption that messiah will re-establish a physical and independent kingdom for our people, and Jesus has repeatedly said that his kingdom is in spirit and not of this world.

The sensitive area, of course, is concerning the repeated situations wherein he seems to be fulfilling prophecies, and the more erudite of his followers delight in noting and publicizing these coincidences. I did once observe to Jesus that, in view of his very superior knowledge and memory of our Scriptures, he surely was aware of these incidents as he entered into and became involved in prophecy-fulfillment. I think this was the only time I have ever felt that Jesus was truly embarrassed.

Very quietly, he replied to me, "Uncle Joseph, you are asking a question I have many times asked myself, without answer. I can only say that in each of those situations I have felt a powerful *compulsion* to act in fulfillment of prophecy, and seemed unable to resist, doing so."

A number of situations happened in Jesus' ministry wherein the culmination should have spoken volumes of validation to the priests and elders present—that Jesus was in some way special to God. I refer to his avoidance of mob violence against himself. In the very first weeks of his formal ministry, right after his baptism by John bar Zacharias and his purification period in the desert, he had such a confrontation in the synagogue at Nazareth. After serving as public reader from the scroll of Isaiah, in which he read the prophecy of the Messiah's coming, he sat down according to custom to give his comments on the reading.

His comments could hardly have been more challenging. He first told them that right then the scripture was fulfilled in their presence—that is, that *he* was the Messiah that was prophesied, but that no prophet is accepted in his own country. He then reminded them that Elijah did not help a widow of Israel during the famine, but a Phoenician widow of Sidon; and that Elisha did not heal a leper of Israel, but Naaman, a Syrian. His implication was clear: he was Messiah, but his Jewish audience might not be the initial recipients of his bounty.

For this insult, the entire congregation rushed him from the synagogue and to a nearby cliff, over which they proposed to hurl him. As happened a number of times later in similar situations, he simply disappeared while six or eight strong men had hold of him. My inquiry of these incidents brought no more than the cryptic statement, "He must have passed through our midst and went his way; we know not how."

Once I asked Jesus for an explanation, thinking, it may have been a magic trick he had learned in his travels. But his simple answer was, "The powers of The Father protect me until my time is come."

⊹   ⊹   ⊹

I can't claim that our race ever eschewed violence; I guess we've been as bloodthirsty as any, over the centuries. But it was usually straight-out killing without torture, and I think there's been an element of mercy and of forbearance exercised by our people on occasion, which one never sees with the Romans. Their cruelty seems rampant. We do scourge with a simple whip. But the Romans use their *flagrum,* with a piece of metal at the end of each thong, so that it tears the flesh with nearly every stroke. We limit the scourging to forty lashes; the Romans recognize no limit.

Our historians and prophets have mentioned the cross, but our people never crucified anyone; we've really never seen crucifixion at close range until the Romans took our country. They order a condemned man to *"patibulum ferre"*—to carry one's *patibulum,* the cross-bar for the cross, which is fastened to the upright, or tree, after the condemned reaches the place of execution with his *patibulum.* We don't even have a word in Hebrew or Aramaic for *patibulum.*

All who know us, and especially the Romans, realize that we Jews are a fiercely independent people. What is less well known is that we are just as independent as individuals, and in this regard Jesus was most forthright in asserting his independence. Now, he realized that hundreds of years earlier, as a nomadic people, we needed strict dietary and health laws if we were to survive; also, he knew that even "laws" would more likely be obeyed if there was a religious compulsion that was thought to be imposed by Jehovah, and not just by an earthly leader or governor. But his intelligence was insulted when these "laws" were continued in effect long centuries after their utilitarian purpose has ceased to exist. He insisted that neither church nor government could legislate morality, and that attempts to do so were farcical. Consequently, he did not hesitate to break and ridicule laws that were nonsensical to him.

No rabbi or priest in the land was more devout in worship of Jehovah, whom Jesus preferred to call his Heavenly Father, nor did he abhor formal worship for its own sake as did his cousin, John, lately known as the Baptizer.[1] But Jesus always examined the facts of each case, and thus readily concluded, for instance, that healing or helping an unfortunate one, even on the Sabbath, should be perfectly proper, though in some instances it might amount to "work," as the Temple scribes and lawyers had defined the word.

Jesus never performed miracles just to show off, but because of his compassion for those who were hurting—he repeatedly refused to heal or perform a "wonder" just as a "sign" in response to his critics' demands.

CHAPTER NOTE:

1. One of the most certain things that can be said about Jesus' ministry is that, although he attempted a radical reformation of Judaism, he had no thought of creating a new religion. Seeing Jesus in the context of first century Judaism is now becoming more practical with current knowledge of archaeological discoveries, Old Testament Pseudepigrapha, the Dead Sea Scrolls, the Nag Hammadi Codices and even recently discovered testimony to Jesus by the historian Josephus. See *Jesus Within Judaism* by James H. Charlesworth, Doubleday, New York, 1988.

✛

CHAPTER THIRTY

More Theology; Jesus Watches a Crucifixion

A.D. 32

NEARLY TWO HUNDRED YEARS AGO a formal treaty between Rome and our people gave Jews everywhere special privileges, which included exemption from military service (largely because of dietary concerns) and freedom to worship and obey our strict laws regarding the Sabbath. But in our Jewish provinces, they permitted all our laws to remain in force and be administered by us, so long as they do not conflict with Roman law; perhaps nowhere else in the Empire has Rome conceded so much to a conquered people.

But the anomaly is, of course, that *all* our law is religious law, making no distinction at all between politics and religion; "the law" covers religion, government, politics, social and economic affairs, as well as the most intimate of personal concerns—it's all of ecclesiastical concern. A purely secular problem is inconceivable under our law—and a Roman can never understand this!

One major weakness is that our law is administered by our priests; this situation causes the Romans much bewilderment and frustration. And, also, this system gives undue power, rarely matched by secular rulers, to priests who, too often these days, are unqualified for governing or have conflicting selfish interests if they are not outright corrupt. This is the situation which led to many conflicts with Jesus. Moreover, he did not hesitate to create such issues, realizing that no one else would do so since it put one in the position of questioning God's representative, the priest, which is blasphemy.

Those of us who have made a substantial study of our religion and have compared it with the other great religions of antiquity and of today, usually take considerable pride in Judaism, for it seems to us so superior in several respects to all others. However, devout as Jesus has been all his life, he is outspoken as to the flaws he sees in our Faith—flaws which in every instance are created by recent interpretations.

One such flaw that bothered him most deeply is the manner in which God is presented to the people. Of course, he realizes the anomaly of urging an intimacy with God because of the risk of making God in *our* image. Nor would he approach the ludicrous by suggesting that the God who created and controls the universe might walk around on two legs as we do. The situation was made even worse, as he saw it, by the dogma that the speaking of God's name is absolutely forbidden. He tried to overcome this by insisting that God's attitude toward us is comparable to that of an earthly father, and consequently, we should call God our Heavenly Father. Yet, he realized that it was not a perfect solution and besides, he got very little acceptance of the idea from the general public.

So, Jesus then tried to explain that God is within all of us. That thought, though, seems to raise more questions than it solves. He said, "The Father and I are one, and only he that hath seen me hath seen the Father"—speaking, I assume, of the Christ-principle or God-factor in himself.

The Twelve, among themselves, said, "We can accept that because Jesus is the Messiah."

"But," he said, "I am in you, and you are in me."

The Twelve thought he was speaking of something abstract like human love and affection, but I believe he was trying to tell us of reality, that the great Truth was the interconnectedness of us and God and all life.

One of Jesus' favorite metaphors was the phrase "kingdom of heaven," which he used in an attempt to explain to the disciples the realm of spirit within, about, and interpenetrating every person—the God-part of us, or "spirit body," which is eternal and which interconnects us with God and with all of life of every kind. Such a concept* is difficult enough for those of us trained by the Temple schools in the meaning and application of our

---

*Robert Findlay of Boturich, Scotland, in his little book, *Turn Again* (CFPSS, London, 1979), says Jesus' "kingdom of heaven" (or kingdom of God) translates as "the realm of spirit within man."

holy scriptures, but the untutored Galilean Twelve found such ideas largely beyond their grasp—though their deeper selves did resonate and glow with pleasure whenever they listened to Jesus expounding on such subjects.

And the difficulty of explaining this truth seemed to be one of the several reasons he has chosen to let himself be crucified—because many of us will accept that he was the Christed One—and yet, he had incarnated, had taken a physical body, so he was someone to whom we can relate.

It's heady stuff, and I'm just beginning to get a fair glimmer myself of what he really meant.

Another basic flaw in today's Judaism which distresses Jesus is the role of women. From childhood, the morning prayer of every Jewish male is: "Blessed be Thou, Oh Lord our God, for not having made me a gentile, a woman or a fool."

Our rabbis continue to tell us that women are not to be taught the Torah, nor to be allowed to touch the sacred scrolls. In our household in Arimathea that teaching was never followed, nor was it in the homes of Joseph bar Jacob in Nazareth or Josiah of Bethany or many others of our family. One of the chief rabbis in Jerusalem has even repeatedly declaimed: "He who speaks much with a woman draws down misfortune on himself, neglects the words of the law, and in the end inherits hell."

When Jesus heard of this teaching he was so infuriated that now whenever he comes into Judea he makes it a point to be publicly seen conversing with women, and does everything he can to vigorously promote the dignity and equality of women. Not only will he talk with women on serious subjects, but he encourages them to have a prominent, public and significant role in his ministry. Moreover, he challenges the scribes and chief priests on the subject of marriage, divorce and adultery, stating clearly that a husband has no fewer obligations and no more privileges in a marriage than does the wife. What a furor that has caused!

Nor are women the only ones oppressed under our law. Children, the poor, beggars, prostitutes, and tax-collectors are totally *without status* under our law. Perhaps most vicious of all is the requirement that a person must be prepared to *prove* his own racial purity. If, even through marriage, there was a mixing of Jewish and pagan bloodlines, it is held to be an illegitimate sexual union and for ten generations the children are deemed sinners. And worse still, those who cannot *prove* racial purity of their ancestors will bear that stigma. Such stigma is the sort of "sin" that Jesus is quite quick to forgive, and he never hesitates to fight for these disenfranchised, whom he calls "these little ones." What he values is humanity, not status and prestige.

In this regard, of course, he attacks an almost sacred institution, for the dominant value in our Jewish life today is prestige. This is a crucial point on which he condemns the Sadducees and the Bet Shammai Pharisees, most of whom live for the prestige and admiration of others. Jesus' healings and his liberating activity are to show that God cares for those who suffer.

✠ ✠ ✠

Our Aramaic language lends itself perfectly to the emotional temperament of the Galilean people, where hyperbole, exaggeration, ridicule and name-calling are an integral part of everyday conversation. And Jesus is very typical of his culture in this respect; he is a masterful storyteller and can sway any audience. One characteristic the public is less aware of is his sense of humor, which he especially enjoys turning on his friends to tease, although never to embarrass or offend.

One day as a group of Judean disciples was meeting with Jesus in the home of Lazarus, a servant interrupted us to say, "Master, people in the neighborhood have learned that you are here, and they request permission to listen as you teach."

"How large a number is there?" Jesus asked.

"About a hundred," was the reply.

"That is too many to crowd into Lazarus' premises," was his response; "let us go out into the orchard, and I will sit on that old stone fence."

Once we were in the orchard and the neighbor folk had joined us, it was soon obvious that they were too embarrassed to ask questions. Thinking to provide Jesus with a point of beginning, Nicodemus asked, "Master, what must one do to have eternal life?"

Jesus then gave his standard response, "Keep all of the Ten Commandments and love your neighbor as you love yourself."

"But, Lord," replied Nicodemus, "I have done all of that since my youth; what more should I do?"

Seeing the twinkle in Jesus' eyes, we friends knew we were about to hear some product of his occasional outrageous humor. Turning from Nicodemus to the crowd, Jesus declaimed with a perfectly straight face: "I perceive this to be a very rich young man who has been badly spoiled by his parents; look at the beautiful raiment he wears; he probably is a ruler of some sort."

Turning back then to Nicodemus, he said: "Yes, I will tell you what more you must do—Go, sell all that you own and give it to the poor, and then follow me."

Nicodemus dropped his head to keep from laughing, because we all knew that perhaps no one in all of Jerusalem gave more to the poor than did he.

Jesus quickly spoke again to the crowd: "There, see! He hangs his head with shame! Verily, I tell you it is easier for a loaded camel to enter the City through the Needle's Eye Gate, than for a rich man to enter the kingdom of heaven."[1]

✠   ✠   ✠

A few months before his crucifixion, as matters turned out, Jesus was visiting for a few days with Lazarus and his sisters, and relaxing after a rather exhausting preaching mission. I happened to stop by and thus was pleasantly surprised to find Jesus there.

As we sat visiting in the spacious and luxurious atrium of their home, Lazarus returned from a brief trip into Jerusalem, and we overheard him complaining to the servant who met him at the door: "I was tired and thought I would avoid the press of the crowds near the Fish Gate by coming out the Ephriam Gate and following a path outside the walls. But as I emerged, lo, the Romans were at Golgotha and just beginning the crucifixion of several luckless criminals, so the crowds were worse than if I had stayed in the City."

We greeted Lazarus who smiled wanly, and asked us to forgive him, as he wished to go lie down.

"What a wonderful young man," I commented to Jesus, "it's such a shame that his bodily health does not match his brain and personality."

"His wonderful attitude in spite of his frail health has been a major factor in developing the sweet character we love in Lazarus," observed Jesus, "and besides he will not always have that handicap."

I was puzzled by his last comment, but before I could speak, he continued: "Uncle Joseph, I would very much like to see these crucifixions. Would you walk over to Golgotha with me?"

"Of course," I replied, and refrained from comment on his strange request.

When we arrived at the scene two men were already hanging from their cross-beams lashed to tall posts. "How they labor to breathe," I observed.

"Yes, death finally comes from asphyxiation, as a rule," he agreed. "They survive a few hours, or even days, only if they can relieve the strain of hanging full-weight from their impaled wrists."

At this point, another victim was forced onto his back on the ground and his arms were spread over his cross-beam. While one soldier gripped his forearm and hand, another soldier positioned a square spike in the soft of the wrist and with a hammer's smashing blow, drove the spike through the victim's wrist and into the crossbeam, as a muffled scream broke from his lips.

"How cruel!" I moaned. "Is there not a more humane way to effect his death?"

After the other wrist had been similarly impaled, four soldiers lifted the cross-beam with the criminal hanging from it, and held it over their heads where the upright was notched.[2] Another soldier stood on a ladder behind the cross and quickly tied the cross-beam securely in place. Two soldiers held his feet, one over the other, while a single spike was driven through them into the tree of the cross. Only a moan came from the man's lips this time. After a bit we observed this latest victim struggling for air, and finally saw him get momentary surcease by pushing against his bleeding feet to raise his body and so relieve the abdominal muscle strain, as his bursting chest heaved, expelling and inhaling air rapidly several times before slumping to hang dead-weight on his wrists again.

"It clearly is difficult and very painful, but it is a death that I can tolerate, I am sure," Jesus said.

"So you think this is your fate?" I asked.

"I'm not yet certain, but I think so," he replied. "The Father will tell me."

CHAPTER NOTES:

1. For other Near East interpretations of the "rich man, camel and needle's eye," story, see pp. 34-35 of *Treasures from the Language of Jesus* by Rocco Errico, DeVorss, Marina del Rey, 1987. Also see *The Lamsa Bible* (translated from the Aramaic)—Matthew 19:24, "Again I say to you, it is easier for a *rope* to go through the eye of a needle than for a rich man to enter the kingdom of God." (A footnote explains that the Aramaic word *gamla* means rope or camel.)

2. Most crosses were low, with the victim's feet only a few inches off the ground; see Barbet: *A Doctor at Calvary*, Doubleday/Image, New York, 1950, 1963.

CHAPTER THIRTY-ONE

✠

The Mount of Transfiguration

A.D. 33

IT ISN'T ALWAYS EASY to follow Jesus' teachings. When in the presence of one or two or three of us whose education and mental training he respected, Jesus would speak much more clearly and directly, permitting us to know what he truly believed on certain matters. But he did not hesitate to tell even the Twelve that he would show them but a few of heaven's mysteries, because they could not understand or accept them. With the public he would only talk in parables and on simple subjects such as God's love, man's love, faith, eternal reward, and the like. He said he was follow-ing the leading of the great (and his favorite) prophet, Ezekiel, who talked of wheels within wheels.

Like Ezekiel, Jesus preferred to refer to himself as "the Son of Man." However, Ezekiel's reason was quite simple, since this was the name by which God called *him*. Jesus' reasons, on the other hand, were probably much more complex. When Jesus spoke to the scribes and priests and other leaders, I feel that he wanted them—by his use of the term "son of man"—to be reminded of Ezekiel and to compare him with Ezekiel—and particularly, he wanted them to remember God's admonition to Ezekiel to speak the truth and be not concerned with whether his listeners hear or refuse to hear.

Also, by this figure of speech he was suggesting to the religious leaders that, like Ezekiel, he was warning his audience to change their ways—with a subtle, half-veiled threat, since they would remember how accurately many of Ezekiel's prophecies had been fulfilled. Moreover, he memorized much of the scriptures perfectly and could quote them more readily and accurately than the leaders could, thus providing them by inference a further comparison with Ezekiel, to whom God had given a scroll of scriptures to eat.

He knew that the scribes always suspected everyone of deviousness, and that they had tried to read special and extra meanings into Ezekiel's use of the pseudonym, Son of Man—some of them said the term meant one who understands the true spiritual nature of mankind—others said it meant a supernatural figure who would preside over the end of the world. In simple fact, I am fairly sure that for the most part Jesus was merely being true to his heritage; the plain, hill people of Galilee very often used the term "son of man" as a circumlocution meaning oneself—instead of saying "I"—presumably because they are basically a modest and unassuming people. But Jesus was well aware of the suggested other meanings of the term, and it amused him to use it especially with sophisticated audiences to puzzle and to infuriate them.

Talking in our Aramaic language, especially to the less educated and more simple people of Galilee, Jesus kept his language very simple when he delivered discourses to the multitudes. However, when he argued with the scribes and priests in Hebrew, our formal language, he often felt handicapped without the colloquialisms and richness of the Aramaic. Especially was this true when he attempted to talk of spiritual things, when the naivete and simplicity of the Galileans made his message more readily acceptable. With them, a message from a deceased relative or an angel in a dream or a vision was completely believable. If, while resting, one of them found himself miles away at a sick friend's bedside, he accepted it as reality. If a relative appeared briefly with a word of assurance or of warning, and later it was learned that this relative had just died, the observer accepted it as reality.

Consequently, when Jesus talked to the Galileans of "life" and "death" they knew he spoke in spiritual terms. They knew that by "life" he meant eternity spent in the presence of God in the heavenly realms, and that by "death" he meant a self-alienation from God. These terms presented no problems for the Galileans, and they understood that Jesus was not talking of the superficiality and temporariness of the physical body.

Just about a month before his crucifixion, Jesus was accompanied to the top of Mount Tabor by Peter, James and John, whom he smilingly

called his "spiritual power support." They had been briefly visiting with his
former neighbors in Nazareth, from whence they followed the long ridge
which connected with Tabor, thus avoiding about half the climb of this
nearly two-thousand-foot-high "holy mountain." This route took them to
the peak in considerably less than an hour.

The disciples have recently been referring to the experience of that
day as the "Mount of Transfiguration." Although Jesus had asked that the
experience there not be mentioned to the public during his lifetime, he was
quite willing that we of the inner circle discuss it as we wished.

James, the least emotional and most articulate of that trio, had tried to
describe the occurrence for me one day as we relaxed in Lazarus' gardens.
He explained that on the day previous to the climb Jesus had been telling
the Twelve that in just a few weeks he would be crucified by the authorities, and then would arise from the dead on the third day thereafter. The
disciples spent many hours protesting and arguing with Jesus. They argued
that although some of the prophecies spoke of the Messiah's death, not all
of them did—and shouldn't a Heavenly Father of love spare him such a
trauma—weren't there other ways to accomplish his purposes?

These arguments certainly didn't convince Jesus, but they clearly distressed him, and the trip to the mountain-top the following day seemed to
be for the purpose of clarifying Jesus' mind on this matter. In any event,
from that day onward Jesus seemed to have no doubts about his death and
would engage in no further discussion on the point. Also, he continued to
remind them that his death was soon coming.

On the mountain-top, according to James, Jesus prayed aloud briefly
for God to confirm and clarify the ending of his earthly mission. Then he
guided them into silent meditation in the fashion he had taught us, asking
God to reveal His will during the silence. The three each felt that they must
have slept. When Jesus asked if God had spoken to them, each replied in the
negative. Jesus did not rebuke them, saying that he also had heard nothing.

Next Jesus told them to close their eyes and hold their hands out to
him, sending him their spiritual power. After some time had elapsed a
sound like a great wind was heard and the three opened their eyes. When
they did so, they felt frozen with awe at the sight before them: Jesus'
robe seemed brilliantly white and a radiance shone from it; James said he
once had been on the high slopes of Mount Hermon where ice lay the
year 'round, and the noonday sun on the ice was almost blinding to the
eyes—this, said James, was the best comparison he could use to describe
the radiance of Jesus' robe. But, Jesus' face, he said, was so luminous, like
a reflected lamp, that the facial features could barely be seen.

After a minute or two it was possible to see two other persons standing close to Jesus as if in conversation, but no sounds could be heard. Even in the absence of words, he said it was strongly impressed on his mind that these were Elijah and Moses. Their figures were not as brilliant as that of Jesus, and, although clear and certain, they seemed almost diaphanous. When I asked him to explain this, he said that he could see rocks and bushes behind Elijah and Moses that their bodies did not conceal—that he could see through them as well as see them.

James had difficulty estimating how long he watched the three figures, but from subsequent discussions with Peter and John, who confirmed all points of his story, he concluded that it might have been fifteen to twenty minutes. The appearance was disrupted and terminated, as might be expected, by the impetuousness of Peter who finally burst out with the suggestion of building three shrines on this spot. Upon this interruption, the visibility of the figures of Elijah and Moses quickly faded into nothingness and Jesus' figure became normal in appearance.

Just two days before his crucifixion (as it turned out), I had an hour alone with Jesus in Bethany, and asked him to explain that mystical event. He responded: "I very well knew that I could be in error or could be indulging in wish-fulfillment as long as I was in the physical body, and the protests of the disciples convinced me that I must get heavenly reassurances before I proceeded with a submissive approach to my probable death at Jerusalem.

"On the mountain-top," he continued, "when neither I nor The Three received any heavenly guidance in meditation, I knew that I must call up advisors from heaven, much as did King Saul in days gone by. So, I asked the Father to send Moses and Elijah to counsel me, which he did, with the aid of The Three serving as my spiritual power support. When Moses and Elijah appeared, I told them that, in spite of varying interpretations of prophecy, it seemed clear to me that permitting myself to be killed by the authorities would be consistent with prophecy and would certainly flow naturally from the desires of my enemies on the Sanhedrin. I explained that I was revolted by the practices related to blood sacrifice as still performed in the Temple—that if, in love, I offered myself as the ultimate sacrifice, perhaps I could end this barbaric ritual for all time. A profession of belief with deeply-felt relationship to God, a practice of agapé love and right living, ought to be the only criteria for overcoming people's failures, in my view, and to ensure an eternity with God.

"Moses responded to me, 'Master, I gave the law to humanity with promises of prosperity and eternal life to all who strictly obeyed it. But in spite of detailed additions and stern penalties for disobedience, the system has not worked. Maybe your love and willing death will touch the hearts of people and win them to eternal life. I'm for you and hope your plan will work.'

"Then Elijah responded: 'Master, I tried on Mount Carmel to prove the power of God, and to kill off his enemies. At first, it seemed I was successful—that force and coercion might induce righteousness, and I have been called the "father of prophets" for my efforts. But I now see that it will take something different to touch the hearts of wayward humanity enough for them to truly accept the abundant life and live like children of the Father God. Maybe your way will work; I hope so!"

Reflecting on what he told me of the Transfiguration, I recalled that he had often spoken to us of his abhorrence of animal sacrifice in our Temple. He recognized that when this symbolic ceremony was inaugurated more than a millennium ago by Abraham, it was a great advance over the then-common human sacrifice practiced almost universally, and which often was blended with fertility rites, as with the spreading of sacrificial blood on the fields.

However, Jesus seemed to feel that it was time for a further advance— that God did not require appeasement by sacrifice in this enlightened age. He may have been influenced, to some extent, by the practice of the Essenes who sacrifice only fruit or grain.

CHAPTER THIRTY-TWO

✠

Raising of Lazarus; Lazarus' Story

A.D. 33

S OME TWO WEEKS BEFORE THE CRUCIFIXION, as matters turned out, my friend and kinsman, Lazarus of Bethany, was spectacularly raised from the dead by Jesus.

Throughout his ministry Jesus had resisted all popular demands and all challenges from his critics to perform miracles just to give them a "sign." Usually his miracles were in response to a real need he was too compassionate to ignore. The miracle of raising Lazarus was, to my mind, a different proposition.

From birth onward Lazarus had been a true weakling, but I never heard him comment on it, much less complain. Because of his frail and delicate nature he frequently was beset by sickness of various sorts but rarely was willing to go to bed or display a handicap, much as his sister, Martha, implored him at times to rest himself. Although not strong enough as a boy to engage in rough games, one would rarely be aware of his failure to participate because he always seemed to be enthusiastically involved, when in fact it was always in a supporting role.

His intelligence, personality and spiritual interests were the factors which seemed to draw him and Jesus into a close relationship right from their first meeting. Among followers of The Way, he was often known merely at the "One Jesus loved"—no other person ever was so described in

Jesus' lifetime,[1] and from Jesus' early twenties onward he stayed nowhere else in Judea except at the home of Lazarus. So, one might ask, why did Jesus not, by a miracle, give Lazarus robust good health? I doubt he would have answered such a question had it been put to him, and I certainly never knew of him to so favor his friends, though many of them had physical needs.

I said the raising of Lazarus was a different proposition, and I think that that was clear. He was preaching across the Jordan at the time, in Perea, at Bethabara, less than a day's journey from Bethany. The accounts of the disciples with him satisfy me that he was indeed using his strong clairvoyant powers to monitor the condition of Lazarus—that he could have returned and healed him had he wanted to—that he delayed his return even after he knew that Lazarus was dead. He would not put so good a friend through the trauma of dying, nor the sisters Martha and Mary through the suffering attendant on Lazarus' death, except for good purpose.

And that purpose was certainly an object lesson for the Twelve; he had been telling them for several months that he would be killed by the authorities, but he would return from the grave. None of us could anticipate the full measure of his passion nor the power of his return, much less the future value he saw in his sacrifice. But the Twelve seemed adamant; they would not even consider such a termination for his ministry, and could not conceive of a spectacular return. The raising of Lazarus after four days in the tomb, and closer to five days from the time of his death, was to provide for the Twelve the proof positive of his control over death—his own, or that of anyone.

Did he succeed? I doubt it. I don't think they got the point, but Caiaphas and Annas certainly did, and it worried Pilate. Those three schemers saw the handwriting on the wall. Who but a God-man could control death and give back physical life? That act really doomed both Jesus and Lazarus in their eyes.

I do think the matter got out of hand, though, and didn't come out just as Jesus had intended. I think he didn't take the feminine factor fully into account. I believe he intended the raising of Lazarus to be a private affair, involving just the family and the Twelve—but it couldn't be contained.

The funeral itself had involved practically the whole village of Bethany, because Lazarus was a very popular man—a man who doubtless was disliked by no one. But during the whole ceremony, both Martha and Mary repeatedly bewailed the fact that Jesus had "let" his death happen—that Jesus had been sent for but had not come to heal Lazarus as he had healed so many others—and they voiced this concern loudly, for all to hear.

Then, when Jesus did return, was it a subdued event? Not at all. As soon as someone at the edge of town saw Jesus and the Twelve approaching, it seemed that everyone shouted the news and raced to tell Martha and Mary, And did *they* wait patiently for him to arrive? Of course not.

Martha raced across the village to meet Jesus, and proceeded to tell him, for all to hear: "If you had been here, my brother would not have died!"

After exchanging a few words more with Jesus, she turned and ran back to the house and sent Mary to do the same. Mary dutifully ran to Jesus and also said, quite loudly: "If you had been here, my brother would not have died!"

When Jesus and the Twelve finally arrived at the gate of the house, most of the town was right behind them.

The only cool head in town was Simon, whom the townfolk were still calling "the leper," even though Jesus had healed him nearly two years previously. When he saw what was happening, he stepped in front of the gate after Jesus and the Twelve had passed through it, and blocked passage to the townspeople.

"For shame," he cried. "Can you not consider the feelings of our good neighbors and of the Master Jesus and grant them some privacy."

"But he's going to the grave!" several of them shouted. "We want to see what he will do!"

Although the garden of the house was enclosed by a high stone wall, everyone knew that the family tomb was an enlarged cave in the orchard some distance behind the house; and so more than a hundred people ran around the wall and through the orchard, and reached the tomb before Jesus did.

Jesus asked that the round stone door be rolled aside, and several men jumped to do his bidding, since the tomb was not sealed. Then Jesus called: "Lazarus, come out!"

After two or three minutes of silence there was a shuffling sound, and indeed Lazarus hobbled forth, dragging his long shroud.

When Jesus commanded, "Loose him!"—several leaped forward to untie the *keiriai* strips of cloth that bound his ankles and wrists, and the *sudarion* jaw-band that was knotted over the top of his head, and pulled the long shroud away.

Needless to say, wagging tongues reached Caiaphas with the news in much less than a hour's time.

Lazarus had died shortly after midnight as the third watch of the night was just beginning. And so, pursuant to our law, he was buried that afternoon—consequently, I was not there for the funeral since I was in Arimathea at the time. Neither did I have any warning of Jesus' return from Perea and so I was not on hand for the raising of Lazarus. However, some ten days later, three or four days before the Passover, I had the opportunity of a visit in my Jerusalem townhouse with Lazarus. He, accompanied by two of his husky and armed man-servants, had quietly come to the Temple to offer prayers of thanks and stopped in to see me before returning home. Our conversation for the next two hours was a most amazing one.

When we embraced I felt a strength in his arms that I had never known, and I immediately asked: "Aren't you actually stronger than before your death?—you feel so to me, and you look it, too!"

"Dear brother Joseph," he replied, "this is the truly amazing thing about my return. I have strength, I have vitality, I have stamina. Never before in my life was this true. In the few days since my return I have had a couple of occasions to work in the shop and in the field for a few hours with my men. Never before could I do that. And strangely enough, my muscles are hard as if I had worked vigorously all my life. I even felt exhilarated by the working. For me the miracle is still going on!"

"This is fantastic news! I am so very thrilled to hear it," I told him. "What has Jesus said to you about it?"

"Very little," Lazarus said. "Actually, he's not been around much since then. About his only comment was to tell me not to describe my experience to the Twelve. He said it was a personal experience that I'd probably not want to share with very many persons, and that he wanted the Twelve to learn faith first. He said, 'I wanted them to see the glory and power of God, but signs bring no conviction, and neither will they be persuaded though one rose from the dead, if they have nothing more than that.'"

"But Lazarus, my friend," I expostulated, "then you did not just sleep for four-and-a-half days—you had an experience, didn't you?"

"An experience beyond compare!—yes, I certainly did, and it is still rocking me back on my heels whenever I think of it," he replied. "Shall I tell you of it?—I've not yet told a single person."

"Yes, of course, I want very much to hear it, and I'll tell no one else as long as we both live, without your permission," I said.

"It is still very vivid in every detail," he began, "and although I can't prove it or explain it, I am absolutely convinced I lived the experience and did not dream it—it was nothing like a dream.

"I was lying in my bed in great pain and with a fever that was burn-ing me up," he continued. "I now know the fever had been with me for three days and nothing would relieve it. Suddenly, shortly after midnight, I heard a sharp, snapping sound, and at once I was without pain, and cool—moreover, I was above my bed, near the ceiling and looking down. Seeing a body in my bed I was surprised and looking closely realized it was *my* body! I saw Martha take my hand, and then in an obvious fright she felt my chest, and then laid a feather on my upper lip. Suddenly she screamed, 'He's dead,' and two serving girls came running. I tried to tell Martha I was fine, but she wouldn't listen. I tried to pat her shoulder but my hand went through her body. Then I realized that I must be dead!"

"But you say you felt fine?" I asked.

"Yes, not a pain nor a care," he replied. "I was a little concerned when I realized I was dead, but immediately I heard a roar, like a tremendous swarm of bees, and found myself travelling very fast down a long, dark passageway."

"Did that frighten you?" I asked.

"Not a bit," he replied. "I was seeing a beautiful light at the end of the passageway, and I was anxious to get there. When I arrived, I found that indeed the light was a brilliant glow coming from the person of Master Jesus. I remembered then the story told by Peter, James and John of how Jesus was illumined on Mount Tabor when he was visited by Moses and Elijah. The light was so brilliant I could barely see him—but I recognized his smile.

"'Master,' I said, 'what shall I do here?'

"'Rest if you like,' he responded, 'or visit the many mansions in our Father's house; it's a wonderful house!'"

"So, what did you do?" I asked in my eagerness.

"I didn't really have a choice," he replied with a smile, "for there at once were my father and mother, and behind them were others who had died before me."

"Did your parents look as you had last seen them?" I wanted to know.

"I'd have to say, yes and no," he replied. "They were as natural as could be, but younger than when they died. And the wonderful thing was, my father's body seemed perfect—you'll recall that he died in an accident in which he was horribly injured, but no evidence of the injuries was to be seen."

"Did they stay with you long," I asked.

"Not really. There was just this wonderful welcome, and then they were gone," he replied. "So then I set out to see the wonders of heaven. I think there would have been a guide for me if I had wanted one, but I seemed all right on my own. It would take too long to describe everything I saw, but there seemed to be no limit of the things to do there. I saw choir directors teaching songs and singing, and others teaching skill with musical instruments; there were classes for the learning of anything one wanted to know; there were training sessions for spirit helpers who would try to influence and help those still living on earth. I was just enthralled by the possibilities, and then I heard Jesus' voice saying: 'Lazarus, come out!'

"And the next thing I knew I was walking out of my tomb!"

CHAPTER NOTES:

1. The "disciple Jesus loved" is mentioned only in the Gospel of John and, although most Christians have always assumed that the author of the fourth Gospel was referring to himself, internal evidence of the New Testament does not in fact tend toward such a conclusion; actually, several present-day NT scholars are convinced that John bar Zebedee was not the "beloved" one for substantive reasons—and other candidates, including Lazarus, have been proposed. Moreover, a number of NT scholars consider that the Gospel of John was authored/edited by two or three persons, none of whom was John bar Zebedee, for very basic reasons (See "Did Lazarus Write the Gospel of John?" *Spiritual Frontiers,* XII-1, pp. 14-19). The Roman catholic scholar, Rudolf Schnackenburg, in the third volume of his *The Gospel According to St. John* (N.Y.: Crossroad, 3 vols., 1968, 1982), came to the conclusion that the Beloved Disciple (who was not the evangelist, John, but the authority behind the Gospel) was not one of the Twelve (pp. 375-378). Also see pp. 33-34 of *The Community of the Beloved Disciple* by Raymond E. Brown (N.Y.: Paulist Press, 1979).

2. In the last two decades of the twentieth century, with the advent of much new archaeological and historical data, it has become fashionable for some scholars to question the historicity of many very basic facts, events and persons of early Christianity. Extreme skepticism in the name of scholarship is found in current writings that question whether Lazarus is a *bona fide* historical character; typically, G.H.C. MacGregor states in his Moffat Commentary on John: "It is inconceivable that the greatest of all recorded miracles, performed during the last critical week, and in the presence of crowds of people, would have been omitted by the first three Evangelists."

But one might question the writer's possible naivete for lack of understanding human nature—simple jealousy is probably the answer. Young Mark (probably thirteen) may have been unduly impressed by "the thunderers" (Zebedees) of Galilee, and little is written in the Synoptics of Jesus' ministry outside Galilee.

I will cite just two items of *hard evidence,* to the contrary: (a) Caesar Baronius, Vatican Librarian, who had no axe to grind, in 1596 wrote his *Annales Ecclesiastici* based on Vatican records; he described the arrival in A.D. 35 in Marseilles of the refugee company from Judea that included Joseph of Arimathea and Lazarus of Bethany, with his sisters Mary and Martha. (b) Professor Paul L. Maier, renowned Bible historian of Western Michigan University, is reported by *U.S. News & World Report* of Dec. 20, 1993 (at p. 65) as noting that, while Bethany was destroyed when the Romans attacked Jerusalem in A.D. 70, it was rebuilt by the Arabs who today call it "el-Azariyeh" which means "the place of Lazarus." Maier asks, "Why would they change the name of the town unless something spectacular happened there?" Lazarus was real!

And finally, MacGregor's statement implies, what other skeptics have bluntly stated, that as to Jesus' miracles generally and raisings from the dead specifically, the miracle claims (except for the psychosomatic healings) should be demythologized. But they glibly skip over Bible passages that are sharply clear: Jesus told the disciples plainly: "Lazarus is dead, and for your sakes I am glad I was not there, so that you may believe." Also, when John the Baptist was in prison and sent his disciples to ask Jesus if he was indeed the Messiah, Jesus is recorded as replying: "Go and tell John what you see and hear—that the blind receive their sight, the lame walk, lepers are cleansed, and deaf hear, and the dead are raised." In Matthew 10, Jesus instructed the disciples: "Go out and heal the sick, raise the dead." Would he expect them to do something he didn't or couldn't?

Elijah raised the widow's son (I Kings 17). Elisha raised a boy (II Kings 4) and, after his own death, Elisha raised a man from the dead (II Kings 13). Tabitha died in Joppa; church leaders sent to Lydda, ten miles away, for Peter to preach her funeral; he came, but raised Tabitha from the dead, instead (Acts 9). While Paul was preaching, a boy fell to his death outside the church; *after the service,* Paul raised him from the dead (Acts 20). Nicholas, Bishop of Myra (A.D. 280-350), while aboard a ship in a storm, saw a seaman fall to his death; *after the storm,* he raised the seaman from death. In 1971 in Madras, India, Walter R. Cowan in his mid-80s, died of pneumonia in the early morning hours of Christmas; taken to a hospital he was pronounced dead and his ears and nose were stuffed with cotton; his wife, Elsie, went to Sai Baba, who promised to visit Walter at 10 a.m.; when she got back to the hospital, Walter was alive and Sai Baba had just left. In his book, *Raised from the Dead,* Fr. Hebert lists more than four hundred cases of persons restored to life after apparent death—some more spectacular than the raising of Lazarus.

Early Christians apparently accepted the story of Jesus' raising of Lazarus from the dead (as reported in the Gospel of John and the Secret Gospel of Mark) as a factual account, since more than 100 images of this scene adorn the walls and sarcophagi of the Roman catacombs *(Bible Reviews,* XI-2, April 1995).

CHAPTER THIRTY-THREE

✠

Jesus' Triumphal Entry; Arrest

A.D. 33

O N THE FIRST DAY OF THE WEEK, just five days before Passover[1] this year, as Jesus and the Galilean Twelve were near Bethphage just east of Jerusalem, James, John and other of the Twelve began urging that his entry into the City should be ceremonial and very impressive as befitting the Messiah. Some suggested that they borrow a Roman chariot or at least a white horse for him to ride.

How sure are you that I am Messiah?" Jesus asked; "Would Isaiah approve of such a display?—or would Zechariah?—or Ezekiel?" They seemed not to get his meaning, so he told Andrew and Matthew to go into the village, to the house of one of the brethren named Joel, and ask for the grown but unbroken colt that would be tied with its mother, a burro, at Joel's gate, and to bring the colt. When it was procured he mounted the young burro and began slowly to ride into Jerusalem.

I have since learned that the Zebedee sons had planned for such a maneuver, though they had hoped for a more ostentatious procession, and that they had arranged that all the brethren in the area, and all of their families and friends, would line the street and shout hosannas, calling to Jesus as the Messiah.

Because these were the annual Holy Days there were a great number of families camped near Jerusalem that had come great distances, and many of those from the east and north and northwest had previously heard Jesus' message or knew about him.

Unfortunately, the Zebedee sons were not the only ones who were trying to maneuver Jesus and to capitalize on his probable popularity for their own purposes. Such also were the Zealots, whose allegiance was given to Bar-Abbas the local Zealot leader, who, with his rough Galilean followers, unsuccessfully stormed the Antonia (the fortified barracks of Pilate's troops, adjacent to the Temple) the following day. When Jesus' brother, Simon (called "the Zealot") realized that Jesus was willing to make a ceremonial entrance into the City, he quickly alerted a large number of Zealots to participate with the local crowds, and to call on Jesus as Judea's savior and new King to throw out the Romans.

Judas bar Simon, sometimes called Iscariot, could not make up his mind whether to actively support the efforts of James and John or that of the Zealots, but he could see that the servile stance apparently favored by Jesus would provide little opportunity for development of an important role for himself. Consequently, as the procession broke up near the Temple porch, he slipped quietly into Caiaphas' chambers (it was not generally known, but Judas was the son of Caiaphas' brother[2]).

Shortly after the Resurrection, when my servant, Hosea, returned from making inquiries of his relatives in Caiaphas' household, and of the clerk in Caiaphas' office who is a secret follower of The Way, he was able to report to me fully respecting Judas' visit to his uncle after Jesus' triumphal entry. I suppose Judas exaggerated a little, but he didn't have to exaggerate much to say that there were many calls from the crowd for Jesus to proclaim himself king and to throw out the Romans.

As High Priest and chief executive of the Sanhedrin, Caiaphas needed no excuses to support his decision to arrange Jesus' death. However, he didn't want ultimate responsibility for that act, and the popular support for Jesus that his demonstration had whipped-up further reinforced that resolve. But Judas' information quickly convinced him that enough evidence might now be available to importune action by Pilate.

As the servants overheard it, Caiaphas then told Judas that an attempt to overthrow Roman rule for religious reasons (by a Messiah) would be blamed on him, Caiaphas; therefore, Jesus must be put in protective custody, so that nothing rash would happen, either to Jesus or to the peace of the City. However, he pointed out to Judas that this must be done carefully—that one bushy-bearded Galilean looked much like another, especially since most of the Twelve were related to Jesus and each other, and all of them spoke with a heavy, Galilean accent. So, would Judas be willing, the night before Passover, to identify Jesus for the Temple police (obviously, it would be unwise to arrest him in daylight)? Judas had agreed.[3]

Had there been any lingering doubts in the mind of Caiaphas as to his own best interests vis-a vis Jesus, Jesus himself resolved them the following day when without warning, he went into the Temple and, using a piece of rope as a whip, attacked the sellers of oxen, sheep and pigeons (for Temple sacrifice), and the money-changers who provided acceptable coins for payment of the Temple tax. While there, he loudly charged that those activities were contrary to Scriptures and an abomination to God. Driving these hucksters out of the Temple, he freed all the animals, and upset all the tables loaded with coins, which were pounced upon by the bystanders.

These extremely profitable businesses were run in partnership with Caiaphas and the chief priests, and so, should the patronizing of such activities be curtailed, even to a small degree, this illicit income would be diminished. Naturally, also, Caiaphas assumed it was no coincidence that this was the very moment Jesus Bar-Abbas and his Zealots attacked the Antonia, so that all Temple guards were away from their posts helping to put down the nearby riot and thus were not available to deal with Jesus. Also, it should be noted that the arrest of Bar-Abbas at the conclusion of that melee certainly had not significantly blunted the Zealot offensive of the moment.

It was clear that the Twelve and the Zealots had both—for different reasons—urged Jesus to take advantage of the Passover crowds for a public display—and both hoped for a declaration from Jesus which each could use to advantage. But why did Jesus agree to start the parade into Jerusalem— which some have subsequently been calling a Triumphal Entry?

Upon reflection, and taking into account the attitudes of Pilate—as I know the man—I think Jesus had become convinced on the Mount of Transfiguration that his execution by Rome was essential to fulfillment of his mission, and that the apparent popular support which a parade would generate might worry Pilate just enough to ensure that he would condemn Jesus. And, in retrospect, I think Jesus was right—Pilate was still full of doubts on that morning of pseudo-trials—was not sure Caiaphas and Annas had demonstrated Jesus to be a danger to Rome—but memory of the wild enthusiasm of the parade crowd just five days earlier, may have tipped the scales in Pilate's mind against Jesus.

✠   ✠   ✠

Since his ceremonial entry into Jerusalem on the first day of the week, Jesus and several of the Galilean Twelve were staying at the palace of Lazarus in Bethany. On the fifth day of that week, that is, Nisan 13th, after the Days of Unleavened Bread had commenced, Jesus sent Andrew and Thomas to Nicodemus to say that they would have supper that evening at his townhouse near the Essene Gate. Although Preparation day fell on the following day—the sixth day of the week—Jesus doubtless "knew" that he would be unable to celebrate Passover then. Moreover, most Galileans, as well as the Essenes, preferred this day for the ceremonial supper.

Also, to advance the Passover Supper by one day for personal convenience was not too unusual, but I was unaware of Jesus' intentions and so I missed his "last supper" ceremony. Being quite taken up with business matters at my Jerusalem townhouse I was not even aware of the passage of time that evening until, near the end of the second watch of the night, as it turned out, there was a frantic knocking on my outer door. Since the servants had long been in bed, I opened the door myself, to find a frightened young boy, nude save for his loincloth.

"Lord Joseph!" he blurted, "I am Mark, son of Mary. May I come in, please?" Then I recognized the precocious thirteen-year-old, whose widowed mother was sister of one of my trading partners, Aristobulus bar Nabas of Cyprus, and of Joseph Bar-nabas the disciple.[4]

I pulled him into the house and locked the doors. Taking a spare robe from the hall cupboard, I wrapped it around his shivering body. I soon realized that his shaking was from fright, not cold, as he told me the fateful news that Jesus had been arrested.

Suspecting that this was an illegal action and thus that events would move slowly, I took the time to have Mark describe everything that led up to this shameful event. He explained that his mother, together with several other women of The Way had been invited to assist the servants of Nicodemus in serving supper to Jesus and the Galilean Twelve at the Nicodemus townhouse. He recounted much of the conversation, which had followed the formal reading for this high holiday of the scroll of Solomon's Song of Songs; thereafter, Mark described the ceremonial supper of bread and wine instituted by Jesus.

I realized that "Eat my body … drink my blood," to the Aramaic speaker means, "Share my suffering, make my teaching a part of you"—but I sensed that Jesus had meant something more.[5]

"That is odd, Mark," I said, interrupting him. "Why something as common as bread and wine? Everyone eats that at every meal."

"Yes," replied, "that seemed to be Jesus' reason. He said, 'For as oft as you break this bread and drink this cup, you will remember me.'"

"Ah!—how wise," I nodded in agreement, "so we can never eat a meal without remembering him. Beautiful!

"But, Mark," I continued, "did they not eat the sacrificial meat, which is the chief item for a Passover Supper?"

"No, they didn't, Master Joseph," he replied, "and I was in the room the whole time, so I'm sure."

"That's most curious," I mused aloud; "so, this was quite purposefully a new tradition he was starting—perhaps to replace the Passover Supper for his followers—and perhaps even to signal an end to all animal sacrifices. And what else, Mark?"

He described the conclusion of the supper; that they went to the olive grove on the little hillock just outside the Golden Gate, to pray; that finally Jesus led them down the hill to the gardens of lush grass surrounding the Oil Press, known as Gethsemane. Here he took Peter, James and John farther into the garden to pray and meditate, while the rest built a fire of broken oil-keg staves to warm themselves, for the evenings were still quite cool in Nisan. It was getting late, and some of them slept as they waited.

Mark then said that suddenly he could hear a sound approaching that was the distinctive, clanking noise of armored, uniformed guards, and then the hurrying figures of servants carrying torches were seen. About a dozen armed Temple guards appeared, and with them was Judas who had left the Passover Supper before it was finished; in the background two of Pilate's soldiers were to be seen, although apparently they did not wish to be directly involved.

"Where is the Teacher?" Judas asked. One or two pointed, and the guards with the servants and Judas moved off in that direction.

"There was some shouting," explained Mark, "and then the guards returned, and two of them were pulling Jesus along between them. Peter had a sword and swung at one of the guards with it; he missed, but struck the ear of a servant—I guess fishermen don't know much about military skills. We all ran then, and one of the guards caught hold of my tunic, but I twisted loose and came naked—it was closer here than home, and my mother would no longer be at Nicodemus' house."

From the Gethsemane olive press gardens, Mark had followed the Valley of Kidron and the Valley of Hinnom outside the City walls, fully halfway around, to come in the Essence Gate nearest my home. From his description of events I judged that Jesus had been arrested about an hour and a half before the end of the second watch of the night, for it was now about the beginning of the third watch.*

---

*The Jewish "day" began at sundown (about 6 p.m. in April) and the first watch was from 6 to 9, the second watch from 9 to 12, and so on.

I thanked Mark for coming and said I would walk him home if he would wait a moment. I awakened my trusty Hosea and told him to go quickly to notify Gamaliel, Nicodemus and Sirach that Jesus had been arrested by Temple guards, and ask them to meet me at the courtyard of Caiaphas' palace. I felt sure the Chief Priest would attempt a rump session, since a formal session of the Great Sanhedrin, with a quorum of 23 present, could not legally be called before morning. Of course, he wouldn't try that anyway, because a capital case must be carried over to the second day, which in this instance would be on Passover and therefore forbidden. For these reasons I initially felt there was no urgency, except to see what we could do informally to effect Jesus' release.

As we walked toward Mark's home he continued to tell me more details of that fateful evening, and it seemed clear to me, as Mark talked, that Jesus knew this was the last evening of his ministry.

I voiced this thought, and Mark agreed: "Oh, yes, I think he knew that the Jews were about to take him."

"Mark, why do you say, 'the Jews'?" I asked, "we are all Jews, you know."

"Because that's what they say," he replied.

"But I'm sure you never heard Master Jesus blame his own race for such opposition—or even a tragedy as might befall him. What specific ones used such words, Mark?" I asked.

"Well, I guess it was mostly John bar Zebedee, for a month or more, and Matthew the publican has been saying it too, the last few days, I think."

"A very odd expression, Mark," I mused aloud, "though I suppose we should never be surprised at the words of a hothead like John—and, come to think of it, I guess that Matthew must deeply resent his whole race for condemning him because he chose to work for the Romans as a tax collector; I understand they banned him from the synagogue in Capernaum, too.

"But, Mark," I continued, "I hope that you will have the good sense to forget such an expression, regardless of what now happens to Jesus. When you are older you will understand that Jesus often preached with exaggeration, hyperbole and ridicule for emotional effect—but he well knew that the thousands of his loyal followers were all Jews, while his committed enemies were only a few dozen whose authority and illicit income was threatened by Jesus, and who are beholden to the largess of Caiaphas. Now, promise me, Mark, that you'll forget this unrealistic expression, 'the Jews' in condemning Jesus' enemies."

"Well, all right, Lord Joseph," he replied, but I didn't in fact sense any conviction in his tone. After all, John bar Zebedee, with his bombast and emotion, was, I am sure, a real hero to young Mark. Moreover, Mark, having been raised in Jerusalem mostly, and briefly in Cyprus, had no real understanding of the emotion of the Galileans and of the symbolism and hyperbole in their speech that Jesus most often used in his public harangues with his detractors.

Once the door of his house was opened to him, I turned and retraced my steps at a brisker pace, and with a sense of foreboding beginning to settle in me. I hoped, though forlornly perhaps, that Hosea might have brought some encouraging news.

My three friends, whom I had sent Hosea to notify of our disturbing news, were, like myself, members of the Sanhedrin; for that reason our belief in The Way of Jesus had to be kept secret for the time being. Like myself, Sirach had known Jesus since before his public ministry began, because Sirach's wife, Seraphia (daughter of Leah and granddaughter of Bianca) was a cousin of John the Baptizer and a cousin-twice-removed of Jesus.

CHAPTER NOTES:

1. Passover is the Jewish Feast of Unleavened Bread, the feast lasts for seven days after the Day of Passover (total of eight days), and commemorates the deliverance of the Jews from Egyptian bondage; Pharaoh agreed to their release after the seventh plague which involved the death of all firstborn in the land, from which the Jews were spared because they had marked the lintels of their doors with sacrificial blood and thus the angel of death knew to "passover" that household. Attendance at this Feast in Jerusalem was compulsory for all males; it was the most important religious event of the year. Jesus's passion, crucifixion and burial occurred from about 11 p.m., Thursday, to 6 p.m., Friday, just before Passover began.

2. See the "Story of Joseph of Arimathea," *The Aprocryphal New Testament,* M.R. James, Clarendon Press, Oxford, 1924, 1972 (p. 161).

3. The "hill folk" of Galilee all looked noticeably different than Judeans, both as to dress and the style of men's hair and beards; to the Judeans, all the Galileans looked "alike."

4. John Evangelist Walsh, in his book, *The Man Who Buried Jesus,* Collier/Macmillan, 1989, confirms that at the time Mark was "a boy of about twelve."

5. Aramaic scholar Dr. Rocco A. Errico adds that Jesus' words imply a spiritual fellowship *at the table* which would belong to the people of the kingdom of God, in lieu of sacrifice and priestly ceremony at the Temple.

CHAPTER THIRTY-FOUR

✠

Mock Trials of Jesus; Scourging

A.D. 33

I STOPPED ONLY BRIEFLY at my home to be sure that Hosea had been able to deliver my messages.

"Yes, Lord," Hosea said. "I was able to speak to each of the three, and they assured me that they would go quickly to Caiaphas' palace, and would meet you in the courtyard there."

The cock in our rear garden began his pre-dawn cacophony at this moment, so I knew that we were into the last hour of the night.

I asked Hosea to send me Reuben, whom I wished to accompany me to Caiaphas' palace in the westernmost corner of the Lower City. This young servant was always a comfort to have with me in dangerous times, for he was beautifully muscled, quick as a cat, and was good for my spirits as well because of his constant good humor.

Reuben had had a full night's sleep, and I almost none, and so I was hard-pressed to keep up with his long, purposeful stride, as we started on our short walk to the premises of Caiaphas. We turned into his courtyard and were searching for my friends among the already-burgeoning throng; the gray morning dimness was giving way to light as dawn approached in the east, to mark commencement of the first daytime watch of this sixth day of the week.[1]

Reuben's height gave him the first glimpse of them, and he swung me gently by the shoulder, pointed, and said: "There, Lord Joseph. By the thorn tree near the outer wall are Nicodemus and the others."

I let Reuben lead the way, brushing aside these curious people who always gather at the scene of any cruelty or punishment, as if by the watching and shouting they could somehow work off their own private angers, frustrations and hostilities.

All three gripped my hands and arms silently for a moment, as we shared feelings we were not yet prepared to voice. "What has happened?" I asked, as I stared across the yard at Master Jesus, who was slumped motionless, with head bowed, on a stone bench, while two soldiers stood nearby.

"We've had time to get only fragments of the story"—Nicodemus spoke in a low voice filled with emotion. "As I piece it together, Pilate was partially briefed in advance and has tried to stay aloof from the matter, but knowing all the while that he cannot. He sent two soldiers to observe while the Temple guards arrested Jesus near the Gethsemane olive press.

"It was an hour before the end of the second watch," he continued, "when they brought Jesus, alone and bound, to the chambers of Annas."

"But Nicodemus," I interrupted, "if he is to be formally charged, why were not all of us notified?"

"I believe it is now obvious that nothing has been nor will be done formally," he replied. "The actions taken so far involve only the *color* of formality, obviously for the mere purpose of misleading the public. As you know, we all learned later that Caiaphas' toadies among the chief priests secretly voted to arrest Jesus some time ago, and notice was promptly posted in a few select places where it would draw little comment. The required forty days having run, they now can make a superficial claim that last night's arrest was legal. As you know, the Sanhedrin sits twice a week as a court, but I am sure Caiaphas has no intention of brining Jesus to a formal trial."

Gamaliel then interjected: "Let me add that trial for a capital offense may be held only in the daytime and must be suspended at night; moreover, no such trial can be held the day before the Sabbath, since the action must be repeated on the following day."

"Returning to your question of what has happened," added Nicodemus, "the third watch of the night* was taken up mostly by Jesus' appearance before Annas, who, of course, has no status at all as a magistrate or

---

*The three hours after midnight.

hearing officer. Judas of the Twelve was in attendance at Annas' interrogation of Jesus, and he offered Peter the opportunity also; but Peter preferred to stay in the courtyard, and has since left the premises. We understand that Annas repeatedly attempted to get Jesus to state the religious beliefs he has been teaching, while Jesus responded to every question by saying that he had spoken openly and in the synagogues—that Annas should question persons who had heard him.

"As you know," Nicodemus continued, "Jesus was perfectly proper in his responses, because it is illegal to ask the accused to testify against himself and at least two prosecution witnesses must agree on all points supporting the formal charge—and there was no formal charge."

"One of our people was present," interrupted Sirach, "and he tells us that when Jesus continued to refuse an answer, a nod from Annas seemed to signal some of the hangers-on here in the palace of Annas and Caiaphas, and these of the rabble attacked Jesus with their fists and spat upon him saying, 'Why do you insult the priest?—why do you not answer his questions?'

"The Temple guards are required to maintain order," continued Sirach, "but they merely looked the other way and let the abuse of Jesus proceed for several minutes. You can see as he sits on yonder bench, still bound, that his face is badly injured from the brutality against which he could not defend himself."

I briefly told them of the activities reported to me by Mark. Then, I asked: "Why the present delay? And clearly, the guards will not let us go minister to Jesus."

"That's right," responded Nicodemus. "We tried to approach him earlier and were rebuffed by the guards. We understand that a hearing is to be held before Caiaphas, and I suspect that he is gathering as many Sadducee members as possible and admitting them through a side-door."

Suddenly, a trumpet blast from the Temple ramparts across the way confirmed the sun's appearance and signaled the day's official beginning.

"We'll probably see some action now," commented Nicodemus—"more of the *color* of propriety."

The ornate bronze doors, nearly twice the height of a man, now swung open at the entrance of the Sanhedrin's chamber. We hurried to take our accustomed seats behind the marble rail and noted that the proceeding would be public as the rabble were being permitted to crowd in to their allotted space and to overflow beyond it a considerable distance. It was most unusual to see at daybreak so many persons in attendance who obviously would normally have no interest in the affairs of government—this situation surely had been carefully planned and staged.

A subordinate priest solemnly but quickly declared the Sanhedrin in session for a public inquiry concerning Jesus ben Joseph,* a Galilean. Caiaphas then lost no time in calling several witnesses who, with no consistency among themselves, claimed that Jesus said he was the son of God, said he would destroy the Temple, said he could forgive sins, said Caesar could be given taxes but not honor, said the laws issued with the authority of the High Priest need not be obeyed.

At this point, Gamaliel interrupted to say that since no formal charge had been read, the witnesses' testimony seemed irrelevant.

With a fierceness that caused gasps around the room, Caiaphas retorted: "*Rabban* Gamaliel, do you presume to tell the High Priest how to conduct his office?" He emphasized the title *rabban* with a sneer, as much as to suggest that the honor of this title was unmerited, even though no other rabbi had ever been accorded the title of *rabban*.**

Gamaliel flushed a deep red and murmurs were heard around the chamber, but Caiaphas continued: "Captain of the guard, take the prisoner to Governor Pilate for judgment and punishment immediately; I will advise the Governor of the charges. The Sanhedrin is adjourned."

We were aghast, but we hurried with the crowd to the nearby courtyard of Pilate, whose residence and offices were contained in a part of the palace of the tetrarch, Herod Antipas.

This action seemed to be no surprise to Pilate, who was waiting in the doorway of his praetorium, though he seemed to resent it as an intrusion, and asked: "What accusation do you bring against this man?"

Caiaphas spoke to Pilate briefly in low tones; then brusquely Pilate responded, "Unbind him. I will examine him myself."

And, so saying, he took Jesus into the praetorium where Caiaphas and the rest could not follow because they would thus be defiled and unable to eat the usual Passover supper that evening.

Within no more than five minutes, Pilate returned to the courtyard with Jesus, saying to Caiaphas, "I find no fault in him—judge him yourselves under your law."

"But he speaks against Caesar," protested Caiaphas.

"The man is from Galilee; we'll let Herod decide," snapped Pilate with a half-smile, as if it would be a good joke to foist this unpleasant task on his counterpart.

---

*For everyday speech, most of us use the Aramaic word *bar* to mean "son of"—but in formal matters where Hebrew is used, the word *ben* is the proper usage.
**The rabban also had the function of *nasi*, the chief presiding officer of the Great Sanhedrin.

At a nod from Pilate, two of his soldiers took Jesus by the arms and propelled him—but not roughly—to the atrium of Herod's audience chamber. The chamber was not large, but quite a few of us were able to crowd in before Herod appeared and ordered the doors closed.

"Well, Jesus of Galilee," boomed Herod; "long have I heard many wondrous things of you—among such, that you are Messiah. So, make me a sign, that I may believe and do you homage."

Jesus stood mute.

Herod then asked many specific questions, but Jesus answered not a word. Several Sadducees from the Sanhedrin were there, and they proceeded to make many charges against Jesus.

Herod listened quizzically, and then to Jesus said, "So, how say you? Are these things true?"

Jesus spoke not a word.

Herod laughed with a great guffaw, and turning to the captain of his palace guard, said: "If he would be king, array him appropriately and escort him properly back to Pilate with my compliments and felicitations."

His soldier-guard was obviously prepared for this suggestion, and with much laughter they brought out a purple robe that was badly moth-eaten and put it on him. One of them handed Jesus the stalk of a large reed with its ball of roots still attached, saying, "Here is your scepter, Oh, King!"—and the guards knelt before him.

"But wait," cried another; "we must have the coronation." And so saying he brought forth a miter-crown, made wholly from the branches of a thorn tree, and, wearing leather gloves to protect himself, he viciously mashed the thorn-cap onto Jesus' head. The guard and the rabble laughed uproariously and cheered and applauded. Jesus' eyes were closed, but he made no sound and showed no emotion; I felt sure he had put himself into a deep state of meditation, withdrawing his conscious awareness and sense of pain.

I literally felt those thorns scraping the bone of my skull; it was excruciatingly painful for me and I immediately felt as bad a headache as I have ever had. From the pain in their faces, I know the others in our little group were suffering too. Looking around, I believe at least half of the Sanhedrin members were repulsed by such brutality.

The palace guard then promptly moved Jesus back to Pilate's porch, prodding him with their swords to ensure a fast pace.

Pilate himself seemed slightly repulsed by the sight, but gave no orders to his own soldiers, who took Jesus from Herod's guards, and stood around him grinning and making jokes among themselves.

Speaking to Caiaphas and the other Sadducees from his porch, Pilate said: "His crimes against Rome, if any, seem minor, so I will flog him and let him go." He nodded to the officer in charge of his soldiers and turned to go into his quarters, but Annas and Caiaphas blocked the way.

The officer ordered Jesus stripped to the skin, taking off his loincloth and the crown of thorns, as well—and then had his wrists tied to a post. Two burly soldiers themselves stripped to the waist, took up scourges, each made with two leather whips tipped by rough metal *flagra*,[2] and, taking turns, they methodically began to scourge him unmercifully. The metal tips of the *flagra* dug into the flesh with every stroke, and at each blow blood forcefully spurted from the wounds and rained for several feet across the courtyard.

Meanwhile, on the porch, Annas seemed to be doing most of the talking, trying to convince Pilate that Jesus should be executed. We were not close enough to hear, but later were told he was emphasizing those charges most nearly to be an offense of sedition against Rome.

Most of Jesus' verbal attacks on authority seemed of little interest to Pilate, but he was clearly concerned about Jesus' physical attack on the concessionaires in the Temple while his own troops were repulsing the Zealots at the nearby Antonia. Also, that and other happenings seemed to argue for at least a working relationship between The Way and the Zealots who were clearly seeking to overthrow the rule of Rome. In addition, Pilate knew that the Temple Tax and the High Priest's share in the profits of the Temple concessionaires was the source for the regular tribute to Rome, and the Emperor would take a dim view of any situation that delayed or diminished those payments. Finally, he had to be worried that the Zealots might be using Jesus, knowingly or not, to stir up the people, so that an armed uprising could be generated by the Zealots.

Having had two reprimands from the Emperor, these factors weighed heavily with him for he would likely not survive a third reprimand. At this point Annas made his subtle thrust, saying to Pilate: "It might not be well for you in Rome, were it thought you were not a friend of Caesar." The rabble, apparently on cue, then took up the chant, "Pilate is no friend of Caesar."

Pilate glanced down at his huge ring, bearing the words, "Friend of Caesar." 'We could see that he blanched a deathly white, and then in a moment a deep flush diffused his face.

Calling to the officer, he asked, "How many strokes?"

"Eighty-five," was the answer; which meant one hundred and seventy cuts from the twin whips of each scourge.

"Enough! Crucify him," was Pilate's curt response, and he wheeled and strode into his quarters. Pilate had no need for charges, formal hearing or standards of guilt under Roman law.

CHAPTER NOTES:

1. Jesus' "last supper" was on Thursday. The crucifixion was on Nisan 14 (Friday, April 3, A.D. 33); Jesus hung on the cross from 9 a.m. until 3 p.m.; the entombment had to be before the Sabbath started at approximately 6 p.m.; the Sabbath ended about 6 p.m. on Saturday; the Sabbath was from sundown to sundown—it was Nisan 15. Sunday morning (Easter) was the first daylight time after the entombment. Sundown (the day's beginning) was determined by the chief rabbi when three stars became visible; the Shofar (ram's horn) was then blown at the Temple. The year, A.D. 33, as date of Jesus' crucifixion, is now accepted by several authorities: P. L. Maier in *First Easter, First Christmas, Pontius Pilate;* H. W. Hoehner in *Chronological Aspects of the Life of Christ;* this was the 19th year of Tiberius' reign (A.U.C. 787) and the Jewish year 3793.

2. A bar-bell shaped piece of metal.

CHAPTER THIRTY-FIVE

✠

The Crucifixion

A.D. 33

*I*N THE TEN OR FIFTEEN MINUTES of this vicious scourging, each of us had to turn at least once to the wall and retch ourselves dry of bitter vomit. How can I tell you what it was like? Those bits of metal tore into his flesh all the way to the bone, until the flesh hung like ribbons on much of his body; with each stroke the blood was beat out of him in thin sheets of spray. The scourgers were almost as bloody as Jesus and, upon the order to stop, they went quickly to the horse-trough to cleanse themselves.

Jesus now hung slack from his wrists, with no sign of life in him. While the scourging was in progress, Jesus had shown no reaction whatsoever. His body had moved, yes, because his reflexes had caused him to flinch and jerk as the nerves and muscles were torn and lacerated—but he gave no emotional sign at all.

With his sword, the officer cut the cords from Jesus' wrists, and he collapsed in the dirt. Gamaliel approached the officer and asked if we could attend him and seek to revive him.

"All right. But have him dressed in five minutes," was his terse response.

Sirach and Nicodemus rushed to the horse-trough and hurriedly brought a tub of water, while Gamaliel and I stretched him out on the nearest bench. As I glanced up, I saw Caiaphas still standing by Pilate's porch, and with an evil sneer on his face.

After we applied dripping-wet cloths of cold water to his face several times, Jesus finally took in a massive breath of air, held it a moment, and then expelled it, as he managed to open his swollen eyes.

Seeing us, he asked, "Is it over?"

"The scourging is over," I replied, "but Pilate has ordered your crucifixion."

"Of course," he responded with no emotion, though his speech was definitely handicapped by the injuries to his face and lips. "That will not be so bad—if I can manage that walk." And he looked upward and prayed soundlessly.

We bound on his loincloth, and quickly put his tunic and his cloak and sandals on him, as the soldiers approached with the *patibulum* or crosspiece, on which he would be nailed. They tied this onto his shoulders and, although he staggered a little from the weight of it, he was able, amazingly, to move forward when the soldiers ordered him.

He left stains of blood on the paving stones as he walked, for we had had no time or ability to close his many wounds. Moreover, the many thorn punctures through his scalp caused rivulets of blood to trickle down his face, so I was sure he would shortly be blinded by the blood—but we were no longer permitted to come near him.

Two Zealot prisoners who had already been sentenced by Pilate were brought from the Antonia prison and added to the procession, which now started for Golgotha, the crucifixion site outside the walls.

☩   ☩   ☩

It was an act of impulse—one might even say of childish pique—but the anger and frustration had to come out somehow. In any event, after watching Herod's palace guards mash the mitre-cap of thorn branches onto Jesus' head as a mock-crown, and conduct a mock coronation ceremony, I had to do something about it.

Also, I've had too many accidental contacts with that particular variety of thorn tree. The spines grow in every direction, are strong and needle-sharp, and when they spur a person the poisonous resin burns the wound and makes the flesh itch and swell. Besides, I know there's no flesh between a man's scalp and his skull—nothing but lots of nerves and blood-vessels. So, I felt that nauseating, excruciating pain along with our Master when that mitre of thorns was mashed onto his head.

There was a slight bit of consolation to see that the guards and soldiers involved got stuck a few times in spite of the care and precautions they took. But not much consolation. And it was while watching Jesus stagger off toward Golgotha between Pilate's soldiers that I acted on impulse and out of anger.

I told my nearby body servant, Reuben, to run quickly to the house and bring our sharpest axe. In less than five minutes he was back and I instructed him to cut down the thorn tree from which Herod's guards had made the thorn-mitre—to cut it off right at the roots. A foolish act, no doubt, but I felt that somehow I was striking back at them—that never would such a vicious act again be accomplished by use of branches from *that* tree.

In a few swift strokes by my servant, the deed was done, and he asked what he should do with the tree. My mental sensibilities returned in part, as I saw the practical aspects of the situation. Although a thorn tree is worthless and a nuisance, we had indeed destroyed government property and my servant might well be punished for it if discovered. And so, I told him to take the tree with the axe back to my house—and then, the frustration still being with me, I told him to mix a strong solution of salt-water and bring it in a bucket and soak the roots where the tree had been—I had to punish the tree, since I couldn't punish anyone else.

He carefully held the smooth trunk near the butt of the small felled tree, and began dragging it away.

Sirach and Gamaliel moved down the street behind the soldiers toward the place of execution, but I held the arm of Nicodemus. I had been able to sense his quiet empathy as I supervised Reuben's attack on the thorn-tree. My anger was spent, but I was still striving to collect my thoughts.

"Nicodemus," I said, "Jesus is still my ward, though more than thirty-eight years old, and it will be my responsibility to provide for his body after the crucifixion. I have some instructions he gave me, and in addition to following them I will do as I think best, but I'm sure that much of what I do will be contrary to Temple law. Will you help me?"

"Of course I will," he promptly responded without asking to know the details. "Crucifixion is usually a slow death, but the High Priest will insist that the victims' legs be broken this afternoon to accelerate death by asphyxiation, so that the bodies will not be hanging when Passover starts at sundown. Thus, we may have but a brief time in which to do what is necessary.

"I'm sure the Twelve and the women will want a formal anointing, which will not be legally permissible until morning of the first day of the week. This, in turn, means preservative spices to hold down body decay—even though this is, itself, contrary to Temple law—and I hope you'll permit me to provide that item," he concluded.

His prompt response and his desire to make a meaningful contribution touched me. "Of course, and thank you, dear friend," I replied. "And you might send one or two servants with jugs of water and cloths this afternoon to wait for us at my new tomb. I must stop briefly at my house to give instructions and then will meet you at Golgotha."

As Nicodemus turned toward his townhouse to commence actions on the burial project, I saw Reuben with empty bucket, who had just finished his task of dowsing the thorn-tree roots, and I joined him to walk back to my home.

"Those roots will begin to rot in just a few days, Lord," commented Reuben.

"That's good," I said, for want of anything better to say. Then: "Where did you put the thorn-tree, Reuben?"

"In the garden house with the tools," he replied.

"Reuben, is Hosea still at home?" I asked, and he nodded in the affirmative. "All right," I continued, "and be ready in a few minutes to accompany me to Golgotha."

Hosea met us in the atrium, and I could tell by his sad face that Reuben had already told him of the crucial events of the early morning. "Hosea," I said, "I expect to bury Master Jesus in my new tomb this afternoon, but time may be short, so I'll need your help."

From my bed-chamber I brought out several items, and described others I would need him to bring to the tomb.

"I will have to go through the formality of asking Pilate for the body," I explained, "although I'm sure he will grant it to me. Thereafter, I will need to quickly buy burial cloths, because I don't want to take time to do so now. Consequently, I would like you to go at once to Sarah bat Israel in the Street of the weavers, and tell her I will come late this afternoon to purchase the best cloth she has for a burial shroud—it should be nearly three cubits wide and eight or nine cubits long, for the Master has a long body.[1] Also, I will need an ordinary smaller cloth as a carrying cloth."

"Yes, Lord, I'll do so right away," he replied. "I assume Reuben is going with you to Golgotha now, but may Rachel and I come along as soon as I get back from the Street of the Weavers and have everything ready to take to the tomb?"

"Yes, of course, Hosea," was my response, as I started out for Golgotha with Reuben. Reaching the outer door, we found Nicodemus waiting to walk with us—but a bit out of breath from hurrying.

✝ ✝ ✝

As we neared the execution site I saw that a crowd of curious was already gathered. The crucifixions had already occurred, and quite some distance back stood several women of The Way, and with them was my niece, Mary, Jesus' mother.

"Reuben." I said, "go ask one of the women how does it happen that Mary bat Joachim is here from Capernaum."

By a quick glance around, I saw no sign of the Galilean Twelve; having limited understanding of national politics in the Sanhedrin, they doubtless believed that their own lives were in jeopardy.

When I saw Sirach and Gamaliel standing with a few other members of the Sanhedrin, Nicodemus and I moved toward them. But, seeing us, Sirach and Gamaliel came toward us, leaving the chief priests they had been with.

"Many members do not agree with this action," said Sirach, "and most, like us, were not notified of the meeting."

"How did the soldiers treat Jesus?" I asked.

"Brutally. Very brutally," responded Sirach.

"I can't say that I've seen many crucifixions," commented Gamaliel, "but the cruelty toward Jesus can only be described as inhuman."

"In what respect?" asked Nicodemus.

The description by Sirach caused me to shudder from shock and anger: "They lay Jesus on his back on the cross-beam, the *patibulum,* and marked where his wrists were," he began. "Then, with a wood auger, they bored holes a full hand-span* farther apart. After spiking one wrist through the bored hole, three soldiers tied a rope just above his other elbow and pulled with all their strength, while the fourth soldier waited with spike and mallet for the wrist to reach the bored hole.[1]

"I think Jesus must have swooned," he continued, "for both of his shoulders were dislocated with a horrible sound of crunching of bone and tearing of flesh; thus the second wrist reached the other bored hole, and the second spike was driven through it."

"How can the Romans be so bestial?" asked Nicodemus in a shocked whisper, "and they've even put the crown of thorns back on his head."

"As you can see," Sirach resumed, "the three trees are stripped of branches and the top of each is cut off some five cubits from the ground;** there is a notch across the top in which they passed a rope and thus pulled

---

*About eight inches.
**About 8 feet; the cross-beam *(patibulum)* would be set about 7 feet from the ground.

up the *patibulum* with Jesus nailed to it. On the front of the tree was another notch into which the *patibulum* was securely nailed and roped.

"The next step was ingenious, as well as cruel," he continued. "They used chisel and mallet to cut a hole, some three fingers deep in the tree, into which the heel of his right foot was placed—this permitted the back of the right leg to lay flat against the tree. Next, the left foot was placed over the right, and a single spike was driven through both feet, and into the tree."[2]

"I had to look, but I couldn't look!" Gamaliel added in a hoarse whisper. "But what kept you two?"

"We were making arrangements for his burial," I said.

At this point Reuben came up to report: "Mary, Jesus' mother, received a message four days ago in Capernaum that was sent by Jesus himself, and which bid her to come be present at his death. She presently has swooned from shock and is being ministered to by the two Marys and the other women."

"Sirach," I asked, "when was the nailing of Jesus to the tree completed?"

"The third hour," he replied; "just at the end of the first daytime watch. The Romans, counting from midnight, will record it as the ninth hour.

CHAPTER NOTES:

1. The Shroud of Turin is precisely 8x2 Jewish cubits (see p. 3, *Shroud News*, No. 74, December 1992).

2. Visions of famous mystics have reported these plausible actions by the soldiers; see "The Shroud of Turin, Mystical Visions and Retrocognition," by this author, pp. 43-51, SINDON No. 34 (December 1985), Centro Internazionalle della Sindone, Turin, Italy. In Psalms 22:14 it is prophesied: "And all my bones are out of joint."

✠

Death and Burial of Jesus

A.D. 33

I REMEMBERED THE CRUCIFIXIONS that Jesus and I had watched here a few months ago and, although we had not stayed long, I now recognized the same horrible stages of dying, the struggle to breathe.

Jesus was terribly weak from the excessive scourging and the beatings and other abuse, and from his several falls along the way to Golgotha which Sirach had told us about, and especially from the loss of blood. Obviously, major blood vessels had been torn in the wrists, for blood ran continuously in rivulets down his forearms, dripping off all the way to the elbows.

His chest swelled abnormally with air he could not expel, until he could stand it no longer and, with a groan, he would push against his bleeding feet and raise his body nearly a hand-span higher. This eased the spasm in his abdominal muscles so that, with a whistling and gurgling of air through his bloody nostrils and mouth, his laboring lungs exhaled, inhaled, exhaled, as fast as possible to serve his air-starved body. He held this strained position for several minutes until his strength was exhausted when, with a combined sigh and moan he would sink downward leaving his wrists to take the full weight of his body.

I looked at the brigands with whom he was crucified and wondered, at first, why they were having a less difficult time. Then I saw the difference and realized the reasons. They had not been scourged and beaten and so were stronger, but especially, their shoulders and elbows had not been dislocated. Consequently, whenever they needed release of abdominal muscle spasms in order to breathe, they would pull up by shoulder and bicep muscles as well as by pushing against their feet. This combined effort Jesus could not make; he could only push against his feet.

Wondering why my mouth tasted so salty, I suddenly realized that tears were coursing down the creases alongside my nose and into the corners of my mouth.

It was already noon, the sixth hour, and he had hung there for three hours. How could he survive much longer? Of course, he was ruggedly husky and beautifully muscled, but no body could take the punishment he had taken. Nor had he had a bit of sleep during the night.

At this moment, Lazarus, who had been standing afar off, came over to be with Gamaliel, Sirach, Nicodemus and me. His eyes were red from much crying, and he said not a word as I put my arms around him and hugged him to me.

I noticed that the other Sanhedrin members were quietly leaving the area, after one of them had shouted: "You saved others, why don't you save yourself?" But most of them seemed embarrassed by this outburst, for only the rabble had shouted at him until this moment.

All at once the sky seemed to darken. I wondered if we would have rain but, looking up, I could see no clouds at all, yet the sun was definitely losing its brightness.

"What is happening to the sun?" asked Nicodemus.

"Is it the sun?" asked Lazarus. "I thought it was just my eyes—I can hardly see with my eyes so full of tears."

The sun was nearly straight overhead and could readily be seen, but it seemed so dim and gave out so little light—and yet no stars were visible. It was like the period after the evening ram's horn had been blown and before total darkness had fallen.

Jesus seemed to swoon from time to time and then would revive to strain mightily and force his body upward for breath. It was hard to tell if he was aware of our presence, but I think he was. Young Mark was sitting on the ground nearby with pen and papyrus in his hands—presumably hoping to write down any words Jesus might say. I knew that he hoped to eventually write a full account of Jesus' ministry; I had encouraged him in these plans because his considerable abilities demonstrated in the Temple Scribes' School would make him an ideal recorder for such a chronicle. For the same reason I had given similar encouragement to Matthew when he had expressed intentions of doing the same.

There still was no sign of the Galilean Twelve.

Finally, at the ninth hour, in mid-afternoon, a heavy earthquake shook the City. Gamaliel lost his balance and fell to his knees, but we helped him up as he said, in embarrassment: "I must have dozed off, though on my feet, but that quake awakened me."

At once we heard a loud cry from Jesus, and then he said: "It is finished!"

As he spoke these words, I saw on his face a look of relief, probably reflecting as well a feeling of a job well done—and even felt that fleetingly his face showed a look of *joy,* as he was being welcomed into the next life; his head sagged, chin on chest.

Suddenly, full sunlight returned, and yet no clouds were visible anywhere.

A messenger came to the centurion in charge of the crucifixion, who immediately called a soldier. Upon instruction, the soldier picked up a heavy club that had previously been brought along. Striding up to the brigand on the left, he swung the club viciously at the victim's shins, one after the other, bringing forth shrill screams that lapsed into a heavy groan that diminished as his breath was again shut off. Without the ability to push against his feet, the victim's chest swelled as he strained to pull by his arms alone. Finally, with a slight sigh his head slumped forward, chin on chest.

The soldier nodded to himself satisfiedly and turned toward Jesus. Jesus' chin was already on his chest. He was certainly dead, but the soldier strode purposefully toward him.

I ran forward and shouted: "No!"

Holding the soldier's arm with one hand and the club with the other, I said: He is already dead! There's no need to mutilate his body further."

The centurion walked over and asked: "What's the matter?"

I said: "Officer, I am Joseph of Arimathea and a member of the Great Sanhedrin. This man is dead. There is no need to break his bones. He is a member of my family, and I shall go at once to ask Pilate for his body. I am well known to Pilate."

"Very well," he replied. "But if you are to take the body, I am required to administer the death thrust with my lance.* You cannot object that I follow my orders."[1]

So saying, he unsheathed the thin blade at his side and in a single thrusting motion straight out from his shoulder he ran it through Jesus' chest from one side to the other. As he withdrew the blade, a small stream of blood flowed from the wound down Jesus' side and splashed on the

---

*Administered through the heart, regardless of whether the victim was dead or alive.

ground. I seemed transfixed and watched until the blood turned to water as the heart and chest cavity were drained.

"When you come back from Pilate," the centurion said to me, "be sure to bring a written authorization for the body."

"Nicodemus, let us go quickly to Pilate, so I may request the body and obtain a shroud," I said—at the same time waving farewell to Lazarus who was starting down the path toward his Bethany home with the women.

Nicodemus, with a nod, immediately set off with me at a brisk pace.

Pilate seemed surprised when I told him Jesus was already dead. He said, "I have been napping; yet, there hardly seems time for him to have died. I will have to verify it." So, calling a messenger, whom he instructed to run all the way, he turned to me and said: "I knew he was your relative and if he had defended himself I might have been able to spare his life. But without a denial or a defense, the suspicion of sedition against Rome was too strong for softer action. I am sorry."

I said nothing, and Nicodemus and I sat down to await the messenger's return. Very quickly he was back, and verified Jesus' death. Pilate immediately wrote out an authorization and handed it to me saying: "I'm sure you are doing the honorable thing, but I hope Caiaphas doesn't seek vengeance on you for it. He and Annas are very stirred up over this case."

We hurried down the street to the shop and home of Sarah bat Israel in the Street of the Weavers. She met us in her doorway, saying, "Is it true? Have they crucified our Lord?"

"Yes, it is true, Sarah, and we must quickly have the best linen shroud that you have made," I said.

"This is my very best, Master Joseph," she replied, bringing out a long cloth from under a table. "Our beautiful and strong Galilean linen thread, woven in an attractive twill such as they use for expensive silk in the far East. And I have treated it with a *struthium* solution that will prevent mildew and decay—it should last forever. My late husband and I learned weaving in Damascus."[2]

"It is a beautiful cloth," I agreed, "and though it needn't last that long, I will take it. What is the price?"

"Fifty silver shekels, Master," was her response. "I wish I could give it to you without charge, for the sake of our Lord Jesus. But I am a poor woman, with no man to support me."

"That's a pretty steep price, brother Joseph," said Nicodemus. "I think we can do better along the street here."

"No, we haven't time to shop or haggle," I replied, "and for Jesus' sake I would pay even more." Turning back to Sarah, I added: "And I must have a carrying cloth."

"Here, Master Joseph," she responded. "This one you may have for no charge."

We hurried back up the slope to stop by our respective homes. Hosea, Reuben and Rachel were waiting, at my gate with buckets of warm water and extra cloths. Before we had gone far, Nicodemus and his servants came from a side street and joined us; they were carrying the preservative aloes and the fragrant myrrh. As we reached the Garden of Tombs, all the servants turned in the entrance, except Reuben, and took all of our materials except the carrying cloth.

Back at Golgotha I showed Pilate's authorization to the centurion, who nodded after a perfunctory glance, and said: "My men will help you with the body."

One soldier with a pry-bar and a block of wood carefully extracted the spike from Jesus' feet, while another was already up a ladder behind the cross, cutting the thongs which bound the cross-beam in place and pried the spikes loose which held it to the tree. Then four tall soldiers reached the cross-beam and lowered it carefully to the ground. I quickly threw a cloth around Jesus' exposed loins[3] while the soldiers—who had been so brutal earlier—very carefully pulled the spikes from his wrists with their pry-bars. Borrowing a pair of leather gloves from a soldier, I wrenched the crown of thorns from his scalp and threw it as far as I could—and then had to support myself by the upright of the cross while my stomach heaved, though nothing came up.

"Shall we move his arms, first," asked Nicodemus, seeing that the heat of the day had already caused the onset of death-rigor, freezing Jesus' arms extended at angles over his head.

"No, not here," I said. My stomach had relaxed somewhat, and Reuben helped me lay the stiff body onto our carrying-cloth. We did so with difficulty, because from crown of head to soles of feet the entire body was covered with blood, making it extremely slippery.

Nicodemus and I each took a firm grip on the corners of the cloth nearest his head, we being separated from each other by Jesus' outstretched arms. Reuben easily lifted the two corners nearest the feet and brought up the rear of our little procession. We moved with care because of the rough ground but with no waste of time, and very shortly reached my new tomb, where Hosea with Nicodemus' menservants had already rolled the stone door aside.

Gently lowering our burden onto the grass in front of the tomb, I said to Reuben: "Now we'll have to force those frozen shoulder muscles, to bring the arms across the abdomen."

Joseph of Arimathea and associates at the burial of Jesus;
mural in the St. Joseph Chapel, Washington National Cathedral.

Photograph courtesy of Public Relations Office,
Washington National Cathedral, Washington, D.C.

Enlargement (extreme right): Joseph leading the cortege.

He nodded, and as I kneeled on Jesus' chest to keep the body from moving, Reuben held one arm above and below the elbow and, leaning the weight of his body against it, forced the arm around until it lay across the abdomen. As he was moving it, there were snapping and crunching sounds which caused some of Nicodemus' women servants to gasp.[4]

"Don't be silly," Rachel said to them. "That's nothing but frozen muscles letting loose."

Reuben then did the same with the other arm.

"Rachel," I said, "the body is totally covered with blood and too slippery to handle. You had best wash it off as it lays on the carrying cloth."[5]

"Yes, of course, Master Joseph," she replied.

Fortunately, they had brought plenty of cloths, and soon were able to have the body clean and dry, except for the slow oozing of blood from wrists, feet and side. She also had tied the wrists together because work on the shoulders had left the arms limp.

"Master Joseph," said Hosea, "the candles are in the sconces and lighted, the leather mat covers the wet limestone burial bench and the shroud is in place upon it; you can bring the body in now."

"Good," I replied. "Reuben, if you and I each take a shoulder, Nicodemus can carry the feet—but we'll have to go one at a time to get through the doorway."

At the doorway, Hosea reached from inside the tomb to support the head while I squeezed through the opening. Finally we were inside and gently placed the body on its back on one half of the long shroud.

First I placed a modesty cloth over the loins and a face cloth over the head. Reuben smiled with embarrassment and relief, and spoke softly to Hosea: "I wondered if the hands and crossed wrists were supposed to cover the loins—but they didn't! Now I see that the little cloth is to cover him there."[7]

"Of course," responded the older man. "Crossing and tying the wrists, as Rachel did, is only to hold the arms in place once the death rigor goes out of them,[6] especially to make it easier to slide the body into yonder burial chamber once the burial rites are completed."

Then, turning to me, Hosea continued: "Master, should we try to lift his chin up from his chest and straighten the left knee that's up in the air?"

"Better not try to," Nicodemus answered for me. "As a chief priest I've had a bit of experience with this sort of thing and it's not easy to change the death rigor—Brother Joseph will support the head with some of the extra cloths, I'm sure." Addressing me, he then asked: "Joseph, what's that you have there?"

"These are *phylacteries* that Jesus asked me to prepare and place on him. This is one practice that the Essenes especially follow, and which Jesus liked. As you know, they usually contain the special passages from two of the books of Moses in our Torah. Also included is the special prayer Jesus taught us," I replied. "They were all written by Jesus in his beautiful script on the thin rice paper from the East, and these tiny leather cases for them were prepared by my artist, Elias. Jesus wanted one on his forehead and the other on his right arm."[7] After attaching the phylacteries, in these last moments I also removed the Facecloth we had initially placed to soak up blood and, rolling it, laid it at the back of the stone shelf—thinking that later I might give it to Rachel, suspecting that she would probably save it as a memento. Reuben then handed me a downy feather which I placed on Jesus' upper-lip, as was our custom, to assure the certainty of death, unnecessary though it certainly was in Jesus' case.

While I watched the feather for ten minutes, I asked Nicodemus: "Is the aloes now ready?"

"Yes," he responded, "and this quantity in powdered form should be adequate to preserve the body until the first day of the week, without a doubt."

I put the *keirui* (tie) strips and other extra cloths under Jesus' head as support to accommodate the curvature of the upper back and neck caused by the death rigor that had set-in while he was still on the cross. I then put the *sudarion,* the jaw-band, beneath his chin and brought it to the top of the head where I secured it with a double-knot to hold the mouth closed, and stepped back to let Nicodemus take over with the aloes.

After he had thoroughly covered the body with the preservative, he then took a bag of the myrrh and sprinkled it around to give a pleasant odor. The rest of the myrrh he left in the bags.

"Master Joseph!" Rachel called from the doorway. As I turned and stepped toward her, she continued: "Mary of Magdala is here with a profusion of spring flower blooms which she asks be put inside Jesus' shroud."

"Let her come in," I responded, and Mary, seemingly embarrassed, approached the burial bench with a small basket heaped with blooms, and said in a hushed voice: "I know you are anointing him with myrrh and after the Sabbath we will have more pleasant ointments, but Master Jesus always said there was no fragrance to compare with the flowers that bloom in the springtime.

"I couldn't stand to watch the crucifixion but a few minutes," she continued, "so to occupy myself I have been picking blooms of every variety—I must have twenty-five or thirty different ones."

"Place them where you would like," I told her, and she put a handful against his hands, and the balance across the top of his head, like a crown.

"Thank you, so much," she whispered, bowing her head, as she turned and went out of the tomb.

We then carefully brought the other half of the shroud over Jesus' head and down the front of him to cover the feet; where there was excess cloth, especially around the feet, we tucked it in a bit. Then Nicodemus set the extra bags of myrrh, which would be used during the anointing on the first day of the week, along each side of the body to hold the sides of the shroud snugly against the body. He and I and Hosea then kneeled while Nicodemus gave a short prayer. We picked up all of the unused materials, extinguished the candles and went out.

As Reuben and Nicodemus' men were rolling the door into place and wedging it there, Pilate's representative came briskly up from the deep shadows where he had been standing and said: "Governor Pilate has ordered me to seal this tomb."

"That's perfectly all right!" I said. "Thank you."

As the rest of us all moved away toward the Garden entrance, two Temple guards moved up from the shadows and took positions a few steps from the tomb.

"It's just as well," I said. "He said he would arise. I don't want any more responsibility than I already have."

"Agreed," said Nicodemus.

As we moved toward the entrance, we could see Mary of Magdala, and Mary Heli, walk away ahead of us and out of the Garden. Obviously, they had stood near the entrance to see where we had put him.

We had but a few minutes until the Sabbath began. Without regrets, we had all barred ourselves from Passover participation by handling a corpse.[8]

CHAPTER NOTES:

1. The *coup-de-grace* was required by the officer in charge of a crucifixion whenever the body was given to the family of the victim (Barbet: *A Doctor at Calvary*).

2. Galilee grew a strong-fibered flax, and the thread from it was usually made manually on a spindle (hand-spun), not on a spinning wheel. Also, in ancient times linen was bleached with soapwort, which made the cloth more pliable and resistant to mildew, mold, and decay; about A.D. 600 this method of bleaching was discontinued.

3. Crucifixion victims were permitted to wear clothes on the way to the cross, but were stripped to the skin just before being crucified.

4. Morticians call it "breaking the shoulder girdle"—a very common necessity even today, since corpses often arrive frozen by *rigor mortis* and rarely in the position the undertaker will desire; see Barbet, *A Doctor at Calvary,* Doubleday/Image, 1950, 1963.

5. Applying to those years, was a tractate, "Semachot," which decreed: "A woman may shroud and gird the corpse of a man or woman; a man may shroud and gird the corpse of a man, but not that of a woman."—quoted by Joseph Marino in *Jewish Burial Customs,* St. Louis Priory, 1987. Several writers have given a-variety of "authoritative" reasons why the body of Jesus could be washed, could not be washed, specifying the proper and improper details. I have taken a practical approach: the body would have been so covered with blood and so slippery for handling that a routine cleaning (not a ceremonial cleansing) would be essential; Joseph and Nicodemus were violating so many technical rules at this point that propriety would be unimportant to them; *and most cogent,* the Shroud of Turin shows blood *only* where and *precisely* as the marks of passion dictate—there are no smears or "extra" marks of blood.

6. Rigor mortis generally lasts 24 to 48 hours; Jesus was in the tomb presumably until forty hours after his death.

7. Both a modesty-cloth and the phylacteries have been suggested by the observations of several of the investigating scientists, notably Dr. Whanger of Duke University and Dr. Haralick of Virginia Polytechnic Institute. Whanger, in a paper read at the international "Symposium on Science and the Shroud," in Paris, September 7 and 8, 1989, reported finding on the Shroud image, and validating, the blooms of twenty-eight varieties of Judean flowers which bloom in March and April; the blooms are clustered about the top of the head and near the hands of the Man of the Shroud.

8. R. E. Brown's excellent article, "The Burial of Jesus (Mark 15: 42-47)," in *Catholic Biblical Quarterly,* Vol. 50, pp. 233-245 (April 1988), discusses at considerable length what was permissible or not from Roman and Jewish viewpoints respecting the burial of Jesus, honorable or not, and its nature and details. However, he cannot decide "Why would a pious, law-observant member of the Sanhedrin [Joseph of Arimathea] want to bury the body of a crucified blasphemer?" Which seems quite odd, in that Brown does not even consider the repeated apocryphal and legendary explanation that Joseph was then the senior, surviving, male member of Jesus' family and was guardian for Mary and her children (even though they were all adults).

Part IV

The Post Resurrection Period

THE CHARACTERS IN
THE ORDER OF THEIR APPEARANCE

CHAPTER THIRTY-SEVEN

✠

Post-Resurrection Appearances

A.D. 33

T HE REPORTS THAT LAZARUS AND I RECEIVED from various sources confirmed with near-certainty that my days of freedom were limited—that
Caiaphas, Annas and other Sadducees were incensed over my participation
in the crucifixion events. I felt that at the very best I might have two months
in which to work out my arrangements before they would be confident
enough to act against me. Nicodemus in a recent visit advised that information he and others at the Temple had heard there and in the halls of the
Sanhedrin were confirmatory of the ominous earlier reports.

Now that word from Thaddaeus assured me of the safety of the Shroud
of Jesus and the welcome new home it had in the kingdom of Edessa with
the ruler Abgar, I could address myself with a near-tranquil mind to the
business and family problems to be resolved in connection with my projected self-exile. Actually, the basic decisions concerned me hardly at all.
As soon as I realized that exile was the only practical answer, in my mind
the principal conclusions seemed nearly automatic—where I would go (to
Britannia, of course!), who would go with me, and the disposition of my
property and business interests, were very clear in my mind.

These past three weeks had been usefully devoted to developing details
and working out arrangements to implement those basic decisions, and
so I had stayed rather close to Arimathea and had heard but little of the

activities of the Eleven disciples. After a rereading of the exciting letter from Thaddaeus, I decided that it was time I learned more of the Resurrection aftermath and that I share Thaddaeus' letter with Thomas. Accordingly, I sent a servant by mule to his home in Lydda, only ten miles along the road to Jerusalem, on the chance that he might be there, inviting him to come to me for a day or two.

The afternoon was scarcely half gone when my servant returned escorting a broadly smiling Thomas. We embraced warmly for at least a full minute, and then Thomas spoke: "Dear brother Joseph, I was home barely an hour from a visit in Jerusalem when your servant arrived, so I gladly dropped everything for the opportunity to spend some time with you and I can see in your eyes that you have much to tell me; I also have much to say, but please, speak first."

Once we were comfortably settled and some cooling wine had been served us, I attempted to tell him of all my interim activity since I had last seen him at the home of Mary, Mark's mother. I began with the story Rufus Rubicus had told me of the dramatic happening he had seen at the tomb and of Caiaphas' reaction to the guard's story, since there had not been opportunity to tell him of it that night with the Disciples.

"Well!" exploded Thomas. "Rufus' account certainly confirms our belief in a spiritual event that you call 'Resurrection' which marked the Shroud and dematerialized the body; it also explains Caiaphas' smug attitude since then.

"Agreed," said I, "and before going further, I should ask if you heard details of that event they called the 'mount of transfiguration'?"

"Just barely, with neither details nor much sense," he replied.

I thereupon recited the event as I had pieced it together from conversations with James bar Zebedee and Jesus, much as I had described it for the friends at Nicodemus' house.

"Amazing, truly amazing," was his comment, "and I agree it must have been the turning, point for Jesus; and now, what about the Shroud?"

I described in detail the beautiful casket Elias had made for the cloth, and of the timely arrival of the transmittal document from Flavius Rubrius, as well as the special copy from Stephen of the Sayings and Discourses of Jesus. Then, to cap my recitation, I handed Thomas, somewhat dramatically I admit, the letter I had just received that morning, saying: "Here is a letter from our emissary, Thaddaeus, in Edessa, which will interest you, I'm sure."

As he finished reading, he looked at me and roared, "Fabulous!"—and started right in to read it through again.

After the second reading, he handed the document back and said: "We could not have asked for a better or more spectacular reception, nor could we want a better custodian of the Shroud than our brother, Thaddaeus. Wonderful! Wonderful!"

"I agree completely," was my response, "and now, what of The Way, and of the Disciples?"

"I don't mean to deprecate the importance, and even the grandeur, of what you've been telling me and of what I just read, my dear Joseph," he replied, "but you've heard nothing until you hear me!"

"First off," he continued, "was my meeting with the Master in the presence of the others. As I told you I would, I proceeded to spend every evening in the home of Mary, widow of Simeon from Cyprus, and mother of young Mark. A full week and a day after the day of the Resurrection, on the evening of the following second day of the week, the Eleven of us were present in Mary's house and Peter suggested that we try from memory to reconstruct that beautiful sermon Jesus preached on the mountain in Galilee—you remember, when he started by saying, 'Blessed are the poor in spirit...'?

"Yes, I remember being told of it," I replied.

"Well, we spent about an hour at it, and probably got it fairly complete and accurate, with young Mark writing it all down. Then Peter said we would stand in a circle and link arms, and each pray in turn, and he would conclude with his prayer. I interrupted him, saying, 'Just a moment, brother'—and I went to the outer door and to the inner one, to see that both were fully barred. When Peter concluded the prayer session and we opened our eyes, there stood Jesus in the center of our circle!"

"Perfect! Thomas," said I, "and then what?"

"As you might expect," he responded,, "I had taken some joking and some criticism during the week for saying I would not believe in his reappearance until I could examine his wounds myself. John bar Zebedee was particularly caustic because I didn't accept the word of the Ten. Then—there he was! The first thing he said, and with the warmest smile possible, was: 'Thomas, my beloved, put your finger in the holes in my wrist and in my foot, and place your hand here in the gash in my side.'

"I did it, dear Joseph! And his flesh was solid and the wounds were real! And then I embraced him passionately; and his embrace of me was the strong squeeze from a carpenter's biceps and forearms. We held each other for more than a minute," Thomas continued, "and when we released each other, Jesus said: 'Some believe with faith alone. Others must have evidence or sound reason, but *their* belief endures, unshakable. Both are blessed.'"

"What a fantastic experience!" I said. "Did he stay long?"

"Just briefly," Thomas replied. "Long enough only to instruct us to go back to Galilee where he would talk to us at greater length. A knock on the inner door was by Mary, bringing refreshments. We looked to her, naturally, but when we looked back, Jesus was gone and the outer door still barred."

"So, you went to Galilee with them?" I asked.

"Yes, I couldn't afford to separate myself from them as long as Jesus continued to be present," Thomas replied.

"Had there been other appearances by Jesus in that interval of eight days?" I wanted to know.

"Only to Peter, as far as I know," he replied. "And Peter was rather reticent when we tried to draw him out. It must have been very important, but also I sense that Peter is unsure of the full meaning of the communication, which accounts in part for his reticence."

"Do you suppose Jesus confirmed the primacy of Peter?" I asked.

"That was flatly asked of Peter," Thomas replied, "and Peter's answer might be described as, 'Yes, *but*'—for he certainly would not or could not tell us any details. From other, seemingly casual, comments that he made, I gather he has misgivings as to his own abilities for he said a couple of times, 'I'm no spokesman and I'm no preacher!'"

"These are difficult times for us all and the more responsibility the more difficulty," I observed; "I have sympathy for Peter, but I'm sure Jesus knew who he was picking—he had known Peter most of his life. I'm sure he will find a way to guide and to empower Peter."

"I'm sure you are right, brother Joseph," he replied; "but to get back to my story—we returned to the shores of the Lake without incident, and after a couple of days of restlessness on the part of all of us, Peter said, 'I'm going fishing.'

"I spent nearly two weeks loafing along the shore, as did Matthew," Thomas continued, "while the other nine spent their days in the fishing boats with only moderate success; finally some wandered off to do other things until there were only five in two boats, and we two on the shore.

"And no sign of Jesus?" I asked.

"That's right," he replied, "until three days ago. The two boats fished all night near the southern end of Lake Galilee, while Matthew and I slept on the beach nearby. At daybreak they were rowing to shore to share a meager breakfast with us, when a stranger in a white cloak walked from the shore a few steps into the water.

"'Young fellows, have you caught anything?' he called to them—and Peter responded in the negative.

"'Throw your net between the two boats,' instructed the stranger in authoritative tones. Those in Peter's boat promptly threw in a net accordingly, and instantly a school of large fish swam into it. The men in both boats worked furiously, and by beaching the boats were able to save most of the huge catch that was straining the net."

"Was this Jesus?" I asked.

"Well, none of us realized it," said Thomas with a smile, "but I guess you can empathize on that. Matthew and I had our eyes glued to the struggling fishermen, and the fish had all of their attention. As they finally got fish and boats under control and ashore, we all turned to the stranger and saw that he had a good fire going, heating a flat rock, and that on it were cooking fish and dough that was just turning into beautiful bread. Suddenly, one of our number shouted, 'It's the Master!' Indeed it was, and he told us, 'Come and eat'—which we did. I never ate better fish and bread, and while we were eating Jesus took Peter aside and talked long and earnestly with his arm about Peter."

"You couldn't hear what was said?" I asked.

"No, and Peter hasn't mentioned it since," Thomas said. "Then, as they came back to us Jesus said to us all: 'I will meet you on our special mountain (pointing to Mount Tabor) in two weeks' time, and after that I want you to return to Jerusalem and wait there for the Spirit of God to empower you fully for the work that is ahead.'"

"How long did he stay with you?" I asked.

"How long, indeed," said Thomas with a laugh. "We all looked at Mount Tabor as he pointed. When we looked back he was gone, and only the fire was there to remind us he had been with us."

"So, he expects you back at Tabor in about ten more days," I observed. "And you'll be there, I assume."

"Oh, yes, and wouldn't you like to go, too?" he replied.

"I certainly would," was my quick response. "Why don't you come by here and we'll ride up Via Maris, The Way of the Sea, together?"

"Agreed. I would like that," he responded. "We should make it easily in three days to Nazareth; I'll be here at your house by sun-up on the second day of the week."

"Excellent!" I responded. "I'll check with the caravansary to learn if a protected group will be coming through at that time; if none is, I'll arrange for some reliable guards to travel with us."

✠

CHAPTER THIRTY-EIGHT

Appearances to Peter and James

A.D. 33

O F COURSE, Thomas arrived when he had promised—in fact, nearly an hour before sun-up, and so we had time for a satisfying meal before mounting our mules for the one-mile ride to the caravansary on Via Maris at the outskirts of Arimathea.

I explained: "We are indeed fortunate, as a small military mission arrived last evening, returning to the Legate of Syria in Antioch after a month's stay in Egypt. As it turns out, the tribune in charge remembered meeting me briefly a couple of years ago when I chanced to be in the company of our secret brother, Petronius the centurion, and Pontius Pilate. So, he cordially agreed that we could ride with them as far as Nazareth."

"Wonderful!" was Thomas' response, and after a pause: "You know, thrills of excitement have been running over me ever since I was last here, as I recall the so cogent report from Thaddaeus, and think of the profound implications to be sensed in the power of Jesus' mystical, yea, mysterious, burial shroud with its enigmatic markings.

"Of course, I must wait with the others," he continued, "for the em-powerment in Jerusalem that Jesus spoke of on the shore of Galilee, but thereafter I shall be anxious to go quickly to Edessa to assist Thaddaeus—for there must be many challenges and opportunities that are arising there, in which I am anxious to share."

"Ah yes," I responded with pleasure. But I had time for no further comment as we pulled up at the caravansary where the tribune was just checking last-minute details with his staff of about a dozen, who were well-armed and nearly ready to start.

The tribune greeted us warmly, as I introduced Thomas, and we were conducted to our places near the middle of the group. Very graciously, the tribune took from me the lead-rope of our pack-mule, saying that it would be attended at the end of the column along with their pack animals. And, without further ado, we started off at a rather brisk pace—so, I was gratified that our mules were young and strong, and thus would have no difficulty keeping up.

We spent the first night near the town of Yisbub, and early the second afternoon we stopped temporarily opposite Caesarea, so that the tribune and his aide could ride off at a gallop to pay respects to Pilate, whose villa was some ten miles from us on the heights overlooking Caesarea.

After their return, their mounts were given a rub-down and permitted to follow with the pack animals, while the tribune and his aide mounted fresh animals and we started again at a very good pace. By pressing hard we reached the edge of the great plain of Esdraelon, where the River Kishon flows northwestward past Mount Carmel and into the Great Sea; we arrived just a few moments before total darkness, and all were quite ready to stop. After walking around briefly, to work the stiffness out of our muscles and joints, we shared a simple meal with the soldiers, as we had the previous night at their invitation.

Crossing the Plain and the River the third morning, we pressed on, and ultimately left the military troop near the outskirts of Nazareth, shortly after noonday. We had grown genuinely fond of the entire company in this brief time, and expressed to them and the tribune our profound thanks, and my greetings to be conveyed to the Legate in Antioch.

The journey had been much faster than would have been possible with a commercial caravan, and, of course, much safer. Thomas and I had talked almost the entire way of the excitement and wonderment in our lives during the formal ministry of the Master Jesus. Also, this gave me the chance to discuss with him my thoughts respecting plans for my exile, and to receive his observations and suggestions. He assured me again and again that he would be pleased to be helpful in any situation that he could.

"One of the greatest services you can render me," I said, "will be to keep Thaddaeus fully informed of the progress and problems of The Way of Jesus, and concerning all the disciples and their activities, since Thaddaeus will regularly communicate with me in Britannia and convey all such news."

"You may be sure that I will," he replied, "and as I probably will move to the lands farther east, I will regularly send communications to Thaddaeus to keep him up to date."

Thomas had no difficulty finding the other ten disciples at the home of one of Mary's relatives in Nazareth, and she herself had just arrived from Capernaum. After greeting all my relatives and friends, I sought out James bar Zebedee for a private talk—remembering how helpful he had been in explaining to me the events on the "mount of transfiguration."

"James," I began, "Thomas has told me of the appearances of Jesus in Jerusalem and on the shores of Galilee, but I wonder if you could enlighten me as to his private appearances to Peter on the day of Resurrection and of their conversation together on the shore?"

"I'll tell you all I can," said James,, "but it is not much, simply because Peter understood so little of what was told to him. The first occasion, on the day of Resurrection, Jesus appeared to Peter where he was staying with friends near Jerusalem, fearful that the Temple police would arrest him next.

"There were really three elements in both of Jesus' conversations with him. One was to assure him that he, Peter, was to be the enduring leader of the world-wide movement of The Way. Secondly, that he would have to accept, for a time, the precedence of Jesus' brother, James, as titular head of the movement with headquarters in Jerusalem. This was for several reasons: the Temple and secular authorities would recognize James' right of primogeniture as eldest surviving brother; James' piety would impress religious leaders; and James' demeanor and erudition would permit him to be more effective in proclaiming our truths and in disputations with others."

"Although I can see reason for Peter's confusion," I observed, "I am sure he would be the first to acknowledge the sensibleness of those comments about James."

"Oh, of course," responded James bar Zebedee. Peter is quick to disclaim any pretensions toward administration and negotiation. He says, 'I am no diplomat, nor could I convince or confuse anyone with fancy talk. I'm even a poor preacher, though I have hopes in that direction.'

"But the third element of these conversations with Jesus was perhaps the most confusing of all to Peter," James continued. "Jesus insisted to him that he had sheep in strange and distant pastures to whom Peter must minister as their shepherd—that mission, Jesus assured him, would be explained to him in due time by Jesus' own voice in a dream. As they talked on the Shore, three times he asked Peter if he loved him, and after Peter's third vehement affirmative, Jesus said:

"'Feed my sheep in the strange and distant pastures that I will show you.' Peter is continuing to worry over the meaning of these latter words, because he doesn't think Jesus means only the Jews of the diaspora."

"His puzzlement is understandable," I agreed. "But tell me, James, if Jesus' brother, James bar Joseph, is to have such a prominent role, has *he* been advised of it by Jesus? Certainly, James, even more than his mother, Mary, was concerned that Jesus was damaging the family name by his preaching."

"I'm sure that Jesus did appear to James bar Joseph," said he, "but James is not very communicative. I understand that he did share some of the conversation in that appearance with their youngest brother, Jude, but so far Jude, himself, has said next to nothing of what transpired between his two oldest brothers."

"Then I will have to see if my great-nephew, Jude, will confide in me," I responded. "Thank you so much, James, for enlightening me to this extent."

After I had eaten the evening meal with the family of Mary, I asked young Jude if he would walk with me in the cool of the evening as the sun set, so that we could talk privately beyond the edge of town. Obviously, the word had been passed from one to another that Jesus would appear in a day or two, and so there were large numbers that were spending the warm night in the open at the edge of Nazareth, and we had to walk beyond them to find privacy for ourselves.

Jude was a favorite great-nephew of mine, I suppose because he was always so pleasant of disposition and friendly, and also because he had willingly become one of Jesus' disciples—one of the Twelve—right from the beginning. He was now a very burly and husky 26-year-old—one who could probably best even Simon-Peter in any physical endeavor. But, because he was the youngest of the family, he naturally was called Jude rather than his birth-name of Judas. Later, as the personalities of The Twelve began to abrade and exacerbate one another at times, Jude took an attitude of dislike toward Judas-Iscariot. This was most out of character for Jude, and he seemed to be somewhat embarrassed by it, but could not help himself. In any event the feeling was so deep that he didn't want a name that could be confused with Judas-Iscariot, and so he would often say, flippantly or sometimes angrily: "Call me Lebbaeus, or call me Thaddaeus, but don't call me Jude—I'm no Judas!" Since the death of Iscariot, I sensed that he no longer had an aversion to the name, Jude.

"Jude," I said, after we had found a quiet and secluded spot where we could sit and look into the gorgeous color of the western sky where the sun had set a half-hour previously, "I would consider it a great favor if you would tell me what you can about Jesus' appearance to your brother, James, the week of the Resurrection."

"Uncle Joseph, I will gladly tell you all that I can, but it isn't much," he said, as his friendly smile spread across his face. "I'm fairly sure that James has not yet told it to anyone but me—still, he was even more than his usual reticent self on this subject."

"I appreciate that James doesn't talk much about himself or his own feelings," said I with a smile, "unless it is to let someone know that he disapproves of their behavior."

"Yes," Jude agreed, "he is quick enough to do that, as I have reason to know so well. However, since Salome married and is in her own home, Joses married and moved away, and since James so greatly disapproves of Simon's Zealot sympathies (as well as of his having been a Disciple of Jesus—which 'stigma' I am just beginning to lose in his eyes) he has been closer to me in recent months than ever before—in fact, more like the brother he's never been to me, than the head of the household which has increasingly been his role with Jesus gone preaching so much of the time.

"Well," he continued, "to answer your question—only an hour or so previously on that great and mind-boggling first day of the week, James had been told of Jesus' death by a Roman soldier, a secret follower of The Way, who rode to Capernaum on a fast horse, by the short route straight through Samaria. And then, suddenly, mid-morning on that day of Resurrection, Jesus appeared in the house in the presence of James, who was otherwise alone. Jesus was accompanied briefly by our father, Joseph, as validation to James of Jesus' status and right to be honored. Joseph stayed but a short while and then disappeared. Jesus showed James the marks of his Passion and quickly convinced James that indeed he had risen from the dead. James was so overcome with shame because of his unbelief during Jesus' ministry that a considerable time must have passed before Jesus could assure him of forgiveness. This part of their meeting James has said little about. He told me that he was completely convinced of Jesus' messiahship and sought to kiss Jesus' feet. But Jesus lifted him up and embraced him, and said, "Are you not still my brother, and have I ever ceased loving you?"'

"His reluctance to talk about that part of the visit is certainly understandable." I said. "I have heard that even in the synagogues in Nazareth and Capernaum he is known as James the Pious and James the Just."

"True—and James has been vainly proud of those 'titles.'" Jude replied. "But once he could compose himself, James then begged Jesus to tell him what he, James, could do to further the kingdom of heaven and The Way of Jesus.

"At this point," Jude continued, "Jesus told James that he was needed as the leader of The Way in Judea, and as the conscience and religious guide to the world-wide effort of the Disciples. He explained that this was James' duty as the oldest surviving brother, and that he would be accepted at the Temple since it was fitting for him to succeed Jesus as leader, and also that the piety of James would make him more acceptable to the priests of the Temple and of the synagogues—and that their good-will would be necessary for a time."

"James was willing, was he?" I asked.

"Deep down, I don't think he had any doubt or hesitancy," said Jude with a small smile. "That sort of role appealed to him. However, he says that he told Jesus he would go to the Temple in Jerusalem and pray without ceasing to obtain guidance from the Father, whether to accept this commission. He did do that and when he returned he assured me that he was willing to accept that role—and asked that I stand ready to intercede with Peter whenever necessary to ensure tranquility in the movement."

Jude continued· "Jesus had told him that Peter was to have a world-wide role and would not be much in Palestine after a while, and as soon as Peter grows in spirituality and in confidence. I think James senses that he and Peter might often disagree, but he would prefer it not to be face-to-face—he recognizes Peter as a physical man, and knows that he is not. Also, he knows that The Eleven will continue to look upon Peter as their leader."

✝

CHAPTER THIRTY-NINE

The Ascension

A.D. 33

THE FOLLOWING MORNING seemed pregnant with momentous event about to happen, although there was nothing specific I could name that would give one such a thought. Stopping by the house where Peter was staying I asked him when and where we should expect to see the Master.

"Brother Joseph," he replied, "I am new at this business of feeling or hearing guidance, and so I am unsure of my own thoughts, but it is my present inclination that we should start onto the mountain about mid-afternoon."

I thanked him, and moved on to visit with my niece, Mary, at a nearby house that was the residence of her oldest daughter, Salome, and Salome's husband. She seemed glad to see me, but at the same time somewhat embarrassed.

Hoping to put her at ease, I said, "Mary, my very special niece, I am pleased to find you with a serene face and apparent good health. I saw you at the crucifixion, but thought that a poor time to impose my presence, since the other women were attending you and I was quite preoccupied with things to do."

"My dear, dear Uncle Joseph," she replied, "I have wanted so much for the opportunity to tell you of my gratitude for begging the body of my son and for burying it so lavishly. I dread to think what would have happened to him if you had not so acted."

"You have no need to give me special thanks, dear Mary," I said. "What I did was no more than my duty as the guardian of your children, and it was besides a privilege to do the little I could. It was my chagrin that I could have done nothing to prevent his death."

"You did all anyone could have in the circumstances," she replied. "I know now that he felt compelled to permit that event, and I think I would not be able to bear my own guilt but for the complete cleansing and forgiveness I felt from him that morning before your tomb."

"Yes, Mary," I said. "We heard from Mary of Magdala your story of that meeting, and it was both beautiful and touching."

We visited for more than an hour and then I ate a light noonday repast with Mary and Salome, before moving on to visit with others.

About the third hour of the afternoon, I noticed that various groups had begun to move eastward along the ridge which connected Nazareth to Mount Tabor at a point half-way to its crown. I noticed Peter and the other Disciples a short distance ahead of me, and so I followed along. After a half-hour's easy climb, we reached the rounded, grassy summit and began to spread across it. In the approximate center was an outcropping of rock as high as a man, and all seemed to assume that if Jesus appeared he would stand there; it was probably the remnant of an old building foundation, and several fragments of ruins across the mountain-top indicated the likelihood that it had been fortified in centuries past. The Disciples stood at the base of this rock, and I moved over to join them.

As the crowd began to quiet, Peter raised his arms and started to pray, his rich, strong voice carrying easily to the crowd of some five hundred persons. We stood with heads bowed as he prayed. When he finished, we raised our eyes and there stood Jesus on the rock in our midst.

His strong but melodious voice, which we knew so well, began to charm us as before, and the crowd settled down to enjoy his discourse. For myself, I was so enthralled by his presence that I could not tell you a word that he said. As I watched, I tried to decide whether anything about him seemed different, and I could only tell myself that his garments and his skin seemed to glow as if giving off light—and I concluded that this must be much as James, John and Peter had described him during the "transfiguration" they had observed. But he certainly seemed solid enough, and I could not see "through" him as they had seen through Moses and Elijah.

He spoke to the crowd for something less than an hour, gave them a benediction, and then spoke to us in a lowered tone, saying, "I will meet you here in the morning as the sunrises."

I must have blinked my eyes, for suddenly he was gone.

☩   ☩   ☩

The next morning I awoke well before sun-up, and walked back to the mountain-top with the Disciples and a few others. It was the sixth day of the week, six weeks since the crucifixion and forty days since the Resurrection. When we reached the crest, Jesus was already standing on the rock.

As we approached him he began speaking: "Be strong and be not afraid, for I shall be with you always. Return to Jerusalem and wait. Pray and meditate there as I have taught you. Put your affairs in order both at home and in your work together, for there soon will be no time for such. In fullness of time, you shall be clothed with power from on high. When this occurs you will know that the time has come to carry my message to all people—in Judea, Samaria, Galilee, and to the ends of the earth."

He then raised his hands and blessed us, and as we watched, he seemed to be lifted up—but then he seemed to melt into the air, and was no more.

⁜ ⁜ ⁜

It was but ten days until Pentecost, which I planned to spend with the Disciples in Jerusalem, but I started to feel an urgency about my personal affairs, and so the same morning of Jesus' ascension into heaven I began my return to Arimathea without delay, in order to complete the detailed arrangements for my exile.

My family trading and metal-working business was now out of my hands and firmly vested in five dominant persons or families who had long been a part of the venture, and the executive head would be Tobias, brother of the deceased Josiah of Bethany. Tobias was uncle of Martha, Lazarus and Mary; he would continue to operate from the office of the business in Jerusalem, and had bought my town-house nearby (which I would soon be vacating). Although all principals were totally trustworthy, one could never be sure about the loose tongues of some servants and lesser employees, and so I could but accept the likelihood that my actions would reach Caiaphas' ears within a few days.

My home and personal property in Arimathea were already disposed of and sales were final on all of my holdings hereabouts. My investments and cash balances in the hands of bankers in Antioch (Syria) and in Rome had been very significantly increased in the past month, for they would be the assets which would support me and my family the balance of our lives. I had purposely severed all interests in our parent company so that Caiaphas would have no excuse or legal basis for harassing that enterprise. At the same time my personal interest in businesses outside of Palestina (as the Romans called our Jewish homeland) had markedly increased, especially in the shipping firm in Tyre with which we had long been associated, and in the mines of Britannia where I would be participating much more actively.

It was now fully settled which persons would accompany me to Britannia. In addition to several of our most valuable servants, these included my wife, Elyap, and our children Anna and Josephes and their families; my sister, Enygeus, with her husband, Hebron, and large family, were committed to come in a year or two, perhaps by travelling with the entourage of Lazarus.

One of my most difficult decisions was to leave my servant, Hosea, behind; his age and frail health clearly dictated it, as well as the need for his presence that I sensed in his family. I need only have said the word, however, and Hosea would have come gladly and without hesitation. My principal support would be my servant, Reuben, and my son, Josephes, and in their capabilities I had total confidence.

Early on the day of Pentecost, which would begin officially at sundown, I arrived at my town-house in Jerusalem and immediately sent a servant to the home of Mary, widow of Simeon from Cyprus, asking that Thomas come visit with me. Within an hour the servant was back, accompanied by Thomas.

"I rather expected to hear from you today, brother Joseph," he said, after a warm embrace. "I thought I recalled it was your intention to spend tonight and tomorrow in Mary's house."

"That is correct, Thomas," was my reply, "and I thought in the meantime to bring you up to date on my actions, and to find out from you what has been happening with the Eleven."

"We are now Twelve, again," he responded with a grin. "Two candidates drew lots, after Peter's prayer for Divine intervention, and the successful one was Matthias."

"He should be an effective worker," I commented. "And what else did you do?"

"Well, quite a lot, actually," was his reply, "but it doesn't take long to tell it. Geographical assignments of responsibility for each of the Twelve were made after quite a lot of discussion. By and large, I think they make good sense. I was given the eastern area, as expected."

"How much does that include?" I wanted to know.

"It's not too precise, north and south; to the east there is no limit. On the west, Peter will have Syria, as well as his choice of Egypt—but we all recognize that he will have a roving role, world-wide. Parthia, Persia, Armenia and India will be my main concerns; I'll not go northwest into Cappadocia, nor southwest into Arabia."

"That much territory will certainly give you all of the excuse for travel that you could ask," I commented.

"Indeed, so!" he exclaimed; "saddle-sores will be my occupational hazard, I'm sure."

"Who will have responsibility in Gaul," I asked.

"That will be Philip," he said. "His assignment also includes Iberia, and tacitly Britannia if he wants to go there. You will get along well with him, I am sure."

"Yes, he is the most amiable and best educated of the 'fishermen five' that worked the Zebedee fishing business in Bethsaida," I said. "My Capernaum office, just four miles away, handled business matters for Zebedee occasionally and Philip was usually his representative. You knew, I suppose, that Zebedee had the contract to provide fish and other delicacies for Caiaphas' table, and that our firm provides the transport to get the shipments to Jerusalem on time?"

"I knew of the Zebedee-Caiaphas connection," he responded, "but didn't realize that you were involved."

"Yes, although transportation is not one of our usual activities," I replied. "Incidentally, Philip's Greek name means 'horse-lover,' and he will have the opportunity to test its appropriateness while covering the great distances in Gaul and Iberia. I'm sure we will get along well."

"Among the other items of business by the Twelve," added Thomas, "we made tentative assignments of preachers from among the Seventy. Those allotted to my eastern zone give every indication of being great ones."

"I'd say you all have been busy," I agreed. "Was that about all?"

"Not quite," he replied with a grin. "We also appointed seven deacons, and the chief of them is our friend, Stephen."

After expressing my pleasure and agreement with his news, I then described in detail the arrangements I had made, the steps taken and the plans projected. Thomas gave me his views on a number of points, and we finished the noonday meal together before we had completed the discussion.

CHAPTER FORTY

✠

The Pentecost Phenomena; My Arrest

A.D. 33

J UST BEFORE WE LEFT MY TOWN-HOUSE to walk to the home of Mary, I asked a question that had been at the back of my mind for some hours: "Thomas, on the mountain-top, just before his ascension, Jesus told us that in Jerusalem we will 'be clothed with power from on high.' This was the equivalent of the statement he made to you on the shore of Galilee, that you were to 'wait for the Spirit of God to empower you.' So, my question, dear Thomas, is, has it happened?"

He hesitated a full minute before answering: "In my judgment, no. We have spent many hours each day in prayer and meditation. We are closer and more of one mind than we've ever been. We each know more clearly and certainly what to preach as Jesus' message. We are no longer frightened or worried, or concerned about the future. But we are just men—and we have no greater ability or power than we've had in the past. I feel Jesus meant something more."

"I think you are right," said I. "'Let's walk over there now. Pentecost[1] starts this evening; surely something will happen before the Pentecost feast tomorrow evening."

Mary's sizeable home had a large upper room where the Twelve had been staying. When we arrived the room was packed—there were the Twelve, the seven Deacons, plus Lazarus, Cleopas and myself, and I don't doubt there were a few others. I took the opportunity for a few words with Lazarus, and said that because my time was doubtless short, I would like to leave here with him, whenever this meeting was over, and to spend some hours in Bethany with him. He, of course, agreed that such was highly desirable.

"Brothers!" Peter's booming voice quieted us instantly, "The empowerment Jesus promised us will surely come within the next day or two. I have chosen not to eat for the past two days. It is my request that the rest of you fast from this moment on until we have our Feast at the close of Pentecost tomorrow."

Peter then prayed for about a half-hour, and asked us all to sit comfortably and go into the silence for the next hour or two—that he would tell us when the meditation period was over.

Group meditation, as Jesus had taught us, always seemed a powerful spiritual tool, and after we had been in the silence for a half-hour I began to have an almost euphoric feeling. Vaguely, and then with more clarity, I began to be aware of a place and of a musical background that I would have to describe as "heavenly." The place seemed pastoral, yet of great beauty; there were "green pastures" and "still waters" as the psalmist might have seen them, and multi-hued flowers of every kind; the musical sound seemed that of an organ[2] of manifold pipes accompanying a chorus of great melodic quality, yet no words could be distinguished. This experience continued on for a very long time, and yet I seemed vaguely aware of my surroundings in the room and was not asleep.

Peter's voice brought us back from our meditation, and he told us that when Pentecost began in about an hour, we would have a time of prayer. We talked quietly in small groups while some moved about or walked outside for fresh air.

As the blast on the Shofar (ram's horn) from the pinnacle of the Temple nearby signalled the commencement of Pentecost, we all turned to Peter for instructions. I noticed that several more had now joined us, including James bar Joseph* from Galilee, and that a number of the women had also moved into this large room from the other part of the house—included in that group was Mary bat Joachim** from Galilee, Mary of Magdala, Salome and others.

Peter addressed us again: "Brothers and sisters, let us now link arms in a circle—I think the room is large enough for all of us." When we had

---

*Brother of Jesus
**Mother of Jesus

finished shuffling and were in position, he spoke again: "May we each strive now to link our hearts with Jesus, our Christ, and with our minds set on our Father in heaven, let us pray in unison the prayer our Lord Jesus taught us."

This we did, and our words reverberated in the room. In the following silence I seemed to feel a strong tingling in my upper arms, as if something real was passing through the links of our arms. Finally, Peter broke the long silence by saying: "We will now pray in turn, around the circle, and I will make the closing prayer when my turn comes. I can't tell you what it will take, but if our prayers are heartfelt, answers should come."

I think that nearly two hours were consumed in our prayer time, and what had previously seemed a tingling in our linked arms now seemed to shake us as if we all were palsied. As Peter started the concluding prayer, I heard a roaring sound as if the wind from a winter storm was howling through the room. I opened my eyes, as did many of the others, to look for the source of such a sound, and saw none—but the roaring and howling of a wind-like sound continued with high intensity.

I saw nothing different in the appearance of my companions, but over the heads of many of them I began to perceive a mist that seemed to be alive. The mist was pulsating away from and toward the individuals and took on swirling movements that occasionally built up like a cone above their heads—and the movement of this mist in some instances seemed like tongues of flame resting on various heads. I tried to find a rational explanation in my mind for what I was seeing, and thought that maybe the several candles burning in their sockets around the walls were giving color to the mist—maybe, but what caused the mist? Maybe mist was a poor word; it was as if a heavy vapor was coming from the head and encircling it or rising from it, cone-like. Lazarus and Thomas, on each side of me were staring at various others, and I could see from their eyes that they also were seeing something inexplicable.

As Peter said, "Amen," and opened his eyes, he instructed us: "Brothers and sisters, the power is upon us. Stay in the circle and keep your arms linked."

Almost instantly John bar Zebedee began to speak in what seemed a foreign language. After a minute or two, his brother James began to do the same. Almost at once, a similar sound came from Mary of Magdala. And suddenly, Lazarus, hooked to my right arm, began to do likewise. By the time a quarter-hour had passed every one in the room was speaking what seemed a foreign tongue, and most seemed different from the others.

About a half-hour after this riot of tongues had started, Peter's strong voice come through to us: "Friends, let the tongues cease!"

And instantly all was silence. "You see," he continued, "we have the sign of our power, but we are in control. We can let the Spirit speak, or we can stop the speech. Some of what we were hearing was but joy and praise of which we were too full for any words we know to satisfy. But other voices were the actual tongues of foreign languages. Tomorrow, in the street below, will be Jews and others from all over the world, speaking a dozen languages. At mid-morning I will open yonder windows, step onto the small balcony, and speak the message of Jesus in the only tongue I can use fluently—our Aramaic. The dozen or more of you who are speaking a true foreign tongue—and Spirit will tell you who you are—will go down into the street and preach in your foreign tongue as you walk slowly along—those that understand you will follow you. In this way, each language will be spoken to its proper audience in the several groups."

"Now, our work tomorrow is important," he continued, "so, while the women find accommodations in the bed-chambers, the men will each find a spot in this room to get his rest, and perhaps some sleep."

I unrolled the bed a servant had brought earlier in the day from my town-house, and Lazarus did the same. Thomas' bedding had been here all week. We three spoke in hushed tones for a few minutes, comparing what we *thought* we had seen and heard. Apparently, the observations of sights and sounds by the three of us were fully identical. With that comforting, but disturbing, idea, we went to sleep.

I could have enjoyed a modest breakfast upon awakening next morning, but held to the fast Peter had imposed on us. Nothing of significance happened until nearly mid-morning, when Peter again called us to link arms in a circle, while he prayed for about twenty minutes.

As he concluded and we prepared to break ranks, he said: "I will now start to speak. After about five minutes, you that are foreign speakers go out among the crowd and speak as the Spirit gives you utterance. The rest of you kneel in a circle and support us with your prayers."

Suiting his words with action, Peter opened the window shutters and stepped onto the tiny balcony, which was barely wide enough for his large feet. He held up his arms and got instant quiet from the crowd—and he began to speak.

I was not at all surprised that Lazarus was one of sixteen or eighteen foreign language speakers who lined up on the stairway to go among the crowd. The rest of us prayed silently in the middle of the room.

About a quarter of an hour later, we heard heckling in the street, and then a roar from Peter: "Men of Judea!—for I know it is only you that are disrupting our sermon. None from the diaspora, and no Greeks or other foreigners have such poor manners. The preachers on the street that are helping me are not drunk as you claim. It is just mid-morning, still three hours until mid-day—they have not yet had one drop of wine. Don't you know your Scripture? The prophet Joel told us God said, 'I will pour out my Spirit.' That is what you can hear and see happening."

The preaching continued, but the critics were silenced and slunk away—it continued until well past mid-day. Much earlier, however, voices from the crowd began to ask Peter, "What shall we do?" And he responded: "Repent of your sins and you will be forgiven; be baptized in the name of Jesus the Christed One, and you also will feel God's spirit."

Thereupon, Peter told those of us still in the room to go down to the street and talk to the converts, accepting their pleas, and making arrangements for their baptisms. Ultimately, the tongue speakers had to stop preaching and work with the supplicants as we were doing. By the time dusk fell more than three thousand souls had been converted. The women had our Pentecost feast ready and we were all very ready to eat it.

It was fully dark by the time Lazarus and I started the half-hour walk to his palace in Bethany. It was more than a Sabbath day's journey and the Sabbath had just started, but we would be outside the City walls in a couple dozen steps, and we had both ceased to be overly concerned about some of these technical "laws." As we walked we marvelled to each other about the twenty-four hours just passed. Never before had Jerusalem seen such a Pentecost, we thought. And for us, people of The Way, Pentecost would forever be different and newly important to us. As we walked, we also realized how exhausted we were, and decided that serious talk would have to wait until morning.

All of the following day we discussed the steps I had taken and the plans I had made. "The word I get from Nicodemus is that I have used up about all the time I can afford to risk," I said, "and that I should leave without further delay—I just didn't feel I could afford to miss Pentecost here, and now I know I was right in that regard."

"The information I am getting from the Temple confirms that," Lazarus said. "In fact, dear friend, I have to say that your time may already have run out. Please don't give Caiaphas the opportunity to arrest you."

"Well, the Sabbath ends at sundown today. As soon as it is dark I will go to my town-house to pick up a few essential things, and then continue right on to Arimathea under cover of darkness."

"I don't like the idea of your going back into Jerusalem at all," was Lazarus' rejoinder, "but if you must, at least I insist on sending my servant, Benjamin, with you all the way to Arimathea. For the moment, let us eat our evening meal, as I see the signal from Martha that it is ready."

Lazarus was certainly right, as matters turned out. In spite of Benjamin's presence, we were accosted and quickly overcome by Temple police a few steps from the door of my town-house. A few minutes later, and somewhat dazed by the rough treatment, I was thrown into a prison room without windows. Expecting to find myself incarcerated here for several days, at least, I fumbled around in the dark and finally made myself reasonably comfortable—as much as one can ever be comfortable in a jail cell.

CHAPTER NOTES:

1. Pentecost began that year on the sixth of the month of Sivan (approx. June), the "fiftieth" day after Passover, beginning shortly after sundown; this one-day Feast of the Jews marks completion of the wheat harvest; this also was a compulsory event for males. It is a significant date for Christians because on Pentecost of A.D. 33 the "empowerment" of the Disciples occurred, marked by tongue-speaking (Acts 2:1-47).

2. In the third century B.C., Ktesibios of Alexandria, Egypt, invented the *hydraulos* organ, comparable to the ones we have today. He stabilized the wind supply by the use of water pressure. The first purely pneumatic organs were built in Byzantium in the fourth century A.D.

PART V

✠

My Exile;
Shroud Pilgrimages
Begin

THE CHARACTERS IN
THE ORDER OF THEIR APPEARANCE

CHAPTER FORTY-ONE:

Asa: (fictional) relative of Hosea.
Samuel: (fictional) cousin of Asa.
Isaac bar Solomon: (fictional) employed in Caiaphas' office; a secret follower of Jesus.
Lucius Pomponius Flaccus: Legate for Rome in the Eastern provinces, with seat in Antioch, Syria.

CHAPTER FORTY-TWO: (none)

CHAPTER FORTY-THREE: (none)

CHAPTER FORTY-FOUR:

Aggai: robe-maker and First Secretary to King Abgar V in Edessa; became second to Thaddaeus heading the Christian church there.

CHAPTER FORTY-FIVE:

Marcus Italicus: (fictional) Rome agent of Joseph of Arimathea.
Tirotates: (fictional) half-brother of Abgar V, serving as official Historian in Armenia.

CHAPTER FORTY-SIX:

Ephraim, Benjamin, Gideon and David: (fictional) young members of the Joseph of Arimathea community in Britain.
Arviragus: Christian king of the Dumnoni tribe in southwest Britain (Cornwall and Devon); cousin of King Caradoc of the Silures (Wales) whom he succeeded as pendragon of Britain. Married in Rome to Venus Julia, daughter of Emperor Claudius.
Gladys (Emp. Claudius re-named her, Pomponia Graecina): Christian daughter of King Bran of Siluria. Married to Gen. Aulus Plautius who commanded the Roman armies that invaded Britain in A.D. 43. Gladys moved to Rome when Plautius retired in 47.
Bran: king of Siluria ca. A.D. 30 to 40. Son of King Llyr ("Lear" per Shakespeare), abdicated in favor of his son, Caradoc, and became Arch Druid. Declared Britain a Christian nation in A.D. 40. When Llyr died while a hostage in Rome, Bran went voluntarily to take his father's place as hostage. Bran was later consecrated by St. Paul in Rome.
Saul of Tarsus: Pharisaic Jew and Roman citizen, who was agent of Caiaphas and Pilate to persecute Christians; later was converted during a mystical experience at Damascus and became a leading apostle/missionary of Christianity.

CHAPTER FORTY-SEVEN:

King Cymbeline (Cunobelinus): born ca. 34 B.C.; died A.D. 40. Ruler of the eastern tribe of the Iceni in Britain, and was Pendragon (commanding general) of the associated tribes.
King Togodumnus, son of Cymbeline, ruled from A.D. 40 till his death in 43.
King Llyr Llediath: born ca. 25 B.C.; ruler of Siluria (south Wales) of western Britain. Abdicated A.D. 30 in favor of son, Bran. Died in Rome while a hostage, A.D. 48/51. King Lear of Shakespeare.
King Caradoc (Caractacus): born ca. A.D. 8. Rule began in A.D. 40 when his father, Bran, abdicated in his favor. Became pendragon the same year upon

death of Cymbeline. Captured by the Romans ca. A.D. 50 through treachery; taken as hostage to join his family in Rome. Pardoned by Claudius; his parole ended and he returned to Britain in 59.

Cyllinus: son of Caradoc; born ca. A.D. 27. Hostage to Rome ca. A.D. 47; returned to Britain A.D. 49 as Regent in Siluria; later became king. At his death his son, Coel, ruled all of Britain.

Eurgain: daughter of Caradoc; born ca. A.D. 28. Married to Salog, civilian official with Roman troops of occupation, and accompanied him, upon retirement in ca. 47, to Rome. Returned with him to Britain in 58.

Cynon: son of Caradoc; born ca. A.D. 29. Hostage to Rome in 47; returned to Britain in 58.

Linus: son of Caradoc; born ca. A.D. 30. Hostage to Rome in 47. Investiture by Paul as bishop of Rome in A.D. 66. Martyred in Rome, ca. 86/90.

Gladys: daughter of Caradoc; born ca. A.D. 36. Hostage to Rome in 47. Married to Rufus Pudens in 53. Name changed by Claudius to Claudia. Died in Rome in 97.

Emperor Claudius, born 10 B.C.; ruled A.D. 41-54. Ordered invasion of Britain in 43 and led his armies there for a few weeks in August.

Menahem (Manaen): Acts 13:1 lists him as a leader of the church in Antioch and "a member of the court of Herod the tetrarch." The Zondervan *New Int'n'l. Dictionary of the Bible* notes that he was the foster brother of Herod Antipas.

CHAPTER FORTY-EIGHT:

Aulus Plautius: commanding general of the four legions invading Britain in A.D. 43, and in the Fall also became Governor. He married a local princess, Gladys of Siluria (whom Claudius renamed Pomponia Graecine), and retired to Rome in 47.

Venus Julia: daughter of Emperor Claudius; married King Arviragus in Rome, A.D. 45, and returned with him to the Dumnoni tribe in sw. Britain (Cornwall and Devon).

General Vespasian: on the staff of Plautius in Britain, in command of II Legion. He became emperor in A.D. 69.

Rufus Pudens: son of Senator Quintus Cornelius Pudens, was aide to Gen. Plautius in Britain. He married Caradoc's daughter, princess Gladys (whom Claudius renamed, Claudia) in Rome in A.D. 53.

Salog: a patrician Roman; a civilian on the staff of Gen. Plautius in Britain.

CHAPTER FORTY-NINE:

Ostorius Scapula: commanding general and governor, who succeeded Plautius in Britain in A.D. 47.

CHAPTER FIFTY:

Pliny (the Elder): A.D. 23-79. A fellow soldier with Vespasian during the invasion of Britain. A naturalist by profession.

Lucius Annaeus Seneca: 3 B.C.–A.D. 65; a native of Spain. Noted as a philosopher (Stoic), playwright, author and statesman. He was exiled to Spain in 41 by Claudius, but recalled in 49 on the urging of his then-wife, Agrippina I, to become the tutor for her son, Nero, then age twelve.

Cletus: of a patrician Roman family, but born in Greece; he became bishop of Rome (A.D. 86 to 88) after Linus. Sometimes called Anacletus.

Philo: Jewish theologian in Alexandria, having Grecian and Gnostic leanings.

CHAPTER FIFTY-ONE:

Aristobulus: Christian leader/missionary; one of the Seventy. He was brother of Barnabus, brother-in-law of Peter, and companion of Paul. Became bishop of Britain.

Nero: (A.D. 37-68) Was emperor A.D. 54-68.

Burrus was head of the Praetorian Guard under Nero and, until his death in A.D. 62, he and Seneca in effect ran the empire.

Clement I: became bishop of Rome (ca. A.D. 88-97) after Cletus. Clement had been a disciple of Paul. He was a Jew whose early life was in Greece and Asia Minor.

CHAPTER FIFTY-TWO:

Luke: a Greek, who became a physician after study in the medical school at Philippi, and was practicing medicine in Antioch when he met Paul, with whom he journeyed to Jerusalem and Rome. He was the writer of Luke and Acts of the New Testament.

Aristarchus: a companion of Paul on his journey from Caesarea to Rome.

Symeon: the fourth child of Cleopas-Alphaeus and Mary-Heli, and therefore first cousin of Jesus. Upon the death of James the Just (Jesus' brother), Symeon became head of the Jerusalem church.

CHAPTER FIFTY-THREE:

Aquila and Priscilla: Jewish man and wife, sail and tent makers from Corinth, who lived in Rome part of the time of this story.

✠

CHAPTER FORTY-ONE

I Escape from Prison and Prepare for Exile

A.D. 33

"Lord Joseph! Can you hear me?" were the whispered words that awakened me.

In the instant of awakening I realized that such a salutation was certainly not coming from a prison guard.

"Yes, I am here," I answered in a low voice. "Who is it?"

As a gentle hand touched my arm, the whisper came again: "Be very quiet, my Lord. This is Asa, a relative of Hosea; I am a servant in the palace of Caiaphas. I have a donkey at the side of the building, and a rug into which I will roll you so that you will seem to be just a burden on the donkey. When we get through the Water Gate and reach the road to Joppa, we will be met by my cousin, Samuel, who is bringing fast mules for your return to Arimathea."

"I trust that no one will be put in jeopardy on my account," I said.

"We believe not. Samuel will explain it all to you. No more talk now, Lord, we must hurry," whispered Asa as he led me through the prison door and around the building.

The donkey looked casually with seeming disinterest as Asa spread the rug on the ground, I laid on it, and he rolled me over with the rug several times. The difficult part came next as I was unable to help him stand me upright. Once he got me upright, I had no balance, especially since I was standing on a doubled-over part of the longish rug. I heard the donkey snort as Asa maneuvered him into position. Then he patted me on the shoulder and pushed me forward so that I was leaning against the donkey. Next, he gripped me around the knees and raised up, sliding me across the donkey's back until I was "folded" with my stomach approximately over the donkey's backbone. With one hand on me to maintain my precarious balance, he spoke to the donkey who moved off at a fairly fast walk—Asa presumably had the lead rope in his other hand.

I supposed that it must be into the third watch, past the middle of the night, as we had neither heard nor seen signs of life as we emerged from the prison. The donkey's small unshod hooves made very little noise on the stones of the street, and he must have been well-trained to move properly without someone ahead to lead him. I was certainly glad I had not eaten recently, for the bouncing of my stomach on the donkey's back was something less than pleasant.

Perhaps no more than twenty minutes had elapsed when the donkey broke into a trot, so I judged we must be past the City wall. After a few minutes more, the donkey slowed to a walk and seemed to be picking his way over rough ground. Suddenly we stopped, I was patted on the back, two persons lifted me off the donkey, laid me gently on the ground, and unrolled me and the rug.

A smiling Samuel introduced himself to me, and then in the pale moonlight I recognized my dear servant, Hosea, standing nearby.

"Hosea! Oh, Hosea! How wonderful to see you!" I said as I embraced him with all my strength.

"Master, I have brought all the things you intended to get from your town-house," responded Hosea, after he got his breath back. "Rachel sends her best wishes. Reuben went on to Arimathea with all of his belongings a few hours ago, as soon as he was satisfied our friends would get you out of prison. I must return now, so that you and Samuel can leave without further delay. Farewell. And write to us when you can."

"Farewell. I'll never forget you, Hosea," I replied.

We rode at a fast trot for about a mile, and then slowed the mules to a walk so that Samuel could explain events to me.

"Well, Master Joseph," he began, "it all goes back to the errand on which you sent Hosea the day of Jesus' resurrection. Since Asa and I are servants in Caiaphas' palace, he came to us to learn of Caiaphas' plans against you. Within a day or two we knew that he and Annas would try to arrest you once their plans were complete, and so we consulted with

Isaac bar Solomon, who works in Caiaphas' office and is a secret follower of The Way.

"We realized that we would need a plan to free you from the old prison if you were arrested," he continued. "We had no doubt of our ability to free you, but needed circumstances that would not result in harm to our friends. Finally, Isaac explained how it could be done. He said, 'That prison was cheaply built on an excellent old foundation, and the two earthquakes which came at Jesus' crucifixion and at his resurrection cracked the mortar that joins the new and old construction—cracked it all the way around the building—so that the building now sits on, but is not joined to, its foundation. I happened to ask the feeble-minded prison guard if he had reported the damage to Caiaphas. He replied with fear that he didn't dare to—if a new prison were built, guarding it would be too good a job for him. I know he's right in that; he drinks wine to excess and Caiaphas only keeps him because the guard is a cousin of Caiaphas' wife. If Joseph of Arimathea is arrested, I'll give the guard some drugged wine, and convince him the next morning that angels lifted the building to permit the escape.'"

"That seems a very far-fetched story that is being proposed by Isaac," I interrupted to say.

"Of course it is," replied Samuel, "but you have to know the guard to realize how perfect a story for him. Between his feeblemindedness and his drunkenness he lives in a fantasy world all the time.

"Isaac did provide the drugged wine last night as soon as Hosea rushed over to tell us you had been arrested just outside your home," Samuel continued. "The guard was asleep in his cubicle as Asa brought you out of the prison tonight. In the morning, Isaac will help the guard discover your absence, and will *remind* the guard of how he had earlier described seeing angels lift the whole building while a Being of Light escorted you out, and then set the building back down."[1]

"But Samuel!" I exclaimed, "Caiaphas will not believe such a story."

"Of course not," he agreed, "but he will be stuck with it! You see, there are only two keys to the prison—or at least there *were* only two! The guard has none. One is around the neck of the Captain of the Temple Guards, a married man, and he never takes it off, day or night—and he is the brother-in-law of Caiaphas. The other key is carried by Caiaphas, but he is a bit careless; when he takes his afternoon bath, he lays the key with his clothes several feet from his sunken tub, and we know that most times he goes to sleep in the tub and sleeps for a half hour or more. So, the very week of the Resurrection, Asa was able to take Caiaphas' key as he slept in the tub, and rushed it to Isaac, who had a key-maker waiting with him.

In no more than ten minutes a perfect copy was made and Asa was racing back to Caiaphas' tub room."

"My, how risky," I said

"Asa didn't think so. He said that Caiaphas often dawdles at his bath for two hours," was Samuel's response; "he said he would find a way. As it turned out there was no problem."

"Yes, I can now see that Caiaphas will have something of a dilemma in the morning," I acknowledged, smiling to myself in the darkness. "He can't blame either the prison guard or the Captain without proof because of his wife, and he can't admit that he may have been careless with his own key. Above all, the crack around the foundation will seem to support the guard's implausible story."

"Correct," said Samuel; "in the morning Isaac will point out to the guard that you haven't taken the food he pushed through the hole—and then will tell him 'his own story' and urge him to call the Captain to open the door to verify your absence. I think it's a perfect plan—ridiculous as it may be."

✠   ✠   ✠

When we reached my home in Arimathea the sun was just barely up, and the only sign of life was a wisp of smoke from the cooking fire in the kitchen.

I led Samuel to a bed-chamber where he could sleep as long as he liked before starting back to Jerusalem; also, I took from him the bundle of personal items, brought from my town-house by Hosea, which Samuel had carried all the way. Upon opening the bundle, I smiled to myself to see that Hosea had included my thorn-tree walking-staff.

During the previous week in Jerusalem, as we moved about the premises of my town-house to select the bare necessities that I would take on my journey to Britannia; my eyes had lit upon the thorn tree that my servant, Reuben, had cut in Herod's yard Crucifixion morning, and brought to the house as I had instructed. It was as thick as my wrist at the butt and longer than I am tall.

We really had no time to waste on foolishness, but it seemed important to me—and so, I called to Reuben and told him to trim the branches and thorns from the trunk, and to cut off both the bottom and top extremities—that I wished to take it as a walking-staff.

Here it was—and so I would!

✠   ✠   ✠

As the household arose for the day, my son, Josephes, brought me a letter that had arrived for me the day before. A month earlier, I had written to the Roman Legate in Antioch, explained our situation, and asked if he could provide transportation to Massalia for me, my family, servants and our household goods. In addition to the attitude of the Caiaphas/Annas clique, putting my freedom in jeopardy because they were infuriated that I had given a respectable burial to my kinsman, Jesus, I explained also that my long-time associate, ship-master Hiram bar Abram of Tyre, had had the misfortune of excessive storm damage to his excellent vessel, "Astarte," which would not be re-outfitted before Fall, and that I would trust no other ship on the Ocean Sea.

His reply was as follows:

> From Lucius Pomponius Flaccus, Legate for Rome in the Eastern Provinces, with Seat at Antioch, Syria;
>
> To Joseph of Arimathea, in Judea, Commerce Advisor to the Legate; Greetings:
>
> Of course, I had heard of the events of the last two months in Jerusalem from my subordinate, Governor Pontius Pilate, and I must say in passing that, although it was by no means a simple case, I agree fully with the action of Pilate in ordering the crucifixion of your kinsman, Jesus of Galilee. Serious suspicion of sedition must be met by stern measures to preclude an open insurrection.
>
> However, we are a civilized Empire. Since Jesus has paid the penalty for his actions, the matter is closed and the Government holds no animus against his family.
>
> On the contrary, I have always had the highest regard for you, and deeply appreciate, as did my predecessors, the great service you have rendered to Rome over a period of thirty years. Accordingly, it is my pleasure to arrange the transportation you require. I have instructed Pilate to arrange for a coastal vessel to meet you in Joppa harbor at your convenience, and bring you to the harbor of Antioch, where a bireme will be awaiting your arrival, to take you to Massalia.
>
> As a Roman, I am totally unable to understand many of the actions and reasons therefor which I observe in your strange Jewish race, in the name of religion. That your life should be in jeopardy because you provided a respectable burial for a kinsman, after he had paid the penalty for his crimes, is to me inexplicable. Some day both Romans and Jews will regret the treaty that gave Jerusalem unlimited religious power.
>
> My felicitations to you, my dear Joseph, and best wishes for a very long life.

I sent word to Pilate in Caesarea that we would be ready to depart from Joppa within three days, and that I awaited the vessel promised by the Legate Lucius Flaccus. Our belongings were all packed and in our warehouse on the docks, and I felt able to relax. I posted guards night and day on the walls enclosing the buildings of our home, but really had no expectation that Caiaphas would dare invade the privacy of my home.

My reflections then turned from the past to the future, when I would certainly want to spread Jesus' gospel. I could readily tell his story as it had unfolded chronologically, but what would I say of his message? Then I thought of a conversation we had had the previous Fall, when Jesus had visited with me for a couple days of rest. I had written his words down immediately afterward and had them with me; they would provide at least a start. He had said:

> It is not what I am but what I permit God to do through me that counts. Some whom I or my disciples have healed had lived lives of self-gratification that had had the effect of refusing to permit God to live through them—thus, they were vulnerable to possession by earth-bound spirits or demons. By prayer, fasting, life-style and supplication, I have opened myself to possession by God's Holy Spirit, the Paraclete, that in one sense the Greeks call the Christos.
>
> Whenever I most strongly feel that I am doing not my own will, but that God's will is being done through me, are the times when I feel impelled to act and say those things which appear to fulfill in me the prophecies of old concerning the coming of the Messiah. However, I am not comfortable with being called the Messiah of the Jews, because some of the prophecies foretold (wrongly, I feel) an earthly king or military leader. Unfortunately, most all Jews today expect such an earthly Messiah—and such a wish I will not fulfill.
>
> Indeed, I am satisfied that God never intended an earthly kingdom for his Messiah. Much as I revere our Holy Scriptures, I am satisfied that there is error in them and there are flaws in the prophecies. The writers and the prophets just were not always perfectly attuned to God's voice and, over and over in my ministry, I have pointed out the errors and misconceptions in our scriptures, but the pious ones choose to call me a blasphemer.
>
> If my message is to survive, it will be because my disciples will carry it to the gentiles and to the diaspora beyond the boundaries of Judea. In fact, I feel that I am nearer to the Christos, as the Greeks conceive it, than to the Messiah as the priests of our homeland see him.

Yes, this would anchor my ministry.

CHAPTER NOTE:

1. The story of Joseph's arrest and imprisonment, and of his deliverance in this fashion by angels, is told in several apocryphal accounts, notably in the "Story of Joseph of Arimathea," the "Gospel of Nicodemus" (also called the "Acts of Pilate") and in the "Coptic Narratives"; see *The Apocryphal New Testament* edited by M. R. James, The Clarendon Press, Oxford, England, 1924, 1972. The story is also reported in *The Chronicle of Glastonbury Abbey,* edited by J. P. Carley, Boydell Press, Woodbridge, Suffolk, England, 1978, 1985—which is a translation and study of John of Glastonbury's "Cronica sive Antiquitates Glastoniensis Ecclesie"; therein John claims it to be "taken from a book which the Emperor Theodosius found in Pilate's Council-chamber in Jerusalem."

CHAPTER FORTY-TWO

✠

Reminiscences at Sea

A.D. 33

*I*T HAS TAKEN ME THESE SEVERAL DAYS upon the Great Sea, fully to realize that my Judean life is behind me—that doubtless I will never return—that that life is over as if I had died at age forty-nine, as perhaps I almost did!

Now that I have time to think without the pressures of trying to outwit our religious enemies, or even to manage a large and far-flung business operation, my thoughts are turning to the last months of Jesus' ministry in an attempt to rationalize the actions of his enemies. Why did the Jewish leadership hate and fear Jesus?—why did they take those particular actions? How valid and voluntary were the steps taken by Rome, especially through the person of Pontius Pilate?

In all honesty, one must admit that Jesus purposefully attacked the Jewish leadership in very specific ways, which would threaten their power and income if the people began to accept Jesus' charges; for instance:

1. He was harsh in his criticism of their personal lives;
2. He challenged their interpretations of The Law—which interpretations they considered part of the Law;
3. By example, his conduct and that of his disciples violated the Law;
4. His miracles attracted the people to him, and his largess in feeding them without charge held them to him;
5. His attack on the Temple sales and money-changing threatened their income;
6. His weaning of the people away from acceptance of the "interpretive law" of Judaism threatened the steady flow of the Temple tax.

Jesus' claims of messiahship (or claims made on his behalf) were not of themselves deemed blasphemous nor particularly threatening to the Temple hierarchy—there had been many claimants to that title over the years, most of them much more vociferous than Jesus, whose claims seemed understated by comparison, and even ambiguous at times.

No, it was not claims of messiahship that bothered the Temple authorities and caused charges of blasphemy, but the claims of Sonship, and statements on Jesus' *own* authority instead of citing a prophet or God—it was his statements that "I and the Father are one," that "before Abraham was, I am," that "in the beginning ... I was with God"—which infuriated them. Also, his claim of authority to forgive sin was inexcusable to them; only God could do that. These were the blasphemies deserving of death in their opinion.

And, of course, the claims of raisings by Jesus of the dead infuriated them further and deeply worried them at the same time, because such incidents were extremely strong evidence supporting the claims of godhood. A few of the reports could be discounted since the person had been dead but a few minutes or so, and thus there might have been no real death. Also, most of the incidents happened in Galilee, and what citizen of Jerusalem would believe stories beyond credulity that came out of Galilee? But what could the critics say about the case of Lazarus of Bethany who had been in his tomb for four days when Jesus called him up from a distance of several paces—no touching or manipulation, no sleight-of-hand or magic could possibly explain it, nor had Jesus been in the area to arrange a phony death. This was the crowning blow to seal the doom of both Jesus and Lazarus.

Now, the Sanhedrin could condemn for blasphemy and, after proper trial, execute the guilty person by stoning—they needed only to get Pilate's concurrence (without further trial), which was always forthcoming. But such an action against Jesus would have been risky for his official enemies, because Jesus' popularity was too great and a revolt might have resulted. Although such action might be intended as against only the Temple authorities, the latter operated under grant from Rome's agent, and any attack would be considered as against Rome, so a revolt would always fail; the world-wide power of Rome was too great. The inevitable result would be two-fold—opression, and loss of many privileges for the privileged class, and replacement of Pilate. For all his faults, Pilate was pliable and usually cooperative—Annas and Caiaphas would not want him replaced, although they might threaten him and bluff to get their way at times. The recent out-pouring of support for Jesus at the occurrence the disciples were calling the "triumphal entry" to Jerusalem was proof enough that Jesus had a popular following.

The only solution that had appealed to Annas, Caiaphas and their ruling clique was crucifixion *by the Romans*. Such an action, based on a finding of sedition against Rome, would enhance Caiaphas' chance of avoiding significant responsibility and, above all, it should bar any likelihood of martyrdom for Jesus. The populace well knew, and Caiaphas would not let them forget, that the scroll of Deuteronomy clearly stated that anyone crucified was "damned." Moreover, bodies of the crucified should not be cleaned or properly buried, and usually the soldiers threw them into the common lime-pit.

Thus, it was essential for them to establish Jesus' sedition against Rome both in the popular mind and in the opinion of Pilate—this was their effort, and the reasons behind it. I'm sure now that for several days or weeks they were working on Pilate behind the scenes—reminding him first that nothing good ever came out of Galilee—that even two centuries ago, Judas Maccabeus and his relatives stormed out of Galilee to establish a short-lived independent Jewish kingdom. And as recently as a generation ago, Judas the Gaulonite, also known as Judas the Galilean (whose father had been executed by Herod the Great for rebellion), had led his Zealots in an attempted takeover of Jerusalem. Of course, he and his "army" were promptly routed and slain by Varus, then Legate of Syria. And, of course, Sabinus the Procurator in Jerusalem had been deposed for permitting that uprising. And now Judas' son, Manahem, though still in Galilee, was building a following of Zealots with threats of takeover. Manahem's lieutenant, Barabbas, was recently arrested in Jerusalem, as an indication of the seriousness of the situation. And to all of this would be added the fact that at least one of the Twelve with Jesus was a Zealot—his brother, Simon—with suspicion that perhaps two or three others of the Twelve also belonged to the Zealots.

The Zealots, as a political party, were totally committed to the forceful overthrow of the Roman government in our homeland. And this result, in the popular mind, was the mission to be expected of the Messiah, and Pilate was well aware of the sameness of those political views. On the other hand, it was an uneasy sinecure that Herod Antipas held at the sufferance of Rome, and the opposing political party of the time was the Herodians who gave at least lip-service to Rome and supported a continuation of Herod's position and the current governmental arrangements. Herod could be counted on to give no support to either the Zealots or the followers of Jesus, and yet he was not disposed to take aggressive action against either of them.

It was Herod's theory that neither of them could ultimately throw out the Romans, yet, the more minor trouble they caused Pilate and the Legate in Antioch, the better he, Herod, would appear in the eyes of Rome. Similarly, Herod had little in common with the Annas/Caiaphas clique controlling the Sanhedrin, and would not help them in attacks on Jesus, but neither would he interfere, and stood aloof from what he deemed petty squabbling.

In the weeks since the Crucifixion I had heard much talk among the Twelve and others of The Way to the effect that the crucifixion of Jesus was really an act of the Sanhedrin or its hierarchy—that Pilate did not act on his own will but was just a tool of Caiaphas. I must protest such an erroneous conclusion.

Which is not to say that Caiaphas and Annas and a few other Sadducees did not work to bring about that result. Of course they did. But this was not an act of the Jewish people, of the Great Sanhedrin, or even of the Little Sanhedrin. If Caiaphas had held a proper trial and required a proper vote, his wishes regarding Jesus would have been badly defeated; the membership of 71 persons would have voted overwhelmingly against recommending crucifixion to Pilate—probably by as much as 61 to 10. And, although it would have been outside its legal competence, even the Little Sanhedrin of 23 would have voted at least 13 to 10 against recommending crucifixion.[1]

Caiaphas might have gotten a conviction of blasphemy and certainly could have received Pilate's approval for a Jewish execution by stoning, but as I've already said, Caiaphas didn't dare go that route—his own life and certainly his job would have been lost in the repercussions. Followers of The Way and the Zealots would quickly have joined forces formally in reprisal against Caiaphas. Moreover, the crowds that shouted, "Crucify him!" in Pilate's courtyard would have as readily yelled, "Release him!" if Caiaphas had told them to—there was no ground swell against Jesus and Caiaphas knew it.

But, to come back to my premise, Pilate was his own man in ordering Jesus' execution. I've known Pilate too long and too well to think otherwise. It may not have been a strong case against Jesus, but under Roman law Pilate didn't need to "make a case." *Of course,* there were political considerations. Pilate's relationships with the executed Sejanus (who had been thrown to the Senate wolves by Emperor Tiberius, and by the Senate to the City rabble), together with the prior reprimands of Pilate by Tiberius left Pilate sensitive and in jeopardy politically. But conversely, Pilate easily could have stopped Caiaphas' conniving actions against Jesus if he had wanted to do so.

He knew that Caiaphas had had arrest warnings posted against Jesus for more than the required forty days. He sent a detail of his own soldiers to observe the arrest of Jesus, even though he chose not to participate. He and Caiaphas knew each other well, and both knew the volatility of the Jewish people. The events leading up to the Crucifixion were carefully stage-managed by both of them in concert. Pilate knew he could expect a command from Rome to justify his actions, and he was prepared to provide such justification.

Pilate was not eager to execute Jesus, but he was not particularly reluctant to do so, either. Clearly, two factors seemed to tip the scales at the end, if there was ever any doubt as to Pilate's action—one was the insistence of Caiaphas, his appointee with whom he had a good working relationship—the other was the intransigence of Jesus, who seemed to Pilate as either uncaring of his own fate or possibly daring Pilate to act. In any event, Pilate felt secure in his justification—should he have his acts reviewed by Rome. He knew that Jesus could sway large numbers of people and, not content to stay in Galilee, had come to Jerusalem four days previously to show his strength; he could not believe it was coincidence that the Zealots' attack on the Temple treasury the following day drew both soldiers and Temple guards, leaving Jesus unopposed in his violence against the Temple salesmen and money-changers. And he had to consider this latter action as a direct challenge to Rome since the tribute to Rome was paid from those Temple funds.

Pilate seemed to be toying with Caiaphas that morning in the courtyard, with seeming reluctance to execute Jesus—making Caiaphas lay-on a public demonstration, before he finally ordered the crucifixion. But Pilate was basically a soldier, and killing was a way of life for him. Also, he was tough md stubborn with a cruel streak in his nature, and knew well the value of public execution to keep the populace cowed and in its place. No, he was not reluctant to order Jesus' crucifixion, once the strongest case had been made. Nor did he express regret or indicate that he might have been wrong. The case for sedition against Rome may have been circumstantial, but he knew he wouldn't be criticized by Rome for so acting—his worry would have been in the case of not so acting. Clemency in the provinces was not popular with the Roman Senate or the Emperor.

These hints and innuendos of sedition against Jesus certainly might be viewed as weak and unimpressive—at most, suggestive—if there was nothing more to motivate Pilate. Even the possible "coincidence" of Jesus disrupting the Temple businesses of money-changers and sacrifice-animal salesmen at the *very* moment when a strong contingent of Zealots was storming the business office of the Temple in an attempt to seize funds from the Temple treasury could be without significance.

But the "something more," as I've indicated above, was the work of Annas, in presenting half-veiled threats to Pilate which he could ignore only at his peril. This Achilles-heel of Pilate which Annas used, involved complex Roman politics. Some seven years earlier, Tiberius Caesar "retired" to the island of Capri and ruled nominally by correspondence However, Sejanus of the Pretorian Guard was his chief aide and in effect ran the Empire. Tiberius then became suspicious of Sejanus' high-handed actions and had him killed just two years ago. It was rumored that Sejanus was plotting to assassinate Tiberius, and that Pilate was involved in the conspiracy. Pilate's wife, Claudia Procula, was an illegitimate daughter of Claudia, who later became the third wife of Tiberius. Pilate's rumored involvement in the plot against Tiberius may have had family overtones, since Tiberius thus had become the stepfather of Pilate's wife.

Additionally, it was widely rumored that Pilate, formerly of the Pretorian Guard, who was appointed governor of Judea at about the time Tiberius retired to Capri, was in fact Sejanus' man, not loyal to Tiberius. So, less than two years after Sejanus' "execution" by the mob in Rome, Pilate had every reason to fear that rumors carried to Tiberius might cause his deposition and possible arrest—and even his execution—by the near-senile emperor. Annas, politically wiser than his son-in-law, Caiaphas, knew of Pilate's tenuous position in Rome and privately threatened to report to Tiberius any equivocation, delay or failure by Pilate in handling the Jesus problem. Using this knowledge, Caiaphas incited leaders of the mob (who were Temple hangers-on obligated to him), to use this barely veiled threat to Pilate: "If you set him (Jesus) free, you are no friend of Caesar!"

This phrase, "friend of Caesar," was very meaningful to Pilate, because he wore Tiberius' signet ring that was given to only a select few of the Roman inner circle, and these few—identified by the ring—were known as "Friends of Caesar." Hearing this chant from Caiaphas' stooges must have caused Pilate's blood to run cold. When he had twice in the past failed to effectively handle Jewish riot situations, Sejanus had been in Rome to serve as buffer with Tiberius. With Sejanus gone, he could expect no mercy from Tiberius if another serious disorder erupted around Jesus.

No doubt Pilate recognized that Jesus' claim of kingship was of a spiritual nature, not a material kingdom challenging Rome—yet, he was fearful that Jesus could not control the situation that was building up around him. Just how deeply Jesus was involved with the Zealots was impossible for him to determine; if one or more of his Twelve were active Zealots, might not the larger group, The Seventy, be more fully and actively involved? This dilemma and the threats and pressure from Annas were the more influential factors that decided Pilate in favor of a finding of sedition and ordering of the crucifixion.

To summarize my thoughts on these matters—parochial Galileans, which most of the Twelve were, did not understand these technical and subtle maneuvers as Annas/Caiaphas attempted to influence or manipulate Pilate and the Great Sanhedrin. Those two wily ones knew they *could* make out a case of blasphemy against Jesus, but they also knew that Jesus had too large a public following, who might turn on the Temple authorities in such a situation; also, that a stoning of Jesus might result in a Zealot attack on the Temple leadership. For these reasons, Caiaphas/Annas had no concern for the obvious and gross illegalities of the Sanhedrin proceedings against Jesus, which proceedings were designed *only* to convince reluctant members of the Sanhedrin and to present Pilate a plausible threat of sedition plus a *real* threat of a Jewish protest to Tiberius. They didn't want a vote of the Sanhedrin, and knew that a judgment by Pilate did not need a trial at all! Failure to foresee and forestall a "Jesus uprising" would have ended Pilate's career—crucifixion of Jesus was the simple and foolproof way for Pilate to defuse the threats.

CHAPTER NOTE:

1. The so-called "Little Sanhedrin" dealt only with civic matters; the Great Sanhedrin handled matters of State and religion.

CHAPTER FORTY-THREE

✠

In Southern Gaul;
Welcoming Lazarus

A.D. 33

MY MONTHS IN THIS LUSH LAND just north of the port of Massalia* in southern Gaul** have been ones of new interests, pleasures, and the opportunity for needed relaxation and meditation, which I had little chance for in Judea recently. We arrived to find a Spring season at its beautiful peak with the lacy mimosa branches everywhere screening the so-blue sky without hiding it, and the colorful bougainvillea whose small flowers are surrounded by large, showy, colored bracts—the scalelike, modified leaves which compliment its blooms so well. Now, after a moist summer, not too different from that of Arimathea, we are in the midst of a brilliant autumn with leaves riotously painted everywhere—this is an experience I had had by staying seasonably late in Britannia, but never in Judea.

We have tarried these months in southern Gaul in response to the request of Lazarus. He felt that this area was right for the new home of himself and his sisters. Yet, by common consent, they wished to settle in separate locations because their ministries for The Way would be significantly different, one from the other. Lazarus is a natural organizer and will certainly spread missions far into the interior, while the styles of Martha

---

*Marseilles (early spelling was sometimes, Massilia).
**France.

and Mary would be more localized. Mary had previously made clear her intention to provide, near the city of Massalia, a hostel-like facility for the rehabilitation of fallen women, while Martha—though unsure for the long term—felt that initially she would establish an orphanage to give street waifs an opportunity for a proper start in life, probably away from the city environment.

I had not tried to find a site for Lazarus, but felt that the locations I tentatively selected for the sisters would suit their needs admirably—one was a large island between the two arms of the Rhodanus* River, and the other a high promontory on its bank some miles farther inland. Both locations had been settled by squatters who made no claim of ownership and were eager to be employed as stewards of the property for the sisters.

I thought it might be a year before they made the move here from Bethany, and I felt a restlessness to get on to Britannia, especially in view of the large company of family, and others that were delaying here with me. And then, unexpectedly, the Roman post brought me the following letter:

> From Lazarus of Bethany;
> To my dear Uncle Joseph, late of Arimathea;
> Greetings from all of us and blessings in the name of our Christ:
>
> You will be surprised to hear from me with news of our imminent departure, but matters have moved faster and more insidiously than I had expected. We had assumed that by moving the mortgages and loans I held from Caiaphas and Annas to bankers out of the country, and by the bankers serving notice that any execution of me (formally as happened with Jesus, or by mob action as we had feared for you) would result in immediate foreclosure on their obligations, my life would be adequately protected. Unfortunately, we naively misjudged them.
>
> Less than a month ago I was lost in thought as I walked at the border of a narrow street in the lower City. I would not normally have noticed the fast passage of a chariot, but the shout of another pedestrian caused me to look in time to see the horse-drawn chariot bearing down on me. Even so, I usually would just have stepped over against the building wall to let the vehicle pass, but I happened to notice a large puddle of water and to avoid being drenched I quickly jumped into the doorway of a shop I was then passing. An instant later the hub of the chariot wheel ground against the stone wall of the building, leaving a scar some ten paces long on the

---

*Rhone.

wall on each side of the doorway where I stood. As the shopkeeper and I jumped out to look, I saw that it indeed was a battle chariot with heavy hubs and that the driver was in battle dress with the visor down over his face. Traffic at the moment could not explain his action, which clearly was an attempt to crush me against the wall. It may well have been a Roman chariot "informally borrowed" for the occasion, but I was sure that the driver was a hired assassin.

And then, last week I chanced to be in the sane general neighborhood. I was not walking fast, and I definitely had my wits about me. Nonetheless, my survival was a close thing—a few paces behind me a friend called my name, and I stopped instantly as I turned to look. In that instant, a large section of the stone cornice "fell" into my path from the roof of the building I was passing. Had I taken one more step I would have been mashed like an insect.

I am sure my guardian angel was working hard to protect me, but I have no desire to put him further to the test. Fortunately, in recent weeks we have made the final property transfers and are prepared to leave Bethany at once—and it would be hard to imagine more fortuitous arrangements. The two difficult items, of course, were Mary's large and lovely Magdala property and our home place here in Bethany.

As matters developed, a relative of Herodias, Herod's wife, wished to move from Perea to the vicinity of Herod's new city of Tiberias on the Sea of Galilee, and when he saw Mary's home in Magdala was totally captivated by it. This prospective buyer quite naturally approached Herod's steward, Chuza, for advice, not knowing that the latter's wife, Joanna, had been a devout follower of Jesus on his travels, along with my sister, Mary. As a consequence, Chuza told him he doubted the premises were for sale but that, of course, with enough money most anything could be purchased. With such titillation it became a simple matter for Mary to obtain a fabulous price for the place.

You may have heard me speak of Silas bar Esau,* a wealthy man of Jericho, who has often expressed his envy regarding our home here in Bethany. He has been suffering for some time with a stiffness and pain in his joints which makes movement difficult for him. Then, two months ago he was elected Elder in the Great Sanhedrin, which has caused him to seek for a convenient place for lavish entertainment. It was at this juncture that I had an agent tell him in confidence that our home might be available on condition of total secrecy of the transaction for a few months. As you know, our home is owned by Martha, under the terms of the wise Will left

---

*Fictional.

by our father; she, in turn, has privately said that she absolutely will not haggle over the sale price. The result has been a sale to Silas at virtually his own price though a very adequate one—and a fair assurance that our early departure will remain undisclosed.

Moreover, the return to vigorous good health by our wonderful neighbor, Simon "the leper," since his healing by Jesus, has given him the urge for more activity, and so we have secretly sold him all our adjacent lands—the orchards, vineyards, olive groves, fields and pastures with farm buildings. He also will help us keep up the facade of permanence while we prepare for our move. He has arranged our purchase of several sturdy carts that are now in our barns and nearly fully packed with our belongings. The axles have been well-greased with tallow for silent movement, and within a few days now we will leave in the middle of the night, going through the orchard to by-pass the town, and by morning will be well past Jericho and ready to cross the Jordan; we would not risk crossing Judea, Samaria or Galilee to reach the coast.

If our timing is right, we expect to join a well-guarded caravan from Egypt that is travelling up The King's Highway to Damascus; from there we shall go to the Phoenician port of Arvad, where the Legate of Antioch promises to have a bireme waiting that will take us to Massalia, just as one took you last Spring.

We look forward to seeing you all soon, and send our love on ahead of us to you.

✠   ✠   ✠

In due course, they did arrive,[1] and we spent much of the winter months getting homes built and getting them settled in this area of southern Gaul, and in preparing our own belongings for a Spring movement northward across Gaul to Britannia.

Needless to say, during those months together in Gaul, Lazarus and I had many opportunities for extended conversations. And one day I remembered to ask him: "Lazarus, what happened to the account of Jesus' ministry that I encouraged you to write?"

"I finished all that I could write from first-hand knowledge, especially covering the periods when he visited in Jerusalem and ministered in Samaria, Perea and other areas across the Jordan," he replied. "However, for it to be useful in the future it should also cover his ministry in Galilee and the north. So, I left it with my disciple, John of Bethphage,[2] because he is uncle to Zebedee's sons, John and James; they will be able to describe those times for him and to tell of how Jesus trained them."

"I appreciate the soundness of your reasons," was my response, "but I wonder about the strong biases that John of Bethphage has evidenced at times."

"True, he has," said Lazarus, "but I an hopeful that the events of this year will have mellowed him somewhat. The post-resurrection appearances of Jesus have confirmed to him his strong Gnostic beliefs about the permanency of spirit. Yet, I think watching Jesus' very real suffering on the cross may have brought him to accept that Jesus was wholly man as well as his spirit being wholly God. In my conversations with John this summer while you have been gone leads me to believe he is now not so quick to denigrate all things physical."

"That sounds encouraging," I agreed, "and I suppose his apocalyptic views are harmless enough. One way or another, time will soon put into perspective the few statements Jesus made on the subject. I trust he will not publicly release the writings in Jerusalem while the climate there is so hostile."

"I think not," he responded. "We discussed that situation; once his sickly daughter dies, John expects to move to Ephesus in Asia where all the rest of his family now lives. He probably will not release the writings until he is there."

"But is John an adequate scholar, so that he can do justice to a work of such importance?" I wanted to know.

"Probably not," Lazarus agreed, "but he is a very intelligent man, and many of his family in Ephesus now are well-educated Greeks. A younger cousin of John is so highly regarded a scholar that he has become an important scribe in Rome and has taken the Roman name of Tychicus.[3] The latter is much given to philosophical theorizing, but his erudition can be a great help to John in formalizing the writings."

"I presume the writing will bear your name," I commented.

"No, it will not," said Lazarus emphatically. "It is much more important that the writing be preserved and be released in the proper climate. And so, I specifically authorized John to ultimately release the writings under his own name. This pleased him greatly and will, I am sure, make publication certain. I also told him not to identify me as 'the beloved disciple'—he was less than enthusiastic on this point as it has become a favored expression of John's for describing me; nevertheless, I could see that such an appellation was anathema to some of the Galileans, especially the volatile sons of Zebedee, and I don't need accolades from posterity."

I laughed and agreed, "No, I'm sure you don't. But I hope you did include the full story of your raising from the dead by Jesus, for I doubt that either Mark or Matthew will do so if they publish their writings on Jesus."

"I did include the bare story of my raising," he acknowledged, "because I felt it was too important an action by Jesus for me to omit it; but I wrote nothing of my experience in heaven, as I related it to you—in fact, I have told that to no one but my sisters and yourself, and of course, to Jesus."

"Yes, an experience beyond the grave would be difficult for some to accept," I agreed. "And what of my sister, Enygeus, and her husband, Hebron, and family?"

"We spent several hours with them on the way to Damascus," Lazarus replied. "They have every intention of joining you in Britanicus, but it cannot be before next summer. Also, I feel that Hebron is looking for some convenient way to terminate his employment with Herod Philip without angering the king."

Almost as an afterthought, Lazarus then added: "Of course, I realized that our fallible memories too quickly lose even the most important details, and so, before departure, I commissioned a reliable scribe-copyist to make copies for you and me of my Jesus Journal before giving the original to John, as I feel sure we will find important use for it in these new lands in the days to come."

I assured him that his thoughtfulness pleased me immensely.

CHAPTER NOTES:

1. Several of the New Testament apocrypha detail the flight to Marseilles of Joseph of Arimathea and family, and of Lazarus with his sisters. Their flight is also validated in the writings of Rhabanus (Magnentius Rhabanus Maurus), archbishop of Mayence, ca. 784, and is reported with elaboration in several current volumes from London. Also, Vatican Librarian, Caesar Baronius, in 1596, wrote in his *Annales Ecclesiastici* that Vatican manuscripts described the arrival in Marseilles in A.D. 35 of the refugee company from Judea that included Joseph of Arimathea and Lazarus of Bethany and his sisters.

2. The authorship of the book of John and the identity of "the beloved disciple" as discussed in this chapter, is fully proposed by Dr. J. Schoneberg Setzer in his article, "Did Lazarus Write the Gospel of John?" *Spiritual Frontiers,* XII-1, Winter 1980, pp. 14-19. Setzer posits three writers of this Gospel: the first being Lazarus who wrote "a layer of early authentic Jesus material"; the second contributing "an overlay of Christian apocalypticism, including gnosticism and Palestinian Judaism" and showing adulation for the first writer; and finally "by the editing of a Christian Hellenist who has provided the prologue and much of the lengthy discourse material." Bethphage was a village on the Mount of Olives between Bethany and Jerusalem, so it seems at least practical if not likely that John of Bethphage was a disciple of Lazarus; legend tells us he died in Ephesus. "The Gospel of John, in the scholarly mind the most Greek of the Gospels, is in fact Semitic in its syntax and style," reports W. D. Davis in "My Odyssey in New Testament Interpretation," *Bible Review,* V-3, June 1989.

The late John A. T. Robinson in his last book, *The Priority of John* (Meyer-Stone Books, 1985), speaks of the "presumption of priority" of the Gospel of John, in contrast to the usual priority given the synoptic Gospels: "His witness, therefore, alike to the history and the theology is, I believe, to be accorded a status of *primus inter pares* [first among equals] ... as well as being the most mature piece of writing in the New Testament." He also notes that "'The beloved disciple' on whose testimony it is based tends to become an 'unknown Jerusalem disciple'..." though the question of authorship "would be perfectly compatible with several hands having been at work." And further, citing Brownlee, a contributor in *John and Qumran* (ed. by J. H. Charlesworth, London, 1972), Robinson notes: "It has been said that while the external evidence points to John the son of Zebedee, the internal points to Lazarus as the one person in this Gospel of whom it is specifically said that Jesus loved him." And he cites R. E. Brown, who changed his own mind, and in *The Community of the Beloved Disciple* (New York, 1979), firmly agrees that the "beloved disciple" is neither John bar Zebedee nor one other of the Twelve. Robinson then concludes this discussion with "the presumption that the Fourth Gospel could take us as far back to source as any other."

In *The Secret Identity of the Beloved Disciple* (Paulist Press, 1992), the author, Professor Joseph A. Grassi, summarizes and correlates this century's research on "the greatest enigma of the New Testament," and puts the clues together for a "composite portrait"—which matches Lazarus perfectly, though not named by Grassi.

3. Tychicus is named in Ephesians 6:21 as emissary from Paul, carrying the epistle from Rome to the church of Ephesus in Asia, in A.D. 61 or 62, and logistically the Gospel of John easily could have evolved from Lazarus' narrative, embellishment by his disciple, John of Bethphage after reaching Ephesus, and finally the Prologue and discourse material by Paul's disciple, Tychicus, who carried Paul's Letter to Ephesus.

✠

A Report of Thaddaeus from Edessa

A.D. 33

*A*FTER RECEIPT OF LAZARUS' LETTER but before his arrival, our autumn in southern Gaul was marked by delivery of the first report from Thaddaeus on the Shroud of Jesus, and of his mission to Edessa:

> From Thaddaeus and Miriam of Edessa, *now officially called "The Land of The Way of Jesus the Christ"*;
> To our revered Lord Joseph, late of Arimathea;
> Greetings from us both, felicitations from King Abgar and his First Secretary, Aggai, and blessings in the name of our Christ:
> Yes, it is true!—the province of Osroene and the city of Edessa—the entire domain of King Abgar V—is now officially described.as The Land of The Way of Jesus the Christ—it certainly is the first country to be so declared! As you must know, this is a very proud country, which broke away from the great Seleucid Empire some two centuries ago, and is now loosely affiliated with the Parthians of Ctesiphon, far to the East, for its own protection.
> As I told you in my letter to Arimathea, King Abgar was instantly, totally, miraculously, and (we must suppose) permanently healed of all his infirmities in the moment that he first looked upon the Resurrection Image of Jesus' face.[1] After I baptized Abgar and Aggai into the fellowship of The Way the following day, and preached a series of discourses to huge

crowds in and around Edessa, the response has been so great that only in recent days have we caught up with the baptizings—in spite of the help of Aggai the entire time and of Thomas in recent weeks.

(I must also note that I seem to be most eloquent and convincing with my discourses, even though, as you well know, I had never before attempted public speaking—something most certainly must have happened during the consecration ceremony conducted by Peter.)

Within a week of my arrival, baptism had been requested by every member of Abgar's family, household and court, except for his second son, Essau. Although the name, Essau, is a very honored one in these parts, this son is a very haughty young man and he insists on being called Ma'nu, a revered title of some of the earlier kings of Edessa; of course, I am hopeful that in time he also will join our fellowship. I have not been able to keep a count of these large numbers of converts, but I don't doubt the King's claim that more than half of the City has joined with us.

There is so much to tell you that I hardly know how to begin! One of Aggai's most time-consuming duties had been as robe-maker to the King, since ostentation in dress had long been characteristic of Parthian kings. However, shortly after his baptism, Abgar advised Aggai that he would no longer indulge in such a vain practice, it being inappropriate, he felt, for a follower of The Way. That decision freed Aggai from all except ceremonial duties for the King, and it was agreed between them that Aggai would become my principal disciple and devote most of his time to assisting me, which has made for a most fortuitous and pleasing result.

Moreover, that step has also solved a small problem that had been something of a personal concern for me. You will recall I had promised Elias bar Jacob in Arimathea that I would find a worker in rich fabrics to make a cloth-of-gold overlay for the Shroud; such, with a hole in the center to show the Face, would enhance its mystique and beauty, while the wide expanse of unmarked and unadorned linen would be appropriately covered. When I happened to mention that promise to Aggai, he replied with a broad smile: "Look no further, brother Thaddaeus. My office as robe-maker to the King was not just a political plum, but a merited assignment because I was recognized as the most skilled worker in fabrics in the kingdom. I, a Jew, and a part of the very large Jewish population of Edessa, was, of course, required by our religion to become proficient in a trade; this skill with fabrics I learned under the guidance of my father, who had pursued it as his lifetime work."

As a result, dear Joseph, King Abgar provided the richest and most beautiful piece of cloth-of-gold in a lattice pattern, and Aggai has made, positioned and neatly stitched the overlay onto the top layer of the Shroud cloth.[2] Naturally, I promptly wrote to Elias of this beautiful overlay.

I hasten to assure you that Aggai has no idea that the Face is only a part of the full-bodied Image and that the cloth is a full burial Shroud. Moreover, neither he nor anyone else here knows that the Image was probably made in the course of the Resurrection event. In this kingdom, only Thomas and I have that knowledge.

One of the most exciting developments, from a personal standpoint, is the discovery that I am now able to perform miraculous healings much in the fashion of those performed by master Jesus. But by no means am I claiming equality with him!—on the contrary, and to my great chagrin, I have had spectacular successes and abysmal failures. Thomas just laughs, and says that this also is the experience of the Galilean Twelve. I had thought that if there were serious health problems suffered by people who, in the future, I wished to see healed, that I would have to let them see or touch the mystical image of Jesus' face. In discussing this latter thought with Thomas, he demurred, saying that he felt it would demean this so fabulous and precious relic to use it for such purposes—and it was at this point that Thomas said: "*You* can heal now, you know. That was one of the purposes of the consecration service Peter and the others held for you in Jerusalem. You have the power; all you need to do is use it so it will grow."

And consequently, under his guidance I have been doing so, and with great pleasure and gratification. Thomas arrived midsummer and promises to stay with me until next Spring to help me and to train me further. I had not realized what a wonderful person he is, and he is certainly building my self-confidence, which naturally makes me think more highly of him!

Thomas has brought me much news of the Galilean Twelve, but I suppose the most surprising development was his report that Jesus' brother James is now the leader of The Way.[3] In separate post-resurrection appearances to James and to Peter, Master Jesus informed them of this new role for James. Of course, I was amazed, because I knew that James had not approved of Jesus' ministry, partly because it was an embarrassment and handicap to his Galilean family. Thomas said that James was present in the upper room at Pentecost when the power of God's Spirit descended on all present—of course, you knew this since Thomas tells me that you also were there. But you may not know that James never returned to Galilee; he merely sent for his family and has continued in residence in Jerusalem since that time. Thomas says that James' stern and pious attitude has already earned him the title of James the Just—probably behind his back—but at least he is better accepted at the Temple than any of the Twelve would be.

Assignments for the Twelve have been at least tacitly agreed upon, although lines are flexible and there will be some overlapping. Thomas, as expected, will supervise all the missionary work from here eastward. Nevertheless, several others will probably come this way for a while. We

are looking forward to a brief visit from Andrew whose permanent assignment is to be Macedonia, but who wishes first to spend a year or so among
the Scythians, far to the northeast from here—and, of course, Thomas is
very pleased to have Andrew's assistance in that huge territory to the east.
Similarly, Matthias, who replaced Judas, and Jude, Jesus' brother, both
are expected to pass through here next year on their way to Armenia, for
further assistance to Thomas, probably on a temporary basis. John bar
Zebedee and Nathaniel bar Tolmai (Bartholomew) will go northwest of
us to Asia, and consequently will not likely stop by here. Both Matthew
and Simon (Zealote), Jesus' brother, will go first to Alexandria in Egypt,
and then possibly Simon will go on to Africa westward from Egypt.

Peter, it seems, will be spending little time in either Galilee or Judea
in the foreseeable future; his efforts will be mainly in Syria at the moment, and later in Asia and Macedonia, and Thomas expects that in time
Peter will certainly be in Rome—so, it seems practical that James be continuously in Jerusalem to give support to the various far-flung missions.
Thomas still looks to Peter as the spiritual head of our movement, and he
attaches special significance to a strange incident that happened in your
old neighborhood.

The story, as Thomas got it, was that Peter was resting and visiting
with a long-time friend, Simon the tanner, in Joppa; I'm sure you knew
him well.[4] Thomas thinks that Peter's extended stay in Joppa was for
more than just rest—that Peter was deeply concerned about the direction
of his own ministry and of the entire ministry of The Way. Peter had real
concern, Thomas thinks, on the question of restricting our ministry to our
homeland—which a few rather loudly urge, or taking it to the surrounding
areas as Jesus did, though briefly—or to the diaspora at large, or the Samaritans, or even to the gentiles; this latter question was a thorny one for
the Galileans, but didn't Master Jesus rather clearly say, in the last months
of his ministry, that we are to make disciples of all nations?

Thus, while resting in Joppa, Peter was probably hoping to sort things
out in his mind while away from the others—and there can be no doubt
that worry is more fatiguing than hard labor.

In any event, Thomas says that while Peter was taking a nap in the
early afternoon, he had a repetitive dream—Peter claimed that it was a
vision while he was in meditation. Whichever it may have been, Peter
saw a large cloth let down through the air while invisibly supported at
the four corners; in the cloth were all manner of tame and wild beasts and
birds; as he saw these squirming animals, Peter heard a Voice telling him,
"Peter, kill and eat."

Peter orally objected since those animals, or most of them, were
unclean according to the Law of Moses as presently interpreted by the

Scribes; but the Voice answered him: "What God has cleansed, call not unclean."

Peter roused briefly from his dream or vision, and then as he closed his eyes, the sight of the cloth and animals returned with the same instruction, "Kill and eat," followed by his same refusal and the response. After these occurrences had repeated a third time, Peter was fully awakened by a servant telling him that a messenger was asking for him.

It turned out to be a courier from centurion Cornelius in Caesarea who asked urgently to see Peter. The courier and escort were invited to eat and spend the night. Next morning, a horse being provided for Peter, he then left with the courier for Caesarea. They rode at a brisk pace all day and into the night before arriving. The next morning Peter found Cornelius and his large Roman family assembled, together with servants and friends. Cornelius greeted Peter profusely and reverently, and then explained: "In the six years that I have been assigned to your country it has been my privilege and pleasure to learn extensively of your religion and to read your books of Moses and of the Prophets. I have learned these things in large measure from my wonderful Jewish servants whom you see here, and I had achieved the skill of reading the Hebrew language as a youth, from my excellent tutor in Rome, who was a Jewish scholar of your diaspora.

"But in the past year I have been hearing more and more of the somewhat revolutionary teachings of the rabbi Jesus of Galilee, who was executed last Spring by Pilate, and I feel that my heart and my soul can wait no longer to hear fully of Jesus' teachings directly from someone who knows. Will you tell us all we should hear about Jesus and his message?"

"But how did you know where to find me?" asked Peter, somewhat bemused by the situation, and not fully comfortable in close association with so many gentiles. "Neither my friends in Jerusalem nor those in Galilee knew where I was."

Cornelius then explained: "I am somewhat embarrassed to answer you, as you may think me mentally unbalanced. But I know I must do so. Four days ago, after reading to my family from the words of your prophet Isaiah at the breakfast table, I returned to my bed-chamber for my customary time of prayer before beginning my duties of the day. Thereafter, when I turned to the door, I found a man before me whose brilliant white robe was glowing as if on fire, and who said to me: 'Cornelius, be not afraid. Your prayers and your exemplary life have been observed by God. Send to Joppa at the house of Simon the tanner, and ask for Simon called Peter to come to you; he will tell you of The Way of Jesus the Christ.'

"I could hear and see him as he spoke, but I could also see through him—could see the door and the door-latch behind him; and then, in the wink of an eye he was gone. I knew then it had to have been an angel, and so I sent for you."

The result was that Peter told all of them of the Good News, and they began to speak in tongues as Peter had heard at Pentecost. And they all asked forthwith to join our fellowship, so Peter baptized them and stayed there teaching them for several days. But when Peter returned to Jerusalem he found that the news of his experience in Caesarea had reached there before him, and that some of the brethren immediately criticized him for eating with gentiles and for baptizing them without circumcision. However, after he had told them the full story, James and the others agreed that it was proper to permit baptism of the uncircumcised—the gentiles. But Thomas is not sure that all of the brethren were really convinced that this is right.

We are not yet sure how that concern is developing in Jerusalem and Galilee, but when other disciples come by here we will know more. Aggai and Thomas and I are also discussing at length the various ways in which we care for the Holy Face, as we now call it, and I will write you again in a few months. For the time being the casket of Elias containing the Face is being kept in Abgar's Treasury.

I commented above on how wonderful I have found Thomas to be; he has educated me especially as to the many-splendored personality of Jesus. As you know, my opportunity for participating in his Judean ministry was limited almost entirely to listening the several times he preached in the outlying towns surrounding Jerusalem. Thomas, however, has been able to describe extensively the informal Jesus, as he talked with The Twelve on both serious and trivial subjects, and as he challenged and entertained, in turn, the hosts and guests at social gatherings and meals in interesting homes throughout the land.

According to Thomas, Jesus was not only an entertaining storyteller on these informal and social occasions, but had a sense of humor that was wide-ranging, from subtle to boisterous. From his public ministry I was aware of the scathing ridicule he could heap on pompous public figures—well-knowing that a leader laughed at is destroyed more quickly than a leader hated. "He taught us laughter, and the value of fun," said Thomas.

"It was easy to see that he loved Peter more deeply than any other," Thomas tells me, "because most often Jesus was poking gentle fun at Peter's impetuousness. And I was pleased," he continued, "that with some regularity he found ways to tease me about my excess of caution, as I usually want to know 'Why,' and be convinced before I act."

Thomas indicated that Jesus' younger brother, Jude, was another that he loved to tease good-naturedly, but that he rarely made fun of the

Zebedee brothers, James and John, except to occasionally use his pet label for them, "sons of thunder," since they were so emotionally volatile,
often acting without thought and out of anger, prejudice or other strong
emotion. Bartholomew of Cyprus, and sometimes Jude, were the only
ones, according to Thomas, who dared—or were witty enough—to turn
the tables with jokes on the Master; on these occasions no one laughed as
loud as Jesus, though Peter and his brother Andrew also loved to laugh.
I'm sure you were well aware of this side of Jesus, but the disclosure was
quite a revelation, and a pleasure, to me."

Much as I enjoyed and valued this long and informative letter, I was
thrilled the most by discovering that Thaddaeus had enclosed for me an
exquisitely penned and beautifully bound copy of Stephen's manuscript,
the "Sayings and Discourses of Jesus." He had certainly found a local
scribe-copyist whose work was beyond compare. But, beautiful as it was,
my real thrill was anticipation that my work to evangelize Britannia would
be aided so greatly by this authentic set of quotations from Master Jesus.[5]

Chapter Notes:

1. Eusebius, Emperor Constantine's Christian historian, wrote (ca. A.D. 325) *The History of the Church,* and in its Book One, Chapters 12 and 13, he describes the healing
of Abgar from his leprosy, which took place in the year of the Resurrection (A.D. 33);
Eusebius says that he translated this information from records in Edessa written in
Syriac. Abgar did live until A.D. 50. Although Eusebius attributes Abgar's healing to a
laying-on-of-hands by Thaddaeus, other ancient records (e.g., *The Doctrine of Addai the
Apostle*) and explicitly descriptive art (see Color Plate 3, p. 128 ff., *Portrait of Jesus?* by
this author, and text at p. 43) suggest that the healing was effected when Thaddaeus,
one of the Seventy, who was sent by Thomas, showed Abgar the mystical Face of Jesus,
described by the Greek word, *acheiropoietos,* "not made by human hands." "The Face,"
later to be called the *mandylion* by the Byzantines, was kept in Edessa as a great Christian relic until A.D. 944, and was the focus for Christian pilgrimages in great number.

2. This lattice pattern overlay surrounding the face of Jesus was an oft-repeated object
of religious art in the early and middle centuries, which today's scientists find is exactly
the Shroud of Turin face; see *Portrait of Jesus?* by Frank C. Tribbe, text on pp. 46-47,
with pictures on p. 248 and the Face of Laon in the colored photographs section.

3. .The apocryphal *Gospel of the Hebrews* seems to support succession by James, true
sibling and full brother of Jesus, as does Josephus' *Antiquities of the Jews,* Chap. IX
paragraph 1.

4. See Acts 10.

5. This is the "Q document" that scholars have presumed must have existed, recording
sayings and discourses of Jesus, and which was used by Matthew and Luke in writing
their Gospels.

CHAPTER FORTY-FIVE

✠

We Become Britons

A.D. 34

T HE WINTER MONTHS AND EARLY SPRING passed so very quickly in southern Gaul because the mild weather permitted us to work almost continuously in renovating and building appropriate premises for Martha and Mary and their servants. Lazarus was with us most of the time but took the opportunity for several trips north and east of the River delta area, scouting the locations he might select for the beginning of his missionary work to spread Jesus' message to the Gauls.

As buds and blossoms everywhere were heralding the progress of Spring, we waited impatiently for the seasonal flood on the River Rhodanus to subside so that river-boats could make headway upstream. Early traffic on the Great Sea had already begun, and I kept in touch with the port of Massalia in case messages for us might arrive. Consequently, imagine my surprise when one fine day a trim Roman bireme docked with Enygeus and Hebron and their large family and entourage aboard.

When our exclamations and embraces of greeting finally subsided, I inquired of Hebron: "How did you manage to leave Herod Philip's employ?"

"The easiest way ever," he replied with a broad smile. "Philip died! I didn't wait around for either medical reports or political rumors, but I would suspect that it was merely rich living that did him in. Yet, quick as we were to leave, his widow, Salome, was even quicker; servants around the palace said that three days after his death, she left for the residence of her cousin, Aristobulus, king of Chalcis to the north."*

---

*Whom she later married.

Needless to say, talking and frenzied preparations occupied us all for the next two weeks until our start north with our enlarged company. Portaging our extensive amounts of baggage slowed our transfer to the northwest-ward flowing River. At its mouth we were fortunately able to obtain the services of two empty cargo vessels which brought us to Meare Island, deep into Britannia's long channel that runs from west to east.* Our stop at Meare was only for a few hours, to obtain foodstuffs and a promise of help from friends of years past, before we pushed on to the island of the Great Tor** at whose foot we would build our community.

After preliminary survey and exploration of our island home, Hebron came excitedly up to me to say: "Brother Joseph, you said no one had ever lived at the foot of this Tor, but come see the small house I have just found that is in excellent condition."

Nestled right on the first slope of the Tor was indeed a beautifully built wattle-house, which of course I recognized immediately.

"This," I said to Hebron, "is the sanctuary Jesus built fourteen years ago when he spent a three-month period here by himself. I agree it is still in excellent shape, but I wouldn't feel right using it for ordinary purposes—I think we'll keep it to serve as our meeting place for religious services."

As I stood on this tidewater plain and looked up—more than five hun-dred feet, I judged—at the stark but majestic cone of the Great Tor, I had the nagging feeling that I had seen it before, *somewhere else*. I shrugged off the thought, and then suddenly the memory came to me—this conical hill, natural and yet mockingly artificial, was superficially almost a duplicate of the palace-fortress created by Herod the Great at Herodium in the Judean desert some half-dozen years before I was born. Of course, there are dif-ferences: Herodium, just eight miles south of Jerusalem, is at the edge of the Judean hills, more than two thousand feet above sea level; also, its top is flat, some two hundred feet across, and hollow like a volcanic crater, but containing a sumptuous palace/fortress complex. I recall hearing my grand-father describe how Herod's workmen built the fortress and palaces on top of a natural hill, and surrounded it with two concentric circular walls rising nearly a hundred feet above bedrock and flanked by four military towers; when it was completed, they then carried gravel and earth to pour down the sides—blending with the natural slope of the hill below and nearly cover-ing the outer wall, so that little more than the towers were visible from a distance. Once, as a youth, my father arranged for me to take a fascinating

---

*Bristol Channel.
**Glastonbury's conical hill.

tour through this structure, imposing still, though deteriorated by disuse; I found that it even had inside access to underground water supplies. Musing on it now, I wondered if the Great Tor before me could similarly have been a man-made addition onto a natural hill—I know from my first explorations, when I came to Britannia as a youth with my father, that there are ruins of some sort of structure on the top of the Tor. I wonder![1]

☩ ☩ ☩

Hebron and my son Josephes had been to Britannia with me in past years, but for all the others this was a strange land that had surprises for them nearly every day. One of their biggest surprises was the mild summer weather without the enervating heat we always had experienced during Judean summers—this land was green all summer and hardly a week passed without rain!

On a quick trip to visit Cymric's tin streaming operation, I assured him that by Fall I would begin to take on a more intimate involvement in the marketing of tin for our joint interests. The immediate concern, however, was selection and agreement on the home-sites for our respective family units and the commencement of construction of our dwelling buildings, as well as community buildings in support of our agricultural and food gathering activities—and the latter activity, fortunately, had the enthusiastic and generous support and advice from the people of Meare. I selected for Elyap and me a location near Jesus' sanctuary on the first slope leading up the Tor, and, somewhat symbolically, I drove my thorn-tree staff into the soft ground as a marker for the spot of our rest and an end to weariness of spirit—this was the staff Reuben had hurriedly fashioned for me from the thorn-tree after he had cut it down upon my emotional command—for it was the tree from which Herod's lackeys had fashioned a crown of thorns they mashed upon Jesus' scalp. I digress to note that well before commencement of the Fall season that strange staff had taken root and put out branches and leaves—and with wry, memory-inspired thoughts, I decided to let it grow as a permanent reminder to us of Jesus' love, and obedience to God's guidance to him.[2]

Reuben's many practical skills and his permanent good humor perfectly fitted him to become the administrator of our community, so that within a short time the rest of us would be free to pursue the missionary efforts among the Britons that I foresaw as our mission in this land. For the time being, planning and overseeing the necessary housing program, and our agricultural efforts so we could quickly approach self-sufficiency, kept

Original Glastonbury Thorn (right), destroyed by a vandal;
present Glastonbury Thorn (left), grown from slip of the original Tree.
Photos courtesy of Goheen Antiques

Thorn Tree grown from slip of the original Glastonbury Thorn,
with Washington National Cathedral in background.
Photo taken by Frank C. Tribbe

me fully occupied through late Spring and the early Summer months, but as a permanent resident of Britannia I had different interests and priorities than when just a visitor, and so even in those first weeks I managed to have several conversations with the elders at Meare and with my old mining associate, Cymric, concerning religious matters. They identified for me the several Druids, or priests, with whom Jesus had talked the Summer he spent here, and told me how to find the Arch Druid. Also, to the extent of their limited abilities, they gave me much information about their religion.

But then, one day, when I chanced to look up from my labors, I beheld a young Druid in his distinctive garb standing at the edge of the clearing and smiling a sweet welcome to me. Although he was a stranger, he quickly reached out to embrace me as I approached. Carefully, being aware of my limited command of his language, he bid me and my company welcome and stated that their spiritual leader, the Arch Druid for this area, would be honored to have me come visit with him.

I decided to go at once, and told Elyap not to worry if I did not get back 'till the morrow. A waiting horse drawn cart took us in a somewhat northeasterly direction into the hills, and the messenger told me that a trip of a couple of hours was in prospect. The transport was not too uncomfortable in spite of the uneven terrain, but the constant loud groan of the turning axle minimized conversation. Nevertheless, the messenger gave me to understand that I would be among friends as I was well known to them through my shipping activities and my dealings for many years with old Cymric in the tin mining operations to the southwest.

When we arrived I was taken at once to the home of the Arch Druid, whom I found to be a thin wisp of a man of great age but whose blue eyes were the kindest in appearance of any man, save Jesus, that I had ever known. His voice was just above a whisper and he welcomed me with an apology for not standing to embrace me because of his weakness. He was flanked by a half dozen senior Druids each of whom rose and embraced me in turn, obviously in the order of their rank; their beaming smiles and strong embraces left no doubt as to their friendliness.

"And tell us of your so beautiful nephew, Jesu, whom we have missed but have well-remembered for these fourteen years since he lived among us," gently said the Arch Druid.

"I have both wonderful and distressful news of him, but it is a somewhat lengthy story," I replied.

"Nothing would please us more than to listen for hours to such a telling—you know, of course, that we use little writing and the spoken word is our greatest pleasure when used for an important message," he replied.

And so, carefully, and with as much detail as I could muster, I told the Druids of Jesus' ministry and message, of his passion and crucifixion, his resurrection and subsequent appearances, the Pentecostal empowerment, his Shroud with its mystical images and the steps taken to protect it, my own imprisonment, escape and exile

There was not a word of interruption and daylight was fast fading by the time I finished my account, but there was no movement or sign of boredom—on the contrary, every face glowed with rapt attention and interest.

All waited for the reaction of the Arch Druid, who finally spoke: "So beautiful a telling!"—his voice was vibrant with emotion, though barely audible.

"And it was all so appropriate," he continued. "When Jesu was with us we spoke often of our Druidic belief of man's need for atonement for sin, and he often would protest that sacrifice of innocent animals should not be used to achieve atonement—that, rather, it was an insult to a loving God. Yes, his action was fitting—a perfect atonement for all. He must have been the Messiah—you claim too little for him!"

I laughed, and squeezed his hand, as he signalled that the evening meal should be served.

As we ate, the Arch Druid spoke softly to me from time to time, explaining their religious beliefs to me. "You see," he said, "we believe in One God, the Creator of the universe, and that we are immortal souls that will survive death of the physical body. We also have a very high regard for truth; our motto is, The Truth Against the Whole World, and we often train our young Druids by asking them to debate the question, 'What is Truth?'"

"Your religion seems very similar to mine," I told him. "The Romans call you Celts, just as they do the tribes in Gaul across the great Channel to the south. What can you tell me of the history of your people?"

"All of our wisdom is committed to memory," he replied. "Since our meal is nearly over, I will ask one of the young Druids to recite for you a long poem that gives our history. We find that the poetic format makes for easier memorization."

The musical effect of the young man's recitation was very pleasant to the ear and the colorful story he told seemed to cover several centuries. I could not recognize the names of people and places, but I was greatly intrigued by the apparent movement over great distances, always in a northwesterly direction. It was a very long story that the young man recited, and so it was bed-time before he finished; I was glad it was too late to talk any more, because there were many ideas his story had stirred in my mind which I wanted to think about—and indeed that thinking kept me awake in my bed for most of the night.

My thoughts harked back to the early Spring in my thirty-fifth year;* Tiberius had been emperor but five years, and Abgar V had been on the throne of Edessa for six years in his second reign.** Through arrangements made by my Edessa agent, Tobias bar Tobias, I was spending a pleasant social evening in Abgar's company, after a brief but highly satisfactory business transaction that had been developed by Tobias and which had been the purpose of my trip.

I happened to mention my need for a new source of the valuable writing material, parchment, which was highly desired at the Jerusalem Temple and by various scriptoria in our country. This was of limited supply since it came almost entirely from the Asian city of Pergamum, just a short distance inland from the Aegean Sea. The workers there specialized in producing these thin sheets from the skins of kids, but because their last king had ceded the city to Rome some century and a half ago, for us that source had practically dried up.

At this point in our conversation King Abgar commented: "Lord Joseph, I believe I can suggest a solution for you, though the source I propose would involve much travel. It is the kingdom of Armenia, whose capital is Artaxata, far to the east and nearly at the southern shores of the great land-locked sea the Romans call Caspian. The present ruler, Artaxias III,*** was placed on the throne nearly two years ago by Rome, and he had been my guest here for several months beforehand, so I think he will favor you when he reads the letter I will give you as introduction. Additionally, my half-brother, Tirotates, has been official Historian in Armenia for many years, and I'm sure he will gladly be your host and may additionally be of some assistance."

As a result, the following day I had Tobias send a message to my office in Arimathea, saying I would be gone for another three to four months, and, while awaiting the letters Abgar was preparing, Tobias arranged for me to accompany a small, fast caravan that was leaving in three days for Artaxata. We purchased a good horse and a large pack mule, and quickly collected the provisions I would need.

Weeks later when I arrived in Artaxata, I found that the letter from Abgar worked a charm on King Artaxias, and he could not have been more helpful. We both thought it would be desirable that I take a sizeable first shipment of parchment back with me, but then an obstacle delayed me: the factor representing the sellers of parchment was unwilling to take my

---

*A.D. 19.
**He reigned 4 B.C. to A.D. 77 and again, A.D. 13-50.
***Ruled A.D. 18-34.

Letter of Credit on my bank in Rome without it being validated; his position was not unreasonable since I had not done business in their country
before and, although involving a slight embarrassment, the King's assurances were not acceptable since he was newly on the throne and had not
previously known me. Official Roman couriers did not come here often,
but fortunately one did arrive two days later and planned to return immediately to Rome. Thus, I was able to send a message to my long-time agent
in Rome, Marcus Italicus, asking him to have the bank validate my enclosed
Letter of Credit and return it promptly to me in Artaxata.

But it was the weeks of waiting in Artaxata that provided the thoughts
which filled my mind that night in the Arch Druid's guest house. It had
seemed but a casual inquiry at the time, when I asked my host, Tirotates,
whether, in his capacity as court Historian, he had come upon any records
that might relate to the events seven and a half centuries ago, when the
Assyrian hosts had over-run the lands of the ten northern tribes of Israel
and carried most of their population off into captivity.

"Why, yes, Brother Joseph, our scrolls of history in the King's library
contain quite a bit of information about that event. You see, I believe that
I am a direct descendant of those captives who, of course, were forced
to intermarry with the inhabitants of this northern territory we now call
Armenia. Tiglath-Pileser III of Assyria,* from his capital, Nineveh, quite
a way to the southwest of us, began the over-run of Israel (then ruled by
King Pekah), and carried off Jews from the tribes of Gilead, Naphtali,
Reuben and Manasseh, and from Galilee. Completion of the overthrow by
Shalmaneser V and finally by Sargon II,** of Israel and its capital, Samaria,
was in the ninth year of the reign of Hoshea as king of Israel. And the
interesting thing is that the captives were brought to this very area—to the
towns of Halah and Habor and neighboring places that were then known
as cities of the Medes."***

"So, all the people here in present-day Armenia are our Jewish relatives?" I asked, with excitement.

"Probably not today," he replied. "You see, the Assyrians just herded
them into this area and left them, apparently without military guards of
any consequence, and did not count on the rapid increase of the Israelite population nor their fierce independence. Their captors presumably
thought that having brought the Jews such a great distance the captives

---

*Ruled 745 to 728 B.C.
**In 720 B.C.
***See II Kings 17:6.

would be exhausted and docile. But the result was that in the next fifty to two hundred years, in at least two great movements, this 'captive' people completely dominated the area and then broke northwestward. One group went northward on the east side of the Sea the Romans call 'Black' and within a century became known to their neighbors as Scythians. The other group went westward first and then north along the western shore of that Sea and became known as Cimmerians. They seem to have merged to some extent where they met on the northwestern shores of the Sea. In any event, most of them, moving westward then became known as Celts. But it is my personal belief that their descendants, even today, are our relatives of the Israelite race."[3, 4]

"This is a fascinating account," I responded, "but why do you suppose the Israelites were brought to this remote area instead of being taken to Nineveh as slaves—and why did the Assyrians not come back and annihilate them once the Israelites began to show aggressive intentions?"

"Your second question I think I can answer, but the first must remain a matter for speculation," he replied. "Basically, the kings of Assyria were fighting men and I think they did not want to spare their soldiers to serve as guards over slaves and prisoners, and they probably had enough Babylonian slaves who shared the same language and culture and whose homeland was but a few miles distant. In any event, *this* country is where they did bring the captives from Israel. Banishment of the cream and bulk of the population to this area was punishment of Israel—no more was intended."

"On the second question," he continued, "I believe I can be more certain. The Assyrian rulers were just too busy with more important matters. Sargon II was the king who brought the Israelites here;[*] for the remaining fifteen years of his rule he had his hands full putting down a revolt by the servient Babylonians who had obtained assistance from the Elamites—it was with difficulty that Sargon finally subdued them. Additionally, he had to put down a revolt in Gaza where the revolutionaries were supported by the Egyptians; and his greatest military effort was the successful destruction of the Hittite empire in the northwest near the Aegean Sea. Thereafter, his son, Sennacherib, spent twenty-five years putting down revolts.[**] The combined forces of Judah and Egypt immobilized him for quite a while, and then a celestial catastrophe—who knows what it was?—nearly wiped out his whole army. While licking his wounds, he was assassinated by two of his sons. His son, Esarhaddon, succeeded him, and had to fight

[*]In about 720 B.C.; he ruled from 722 to 705 B.C.
[**]Ruled 705-681 B.C.

Egypt twice. Forty-five years too late he did fight the Cimmerians—our relatives—but by then they were beyond the Caucasus Mountains and Esarhaddon had to let them go. His son, Ashurbanipal,* rounded out a full century of Assyrian dominance over our people, but by then the Cimmerians and the Scythians both were beyond the Sea called Black and out of Assyrian reach."

CHAPTER NOTES:

1. The Herodium data is based on "Jewish Rebels Dig Strategic Tunnel System" by Ehud Netzer, *Biblical Archaeology Review,* XV-4, Jul/Aug 1988; and the Glastonbury contrast found in *Avalonian Quest* by Geoffrey Ashe, Methuen, London, 1982, and others.

2. The "Thorn of Arimathea" at Glastonbury, England, inexplicably bloomed in December as is appropriate for the Judean (Levantine) thorn, and again in May like the British thorn, and lived until destroyed by a pious Puritan in ca. 1600. Many slips from the original tree were grown and are still alive today (see *A Guide to Glastonbury,* Avalon Press, Glastonbury, 1954).

3. The "explanations" in these paragraphs that connect the "Ten Lost Tribes of Israel" to the Celtic peoples of Europe and Great Britain are based in part on the data fully set forth by E. Raymond Capt, with illustrative maps, in his book, *Missing Links Discovered in Assyrian Tablets,* Artisan Sales, 1985 (256 pp.), and in the final chapter, "Migrations of Israel," of his short book, *King Solomon's Temple,* Artisan Sales, 1979. Also see, *The Drama of the Lost Disciples,* by G. F. Jowett, Covenant Publishers, London, 1975.

4. Several of the historical points covered In this chapter and the next are supported by statements made by Professor Oliver L. Reiser in his book, *This Holyest Erthe,* Perennial Books, London, 1974:

   a. That the Druids preferred memory and oral recitation over writing for important records and information (page 3).
   b. That there is a strong probability the Celtic race originated in the Near East (p. 4).
   c. That Joseph of Arimathea brought Christianity to England (page 15).
   d. That Jesus visited southwest England in the company of his relative, Joseph of Arimathea (pages 6, 15).
   e. That Druidism, Judaism and Christianity shared many similar beliefs; Druidism and Christianity were very compatible, and merger of the former into the latter was simple, natural and without conflict (page 39).

Also, see *Celtic Mysteries: The Ancient Religion* (by John Sharkey, Avon, N. Y., 1975) for the proposition that the Celts/Druids relied on memory for the preservation of oral tradition of everything important—for such matters they placed a taboo on writing. And see *King Arthur* by Norma Lorre Goodrich (F. Watts, N. Y., 1986), wherein Joseph of Arimathea is mentioned more than twenty times—for the strong probability that

---

*Reigned 688 to 626 B.C.

Joseph was in England and died there and possibly took Jesus there in his youth or young manhood; numerous sources are cited. Also, see Immanuel Velikovsky's *Ages in Chaos* and its projected sequel which was to be *The Assyrian Conquest,* the completed manuscript for which has never appeared in book form; however, much of it has been published as four articles in *Kronos* journal (Glassboro, N. J.), i.e., Vol. III No. 3, pp. 3-33; Vol. V No. 3, pp. 1-10; Vol VIII No. 2, pp. 18-20; Vol. IX No. 3, pp. 1-5; his efforts to harmonize Egyptianologists' and Biblical chronologies was ridiculed by orthodox science during Velikovsky's lifetime, but in the past decade competent scientists have slightly revised and largely validated his efforts (see the work of John Bimson and David Livingston), as reported in journals such as *Catastrophism and Ancient History* (Los Angeles) and *Society for Interdisciplinary Studies Review* (London); Velikovsky's chronologies, as since modified, tend to support Capt's migration sequences for the ten tribes of Israel that moved northwestward across Europe. Nor is the Israel/Celt migration scenario necessarily inconsistent with the tentative conclusions of Henriette Mertz *(The Naphtali,* Chicago, 1957), to the effect that one Israeli tribe, the Naphtali, reached America and became the "white Indian" tribe of Mandan in North Dakota. In Israel, the Naphtali were the northernmost tribe, having a common border with Phoenicia on the Mediterranean shore—home of the greatest seamen of antiquity— and the Naphtali capital of Dan was just twenty-five miles from the Phoenician seaport of Tyre. Both Capt and Mertz point out the probability that not *all* Israelites were carried into captivity by Assyria—that before, during and after the Assyrian captivity, there were numerous migrations westward by the Semitic Hebrews, including groups that have been traced to Ireland, which in turn may have been a stepping-stone to America by many ancient migrations—Phoenicians, Brendan the Bold, Prince Madoc and others (also see *They All Discovered America* by Charles M. Boland, Doubleday, 1961; *Madoc and the Discovery of America* by R. Deacon, F. Muller, London, 1966; *America B. C.* by Barry Fell, Quadrangle, 1976; *Before Columbus* by Cyrus H. Gordon, Crown, 1971).

The legends of Joseph of Arimathea at Glastonbury are cited and discussed at length with apparent approval by John Michell in *New View Over Atlantis,* 1983 (Thames & Hudson, London, and Harper & Row, U.S.A.), pp. 167 et seq.

Also see, Barbara Tuchman in *Bible and Sword,* N. Y. University Press, 1956; Ballantine, 1934: "Perhaps the answer is that he [Joseph of Arimathea] actually did make his way from Palestine to Britain." (p. 14) AND "It may even be that he rightfully belongs there, for, as so often happens when modern science goes to work on the stuff of legend, the available facts tend to confirm the legend." (p. 21)

Also see "Glastonbury, Christianity's Stepping Stone to Rome?" by Frank C. Tribbe, pp. 43-50, *Glastonbury Treasures,* Stonehenge Viewpoint, Santa Barbara, CA, 1988.

Joseph is mentioned in several ancient Welsh genealogies and is named in the triad of "Three Saintly Lineages of the Island of Britain" *(Trioedd ynys prydain* 81), per Gladys Taylor in "What Happened to Judah?"—British Israel World Federation.

✠

Christianity in Britain and the Near East

A.D. 34/5

T HAT CONVERSATION OF FIFTEEN YEARS AGO came back to me clearly and completely now as I lay thinking of the Celtic religious beliefs as the Arch Druid had explained them to me, and the Celtic history as recited by the young Druid. These thoughts excited me so that I was tempted to awaken my host to resume our discussion. Eventually, I did sleep, however, and in spite of the brief rest that night, I was fully awake again when I heard the cook begin preparations for the morning meal.

I was eager to resume the conversation with the Arch Druid immediately after we had eaten, but I was unprepared for his eagerness to do likewise.

"Your nephew, Jesu, told us much about your religion," he began, "and also of his personal views which we agreed rang true in our hearts. You commented last evening on the similarities of your religion and mine, and indeed, Jesu and I agreed to the same effect. Which raises the logical question: Could we have had a common beginning? What think you?"

Then I rapidly told him of the Assyrian captivity and the carrying-away of the Israelites from our homeland, and of my conversation with the Historian in Artaxata concerning the probable happenings thereafter.

"How can we doubt it?" he asked with fervent intensity as he gripped my hands, and his blue eyes seemed on fire with excitement. "We must be of one people and of one religion."* And after a moment's pause, he added a most sincere question: "Can my Druids help your construction and planting activities, in order that you and your men can return very soon and tell us more carefully and completely of The Way of Jesu, and pray for our empowerment by the Holy Spirit of God?"

His eagerness almost made me laugh, but I smiled broadly as I assured him that we would be happy to have help and that it would be our pleasure to tell his people the good news of The Way.

✛ ✛ ✛

Our first growing season in Britannia followed by our harvest was exciting and filled with new experiences, and there was pride all around upon completion of our extensive construction program. Both activities went smoothly, thanks in large part to the sizeable group of husky Druids which appeared each morning to counsel and assist us. At the same time, Reuben selected work crews from among our own youth according to their skills and interests, and each month as construction jobs were concluded more could be assigned to permanent responsibilities. Very early in the season Reuben was able with great confidence to name Ephraim, the twenty-two-year-old third son of Hebron and Enygeus, as head of the farming operations, assisted by his twenty-year-old brother, Benjamin, to be concerned with orchards and vineyards, and fifteen-year-old Gideon, son of my Josephes, to handle our variety of animals; of course, there were many other youth in our company who worked along with these young leaders. Equally important, was Reuben's designation of my son-in-law, David, Anna's husband, as chief hunter to bring in the kill of wild animals, birds and seafood that would be constantly needed for our tables.

Happily, these arrangements freed Josephes, Hebron and me to spend the First Day of every week at the Druid's Center, teaching them of our Holy Scriptures as clarified by the enlightenment of Jesus. Well into the Fall season we began to notice new faces among those attending these weekly services with the Druids—obviously, these were Druids from other centers. And finally, as Winter came on apace, the old Arch Druid called me aside to say: "Dear Brother Joseph, as you will have noticed, we have had visiting Druids with us in recent weeks from surrounding areas, to hear your fascinating teachings. And, as I expected, a group whose Center is attached

---

*The Druids were readily converted to Christianity; see *Dedicated Disciples* by H. W. Stough.

to the court of Arviragus, king of our nation, the Dumnoni, whose seat is south and west from here,* asks if you will come for a few days to talk with them and their arch-druid. Also, I would infer from their words that a further invitation from Arviragus himself seems likely. What say you?"

"Dear friend," I replied, "you know my answer is, 'Yes.' This is exactly what I have hoped for. We will plan to go to them day after tomorrow. And will one of your young Druids be our guide to get us there with ease?"

That night happy thoughts filled my mind and kept me from sleeping for a long while; I was just plain excited, as this was exactly the sort of opportunity I had prayed for.

After two full days of reporting, explaining, teaching, and answering questions, the Arch Druid of the Dumnoni and his senior staff were unanimous in requesting that we accompany them into the presence of young King Arviragus. No host could have been more cordial; the King was smiling broadly and spoke: "My dear, revered Joseph, we have never met but my father before me and I have heard nothing but good reports of you for many years. No traders who have come to our mining fields have been more honest or fair in dealings with our people, and perhaps none have been more successful in business, which has been most helpful to our economy. And now, for several weeks, our Arch Druid has been reporting to me of your religious teachings, and has just summarized for me the beautiful sessions of these two days while you and your associates have been our guests.

"After the evening meal, which we ask you to eat with me here," he continued, "I hope you will spend the hours before bedtime helping my own understanding of your teachings."

Before I could respond, he nodded toward a doorway, which was the signal for the entrance of a most beautiful young woman of about the same age as the king—both in their early twenties. Arviragus resumed: "Sire, may I introduce my lovely cousin, Gladys, who comes from the kingdom of the Silures just across the Channel of water to the north,** where she is daughter of King Bran. And dear cousin, this is Joseph of Arimathea who is no longer an occasional visitor from a far away land, but now graces us with his permanent presence."

"Honored Joseph," she spoke with a most melodious voice, "I am very pleased to meet you, for my uncle, Arviragus' father, before his death, always mentioned you when I visited this house."

---

*Devon and Cornwall.
**Wales.

I was stunned, and told them so as soon as I found my voice, to learn that I had been so well known in this country, since I had been merely a traveling businessman, and engaged in little activity here in the past except as concerned my business.[1] And, of course, I introduced Josephes and Hebron.

The Arch Druid stayed to join the dinner party for Josephes, Hebron and me. I found Gladys to be a most engaging person, and soon learned that she had studied for several years in the Druidic schools and was far more fluent than I in Greek and Latin.[2] In fact, she offered to converse in Greek to make the discussion easier for us, but I assured her that we needed all the practice we could get in the use of the local language.

Our discussions of that evening and the following day were as wide-ranging and scintillating as any I could remember for many a year, except for a few of my conversations with Jesus. Both Arviragus and Gladys were seemingly thrilled when I told them the story of their Celtic race as I theorized it—that by blood and religion we were one people, and that Jesus seemed to be the prophesied fulfillment for us both.

By mid-afternoon there was a lull in the conversation, and before any man could speak Gladys held up her hand for silence and addressed the King: "Cousin, I really don't know your intentions or desire, but for me, I will wait no longer. I wish to be a follower of The Way of Jesus, and I want Brother Joseph to baptize me today." And she turned to me as she spoke the last.

Arviragus smiled broadly and said slowly: "Beloved cousin, no one will ever be ahead of you, but that's all right with me. This is one king who doesn't mind being second. Yet, I shan't be far behind. I also wish to be of The Way, and I will have Joseph baptize me as soon as he has accomplished it for you."

✛　✛　✛

That first British winter was a busy one for our community, and for us missionaries. Our teaching sessions in the several Druidic communities and in the court of Arviragus, were now expanded north of the Channel into Siluria and especially among the large family of King Bran.[3] Bran told us that he was much more interested in religion and matters spiritual than he was in rulership, and that before many years he was going to abdicate in favor of his handsome and brilliant eldest son, Caradoc,* now twenty-seven and with a growing family of his own.

---

*In Welsh it is spelled, Caradawg.

As Spring arrived we all were poignantly and sorrowfully reminded of Jesus' passion two years before, as well as the joy of his resurrection. When the first ships of the season began to arrive at Meare and other nearby ports of call, we began to watch for familiar sails and were pleased before long to see the *Astarte* captained by my old friend and partner, Hiram bar Abram. After the exuberance of our reunion subsided somewhat, Hiram quickly interposed the news that he had a thick communication for me.

"It's from your agent, Thaddaeus, in Edessa," he said. "'He anticipated that I would be making a trip to you early this season, and got the letter to Tyre by fast courier just the week before I sailed. I'm sure you will find much of interest in it."

When I had the opportunity to break seals and begin to read his long report, I quickly found that indeed there was much of high interest that Thaddaeus had to tell me. He began by saying that he had both good news and sad news, and indeed that was so. After giving me some most gratifying words about my former business associates in Arimathea and Jerusalem, he wrote as follows:

As for the wonderful and mystical Shroud of Jesus, Thomas has suggested that we not expose "The Face" to the general worshippers. We will keep it securely locked away except for high holy days such as the annual anniversary of Jesus' resurrection; and even then, no one but leaders of the congregation will see The Face—the worshippers will see only the casket with its drapery of cloth-of-gold in grille pattern.[4] Our plans for construction of a suitable place of worship are going forward, and before another year has passed we hope to have the building completed and be conducting services in it.

The people of Edessa and of the countryside of Osroene soon came to know that their once-ailing king now is enjoying robust good health, and that it was a mystical Face of Jesus which I had brought that was the instrument of the healing. I continue to lay-on-hands each day to heal those in need, but I make it quite clear that the power which healed Abgar came from God through the Face, not me. For good or ill (and I know not which), these circumstances are building up a considerable mystique about The Face, so that the special times when its casket is on view are coming to be especially noted by the populace, and large crowds attend our services at such times. In fact, this reputation is spreading to the surrounding area, especially eastward, and pilgrims are beginning to come from many countries of the east—Parthia, Mesopotamia, Elam, Media and Armenia; and from the cities of Duro-Europos, Nisibis, Palmyra, Susa, Ecbatana and Ctesiphon.

As for what the Face is, how it was made, and why it came here, I am saying as little as possible. I acknowledge that it is the Face of Jesus, which he and the Father-God made in some mystical way. Even if I wished, I could honestly say little more! I have written Thomas to give me guidance on this matter, because I am sure that in time some of the Twelve will again pass through Edessa and will insist upon more information and the opportunity for examination of the Face. I suppose that eventually we will have to acknowledge that you found it in the Tomb on Resurrection morning, and that you, Lazarus and Thomas entrusted it to me for safe-keeping. Without volunteering that it is part of the full burial shroud, we might establish its bona-fides by citing the healings of Hosea and of Abgar.

Last year I wrote you of the vision seen by Peter in Joppa, which received the formal endorsement of James, the Lord's brother, in Jerusalem, so that gentiles may be baptized into The Way without first becoming Jews. This was cheering news to most disciples, and especially to Andrew who stopped here in Edessa briefly on his way to Scythia, and to Matthias and Jude who stayed with us for about a month before departing for Armenia to assist Thomas who was already in the East. Andrew also told us of the early ministry of Philip, one of the deacons, among the Samaritans who are so greatly hated by Judeans of the Sanhedrin because of their mixed-blood—and that James bar Zebedee had already left for his designated area of Sardinia and Iberia,* while Philip the apostle plans next year to go to Gaul for a while to assist Lazarus in expanding his ministry.

However, Matthias and Jude were also the bearers of tragic news. We all knew how fearlessly deacon Stephen spoke the truth to every audience. This finally became more than Caiaphas would tolerate. Caiaphas and the Sadducees had been afraid to act directly against Peter and John for healing in the Temple, because of their popularity, but had since decided that indirect action, especially against such as Stephen, would be feasible. Accordingly, they induced a firebrand from Tarsus, Saul by name, to lead a large number of Temple riffraff, who owed favors to Caiaphas, to seize Stephen. Not daring an open trial, the mob was guided to rush Stephen out a nearby City gate and then stoned him to death as a blasphemer before the Roman guard could be called.** Thus The Way has lost one of its most powerful voices, and Caiaphas is able to shrug and say "the people" took matters into their own hands. Of course, that tragedy also eliminates one who knew the full secret of the Shroud of Jesus. Now, save for Miriam and Elias, only you and I, Lazarus and Thomas are aware of the story and the relic behind The Face.

• Spain and Portugal.
** Acts 7:58.

Peter has gone on to Syrian Antioch and we already are hearing of his great work there, among both Jews and gentiles. However, rumors which reach us here suggest that Caiaphas may give Saul of Tarsus a special commission to go to Damascus, and even Antioch, for the purpose of arresting all of our brethren that he can find—we pray it will not happen.

You know how the people of Antioch are given to using the slang and gutter language of the Greeks who dominate the business community. We are told they have now made up a Greek word, *Christian,* as a epithet of derogation against followers of The Way.* But, you know, dear Brother Joseph, I rather like that name. I agree with you that our Lord Jesus was perhaps nearer to the *Christos* in the Greek language than to the Hebrew *messiah* as the Temple hierarchy and the general populace in Judea describe him. I would like to see us embrace and proclaim Christian as our name!

CHAPTER NOTES:

1. Joseph of Arimathea was probably of the third generation to head this family business involving tin mining and export from Cornwall (see *Dedicated Disciples* by H. W. Stough). Such operations were commercially active as early as 1800 B.C. The earliest mining was by streaming and by working open veins amongst the rocks and evergreen shrubs (sometimes called gorse or furze).

2. It is recorded that she was so fluent in Greek that later, in Rome, the Emperor Claudius renamed her Pomponia Graecina and encouraged her marriage to his top general, Aulus Plautius. She authored several books in Greek and Latin as well as in her native language. *(The Early Church* by Gladys Taylor, Covenant Pub., London, 1967, 1987)

The Celtic Druids were fully capable of precise technological achievement, as has been reported by numerous ancient historians, including Pliny and Hippolytus; Julius Caesar wrote: "They hold long discussions about the heavenly bodies and their motions...." In 1897, through a fortuitous archaeological discovery in a vineyard near Bourgen-bresse (Dept. of Ain), France, it was discovered that the Celts used the standard 19-year calendar system, as did the Babylonians, Hindus, Jews, Greeks and Romans (Having fixed celestial factors of: 19-year cycle, lunar year of 354.37 days, solar year of 365.24 days, lunar month of 29.53 days, 235 lunar months in the 19-year cycle, and 24-hour days). The discovery has become known as the Coligny Calendar; it is so precise that, though it differed considerably from the Greek calendar, it was markedly superior to it (reported in *Horus Magazine,* III-1, Winter 1987).

An Associated Press dispatch of September 5, 1986, quotes archaeologists, who have excavated a Celtic fort in southwest England, that these Celts lived in a sophisticated society with clear class distinctions and complex technology. The forty-six-acre fort of the Durotriges tribe, when excavated, was found to embrace six to seven hundred houses within its circumference.

---

*Acts 11:26.

3. St. Gildas, British historian of the sixth century, wrote that the British Celts were descendants of the lost tribes of Israel, and that Joseph of Arimathea and associates brought Christianity to Britain about the years A.D. 34 to 37. St. Freculphus, a French bishop in Lisieux in the ninth century, wrote of Joseph of Arimathea's missionary work and, in turn, was quoted by William of Malmsbury, British historian of the twelfth century. Hugh Paulinus de Cressy, French monk of the sixteenth century wrote in his *Church History of Brittany* of Joseph of Arimathea's missionary work in Britain. Also, see current works which include *Avalonian Quest* by Geoffrey Ashe, *Chronicle of Glastonbury* by J. P. Carley, *Two Glastonbury Legends* by J.A.T. Robinson, and *A Biographical Dictionary of the Saints* by F. G. Holweck.

Gildas' statement about the early evangelization of Britain by Joseph is quoted in *A History of the English Church and People* by Bede, at p. 65. The 9th-century report of same by historian Freculphus is to be found in *Trias Thermaturga,* at p. 156b.

4. Also, see Note 2 at end of Chap. 44. Many dozens of copies of the Shroud Face were made by artists, especially during the period A.D. 525 to 1204, and on many of them the Face was surrounded (as the original doubtless was) by a distinctive lattice or diamond pattern that later was sometimes described as a "grill" pattern; that pattern closely resembles one of the customary patterns found in the cloth-of-gold used by Parthian kings of that period for their ceremonial robes (see *Portrait of Jesus?* by Frank C. Tribbe, Stein & Day, 1983; and *Shroud of Turin* Wilson, Doubleday, 1978). It seems likely-that the Shroud was folded and kept in a shallow casket or deep frame with only the Face showing. In the Middle Ages a plethora of legends grew up in western Europe and England about the "Holy Grail"; unfortunately, the legends were not consistent, and the Grail was variously stated to be a cup, a chalice, a cruet, a platter, a dish. In his book, *The Shroud and the Grail* (Weidenfeld & Nicolson, London, 1987), British etymologist-genealogist Noel Currer-Briggs suggests that *the Shroud casket itself* was the Holy Grail; apparently, only a few priests or custodians in those years even saw the Face and none was aware of the full Shroud folded beneath. He speculates further that the name was a corruption from the medieval French *greille* and early English *grille* that were in fact merely attempts to describe that lattice pattern of the overlay (with hole in the center for the Face to be seen).

CHAPTER FORTY-SEVEN

✠

More Christians in Britain and One from Tarsus

A.D. 40

As Fall shades into Winter in Britannia it is hard for me to realize that seven years of exile have passed since we left Judea, and that early in the coming Spring we will commemorate the eighth anniversary of our Lord's passion and resurrection. Emperor Gaius Caligula gave us somewhat of a scare this Summer as he mounted troops across the ocean Channel to invade these fair shores. But, as with all other acts under his sovereignty, he played the dunce—because the troops mutinied and refused to board the boats, so Caligula went back to Rome to pout.

Caradoc tells me that Rome's timing was excellent, because upon the death last Spring of King Cymbeline (whom the Romans called Cunobelinus) of the Iceni tribe (Belgae, in Latin) a natural hiatus had occurred. Of course, his son, Togodumnus, became king of the Iceni—the easternmost province of Britain. But, under a long-standing agreement, the authority of "Pendragon" (commanding general of all British armies for defense of the country) shifted on the death of Cymbeline to the westernmost province, the Silures, of which Caradoc is now king.

Bran had served as king of the Silures only ten years but, had as he had told me at our first meeting, his interests ran to the spiritual and contem-

320

plative, not rulership and fighting. Consequently, early last Spring, when messengers reported that Cymbeline was dying, Bran abdicated in favor of his eldest son, Caradoc, so that the military role would be in firm hands. Nevertheless, Caradoc's Spring and Summer were taken up mostly with courtesy calls on the military leaders of the Iceni, Brigantes, Atrebates, Dobunni, Durotriges and Dumnoni—and if the Roman troops had crossed the Channel in early August, as was apparently planned, he certainly would not have been ready for them. I for one will not be surprised if someone assassinates this mad emperor.

In these few years I have developed so much love for the Britons—and it is not limited to any special group or class. Over the many years of working with old Cymric and his miners and the ship-masters and citizens of Meare, I knew little of others. But now, the several communities of Druids, and the ruling families who have practically adopted us, bring me to the conclusion that no finer or friendlier people exist anywhere. A year after I baptized King Arviragus, he celebrated the anniversary by giving to our exile group the huge tract of land where we are established, tax-free forever.* He described the written grant to us as covering twelve hides of land,** which the Romans would count as about 777 hectares. The giant tor and the flat land around it actually constitute a large island, for the tidewater streams meander in every direction off our placid, large channel.*** Often in the mornings we can stand at the foot of the tor and find ourselves surrounded by a low fog riding on the streams; the first rays of sunshine reflect off the fog, giving it a glassy look, and natives here sometimes call ours the Glass Island for this reason. Also, there is a bountiful supply of wild fruit growing on the trees here, the name of which we are told is, *apple*—and so our spot is also called Isle of Avalon (apples).[1]

The large family of King Bran (and his father, Llyr) have not only been most hospitable, but have been very receptive to The Way, which Thaddaeus suggests we call, Christianity. I have baptized Llyr and Bran, the latter's daughter, Gladys, and two sons. Son, Caradoc, is as friendly as anyone here, but he laughingly says he is too busy right now for religion; nevertheless, he seems pleased that his wife has been baptized, as well as his two oldest children (son and daughter), Cyllinus and Eurgain; the other three, Cynon, Linus and Gladys, are anxious to be old enough for this experience.[2]

---

*Strong validation is to be found in the book, *The Legendary XII Hides of Glastonbury* by Ray Gibbs, Llanerch Ent., Felinfach, Wales, 1988.
**About 1,920 acres.
***Bristol Channel.

✤ ✤ ✤

A.D. 41

As Winter's last blasts are waning, an early ship from north Gaul came in to Meare with the news that Emperor Gaius Caligula was murdered by tribunes of his own guard during the first month of the Roman year,* and that the Praetorians immediately chose Claudius (nephew of Tiberius) as successor. We were unsure just what this news might mean for us, but Caradoc was gone more than ever in the following months as he bolstered Britain's defenses with a sense of urgency.

I thought his preparations wise, since my agent in Rome, Marcus Italicus, had commented more than once that Claudius was not a foolish and abnormal one, as claimed by wags about Rome. He had been sickly from birth and had physical impediments including a stammer and a tendency to extreme nervousness,** but he was a studious person, fascinated by military tactics and strategy and wrote extensively on history. I suspected that he might very well launch a serious invasion of Britain to prove he was not the moron many slyly suggested.

I write to Thaddaeus each chance I get, and regularly receive one or two letters from him each year; the first visit this Spring by Hiram and his *Astarte,* brought one such, brimming with news. After salutations, it began:

> The mad emperor is dead! What a relief. You have no idea how near we were to war. Caligula had ordered the Legate to commission a statue of himself (the emperor) and to install it in the Temple in Jerusalem.*** Though Caligula had replaced the highly competent Vitellius as Legate in Syria with Petronius, even the latter knew that nothing would unify and infuriate the people of our homeland like the emperor's statue in the Temple. Consequently, the Legate dragged his feet and made excuses to Rome, stalling for all he was worth to delay completion of the statue. I'm sure he was as relieved as everyone else here in the Near East by the emperor's death.
>
> Caligula's short reign of three and a half years nevertheless involved a number of changes out here. Pilate's irrational attack on the Samaritans at

---

* Apparently at 7 A.M. on January 23, A.D. 41, according to Seutonius' *The Lives of the Twelve Caesars.*
** He had suffered infantile paralysis.
****Columbia Encyclopedia,* Third Ed., Columbia University Press, New York, 1963.

Mount Gerizim resulted in his being ordered to Rome by Vitellius, who then sent Marcellus to Jerusalem as governor. Pilate was fortunate that Caligula was on the throne by the time he arrived, and we understand that Pilate was permitted to quietly retire. Marcellus replaced Caiaphas with Jonathan as high priest. As you know, Jonathan is a vain and worldly man who, as son of Annas, had expected to succeed his father, when Pilate named Caiaphas instead. In spite of his meanness, Caiaphas was fairly competent and more respectable than Jonathan. The change was short-lived, however, for a few months later Vitellius himself replaced Jonathan with Theophilus; we hope he survives for a while!

Governors, tetrarchs and high priests, all of low estate, continue to be the bane of our homeland. One of Caligula's first acts was to give Herod Agrippa the tetrarchy of the recently deceased Philip, plus the title of king. Then he exiled Jonathan's friend, Herod Antipas, to Iberia and gave his tetrarchy to Agrippa also. Now, our latest post from Rome tells us that Emperor Claudius has given Judah to Agrippa as an addition to his kingdom—Roman governors were better, I'm sure.

A.D. 35

In an earlier letter, Thaddaeus wrote of Christianity's biggest news since the crucifixion-resurrection-Pentecost events. It concerned Saul of Tarsus:

As I greatly feared when I wrote you earlier, Caiaphas did indeed commission Saul of Tarsus to go into Syria and arrest the leading Christians. But even the most optimistic of us could not have guessed how the hand of God would intervene.

I would hardly credit this story had it not come to me from the lips of Menahem (whom the Greeks in Antioch call Manaen) when he visited with me this month. Since you may not have heard of him., I will explain that he was the son of a slave in the household of Herod the Great, when Herod freed the slave and all of his family for some great deed rendered to the king. Be that as it may, Menahem was raised as a foster-brother to Herod's sons* and was very close to Antipas, who later got Menahem a well-paying job as a Guard of the Sanhedrin. In that capacity, he was chief

---

*See "Manaen" in the Zondervan *New International Dictionary of the Bible,* and Acts 13:1.

of the military escort sent with Saul to Damascus under commission from Caiaphas.

It is Menahem's story to me that, as they approached within two hours' ride of the gates of Damascus, Saul suddenly gave a loud cry, threw his arm across his eyes as if blinded by a great light, and fell off his horse to the ground. It was mid-day and sunny, but as Saul fell from his horse, suddenly a low cloud seemed to be hovering over them and from it Menahem and the others heard a roaring noise that was like a voice speaking but they could distinguish no words. Saul asked who was speaking, and the voice seemed to respond, but again his companions could understand nothing.

At once the sun shone strongly again, and Saul groaned and attempted to rise. Menahem assisted him to his feet, but Saul was staring wildly and said he could not see. His companions put him on his horse and led it into the City.

Saul then spoke, saying: "You must take me to the house of Judas on Straight Street," and they did.

Menahem knew that Caiaphas would hold him accountable, and so he found lodgings across the street and went in to Saul every few hours to know his condition. For three days Saul would not eat or drink, and then a man named Ananias came, saying he had been sent by the Lord to heal Saul of his blindness. As Menahem watched, Ananias laid hands on Saul and spoke to him and immediately Saul could see. Saul was baptized and then spoke for several days in the Damascus synagogues, telling that Jesus had challenged him on the road and had sent Ananias to heal his blindness. The people of The Way accepted Saul as one of themselves, but other Jews in the synagogues were highly critical of him.

Saul left the City, saying he was going into the desert for a time of purification and contemplation. Menahem also was converted to The Way and was baptized and told the other guards he would not return with them to Jerusalem. He studied with Ananias for some months, but was not welcomed in the synagogues, and so he went on to Antioch to work in the Christian churches there.

✠   ✠   ✠

A.D. 36

A year and a half later Thaddaeus wrote:

News that is puzzling, but not tragic, concerns Saul of Tarsus, again. After a year and a half spent in and near the cliff-locked, Arabian city of Petra, Saul came back to Damascus, seemingly ready to take up a life of preaching The Way of Jesus.[3] Most of the brethren in Damascus meet in home-churches because the synagogues have become so hostile to our teachings. However, Saul was not to be dissuaded, and boldly began to preach Jesus' message in the synagogues there, and also to state that His salvation was available as well to the gentiles.

The leaders of the synagogues plotted to kill Saul, but friends warned him, and when it was found that his enemies were also watching the city gates, friends took him by night and lowered him from the city wall in a basket. Saul then went to Jerusalem to join the brethren there, but they were afraid of him and shunned him because they doubted his story of conversion by Jesus. Disciple Barnabus believed him, however, and in a special appearance before James and the apostles who were present, he was accepted and authorized to preach. Nevertheless, the Jews who had not accepted The Way were angered by Saul's bold preaching of Jesus' message and sought to kill him. The brethren then led him away at night, and from Caesarea put him on a vessel bound for his home city of Tarsus, where he apparently will stay awhile."

☩   ☩   ☩

A.D. 42

In the year following Thaddaeus' report on the changes occurring in Judea during the reign of Caligula, he wrote me of other events:

The bad news first, dear Brother. Here in Edessa we have just learned of another tragedy. James bar Zebedee, called "The Greater" by some who were impressed by his great size, was one of the earliest missionaries to foreign soil, having gone to Sardinia and Iberia late in the year of Jesus' death. Reports are that the Good News of Jesus was received with enthusiasm by both Jews and gentiles of those lands, and many churches were begun in the homes of new leaders there. However, nine years having passed since that last Passover with Lord Jesus, he determined to come back for Passover at the Jerusalem Temple.

Not without reason did Jesus call him a "son of thunder." He was hardly arrived back, when he began preaching Jesus' message on the porches of the Temple and in the strongest possible language—reminiscent of the invective preached by Stephen. But he most infuriated the leaders of the Temple by insisting that Jesus would soon return from Heaven and establish his kingdom. This was a claim Herod Agrippa would not tolerate, and he had James beheaded by the executioner's sword. Thus, we have our second martyr, both in Jerusalem.

CHAPTER NOTES:

1. Glastonbury is the modern British name for Avalon; its Welsh name was, "Yniswi-triu." The Glastonbury tor rises 522 feet above sea level. Silt from the River Severn has now filled the marsh, making solid-ground that joins all the former islands of the estuary. The present town of Glastonbury is close to the city of Bristol to the north. South of Glastonbury is the nearby town of Bath, known from antiquity for its healing hot springs (temperature, 116° F.). After the Romans finally reached this area in A.D. 75, they considered the springs sacred, and named them Aquae Sulis for the old Celtic (on the continent) deity, Sulis; the springs reached the surface through three vents.

2. For the likely importance of the probable exile of Joseph of Arimathea, see this author's documented speculations in the article, "Glastonbury—Christianity's Stepping-Stone to Rome?" in the Glastonbury Anthology, *Stonehenge Viewpoint* No. 81, 1988, Santa Barbara, California.

3. Zondervan's *New International Dictionary of the Bible* suggests that Paul's visit to Arabia, mentioned in Galatians 1:17, probably should be placed between Acts 9:22 (his "several days" of preaching in Damascus) and Acts 9:2-3 (when the Jews of the Damascus synagogues plotted to kill him).

CHAPTER FORTY-EIGHT

☩

Caradoc Versus Emperor Claudius

A.D. 43

During the Spring ending the second year in the reign of Claudius, pendragon Caradoc was in his home area for a few days and I had the opportunity of a serious talk with him about his military effort.

"Caradoc," I said, "you seem committed to an all-out, lengthy, military resistance to the probable invasion by Rome. Have you thought fully of the consequences for your people?"

"I have thought of little else for some months, friend Joseph," he replied, "and I am greatly grieved by the certainty of extensive casualties and the suffering of the non-combatants—but I see no alternative, and all of the tribes are in agreement."

"Of course, I have no military qualifications," I responded, "but I have seen quite a bit of the massive military power of Rome and know of their stubborn ruthlessness. They might start a campaign here with a half dozen trained legions—incidentally, whose only life-time occupation has been warfare under skilled leaders—but the important factor is that if you have some initial success they could, and would not hesitate to, bring in a dozen more legions with which to overwhelm you. Rome has existed for five centuries, and they may have lost a few battles but they have never lost a war; and now, for eighty-five years Rome has been ruled by the Caesars, who have been the world's greatest fighting leaders. I have no love for

Rome, friend Caradoc, my own nation has suffered mightily under the Caesars, but I feel you cannot win, and I hate to see the bloodshed of your wonderful people."

"I believe everything you say, dear Joseph," Caradoc replied, "and in our war councils I have stated the same arguments you present, but we are a fiercely independent people and on this point we are utterly united. We Silures, here in the west, are perhaps the least militant—in our hills, with our channels and seas to isolate us, we might sit and dare them to come to us, if we were alone; but the Iceni and other Belgic tribes of the southeast do not have any natural defenses and they well remember the invasion by Julius Caesar, just less than a century ago—so the anti-Roman feeling has been endemic for at least that long.

"Moreover," he continued, "we are well aware of the effects of Roman rule on our brothers, the Celts of Gaul and Germani. It is the belief and policy of Rome that other races are entitled to no consideration at all—allies, client-kingdoms or conquered kingdoms, alike. To Rome it is quite justifiable to oppress nations, break treaties or exterminate whole peoples. So we know that our choices are to submit and hope for the best, or to resist, if necessary to the point of extinction. Just because they desire to rule the whole world, it does not follow that all others should readily accept servitude. And has that servitude been comfortable in your home country, friend Joseph?"

"By no means," I agreed; "Rome has certainly ground down our people in every way, and economically most of all. They impose a land tax, property tax, customs duties, imposts on farm products, and in addition we must pay the cost of the occupying army and civil administration. And if we are too poor to pay, Roman bankers are there to make loans at exorbitant rates, and their soldiers assist them in collection. About the only concession the Jews have, is exemption from military conscription, for that burden, too, usually falls on conquered peoples."

"And so, we will fight," concluded Caradoc. "It is not an easy decision to live with, but one we readily made. As you know, we are a very religious people and judging from Rome's treatment of the Gauls, one of their first efforts here would be to stamp out our religion, whether it be Druidism or Christianity. No, we will fight."

"Your principles are sound and your facts are right," I responded. "Just last year, I am told, Emperor Claudius delivered an Edict to the Roman Senate, proclaiming that acceptance of either Druidic or Christian faith is an offense punishable by death.*

---

*According to Corbett in *Why Britain?*—below.

✠ ✠ ✠

In late Spring and early Summer we had continuous reports of Roman troops being marshaled on the shores of north Gaul. Again, there were rumors of mutiny but this was a different emperor and Aulus Plautius was a different commander.

Here in the west, with our islands and hills, creeks and marshes, we thought little and worried less about the inevitable invasion. But the leaders thought of little else, and one late Spring day Llyr told me he was concerned that all was not well with our troops.

"But your grandson, Caradoc, is an able commander, is he not?" I asked.

"None better in Britannia, I am sure," he replied. "But he is not getting the respect as pendragon that he should. Young Togodumnus weakened our unity by attacking his unsuspecting neighbors, south across the River Thames, to enlarge his own kingdom. This he did before his father, Cymbeline, was hardly cold in the grave. Now he says his Iceni troops will take orders from him, not Caradoc."

"How is Caradoc taking that?" I asked.

"As well as he can," he replied. "He will bring the northern tribe of Brigantes straight south to flank the Iceni, to avoid friction with our own Silures that will hold the west flank. But this risks any strong attack along those seams where there is no integration or overlapping of troops separately controlled."

✠ ✠ ✠

Early summer saw the invasion, as anticipated. Caradoc maneuvered the British armies in a series of planned withdrawals to take advantage of the eastward flowing Thames and Medway rivers. The rivers did not slow General Plautius as much as should have been the case, but Llyr explained to me that Togodumnus had expelled both his brother, Adminius, and the Atrebate king, Verica, to Gaul, and both were obviously giving advice to Plautius. Oddly, Plautius consolidated his position but did not try to advance. Both Roman and British armies then were unmoving but restless for several weeks. At this time, Llyr explained to me that Plautius had sent for the emperor, apparently according to plan, and that Claudius had brought fresh troops, and was assuming control for appearances sake.

Then, during the succeeding weeks of late summer we observed Arviragus' return with his Dumnoni troops and Caradoc with his Silures troops, in good order and apparently in good condition. As news filtered back from the battle zone and the western army groups dug in at fortified positions in the hills, Llyr described to me what had been a partial debacle. Claudius not only brought fresh soldiers but a troop of battle-seasoned elephants.[1] None of the British had ever before seen such animals and very few had even heard of them. Plautius and Claudius very professionally hit the seam between the Iceni on the east and the Brigantes in the center; they led with the elephants, followed by cavalry. The Brigantes fought stubbornly but had no means of combatting such a weapon; the Iceni were in complete rout and Togodumnus was killed, so to avoid disaster the Brigantes had to give ground or their flank would be turned. Caradoc and Arviragus held their ground until it was clear that the bulk of the Roman forces were wheeling to the right, eastward, to chase the routed Iceni; under cover of darkness Caradoc and Arviragus withdrew as we knew.

Claudius and Plautius quickly followed and slaughtered large numbers of the Iceni fighting men. Claudius signed treaties with the Iceni and some dozen smaller tribes in southeast Britannia, installing client-kings in each of them. Claudius appointed Plautius governor in addition to his military duties, and the emperor started back to Rome after but a few weeks in Britannia. Plautius next sent the II Legion under General Vespasion slowly along the southern coast to subdue the area; later he turned northwestward, and then northeastward to establish a zone of security running southwest to northeast across southern and central Britannia but never reaching our area and the kingdoms of Arviragus and Caradoc.[2]

✠   ✠   ✠

A.D. 45

Claudius the unpredictable, declared a six-months' truce in Britannia, called Arviragus to Rome and gave his daughter, Venus Julia, to Arviragus in marriage. Weeks later Arviragus was back with his bride, a very lovely maiden, apparently resolved to be a loving and useful wife. Before long Arviragus sent word that she was willing to have a visit from us to instruct her in Christianity and baptize her, which we were pleased to do.[3]

It seems obvious that Plautius has no present intention of pressing the invasion into the hinterlands and is using his efforts mostly in making the southeast of Britannia into a truly Roman province behind his zone of security. The Roman post which anchors the southwestern end of Plautius' zone of security is called Corinium,* and he has recently placed his young

---

*Modern-day town of Cirencester in Gloucester.

aide, Rufus Pudens, in charge of the Post. This handsome young man, scion of an important patrician family and son of a Roman Senator, was just nineteen years old when he arrived in Britannia two years ago, but clearly General Plautius thinks highly of him.

Early on, Pudens let the natives know that he was quite interested in meeting socially with the ruling families of the area. Consequently, Arviragus, with his young bride, went calling on Pudens, thinking that she would enjoy being in the company of Romans occasionally—which she was. The result, of course, was that Pudens soon made a return courtesy call at Arviragus' court, where he learned also of the large Llyr/Bran/ Caradoc family in Siluria to the north, and expressed an interest in meeting them. Although Pudens could not be expected to visit Siluria, since it was considerably north of the zone of security, Arviragus' assurances of Pudens' sincerity and peaceful intentions soon brought a visit to the post at Corinium by Llyr, his granddaughter Gladys, and two great-grandchildren, eighteen-year-old Cyllinus and nine-year-old Gladys from Caradoc's household. Pudens was enthralled by his rapport with this group of visitors but, oddly, it was Cyllinus, three years his junior, and nine-year-old Gladys with whom he found the most affinity. Various others of the Silures royal family came regularly and frequently, often staying for days at a time with Pudens. Before long, Bran began joining in these visits, and soon Pudens asked Arch-Druid Bran to describe the British religion to him. Bran, having been an enthusiastic Christian for five years now, explained the old Druidic teachings and the transition to Christianity that resulted from my missionary work in Britannia.

And so, inevitably, I was drawn into these discussions and found Pudens to be a most sincere and brilliant young officer. Coincidentally, on my first visit, I had been in Corinium but a day or two when General Plautius chanced to pay an official visit. Pudens was not at all chagrined and seemed to be on close personal terms with his general. In any event, Plautius, too, was very soon participating deeply in our discussions, though I couldn't be completely sure whether it was his religious interest alone, or his romantic interest in Bran's beautiful and intellectual daughter, Gladys, that intrigued him most. If there is such a thing as love at first sight (and my meeting with the lovely Elyap convinces me that there is), then surely it happened right away between Aulus Plautius and Gladys, daughter of Bran. Hardly a week passed that Summer without a visit of Gladys to Puden's post when Plautius was there, or her visit to Plautius' headquarters near Londinium.* By early Fall, no one could doubt the seriousness

---

*London.

of their courtship, and so I was not surprised one day to be summoned to Corinium to consecrate and baptize both Plautius and Pudens. Gladys had told Plautius she would not marry him until he became a Christian, and Pudens said he had only deferred such action himself on the question of propriety for a military officer on duty in a foreign country—but the precedent set by his general resolved that question. Strange to tell, Plautius' religious decision and his forthcoming marriage had received full and official approval from Emperor Claudius.

For propriety's sake, Gladys had been taking Caradoc's seventeen-year-old daughter, Eurgain, with her on the trips to Corinium and Londinium. I had baptized Eurgain four years earlier, and she had become a more zealous missionary than any of my staff, and so it was no great surprise later that year when she appeared on our island with a civilian member of Plautius' staff by the name of Salog, requesting that I consecrate and baptize him. He was a Roman patrician and businessman who worked in coordination with the military. Late that year Bran and a Roman chaplain jointly officiated at a double wedding for Plautius and Gladys, and for Salog and Eurgain.

CHAPTER NOTES:

1. Several report the use of elephants, notably Sheppard Frere in *Britannia-History of Roman Britain,* Harvard Univ. Press, 1967; and *Roman Britain* by P. S. Fry, David & Charles, London, 1984, Barnes & Noble, Totowa, N. J., 1984.

2. The Plautian zone of security ran roughly from modern Cirencester (Corinium) to Lincoln (Lindum)—the *Roman Conquest of Britain,* by D. R. Dudley and G. Webster, Dufour Editions, Chester Springs, Penna., 1965; also, *Roman Britain* by H. H. Scullard, Thames & Hudson, London, 1979.

3. In *Why Britain?* by Percy E. Corbett (RJ Press, Newbury, England, 1984) we are told that during the six months' truce, in ca. A.D. 45, Claudius arranged three marriages with Christian Britons which merged them with highly placed Roman families. The explanation seems to be in the personality of Claudius himself. All analysts and historians seem to agree that Claudius' reign was *primarily* noted for his vacillation and inconsistency; his rulings and actions were frequently exactly the opposite of acts on previous similar matters. To the same effect, see *The Early Church* by Gladys Taylor, Covenant Publishing Co., London, 1969, 1987; *The Lost Chapter of Acts of the Apostles* (The Sonnini Manuscript), ed. by E. Raymond Capt, Artisan Sales, Thousand Oaks, Calif.; *Did the Virgin Mary Live and Die in England?* by Victor Dunstan, Covenant Publishing Co., London; *The Drama of the Lost Disciples* by G. F. Jowett, Covenant Publishing Co., 1975; *St. Paul in Britain* by R. W. Morgan, Covenant Publishing Co., 1960.

✠

CHAPTER FORTY-NINE

British Christians in Rome

A.D. 50

SIXTEEN YEARS HAVE ELAPSED since we arrived as permanent residents of Britannia, and in this Springtime season we are celebrating the seventeenth anniversary of the Resurrection of Lord Jesus from my new tomb in Jerusalem.

The decade just passed has certainly been filled with momentous events, but as I try to peer down the long road into the future I feel sure that the recent secure establishment of a Christian center in Rome is by far one of the most important happenings in my lifetime—and indubitably, the most significant since the Resurrection. And, although I've not been in Rome for years now, it is a most gratifying feeling to know that my efforts were crucial to that result.

Who could have anticipated the importance for the whole Roman world that would result from our missionary efforts here in Britannia that began the year after the Resurrection? And who would have thought that the seeming tragedy of Caradoc's capture in defense of Britannia would also be a key factor in that result? And yet, over the past three years nearly the entire Llyr/Bran/Caradoc family has been taken to Rome as captives/hostages, and most of them had previously become stalwart Christians, baptized here in Britannia by my hands. And now, that family is the darling of Rome and the immense palatial estate in Rome in which it is resident bids fair to become a Christian center to rival Jerusalem and Syrian Antioch, if not surpass them. And so, I must now write in selective detail of these years just passed.

☩ ☩ ☩

A.D. 47/48

There were other tribes with their own kings in the southwest quarter of' Britannia and Druidic communities within them, to which we took Jesus' message of Christianity with fabulous success. But in early Spring as we were celebrating the fourteenth anniversary of Jesus' resurrection, events of change were on the move in Britannia. Plautius had been authorized to retire and return to Rome, where it was hoped the Senate would give him a "Triumph"—though, of course, not a *full* Triumph as was given Claudius. Both Salog and Pudens returned to Rome with their general—Plautius and Salog taking their Christian British wives with them.

Before departing for Rome the twenty-three-year-old Pudens, dressed as a civilian secretly visited Caradoc's capital, Trevman,* to ask the Pendragon for betrothal to his eleven-year-old daughter, Gladys. Caradoc was reported to have replied: "Sir, I will fight the armies of Rome until my death, but I cannot deny my daughter's love for you, nor yours for her. I believe you to be an honorable man, and so I grant your request and my daughter will came to you in due time."

Late in the Summer we learned of the arrival of Rome's new commanding general and governor, Ostorius Scapula, and very soon it became apparent that a new phase of the invasion was beginning. First, it was obvious that Ostorius would no longer sit behind Plautius' zone of security. We, on our Isle of Apples and the kingdom of Arviragus, cut up by so many marshes and tidewater creeks were never seriously threatened. But Arviragus had to take his troops across the Channel to help Caradoc defend the Silures hill-country with its many forts. By the following Spring, Ostorius was pounding them mercilessly. Moreover, Ostorius did not have the respect for civilians that we had seen in Plautius.

Before the next Summer arrived we were saddened to learn that the entire Llyr/Bran/Caradoc family (except for Bran, himself) had been captured and were taken to the southern coast for shipment to Rome as hostages.[1]

---

*In the parish of Llan-Illid in Glanmorganshire, Wales.

✝ ✝ ✝

A.D. 49/50

Caradoc and Arviragus fought on for another year, but the sheer numbers of fighting men that Rome was able to commit to action began to tell on the Britons. The Winter which marked six and a half years from Plautius' first landing saw the Romans breach one fort after another in the Silures hills.

Late in the Winter we received some very sad news. King Llyr, whose health had not been good in recent years, had been weakened by the trip to Rome as hostage and died within a few months of arrival. Upon receipt of the news, Bran immediately set out to offer himself as hostage in lieu of his deceased father;[2] I think Rome was shocked by such high moral standards—because Bran was Arch-Druid, he was the only member of the family who had not been initially captured and taken as hostage.

Not counting small children, the hostages taken to Rome had included Llyr; the wife of Caradoc; Caradoc's sons Cyllinus, Linus and Cynon; Caradoc's daughters, Gladys and Eurgain; Caradoc's two brothers; Caradoc's sister Gladys.

Finally, as Spring was beginning, we learned that Arviragus was back in his own capital with the remnants of his fighting men. I went to visit him and asked for his appreciation of the situation.

"My dear Joseph," he replied, "it's just a matter of time now. The power of Rome was too much for us. As our forts began to fall, our losses of manpower began to make defense of the remaining strongholds impossible. Caradoc finally told me to take all the men I could find westward to the Sea,* and back through our own Channel ** to the safety of our marshes—which I have done. He, with a small personal guard, was going to flee northeastward to the area of the Brigantes in hopes that Queen Cartimandua would permit him to take her armies."

"But," I protested, "hasn't she signed a treaty of allegiance with Rome?"

"True," he replied, "and that presents a gamble, but Caradoc feels that her officers will support him in continuing the fight."

---

*The Irish Sea.
**The Bristol Channel.

A.D. 50

The gamble did not pay off. In late Spring we finally learned that Cartimandua had promptly placed Caradoc under arrest and delivered him in chains to the nearest Roman garrison. Her action was quite a surprise. Everyone had assumed that she would either permit her troops to decide for themselves whether they would go under Caradoc's command, or would say, "No," to his overtures and force him to go elsewhere. But to arrest a neighboring monarch and deliver him to Rome was most unexpected.[3]

Later in the year we had a pleasant double surprise. First, was the arrival from Rome of Cyllinus, Caradoc's eldest son, to serve as Regent in place of his father, but with no instructions of a military sort; this latter seemed to leave Arviragus free of any restraint from Cyllinus, to continue the war against Rome as pendragon, which post he had assumed upon the capture of Caradoc through Cartimandua's treachery.

The bigger surprise, however, was the news brought by Cyllinus about his father. We had had little hope for the lives of the family taken as hostages and assumed that Caradoc himself would doubtless be tortured and eventually executed as was Rome's custom. However, our expectations couldn't have been more wrong! Caradoc had requested permission to address the Senate; Claudius not only agreed, but he and his empress were present to listen. Caradoc spoke eloquently, and concluded with the statement: "If you were to put me to death, I should be forgotten. But if you preserve my life, I shall be an everlasting witness to your clemency."[4]

Claudius thereupon pardoned Caradoc and all his family subject only to their commitment to war against Rome no more and to remain in Rome until authorized to leave. Shortly thereafter, Claudius arranged that the family be given a huge estate in Rome where Roman soldiers were not permitted to enter. The effect of Claudius' various actions seems to have been equivalent to the taking of them all into the imperial family. In addition to the three marriages previously arranged by Claudius, after the family arrived as hostages he renamed Caradoc's daughter Gladys, as Claudia, to take the place of his own daughter of that name who had died earlier. He renamed Caradoc's sister, Gladys, as Pomponia Graecina—the latter name because he was greatly impressed by her fluency in the Greek language. The estate that they were given was called Pallatium Britannicum.[5]

Cyllinus pleases me greatly by reporting that Eurgain and Gladys/Pomponia, with the full support of their Roman husbands, have been missionaries for Christianity right from the time of their arrival in Rome three years ago when their husbands took retirement. Also, that the family estate, Palatium Britannicum, has immediately become a Center for the propagation of the Christian faith, with Bran officiating under the authority I had conferred on him.

Cyllinus reports as a humorous sidelight that Pomponia made no secret of her Christianity, and when she arrived in Rome with her new husband, General Aulus Plautius, his political enemies formally charged that under existing law she was a criminal by virtue of being a Christian. However, as also permitted by law, Plautius, as her husband, chose to serve as magistrate to try her. He found her not guilty of the charged crime.[6]

I was also pleased that Cyllinus says he has become a believer in The Way of Jesus and wants me to baptize him. He tells me that all of his children must follow him in this Faith as soon as they are old enough.

CHAPTER NOTES:

1. The family was captured first and Caradoc later; *The Dictionary of National Biography,* Vol. III, ed. by L. Stephen and S. Lee, Oxford Univ. Press, Great Britain, 1917, 1973. Also, *The Roman Conquest of Britain* by Dudley/Webster, supra.

2. Bran's act of substituting himself as hostage in place of his father upon his father's death in Rome, is reported by several historians, including Henry W. Stough in *Dedicated Disciples,* Artisan Sales, Thousand Oaks, Calif., 1987.

3. Caradoc's capture through the treachery of a neighboring monarch, Queen Cartimandua, is described and analyzed by many historians, including Dudley/Webster in *The Roman Conquest of Britain,* supra.

4. Parts of his speech were presumably recorded by Dio, Tacitus, Petrus Patricius, and Suetonius; one of the best modern texts of it is found in *Rome Against Caractacus* by G. Webster, Dorset Press, N. Y., 1981, 1985.

5. The renaming of the two Gladyses and the naming of the estate is noted by several writers, notably, Gladys Taylor in *The Early Church,* supra.

6. *Why Britain?* by Percy E. Corbett, supra.

family except for his grandfather, Bran, who by then was known to all as Bran the Blessed. Now, after two and a half years in Rome, twenty-year-old Linus is reported by Cyllinus to be a most scholarly and serious young man, and Cyllinus pleased me enormously by handing me a long letter from Linus who, from childhood, has called me, Uncle. He first wrote me several pages of details of the family's life in Rome, and then of his thrill upon being accepted as a student in the school of philosophy of Seneca:

This fabulous development, dear Uncle Joseph, happened in such an interesting way that I must tell you of it. You may recall that while Rufus Pudens was commander of the military post at Corinium, some of us had occasion to meet the general, Vespasian, whose II Legion was quartered a few miles to the east. One of the civilians on his staff was a naturalist by the name of Pliny, about of an age with Pudens whom he had known in Rome. I was only fifteen at the time but I remember how proud I was when Pliny (whose formal name was Caius Plinius) asked me to take him "exploring" one afternoon so that he could take samples of fruits and bushes and wildflowers, and could observe some of the wild animals.

How little we can anticipate the ways important future events are often foreshadowed by trivial happenstance! After a few months in Rome I met Pliny again in the company of Pudens (who will soon be marrying my sister Gladys) and saw him casually every few weeks thereafter; he remembered our 'explorations' in Britannia and was most friendly. And then, a little over a year ago, Pliny said to me: "Friend Linus, I think I have some good news for you. You have asked several times about a tutor in philosophy, and I truly have given it some thought without finding the right person. But now, fortune smiles. Our unpredictable emperor, Claudius, exiled a great man, Lucius Annaeus Seneca to his home country, Iberia, just a few months after Claudius ascended the throne of Rome; the reason for Claudius' action was, as usual, obscure, though probably involved some imagined romantic activity by Seneca. In any event, Claudius has now married his own niece, Agrippina, who insists that he recall Seneca to tutor her son, the twelve-year-old Nero—which, of course, Claudius has done. But Seneca is seeking more students and I have recommended you—I know him well enough, and am sure you will be accepted."

Dear Uncle Joseph, I should have written you sooner of this great, good fortune and of my excitement and pleasure, studying with Seneca, but I have just been *so* busy! Needless to say, I am enthralled by his erudition. He is a successful author and playwright as well as now becoming a statesman of influence in the emperor's household. As a philosopher, he adheres to the Stoic school, which fascinates me, though I am not sure

I can embrace it fully. As you know, Stoicism is divided into three parts, with physics and logic serving as support for ethics; it is basically a materialistic approach to reality, and yet Stoics say that God pervades all, and becomes the reason and soul in the animate creation. That seems internally inconsistent, but I'm sure that Christianity as you've taught it to me shall be the true rudder for my life.

I remember that you told us of the study group Jesus taught in Galilee, involving mostly the young men who would later become his disciples. The idea has always appealed to me, and in recent months I have begun a study group here to foster a better understanding of our religion. One of the group, about my age, Julius Cletus, feels like a twin to me, as we seem to think each other's thoughts when we get into an animated discussion—it is so wonderful! I'm sure he is going to have grandfather Bran baptize him into the Faith very soon.

Cletus has had a very interesting life. He comes from a most illustrious patrician family of Rome, and his father, Anthonius Cletus, was resident in Athens in the foreign service of Rome when my friend was born. They continued to live in Athens for another ten years, the last three of which he was tutored in languages, art and literature by the very best Grecian scholars. However, shortly after his tenth birthday his mother suddenly died of a fast-acting malady which the physicians could not check, and the elder Cletus resigned from his post and returned to Rome. As comfort to each other, for the next four years his father kept young Cletus at his side almost constantly, so that in a kindly, joking way friends began to call the youngster "Anacletus," as a nickname, and older acquaintances still use this appellation frequently.[2]

Knowing from the letters you receive from Thaddaeus how important is the work of both Peter and Paul in the east, some two years ago I wrote to both of them in care of the Christian Church in Syrian Antioch.

My letter caught up with Saul/Paul in Lycaonia, in the Asian province of Phrygia, where he was preaching with Barnabus of Cyprus, whom I know was a special friend of yours. Paul wrote me briefly from there, saying that he was just completing a series of collections from the Asian churches to take to Jerusalem for support of the mother church, and that he would write me at more length after leaving Jerusalem. Finally, just a month ago, I received a long letter from him while in Corinth, apparently one of his favorite churches. He told me that Silas and Timothy are with him, and that all three of them send you warmest greetings; Timothy, of Lystra, of course knew you only by reputation, as is true of Paul, himself, but Silas had met you several times at the home of Cleopas in Emmaus. Paul says he envies me the opportunity of working for The Way in Rome, and that in another ten years, at least, he hopes to visit us here and even go on to Iberia, Gaul and Britain, if he lives and his health permits. Paul's reason for wanting to go to Iberia is to nurture the churches founded there by the martyred James bar Zebedee. Paul says those churches were flourishing when James returned to Jerusalem, and it would be a shame if they shrivelled from neglect or fell into error.

Long before that he has in mind to send Aristobulus to Rome so we will have a powerful preacher here; one of the Seventy, Aristobulus is a brother of Barnabus and father-in-law of Peter, so I imagine you know him well. Paul tells me that he is just in the midst of writing a special letter to his church in Thessalonica of Macedonia, and says that the following—which he is writing them—might have equal meaning for us in Rome:

"What we preach is God's message and not some human thinking. Expect that you will have persecutions to bear. The Lord will be generous in increasing your love and will make you love not only one another but the whole human race. Live quietly, attending to your own business and earning your living, to be seen to be respectable by those outside the Church. Do not grieve for the dead as if there were no hope; you who are living have no advantage over those who have died, for alive or dead we still live united to Christ Jesus. Pray constantly, and in all things give thanks for this is the will of God concerning you."*

A few months ago my letter to Simon/Peter was answered from Alexandria where he is living in the home of Philo and preaching mostly in the synagogues, but also to gentiles in the marketplace. He asks to be remembered to you and says that followers of The Way have never properly recognized your great sacrifice—that of giving a respectable burial to Jesus, well-knowing that you would consequently lose your standing with the Sanhedrin and with Rome, would lose your business and livelihood, and would either lose your life or be forced into exile—that the quick death of a martyr, such as was suffered by Stephen and James bar Zebedee, would be much easier to take.

He tells me that Philo remembers visiting off and on for several weeks with Jesus who spent time in Alexandria while still in his twenties. Peter says he had not been aware of Jesus being there, but he realized that Jesus was often gone from Galilee for months at a time. Peter says that Philo is interested in the good news of The Way and is largely accepting of Jesus' message, but it is doubtful that Philo will ever make a move to separate himself from conventional Judaism, though he smiles and admits that his philosophy of the Logos—largely borrowed from the Greeks—is very close to the Christ as we see it. Peter writes that Philo, now about seventy

---

*Adapted from I Thessalonians.

years of age, is mite feeble and may not live much longer.* Peter says he has no present plans to come to Rome but does not doubt he will do so some day. He tells me that his father-in-law, Aristobulus, is eager to go to Rome, now that-his wife is dead, and when Paul can spare him Rome will surely be his destination. One paragraph of his letter may interest you:

"On the day of the Resurrection, the risen Jesus, in his spirit body, appeared to me alone, and told me many things I am not yet ready to reveal, but one explanation he gave me may avoid a puzzlement for new Christians. Many ask, 'Where was Jesus during the three days of his entombment?' And his own explanation to me was this: 'In the physical body I was put to death; in my spirit body I was raised to continuing life; as a spirit I went to preach to spirits trapped in Hades of the afterlife, and uncountable thousands upon thousands did respond to my Good News of salvation. For as David foretold of old, the Father would not abandon my soul in Hades nor permit my physical body to experience corruption in Joseph's tomb. And so, I was raised to new life on earth for a short while, and in that raising was my physical body wholly consumed, for the glory of God. And soon I will go to the Father, but neither will I leave you.'"**

☩   ☩   ☩

At about the same time I received a most interesting letter from Thaddaeus, which included the following:

I had a most wonderful experience last month that involved that strange man, Saul of Tarsus. As was true on rare occasions when you were head of this business, we found it desirable to facilitate a transaction not involving metal or metal products. An agent of our good friend and shipmaster, Hiram of Tyre, was here in Edessa on other business, and seeing me he asked if we would undertake a special commission for Hiram. It seems that during a late Spring storm, a poorly moored vessel in Tyre harbor broke its moorings and anchor rope, and was blown across the harbor into three of Hiram's vessels, doing considerable damage. The great *Astarte* was unharmed and the structural damage to the three that were hit was not significant, but their furled sails were virtually shredded to ribbons by the repeated brushing back and forth of the rampaging vessel as it was buffeted by wind and waves.

As you know, Hiram prefers the black sails coming from Tarsus in Cilicia, where they use tent and sail cloth, called "cilicium," made from the

---

*He died that year, A.D. 50.
**Adapted from I Peter 3:18,19 and Acts 2:27.

tough, black goat hair of that region. But, unfortunately, Tarsus sail-makers appeared to be fully committed for the season and refused to consider Hiram's needs. And consequently, his agent begged that we help if I had any knowledge of a source for such sails.

Coincidentally, my assistant preacher for The Way, Aggai the former robe-maker for King Abgar, had been in the small seaport of Issus the previous week and happened to have a brief visit with Saul of Tarsus who, accompanied by one, Silas, was on his way to visit Christian churches in Derbe, Iconium and Pisidian Antioch.[3] Because of their mutual professional interests—Saul as a tent and sail maker, and Aggai as a robe-maker—they visited on a very intimate basis about their professions as well as their passionate interest in Christianity. Saul mentioned that he planned to stop first in his hometown of Tarsus for about a month to encourage and try to find new business for his former associates in the tent and sail business of which he was still a part owner—explaining that these workers were quite old and needed the work, but had no experience in finding business.

Accordingly, I took measurements and specifications from Hiram's agent, and assured him that I would visit Tarsus at once and see that the order for sails was placed and expedited. I left the next day on a fast horse and was in Issus within three days, where a coastal vessel promised to have me in Tarsus in another three days; the shipmaster was as good as his word, reaching its Cydnus River docks by mid-afternoon, so that I was able to find Saul's shop before dark. This was my first visit to this essentially Phoenician city, and I found it a bustling commercial world of diversified activity. In my few days there I sensed it to be Hellenistic in attitude though oriental in emotion.

Needless to say, Saul was glad to have such a large order and promised to begin on it at once, ahead of their other work. Saul, who now prefers to be called Paul, is a smallish man with powerful hands, arms and shoulders that seem out of proportion for his slim torso and bandy legs—but the dominant physical feature of the man is a pair of piercing, eagle-like, gray eyes that are ever in motion as he talks, questing from beneath craggy, gray brows and a shock of unruly gray hair. His eyes and dominating personality give him an almost hypnotic presence that commands one's attention, if not an accepting belief. We were soon talking with mutual excitement about our respective Christian mission fields.

CHAPTER NOTES:

1. Data concerning Seneca and Pliny are taken from information provided in *The Columbian Encyclopedia*, Third Edition, Columbia University Press, N. Y., 1963.

2. Cletus became bishop of Rome (A.D. 86-88) upon the death of Linus in either A.D. 86 or 90, and served but two and a half years before his own death. He was of Roman

patrician lineage, although Irenaeus, Eusebius and Jerome state that he was born in Athens. He is sometimes referred to as Anacletus (the prefix "ana" in Latin can mean *again, repeat* or *ditto*).

3. The name, Antioch, was given to sixteen cities by the Greek general, Seleucus Nicator, one of the successors of Alexander the Great.

CHAPTER FIFTY-ONE

✛

Edessa, Rome and Britain

A.D. 50

*T*HADDAEUS' LETTER CONTINUED:

Paul knew somewhat of our situation in Edessa and was soon asking eagerly for all I was willing to tell him about our mystical Face of Jesus.

"But how came this Face to be made?" he asked me,

"It was a mystical event, uniquely created by the spirit of God, which we feel will never be explained by man," I replied. "However, Joseph of Arimathea has the most complete first-hand knowledge. Perhaps he will one day recount it all."

Paul said that it was not in his plans to travel eastward where Thomas and associates seem so effective already, unless the Lord were to specifically instruct him to do so, but he was most interested in the Face. Also, he observed that when he had preached in Pisidian Antioch some two years earlier on his first missionary journey, with Barnabus, some of his converts were from the wealthy mountain city of Laodicea in the adjoining province of Phrygia; they, living on a main trade route with the east, had heard the story of King Abgar's miraculous healing and of a mystical relic called "The Face," which they somehow associated with the healing—they had wanted Paul to tell them more about it, but he could not.

Paul also explained to me: "I will make all the converts I can and establish all the churches that I can in this whole area, but there is a limit to how much one man can travel and nurture his flock. I think the time is coming, in the next five to ten years, that I will nurture them more by writing to them. I seem to be always getting into trouble of some sort when I deal with my flock face to face—I may be able to be more effective in writing, and besides I like to write. In between trips I will one day write an Epistle to the Laodiceans and will tell them the amazing story you have shared with me about the Face of Jesus in Edessa."[1]

Paul had been invited to preach on the grounds of the large and beautiful Tarsus University the following morning, and suggested that I might like to accompany him and Silas, which I was most pleased to do. This is a brilliant, educated, erudite man with a convincing demeanor as a speaker, and his effectiveness was demonstrated by the large number of converts at the conclusion of his talk.

His theology, which he later told me was taught him by Jesus while in deep meditation or trance, during the months he spent in and around the desert town of Petra after his Damascus experience, leaves me with mixed feelings. His mystical Christianity rings true and the idea of Jesus as the incarnated son of God is fully logical, but divinity of the messiah was never a Jewish concept. Paul's suggestions of sacrificial death and vicarious atonement can possibly be found in Jesus' own claims—I will have to think further about that. Paul's position that gentiles may become Christian without first becoming Jews (and without circumcision), and that they need not keep Jewish laws seems to square with the teachings I heard from Jesus—however, although James agreed with Peter and Paul in Jerusalem on this point, I am not sure that James has imposed such a rule on the ultra-conservative element in our Jerusalem churches. Incidentally, Paul insists on being accorded the title, "Apostle."[2]

Some of Paul's other positions I would have difficulty accepting. He looks for Jesus' early return to earth-life; I doubt it, even though some of Jesus' discourses might be so interpreted. It seems that only with reluctance does Paul accede to women's participation in The Way, while Jesus embraced such concept fully, I felt. Even more difficult to accept is Paul's limited approval of marriage and his aversion to physical relations between married couples—even to the point of espousing "virgin marriages." I wonder if this is a form of asceticism that he may have learned from the Essene communities near Petra. All in all, I do not wholly trust Paul, for he is a man of fierce passions and will always have his way; he is impetuous, impatient and immoderate, and though he seems to strive at times for humility there is a hauteur about him and a condescension which ill becomes a follower of the Master. But, I must hasten to add, that he is most persuasive and effective, and doubtless will reach untold thousands whom you and I could not reach at all.

Sadly, I must note, however, that I feel Paul has a martyr complex that seems very basic in his character. I shall not be surprised if one day he is taken to Rome in chains.

And then there was a hastily written addition to his letter:

I am greatly saddened to report that word just came to me from the Palace that Abgar V has died this afternoon, and I am requested to conduct the services for his burial tomorrow. He was seventy-three years old and had had a split-reign, due to the vagaries of international politics, which altogether totalled forty-eight years on the throne.* He thus has lived seventeen years of robust good health since the day I showed him the Resurrection Face of Jesus—when his doctors had not expected him to live more than a week or two.

His eldest son, Ishmael, has now ascended to the throne succeeding his father, and will go by the name of Ma'nu V; I baptized him as I did Abgar, and so we will doubtless see no change in the government's attitude toward religious affairs. However he is now a man of fifty-five years, so convivial of disposition that his festive enjoyments may well shorten his life.** Hence, I must seriously consider thorough-going steps for protection of Jesus' burial shroud. Also, I believe I will implement a long-standing suggestion of Aggai that we bring to Edessa an outstanding Greek portrait painter to make one or more copies of the Resurrection Face, so that the true relic can be put into a secret and safe place for posterity.

It is perhaps worth telling you that a number of simple (but errone-ous!) stories of how the image came to be on the cloth have grown up through the guesses of some 'wise ones' and we have not contradicted them—both as a matter of security for the Shroud, and since it seems desirable to avoid roiling the sensibilities of those of Jewish blood who might still regard a burial shroud as unclean.

---

*Abgar V reigned 4 B.C. to A.D. 7 and A.D. 13 to 50.
**Ma'nu V died A.D. 57.

A.D. 53

The Roman invasion seems less intense now, and is certainly farther away, north and east of us for the most part. Arviragus fights on with the limited troops at his disposal, but with little spirit or hope. His Roman wife supports him fully, but she tells me there is little chance he can continue the defense effort much longer.

I receive letters regularly from Lazarus telling of his exciting missionary work among the Celtic tribes along the mighty Rhodenus River, and tributaries of the northward flowing Rhenus.* His greatest concern these days is the health of his sister, Martha; he is afraid that she is working too hard in the orphanages she is operating. However, we both know that Martha would not be happy if she wasn't working.

My latest letter from Linus (now a mature twenty-three!) is full of news from the capital of the world:

> You may be sure, dear Uncle Joseph, that we at Palatium Britannicum speak of you often—mostly as we quote your wisdom to our students and new Christians. This beautiful palace with its extensive grounds and out-buildings is ideal for our large family and many friends. As I told you in an earlier letter, Emperor Claudius gave this property to father [Caradoc] and promised that Roman soldiers would never enter our gates.[3]

> Grandfather Bran preaches the Good News of Jesus whenever a new group appears, and I am teaching classes of young people nearly every evening. I must admit, however, that neither of us puts in as much time and energy as sister Eurgain. She goes all over Rome every day preaching and challenging every person or group she can find. Her husband, Salog, accompanies her most of the time, principally to be sure she is safe from ruffians; he smiles and supports her, but tells me, "I'm just not the evangelical type." The scrolls you have furnished me are a big help, and James bar Joseph has sent several from Jerusalem that I had asked him for.

> It is only a few weeks now until the marriage of Rufus Pudens to my sister, Gladys; of course, the Emperor renamed her, Claudia, but she will always be Gladys to me! Rufus' father, the Senator, insists that it must be a large and formal and very proper wedding—Gladys just says, "All right, but it's going to be here in our home, and my father is going to perform the ceremony."[4]

> I have saved the biggest news 'till the last—Aristobulus has finally arrived. After ten days I'm still asking him questions and he's still smiling

---

*Rhine River

and answering. As father-in-law of Simon-Peter, brother of Barnabus, consecrated by Jesus as one of The Seventy, and travelling companion of Paul, he is for me a gold-mine of information. Of course, I'm sure you know as much, but when I left Britannia I was too young to know the questions to ask! I've heard Aristobulus preach twice since he's been here—he indeed is a powerful preacher and clearly follows the Pauline thrust of theology. He has brought with him copies of some of the letters Paul wrote to his churches—I'm enjoying them immensely—two of them were written a year or two ago to the church in Thessalonika, and the one I like best is to the church in Corinth, but Aristobulus says it is just a preliminary draft which Paul may not complete and mail for a while yet. He says Paul sometimes sends such a letter as soon as he writes it, and other times he may take a year or more in getting it worded just right—the one to Corinth seems to be of the latter sort.

I know you are not especially interested in Roman politics, but some of the present happenings seem ominous. I am still taking occasional classes with Master Seneca, and I pay attention to the comments he sometimes makes because he lives in the emperor's palace. Of Claudius' three wives, Agrippina, the present one, is clearly the most vicious and has no love or respect for her husband. She is constantly compelling Claudius to take official actions to please her; by far the worst act was the forcing of Claudius to disinherit his own son, Britannicus, and the establishing of her son, Nero, as heir and successor. Having achieved that, we are figuratively holding our breath since rumor has it that she has already poisoned a half-dozen persons who displeased her.

A.D. 54

The warnings from Linus, a few months ago, turned out to be prophetic. Emperor Claudius is dead by poison, and Agrippina seems the likely murderer; she has nothing to worry about, however, because her son, Nero, is now emperor. Nero may be more sane than Caligula, but is certainly more irresponsible at the same time. The only good thing about his administration is that for the moment he is leaving the affairs of government in the hands of Seneca and Burrus—the latter being chief of the Praetorian Guard. Some seventeen-year-old boys might make passable emperors but Nero is not one of them; his escapades with his friends are a public scandal each week.

✠　✠　✠

A.D. 58

Arrivals a few days ago from Rome gave me as much joy as a seventy-four-year-old should ever have! Bran has returned to Britannia accompanied by Aristobulus, Eurgain and Salog. Eurgain, the religious whirlwind, has taken Aristobulus (five years my senior) in tow, and is showing him the possibilities for evangelization. And, as for energy and zeal, she has met her match! No one has more enthusiasm for The Way of Jesus than this old Cypriot. I have really missed Bran, however, and plan to catch up on leisurely conversation with him. As much as anything, I have badly needed his assistance in the training of missionaries; Lazarus and others have continually asked for helpers faster than I can train them, and apparently no one else is doing that on a formal basis.[5] Eurgain will be of help to me in this endeavor if she can stay still long enough to do what she proposes—she says she will establish her own college for the training of missionaries; she even has the name picked out—she will call it Cor-Eurgain. I am sure that Jesus in heaven must be smiling to see the vigorous evangelizing by Eurgain. Much as he loved Mary and Martha and must be pleased with the work they have done in southern Gaul, the fearless fervor of Eurgain must gratify him in his earthly espousal of women's equality.[6]

I now learn something Linus has not had time to write me: the reason both Bran and Aristobulus could be spared from Rome is that a few months ago Clement arrived in Rome as promised by Paul. Clement's early availability resulted from the jailing of Paul; the Governor took Paul into custody in Caesarea last year, ostensibly to protect him from the Sanhedrin, but there seems to be no likelihood he will be released soon. According to Bran and Aristobulus, Clement is everything Paul claims for him and is well liked by Linus and all the rest. Although a powerful preacher and a brainy one, he is not yet the scholar that one sees in our Linus, though some five or six years younger than Clement.[7]

CHAPTER NOTES:

1. Suggested as contents of the "lost" letter from Paul to the church in Laodicea; see *The Fall of Jerusalem* by S.G.F. Brandon, SPCK Publishers, London, 1951, 1981.

2. In this story I follow the tradition that "apostle" is someone who learned directly from Jesus. "As between Hellenistic sources and the Hebraic-rabbinic sources, it was the latter that most illumined Paul," according to W. D. Davies in "My Odyssey in New Testament Interpretation," *Bible Review,* V-3, June 1989.

3. *The Early Church* by Gladys Taylor, Covenant Pubs., London.

4. The Roman poet "Martial" (Marcus Valerius Martialis) was a close friend of Pudens and Claudia; in one of his published poems he wrote: "Our Claudia, named Rufina, sprung we know from blue-eyed Britons." Pudens and Claudia had four children: Novatus, Timotheus, Prassedis, and Pudentiana; the entire family, except for Claudia, were eventually martyred. After the Roman, Hermas, wrote the apocryphal book, *The Shepherd,* he was sometimes called "The Pastor"; later, he wrote *The Acts of Pastor and Timotheus* (himself and Puden's son); Baronius, Vatican Librarian of the late sixteenth century, validated this book.

5. *In Why Britain?* Percy E. Corbett accepts the legends which credit Joseph of Arimathea with training in Britain these first bishops for Europe (mostly Gaul): Trophimus to Arles; Maximin to Aix; Eutropius to Aquitaine; Parmena to Avignon; Drennalus to Treguier; Marcellus to Tongres; Mansuetus to Toul; Cadval to Tarentum, Italy; Beatus to Unterseven, Switzerland; Crescans to Mayence.

6. See "Jesus a Feminist?" by Michael Scrogin, *The Messenger,* February 1979, Church of the Brethren, Elgin, Illinois.

7. Clement I became bishop of Rome (ca. A.D. 88-97) after Cletus; these dates are in accordance with the writings of Hippolytus, and later Bible scholar, J. B. Lightfoot, and are concurred in by J.A.T. Robinson in *Redating the New Testament,* Westminister Press, Philadelphia, 1976; earlier scholars had opted for his tenure as A.D. 92-101. Origen identifies Clement I as the disciple of Paul, whom Paul praises as a fellow-worker with whom he labored and whose name is "in the book of life" (Philippians 4:3). That identification is accepted by modern authorities, notably, *A Biographical Dictionary of the Saints* by F. G. Holweck, Gale Research, Detroit, 1969, and the *New International Dictionary of the Bible,* ed. by J. D. Douglas and M. C. Tenny, Zondervan, Grand Rapids, 1987. They conclude that Clement was of Jewish blood and may have lived mostly with Aquila and Priscilla in Rome; if he was in his early thirties when Paul wrote to the Philippians in A.D. 58, he would have been in his mid-eighties at his death. The writing of his own letter to the Corinthians *(I Clement)* would tend to support the suggestion that his antecedents and early work were in Greece and Asia Minor; many say it was written in A.D. 96, but see Robinson, p. 329, for a dating of *early* A.D. 70, before the fall of Jerusalem. Origen records that Clement was with Paul in Philippi but suggests that Clement may not have been present when Paul wrote Phil. 4:3.

CHAPTER FIFTY-TWO

✠

Christianity Wanes in the East and Grows in the West

A.D. 58

ABOUT THE SAME TIME that Bran and party returned from Rome, I received a letter from Thaddaeus in Edessa bearing unhappy news. He wrote:

Just at the end of last year, Abgar's first son, Ma'nu V, died peacefully in his sleep after hosting one of his many parties at which he indulged himself. Two days later I met with his brother who is now reigning as Ma'nu VI; the meeting was most pleasant, surprisingly, and the king told me: "I have no quarrel with Jews, nor with Christians whether they be Jews or not, nor with any other religionist for that matter for I observe that most religions develop in their adherents a respectable and law-abiding attitude. For myself, I have no interest in such. As for you and your church, while you give me the fealty I expect I will not likely cause you any trouble, but neither will I give you special status and privileges as did my father and brother.

"Some say I am a callous man," he continued, "and perhaps I am, but I do not believe I am mean for meanness' sake. However it was that you or your relic cured my father I do not know, but he was dying and instead,

352

he lived. I revered my father and you always honored him. Had you let him die, it would not have profited me—for my brother's rule would have been longer and the kingdom weaker. So, I have no quarrel with you as a businessman or as a religionist."

Although there was nothing threatening in his manner, there is a certain coldness in the man and I am glad that I acted as I did three years ago to protect the Holy Shroud. As I told you, I arranged for one of the premier portrait artists from Athens to come, with two of his assistants, to make copies of the Resurrection Face of Jesus. He was willing to work in secrecy, so that I believe no one here knew the Face was being copied except Aggai, my son Jacob and I. I had the artist make three copies because I was not satisfied with the first two efforts; the artist told me that it was the most difficult job of copying he had ever undertaken, and at the same time *so* gratifying—even exhilarating—he couldn't really understand his own feelings about it. It was necessary that the artist use assistants so that they could measure the dimensions of the Face *which they couldn't see,* while he directed them and looked at the Face *which he couldn't reach.* This anomaly, which we discovered in Bethany right after the Resurrection, clearly contributed to my artist's wonderment, initially, when he discovered this phenomenal attribute of the Face, he asked who had made the original—but I told him that was my secret. "He was a great one," was the artist's only comment.

Afterward, Aggai made cloth-of-gold overlays for all three copies and arranged for the making of shallow caskets so that the copies each were superficially similar to the true relic.[1] The first copy I donated to the church in Laodicea and the second one I sent to Thomas, and it reached him in the ancient town of Madras in Bharat,* the land to the east of Persia.

Fortuitously, Ma'nu V was wanting to do something for the Church at about the time our Face copies were completed. He knew the artist was with me but he didn't know why. I knew the artist was also skilled with ceramics, and so I suggested that I would have him make a copy of the Face on a tile and glaze it. The king was delighted with the suggestion and said: "Let's mount it over the West Gate of the city, since that was the gate by which you first entered."

I agreed, of course, but thought it a gesture not too appropriate for the Church. Since my son Jacob is a stone-mason by trade, I told him to cut the necessary niche in the arch over the passageway to accommodate the tile, while the artist was painting and glazing the tile. Shortly thereafter,

---

*India.

with some chagrin, he reported to me that the upper section of the gate was hollow, and he had broken into it.

Then, dear Joseph, an inspiration hit me: under cover of darkness Jacob and I would put the Shroud, in its casket, into the chamber above the gate and he would cover the hole with the new tile. As matters turned out, I had the artist make two tiles and we put the better one in the chamber with the Shroud,[2] while the remaining one was set prominently above the Gate. Of course, I consulted with Aggai about all of this, but only he and I and Jacob, and now you, know that our true Relic is thus fully protected above Edessa's West Gate.

I must also tell you that pilgrims continue to come here because of the mystery and legends about the Face, which are coming to be widely known. In recent months we have had groups from the Parthian capital, Ctesiphon, in the east, Alexandria in Egypt to the south, and Laodicea and Thessalonika in the west.

This had been the end of Thaddaeus' letter, but a hurriedly written paragraph had then been added:

My dear Joseph, I wish you were here to comfort Miriam and me. I've not been shattered by such a tragedy since the crucifixion of Lord Jesus. Yesterday, Ma'nu VI sent for Aggai and ordered the making of a regal robe of the sort his father had worn in his earlier years on the throne. Aggai was properly servient and apologetic, but refused to perform as ordered, saying that he was now a religionist and not a robe-maker. Ma'nu flew into a rage, struck Aggai and ordered him imprisoned. Early this morning gentle Aggai was beheaded.[3] His son, Ibrahim, deacon in our church, and I are both inconsolable.

✠ ✠ ✠

A.D. 59

Early this year we had the wonderful surprise of return from Rome by our most illustrious Britons: Caradoc, his wife and two brothers. Now age fifty-one, his parole ended, Caradoc looks the part of a mellowed, senior statesman, and says he will give advice to his son, King Cyllinus, only if requested.

Caradoc reports to me that one of the last items of news coming to his attention in Rome was that Emperor Nero had just poisoned his mother, Agrippina—even he couldn't stand her political machinations and bloodthirstiness. Not that Nero would have much room to complain since, only a few months after taking the throne in derogation of the natural rights of Claudius' son, Brittannicus, the latter died of poison and it was common gossip that the deed was by Nero's hand. I pray that Seneca and Burrus remain healthy and in Nero's good graces, for they are all that keep the empire from the hands of our depraved, twenty-two-year-old emperor.

With full formality, Caradoc vested ownership of Palatium Britannicum in his daughter Claudia and her husband Rufus Pudens just before he left Rome, and the former Pendragon of Britannia seems totally happy with life, but extremely glad to be back in Siluria.[4]

✠ ✠ ✠

A.D. 61

The first mail this year from Rome has arrived, including a letter from Linus which finds him soaring to the skies:

Uncle Joseph, the greatest news ever—Paul has arrived! He comes as a prisoner, simply because Procurators Felix and Festus in Caesarea were too timid to release Paul for lack of evidence and give him military escort out of the country. So he had to appeal to Caesar. The leaders of the Sanhedrin have no case against him so we are confident he will be released in at most the two years provided by law when there are no prosecuting witnesses. His journey by sea from Caesarea was in itself fabulous; his ship was wrecked in a storm and Paul was the hero—as acknowledged by all the seamen. His military guard is a centurion named Julius, who by now nearly worships Paul. As an indication that the charges against him are technical only, Paul has been permitted to rent private quarters for himself and Julius near to the barracks of the Praetorian Guard and to have all the visitors he wishes, subject only to his observing house-arrest in his quarters and not leave there. Paul asks urgently that Bran and Aristobulus visit him; will you please notify them of his desire.

Paul preaches on the first day of each week, and every time his little house is full of listeners and the yard is packed also. Rufus, Claudia and Cletus accompany me to each of these sermons, and Clement as well whenever he is in the City. Clement is now our principal evangelist, with Eurgain and Aristobulus back in Britannia; he works the streets of Rome much as Eurgain did, and also ranges into the countryside up to thirty miles in every direction. The sizes of our various groups are now expanded to the point that church-homes and preachers are a serious need. Whenever you have trained preachers willing to come here, we can certainly use them.

After several more paragraphs about Paul, whom he visits daily, and about Paul's companions, Luke and Aristarchus, Linus writes:

> For the past year I have had a most rewarding correspondence with your good friend, Gamaliel. As I've told you before, I have found your training of me provided all that I need to know of Christianity, but not knowing the Jewish faith as a background I have felt somewhat inadequate in some situations. Consequently, I implored the Rabban to tutor me in his faith, which he has done magnificently.
>
> Previously I have mentioned to you my correspondence with Peter, Paul and other leaders. As you know, I am not yet prepared to expound on our faith in writing; my purpose in such correspondence is to gather as much first-hand information about the ministry of Jesus and the early years of Christianity as possible from the leaders while they are still alive. I have had two wonderful letters from Andrew bar Jonah, who is presently in Nicomedia, the beautiful port-city of Bithynia, but he hopes very soon to go to Scythia; as the very first Disciple he has some very interesting things to say. I also have had a lengthy and very helpful letter from the Apostle Philip, now in Sargossa, a city on the northern plains of Iberia; he tells me that James bar Zebedee, was mostly in the southern part of that country. He also tells me that the superlative work of Lazarus in Gaul and yourself in Britain leaves no reason for him to stay in the west, so he will be leaving shortly for Hierapolis in Phrygia.

✠   ✠   ✠

Bran and Aristobulus returned after a very brief visit in Rome, singing the praises of Paul. In a very elaborate ceremony with all the Roman dignitaries of the Church participating, and his little house fully packed with people, Paul consecrated Bran and then invested Aristobulus as bishop of Britannia. As Aristobulus described it: "I knew I wouldn't be able to do justice with any word description of Paul, and so I told brother Bran nothing at all before we arrived. Well, I've heard Paul called a fire-eater and many other things, not all of them complimentary, but I had never seen such a powerful performance as he gave to consecrate Bran and invest me—and if there hadn't been a ceiling I think we would have had to pull brother Bran down from the rafters!"

Bran just grinned broadly and nodded.

A.D. 62

Nicodemus, my wonderful friend from boyhood onward, has kept in touch with me ever since I left Jerusalem, but he has not been a frequent correspondent. I always know that when he does write it will convey something important. His latest letter was no exception, and contained these items:

We are all saddened and my emotions are mixed over today's news, dear Joseph; James bar Joseph has been killed by the Procurator. I believe we were better off when we had governors (like Pilate) who didn't have so much power. You will recall that upon the death of Jewish king Agrippa I, eighteen years ago, Emperor Claudius put our whole realm under a Roman procurator, the first such being Cuspius Fadus, followed by Tiberius Alexander, and then Cumanus, and next Antonius Felix who "arrested" Paul. What a parade! Emperor Nero then appointed Porcius Festus who sent Paul to Rome, but he died earlier this year; Nero appointed L. Lucceius Albinus to replace him but before Albinus arrived, events moved quickly: King Agrippa II appointed Ananus as High Priest and he called a special meeting of the Sanhedrin who tried and convicted James of blasphemy and executed him by stoning. Upon arrival, Albinus rebuked the High Priest (too late to do James any good).

What, you will ask, was James' crime? He was "James the Pious" and high in favor at the Temple, wasn't he? Perhaps his crime was of supporting the wrong group; the ordinary priests were grumbling about the daily Temple sacrifice for Nero, and nearing an open breach with the chief priests who were becoming more pro-Herodian and pro-Roman. This disagreement might have been tolerated by the chief priests except that they saw a loss of control as more of the ordinary priests were becoming Christians and many were developing strong ties with the Zealots. (Also, I should digress to say that it seemed James himself was moving into a closer relationship with the Zealots.) In this volatile situation James was becoming very outspoken in support of the ordinary priests. The interim between procurators gave the Sanhedrin an opportunity to move on their own; in the gamble Ananus lost his job but James lost his life.[5]

As you know, I have been unhappy with James for formally agreeing with Paul about gentile Christians, but then informally tolerating actions of the "Judaizers" who went from Jerusalem to Paul's churches undoing much of Paul's work and causing many problems.[6] Yet, none of us would deny that James has avoided open schisms and held us together. In any event, a few days after his death the leaders of the Church elected Symeon

to succeed James; as brother of Matthew and James the Less, Symeon
also was first-cousin of Jesus. He will certainly be closer to Peter than
was James.

On a less somber note, I should tell you of a background matter that
relates indirectly to Linus' new parishioner (or should I say "overseer"?),
Paul. I refer to the Antiochan, Luke, a companion who undoubtedly is
becoming a chronicler of Paul as well. Of Grecian antecedents, he became
a physician after study in the medical school at Philippi, and continued
his professional practice in Syrian Antioch where he met Paul and later
began travelling with him, though he did not become a Christian on an
immediate basis, but after study and extended reflection. When Paul was
incarcerated at Caesarea, Luke took that opportunity to visit and converse
extensively with Mary and all of Jesus' family, and with all of the Disciples
who were still in the area and others who had known Jesus personally.[7]
Like Paul, he loves to write and will doubtless serve us well in that capacity later. I tell you of Luke mainly so you can share the information with
Linus, who doubtless is already getting acquainted with Luke but will
want to know of him more fully.

Last year I had a very emotional letter from Lazarus, telling of the
deaths of both of his sisters—Martha first, and Mary a month later. Of
course, both were buried in Gaul where they ministered, just north of
Massalia. Just now another letter comes from him which includes the following:

> For nearly a year I have been struggling since the deaths of my sisters,
> not knowing what I would do. I am now sure of one thing—I can no
> longer work in this area where memories of them are too frequent. As
> you know, Barnabus and others in Cyprus have been urging me to come
> there, where I have pleasant memories of boyhood visits; they have ar-
> ranged with Paul that he will invest me as bishop of Cyprus when I stop
> off in Rome on my way, and I have decided to do it. As I discussed with
> you often, I have one of the greatest corps of workers a man could have,
> and most of the younger ones are those trained by you and by Eurgain
> in Britain. I am very comfortable with the thought of leaving this area in
> such good hands—that include: Saturninus in Tolosam;* Martial, cousin

---

*Toulouse, France.

of Stephen, in Lemonicas;* Parmenas in Avenicorum;** Eucharius in Treves;*** Maternus in Tongres;**** Paulus (Sergius Paul) in Narbonam;***** and Trophimus of Ephesus, now in Arelate.****** Farewell, dear friend; I will write often.

✠ ✠ ✠

A letter from Linus brings the disquieting news that Burrus has died and Seneca has retired. Emperor Nero, at age twenty-five, is still an irresponsible adolescent. Who knows what horrors are in store for Rome. I pray for the Christians there.

CHAPTER NOTES:

1. Shroud copies or Face copies were sanctified by a ceremony during which the artist's copy was laid upon the True Relic so that the two were perfectly fitted together in every part; upon dedication the copy became a "touch relic." In the early centuries the original Face was considered too holy for viewing by the public.

2. "The Face" and the tile copy were found in the chamber above the West Gate in A.D. 525 when repairs of the city wall were in progress as a result of extensive damage caused by flood waters that year when the River Daisan overflowed its banks, where the River ran through Edessa (see *Portrait of Jesus?* by Frank C. Tribbe, p. 45.

3. This incident is recorded in the "Teaching of Addaeus the Apostle" in *The Ante-Nicene Fathers,* Vol. VIII, Eerdmans, Grand Rapids, 1951.

4. The New Testament letter to the Romans, rather certainly was written by Paul from Corinth during the winter of A.D. 57-58, in anticipation of a future visit to Rome (see editors' Introduction, pages 258-260, of *The Jerusalem Bible,* Doubleday, 1966). The letter has been described as a *midrash,* a teaching, that clearly was addressed to both Jews and non-Jews in a Jewish synagogue somewhere in Rome (p. 90 of *The Rabbi from Burbank* by Isiador Zwirn, Tyndale House, 1986).

Romans 16:13 states: "Greet Rufus, eminent in the Lord, also his mother aid mine." But who was Rufus, and who was Pudens? A number of Bible scholars have provided tortured mistranslations to "explain away" the obvious intent. However, a few have suggested that Paul did indeed have a half-brother, Rufus, whose full name was Aulus Rufus Pudens, son of Senator Quintus Cornelius Pudens. That rationale would clarify two obscurities:

---

*Limoges, France.
**Avignon; see Acts 6:5.
***Trier, Germany.
****In Belgium; the young man from Nain, Galilee, raised by Jesus.
*****Narbonne, France; see Acts 13:7-12.
******Arles, France; see Acts 20:4-6.
All are identified by H. W. Stough in *Dedicated Disciples.*

One, that Paul, for at least a part of the time between his two Roman imprisonments (in A.D. 61-63 and A.D. 66-67), was living in the palatial estate of Pudens and Claudia in Rome, known as Palatium Britannicum; during that time he wrote II Timothy, whose penultimate sentence reads: "Eubulus sends greetings to you, as do Pudens and Linus and Claudia and all the brethren." Claudia was a British princess, daughter of British King Caradoc (Caractacus); the entire ruling family (including grandfather and grandchildren of Caradoc) were brought to Rome as hostages. After a limited pardon, Emperor Claudius gave the family the Estate in question, and renamed Claudia, whose British name had been Gladys, "to take the place of his own daughter of that name who had died. Pudens became a Christian while on military duty in Britain and later (A.D. 53) married Gladys/Claudia in Rome. Palatium. Britannicum became enclave of the Christians in Rome, and in effect their citadel.

And, *Two,* it would make more plausible Paul's action in A.D. 66 of presiding at the ceremony for investiture of Linus as bishop of Rome. Linus, brother of Gladys/Claudia, and former prince of Britain, had, before the Roman invasion in A.D. 43, along with most of the members of his family, become a Christian at the knee of Joseph of Arimathea in exile in Britain.

The rationale provided by Henry W. Stough in *Dedicated Disciples* (Artisan Sales, Thousand Oaks, Calif., 1987) is that Prassede (Priscilla), mother of Saul/Paul, was widowed and re-married Quintus Pudens in Rome and by him had the son, Rufus Pudens (though Stough lists none of his sources). Thus, the latter would be Paul's half-brother and brother-in-law to Linus, as well as host to Paul and briefly to Peter, and many Christian transients. A similar scenario is presented by G. F. Jowett in *The Drama of the Lost Disciples,* Covenant Publishers, London, 1975; Jowett also states that by this time Paul's mother was now living with her son Rufus Pudens because her second husband, Senator Pudens, had died.

This proposal may be too conjectural and devious, but technically it is feasible: Saul/Paul was possibly born ca. 2 B.C. in Tarsus where his Jewish parents were living because his father was a Roman official. (Paul often makes much of his Roman citizenship.) If, in about A.D. 18, when Saul was age 20, his parents moved to Rome, he might have stayed in Tarsus because of the excellent university, with plans for further study at the Temple in Jerusalem. If his father died in Rome about four years later (ca. A.D. 22), it would not be surprising in those times that the Jewish widow would, the next year, marry Quintus Pudens whom she had met socially in official circles. The timing would thus be right for Rufus Pudens to be born in ca. A.D. 24. Paul was martyred in Rome in A.D. 67. Peter arrived in Rome in A.D. 63 and lived with fellow-Jews, Aquila and Priscilla until the fire of A.D. 64 when Emperor Nero began a pogrom against the Jews and they returned to Corinth; Peter then moved into the Palatium Britannicum until Aquila and Priscilla came back to Rome; Peter was martyred in A.D. 65.

5. *Jesus and the Zealots* by S.G.F. Brandon, Manchester Univ. Press (England) and Chas. Scribners, 1967.

6. Early Christians were of many stripes; some of the names mentioned were:
   A. Judaizers—who believed that a gentile must first become a Jew and abide by all Jewish law, before being eligible to become a Christian; many of these were quite militant.
   B. Hellenists—many Jews of the diaspora and gentiles, both of Grecian culture, who became Christians without forsaking some of their liberal religious views.

C. Gnostics—who professed strong spiritual beliefs in denigration of the physical body; they espoused inspiration and secret knowledge:

a. Docetists—gnostics who believed Jesus was spirit only and just "appeared" to be human and mortal.

b. Montanists—tongue speakers.

c. Marcionites—who gave women a leading role in Church matters.

d. Carpocratians—who thought every sin must be experienced.

7. *The New Int'n'l Dictionary of the Bible,* Zondervan.

CHAPTER FIFTY-THREE

✠

The Focus Is Rome

A.D. 63

THERE CAN BE TOO MUCH ZEAL. Our great friend Aristobulus is dead because his zeal carried him too far too fast. Bran and Eurgain warned him of going farther north than the area peopled by the Silures. He merely laughed and said God would protect him. People of the Ordovices tribe in the north had not been prepared for Christianity by their leaders as had the Silures and the Dumnoni. We'll never know why, but they killed him.

✠ ✠ ✠

Three letters from Linus arrived in late Spring, Summer, and late Fall which report events that impress me as involving great days for the Church, even though they are days of great risk from Emperor Nero now that he has picked up the reins of government dropped by Seneca and Burrus. Parts of Linus' letters are as follows:

> Peter is here! Peter is here! What wonderful days to be alive and to be in this place—the capital of the world. Peter, accompanied by Mark, arrived on foot. We were alerted by friends and went down Via Appia* by cart to meet them where the road crosses the Alban hills—and thus they rode the last few miles. They were not too travel weary since several cart

---

* The Appian Way.

drivers had given them rides in their trek from Brundusium*; they had taken the first ship from Tyre to cross the Great Sea this season.

While we shouted above the noise of the cart, Peter's first questions were about Paul, and he seemed much relieved when I told him Paul was in good health and good spirits, and could have unlimited visitors. Whereupon, he said: "Brother Linus, if my absence so soon after arriving would not offend you, I would like to be taken to Paul's residence in the morning and be left to spend the day with him. I do not know how much we will have to say to each other, but I am hopeful that we can pray together for the needs of the Church. You know the Lord Jesus told us if any two of us could agree on anything and pray for it:, the Father God would be receptive."

Of course I assured him that such an arrangement would be perfectly all right, and that I would send a messenger to alert Paul; also, I was sure Paul would be most pleased to have the visit. I additionally told him that Aquila and Priscilla from Corinth were anxious to see him and that they hoped he would live with them while in Rome. I hastened to add that he was welcome to stay at the Palatium with us for as long as, and whenever, he wished. When we arrived, none could have been more hospitable than Claudia and Pudens who echoed my invitation. Also living with us are Luke and Aristarchus, who arrived with Paul; they greeted and embraced Peter, and Mark whom they had met in Judea before embarking. I personally took Peter to Paul's residence the following morning, and Paul's cordiality was clearly affected with deep emotion, as well as pleasure for Peter's visit.

It was subsequently arranged that Peter would stay with us for a week and then go to live with Aquila and Priscilla, while Mark would stay on here at the Palatium. Mark and Luke had much in common as writers, and as record-keepers and secretaries for Peter and Paul, respectively. I had already found Luke to be a valuable discussant as I explored Christian theology, because of his scholarly objectivity as well as his scientific precision and his understanding of the human animal.

I am continually amazed at the prodigious effort of Paul in nurturing his many churches in Asia, Greece and Macedonia. Luke and other scribes are kept busy with Paul's writings to the churches, and hardly a month passes without a major epistle being sent to one of them—plus many shorter letters responding to their questions and requests.

Luke has shown me many of them before they are entrusted to the Imperial Post for transmission, and I am repeatedly thrilled by the profound

---

*Brindisi, at the heel of the Italian boot.

depth of his insight as well as the tenderness of his caring. And of course, he does not hesitate to point out their errors and short-comings, as well.

I once asked Paul why he did not have an extra copy made of the more important epistles to save for future record and enlightenment.

"Why?" was his sharp response. "To glorify me? If there is anything worthy in what I write, it will survive without any conniving on my part."

Luke stayed in his chambers much of the time as he worked on the voluminous records, lists and notes he had made while traveling in Judea and Galilee for two years talking to relatives and friends of Jesus, while Paul was under protective arrest in Caesarea.

One evening, that first week, I asked Peter about the situation in Jerusalem that had led to the death of James. The story he told was almost identical to that written you by Nicodemus. I asked if he thought James might have foolishly dug his own grave with the Sanhedrin, and he replied: "Brother Linus, there is of course a time to be silent and a time to speak out, but each person must decide what cross he will take up and at what point he will make his stand. James was no more foolish than the rest of us. I only hope that my work is finished before my foolishness catches up with me."

During the week Peter stayed with us in the Palatium before moving to the home of Aquila and Priscilla, I had the opportunity for several deep and valuable discussions with him. One point which had troubled me was the pseudo-independence of Christianity and its relationship to Judaism; I asked Peter's comments on this situation, and especially Jesus' attitudes that might be relevant.

"Brother Linus," he responded, "of one thing I can be absolutely certain. Jesus had not the remotest intention of starting a new religion nor of leaving Judaism; moreover, he was a Pharisee of the Hillel school which, of course, has no power in today's Sanhedrin. Nevertheless, he saw much in Judaism with which he could not agree and he attempted a radical reformation of Judaism.[1] That Jesus was significantly succeeding with the common people was proven by the action of Caiaphas and his small clique in the Sanhedrin who goaded Pilate into an intemperate—though legally defensible—judgment against Jesus.

"The background of the death of James, of which we just spoke," he continued, "doubtless involved the potential for further eroding the High Priest's power on a more vital level—if, as seems likely, the Temple priests and other ordinary priests were being strongly influenced toward Christianity and Zealotry, and James was a very visible catalyst in such defection, the chief priests needed nothing more in order to influence the High Priest to act against James. So, of course, this outrage is causing many Jewish Christians to agree with most of the gentile Christians in saying, 'Why should we any longer be shackled to Judaism?' Similarly, priests who were friendly to Christianity are receiving a thinly-veiled warning from the Sanhedrin. Thus, the potential for a schism—splitting Christianity from Judaism—is clearly developing—and it makes me very sad."

Peter had participated last year in the discussions in Jerusalem that resulted in the selection of Symeon as James' successor,[2] and seemed pleased with the results. I asked whether Symeon had a sufficient grasp of what was going on, world-wide, and Peter replied: "I feel there is no doubt he has. He has been an assistant to James for a number of years and has been living in Jerusalem. He has seen all of the communications to and from the churches. In fact, in our recent discussions Symeon showed me portions of letters from churches in Galatia, Bithynia, Cappadocia and Asia, indicating that the Jewish Christians there felt themselves to be in acute danger from heresy and wanted guidance. Symeon showed me the response he had drafted to them and I found it excellent and told him so; I asked him why he had not sent it. He replied that having been in office but a few weeks it would be presumptuous of him to advise them in strong language. I told him bluntly, 'This is the right thing to say; address it from me, "Simon-Peter, servant and apostle," and send it off.' I think he did so.[3] He needs but to believe in himself a bit more strongly, but he will do well."

Peter likes my Roman/Greek friend, Cletus, and has consecrated him as a minister of the Gospel of Jesus. After Peter moved to the home of Aquila and Priscilla, it became the practice of Mark to go there each morning to see what errands Peter might have for him, and occasionally a letter to write. Peter's speech in Greek and Latin is passable, but he is comfortable at writing only in Aramaic, and so Mark writes for him anything formal.

Peter had been in Rome a little more than a month when Paul arrived at our palace with a sheepish smile on his face—he had been released. During the weeks that followed, Paul and Luke spent much time together planning a trip to Iberia to visit the churches of James bar Zebedee along the southern coasts and in the southern plains of the country. Before the summer was far advanced, they left on that journey, accompanied also by Aristarchus.

I asked Mark to let me see any major letters that Peter might write to the churches—he said with a smile that there wouldn't be many. What a contrast in these two apostles! Paul excites me every time I hear him speak. With Peter, I feel awe in his presence; he has little to say unless questioned, speaks slowly, upon reflection, but his words burn deeply within one.

☩   ☩   ☩

A.D. 64

At mid-summer the shocking news comes to us—Rome is afire! No one seems to know if it was an accident or if it was set.* There are even rumors that Nero or his ruffian friends did it during an orgy—if so, it will never be admitted. Six or seven sections of the city are burning or threatened. So far the conflagration has been nowhere near Palatium Britannicum. It may take weeks to bring the fire under control.

☩   ☩   ☩

A.D. 65

Some nine months after the start of the Fire in Rome, we are beginning to see the shape of the political repercussions. Nero seems determined to blame it on the Christians, even though there is not the slightest bit of evidence that such might be true. Those prominent in the Faith are leaving the city. Aquila and Priscilla were among the first to leave, going back to Corinth. Peter has moved back to Palatium Britannicum. All indications are that Nero will respect the Claudian commitment of asylum for this sanctuary. We certainly pray he will. Linus reports that near the end of the fourth Roman month of the year, Peter had Mark write for him a fairly short letter addressed to gentile Christians of churches in Pontus, Galatia, Cappadocia, Asia and Bithynia who, specifically, were in acute danger of persecution.[4]

Another great tragedy for the Church: Linus writes that in mid-summer Peter was martyred by crucifixion. Soldiers would not permit Linus to approach the site. The story given out was that Peter told his executioners he was not worthy to be crucified in an upright position, and insisted that he be crucified head downward; they complied. Whether true or not, how like Peter! Linus is prostrated with grief. Most Christians have gone into hiding or left the city, except those behind the walls of Palatium Britannicum.

☩   ☩   ☩

---

*July 19, A.D. 64.

A.D. 66

Paul, learning of Peter's fate, has returned to Rome, apparently to dare the powers that be. Nero is off in Greece, but obviously knows what is happening in Rome. The Zealots in my homeland have dared Rome one time too many and a full-scale war is in progress; the empire is represented by General Vespasian (who once showed his military prowess here in Britannia), together with his son, Titus.

And my dear, dear friend, Lazarus, has died in Cyprus.

I would consider this the worst year of my life except for one item of news that overbalances all of the negative. Paul has invested Linus as bishop of Rome.[5] My cup is full to overflowing. This is truly the crowning glory for me. From age five, every year of his life, I have loved and trained Linus. It may be sinful but I am bursting with pride for this thirty-five-year-old man. Bishop of Rome—how grand a sound!

Bishops may come and bishops my go, but Linus has nurtured branches of the True Vine, and Truth will persist. The Church of Rome is now secure. Both Cletus and Clement have the stuff of which good bishops are made. Growth of the Church is assured, persecution or no.

✠   ✠   ✠

Linus writes that before Paul's departure from Rome he and Peter had agreed that Linus should be invested as first bishop of Rome. Paul had considered that such ceremony should be conducted by Peter, but Peter demurred, saying it was only fitting that that pleasure go to Paul who had arrived in Rome first (before Peter) and was a Roman citizen—"Besides," said Peter, "I am no administrator!"

Paul was anxious to be off on his next journey to Iberia with Luke and Aristarchus, but promised that Linus' investiture would be accomplished promptly upon his return. Linus had been fully informed by Peter and Paul but had chosen not to tell me in advance, largely to avoid it seeming a boast, and also because such matters could not be assured in these perilous times.

After the ceremony on Paul's return, Linus did write, giving me undue credit for having so well prepared him for the office.

Linus also confided that, although invested by Paul, as bishop at the seat of the capital of the world, Linus sensed that it was the heritage of Peter that had fallen upon him like an aura—that it was the Big Fisherman whose shoes he would strive to fill—the shoes that had followed wherever Master Jesus had led, in Galilee, in Judea, and unto the ends of the earth.

☩ ☩ ☩

The investiture of Linus as Bishop of Rome serves to remind me of the hours Linus and I spent together just before he departed with some members of his family as hostages to Rome. It was nearly twenty years ago, and he was barely seventeen years of age. Of course, we had reason to fear that all of them would be tortured and killed as a spectacle to sate the bloodthirstiness of the Roman rabble, but for some illogical reason I had a calm confidence that Linus would survive, even if I never saw him again.

In this mood we spent a long afternoon together as I refreshed his memory on the major tenets of our Christian faith, and told him a few intimate details of my last weeks in Judea that I had not previously spoken of. It seemed important and desirable that I explain to him as graphically as I could, of the full Resurrection image of Jesus on his burial shroud, of the actions we took concerning it during Resurrection week, and the highlights of Thaddaeus' experiences as its custodian in Edessa.

He was wildly ecstatic at these disclosures, as might be expected of a studious but lively teenager, and plied me with questions for more than an hour. Ultimately, I explained why we had decided to hold full knowledge of this relic to just the handful of us, and he agreed it was a secret he would keep for life if need be.

However, in view of his new status as Bishop of Rome, I will write him at once, referring to that discussion of twenty years ago, and will suggest that the secret should be shared—at an appropriate time—with his successor. A part of my reasoning being that pilgrimages to Edessa should be encouraged throughout the Church Universal, even though only a touch-copy of the Face was presently being kept at the place of worship in Edessa. This was a relic not to be forgotten.

CHAPTER NOTES:

1. *Jesus Within Judaism* by James H. Charlesworth, Doubleday, 1988.

2. Robinson: *Redating the New Testament,* p. 198.

3. Robinson, in *Redating the New Testament,* pp. 169-199, concludes that I Peter and II Peter could not have had the same author and the differences cannot be explained by different amanuenses; moreover, that II Peter was written first, probably in A.D. 62, and is related in some way to Jude but not to I Peter.

Eusebius Pamphili, writing his *Ecclesiastical History,* begins Chapter 3 of Book Three with this statement: "Now, one letter of Peter, his so-called first Epistle, is admitted as genuine, and the ancient presbyters made use of this Epistle as undisputed in their own writings. The reputed second Epistle we have ascertained to be not canonical;

nevertheless, since it appeared useful to many, it has been studied together with the other Scriptures." Second Peter was admitted into the canon at the Council of Hippo in 393 (See *The Fathers of the Church,* Vol. 19, p. 139, Catholic Univ. of America Press, 1953). At p. 162 of the same volume, Eusebius refers to the selection of Symeon, son of Cleopas, to succeed the martyred James as head of the Jerusalem Church—and writes that Cleopas "was as they say, the cousin of the Savior, for Hegesippus relates that Cleopas was the brother of Joseph"—the editors in a footnote state that Eusebius *assumes* from Hegesippus' statement that Cleopas and Joseph were brothers; they were probably half-brothers (with the same mother)—see the Genealogies, Appendix 1, infra.

4. The book of I Peter was written from Rome at the end of April, A.D. 65, per Robinson, *Redating the New Testament,* pp. 169 and 195.

5. Linus—bishop of Rome, ca. A.D. 66–86 or 90. Irenaeus identifies him as also being the Linus mentioned in II Timothy 4:21. Prince of Britain, son of King Caradoc (Caractacus), he was taken, as a member of the British royal family, a hostage, to Rome in the period A.D. 48-51, where he lived the balance of his life until martyrdom. Irenaeus and Eusebius record that Linus was the first bishop of Rome, subordinate, of course, to the Apostles Peter and Paul. His investiture as bishop came at the hands of Paul in A.D. 66. The date of his death is uncertain, being variously recorded as A.D. 86 and 90.

✠

Epilogue

A.D. 67-82

MANY NEGATIVE THINGS continue to happen, but I am not dismayed. Peter did not die in vain. The Church will live on.

The year after Paul returned to Rome, he was martyred; as a Roman citizen he could not be crucified, and was mercifully beheaded.

The following year Nero returned home from Greece and promptly died a suicide*—perhaps he was just a miscast actor. The blood-flow continued: Nero was succeeded by Galba who was assassinated the first of the following (Roman) year**; his successor, Otho, was a suicide three months later***; followed by Vitellius, who was murdered the last month of the Roman year.**** Emperor Vespasian then began his reign and perhaps we will have peace; as a man of war he knows that violence is not a solution nor produces any; his career shows a man of judgment and I am much encouraged.*****

The next year****** saw more tragedies: Beloved Thomas, somewhere east of Persia, died a martyr, and his body was brought to Edessa for burial. General Titus completely destroyed Jerusalem and demolished

---

*June 9, A.D. 68.
**January A.D. 69.
***April A.D. 69.
****December A.D. 69.
*****Ushering in a century of peace, he ruled for ten years, followed by his son, Titus, for two years, and son, Domitian, for fifteen years.
******A.D. 70.

370

the Temple, ending the Zealot revolt. The death toll was exceedingly high. Some Christians escaped to Alexandria the year before, but most were killed; they, unfortunately, were too closely allied with the Zealots by all accounts I have received, Elias, Lazarus and Thomas all are now dead; the Holy Shroud is sealed in its crypt, and no one knows its full story but Thaddaeus and Miriam in Edessa, myself here in Britannia, and Linus in Rome. And yet, the mystique of "The Face" draws more pilgrims each year.

Later that same year, following the fall of Jerusalem by only a month or two, Mark revised and released his Gospel account of Jesus' ministry. Linus has sent me a copy which I will treasure always. One of his major purposes, for this moment, seems to have been to convince the people and officials of Rome that Christians are not Jews and should not be blamed for the futile war in Judea.[1] I cannot blame him for wanting to forestall the possibility of another pogrom like we suffered under Nero. I do feel he needlessly went too far in repeated blame of "the Jews" for the calamity that befell Jesus; my admonition to him as a boy on the night of Jesus' arrest, on this point, clearly was not accepted or remembered. I do fear that an alienation between Christians and Jews will result, based upon fallacy. That will certainly be of greater long-range harm than the separation of Christianity from Judaism—which Peter sadly foresaw, and which Mark's Gospel doubtless will compel.

Also, Linus sends a copy of Luke's (as yet unfinished) two-part history of Christianity, covering the life and ministry of Jesus and the acts of his apostles.[2]

Now in my eighty-sixth year,[*] I think I am beginning to slow down. I have a beautiful family around me and many good friends, and I hope to read glowing reports from Rome for many years on the accolades for my protege, Linus. But I've had a good life and shall be ready to shuck off this mortal shell at any time.[3, 4]

Sitting comfortably and thinking in this fashion with my eyes closed, I suddenly "see" my great-nephew, Jesus, standing before me in radiant good health about as I remember him ten years before his death. His white robe is trimmed in gold and his face, hands and robe seem glowing iridescently, shimmering and shining forth with light. His face is wreathed in a huge smile, white teeth gleaming; his eyes show pleasure and beam love to me. One minute, two or three, he stands thus and then speaks: "Well done, good and faithful servant!"

---

[*]In A.D. 70.

He dissolves into nothingness. My eyes pop open. What had happened? Was I dreaming, or in meditation? Was that a mystical vision? Above all, *was it real?*—did it *happen?*

And then, I thought I heard his voice, out of the air around me, saying, "Selah! Selah! Selah!"

CHAPTER NOTES:

1. See S.G.F. Brandon in *The Fall of Jerusalem* (SPCK, London, 1951, 1981) and other of his writings.

2. The Acts of the Apostles (of the New Testament) was presumably written by the Grecian "Luke," and was probably completed in the form we know in the year A.D. 63, shortly after Paul was released from house-arrest in the Spring/Summer of that year (the writer may have intended to add further to it, but did not). In any event, it was apparently not released generally until after the issuance of the Gospel according to Mark in late A.D. 70. Both Luke and Acts are addressed to Theophilus—this name is definitely Roman (not Grecian or Jewish), so one may presume the addressee was in Rome, though this need not necessarily be so.

3. The death of Joseph of Arimathea in Britain is variously given as A.D. 76 (R.W. Morgan in *St. Paul in Britain,* Covenant Pub., London, 1960); as July 2, A.D. 82 (G.F. Jowett in *Drama of the Lost Disciples,* Covenant Pub., London, 1975); and as July 27, A.D. 82 (L.S. Lewis in *St. Joseph of Arimathea at Glastonbury,* James Clarke, Pub., Cambridge, England, 1922).

4. The Jewish scholar, Josephus, who was a reluctant military commander for the Zealots in Galilee for six months, in A.D. 66, surrendered, was pardoned, and became a protege of General Vespasian, with whom he returned to Rome in A.D. 69 in time for Vespasian's elevation as emperor. Adopting the emperor's family name, he began calling himself Flavius Josephus, was given the former mansion of Vespasian and an imperial pension to support his literary career. In A.D. 75, with Vespasian's encouragement, he published *The Jewish War* in Aramaic and it was translated into Greek two years later. *Antiquities of the Jews* was published in 93/94; Josephus died in A.D. 100. (See *Josephus— The Essential Writings,* Paul L. Maier tr. and ed., in the Bibliography of this volume.)

✠

Appendices

Possible Genealogies of Related Families

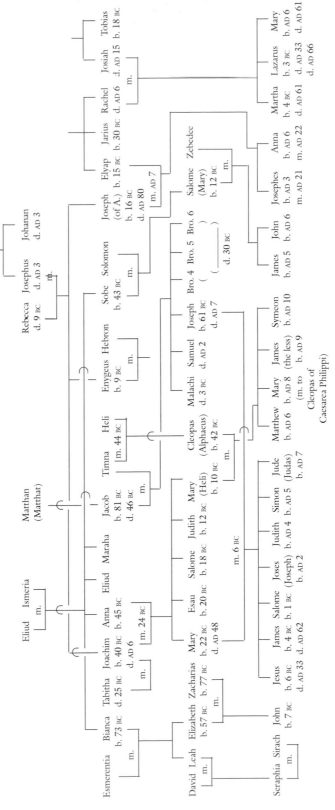

NOTE: There has always been controversy over the question of whether Jesus had brothers and sisters. Catholic author, John P. Meier, in his 1992 presidential address to the Catholic Biblical Assn., stated that "the most probable opinion is that the brothers and sisters of Jesus were true siblings." From 1997 to 1999, three other Catholic Bible scholars' books express agreement.

"The Twelve" of Galilee

According to Matt. 10:2		Mark 3:14	Luke 6:13	Acts 1:1
1. Andrew bar Jonah	fisherman	do.	do.	do.
2. Simon bar Jonah (Peter)	fisherman	do.	do.	do.
3. James bar Zebedee[1] (The Great)	fisherman	do.	do.	do.
4. John bar Zebedee[1]	fisherman	do.	do.	do.
5. Philip	fisherman	do.	do.	do.
6. Bartholomew (Nathaniel bar Tolmai)		do.	do.	do.
7. Thomas		do.	do.	do.
8. Matthew bar Alphaeus[1]	tax collector	do.	do.	do.
9. James bar Alphaeus (The Less)		do.	do.	do.
10. Lebbaeus bar Thaddaeus[2]	carpenter	do.	Judas bar James	do.
11. Simon the Cananaean[3]	carpenter	do.	Simon the Zealot	do.
12. Judas Iscariot	employee of Herod Antipas	do.	do.	Matthias

---

1. Cousin of Jesus.
2. Probably Jude (diminutive for Judas), a brother of Jesus.
3. Probably a brother of Jesus.

The Judean Disciples

(referenced in this story)

Lazarus	"The Beloved Disciple."
Joseph of Arimathea	Elder; Manufacturer/trader; Roman decurion.
Nicodemus	Lawyer-member of Sanhedrin.
Zacchaeus	Banker (former tax collector).
Sirach	A chief priest.
Gamaliel	A chief priest, and Rabban of the Sanhedrin.
Petronius	Roman centurion.
Silvanus	Roman official, initially; Missionary.
Philip	"The Evangelist"—one of the Seventy.
Stephen	Deacon; one of the Seventy.
Simon "the Leper"	One of the Seventy.
Barnabus	One of the Seventy.

Early Bishops of Rome

Linus	British prince	A.D. 66 to 86
Cletus	Grecian-born Roman	A.D. 86 to 88
Clement I	Grecian-born Jew	A.D. 88 to 97

Key British Christians

Llyr Llediath (King Lear): founded first Christian church at Llandaff.

Bran: Arch-Druid, and former king; son of Llyr.

Caradoc (Caractacus): son of Bran, king of the Silures (Cambria, Wales); Pendragon of Britain; fought Rome nine years (43-52).

Arviragus: cousin of Caradoc; ruler of southern Britain; succeeded Caradoc as Pendragon; married Venus Julia, daughter of Emperor Claudius in A.D. 45.

Eurgain: daughter of Caradoc; married to Salog.

Gladys (took name, Pomponia): sister of Caradoc; married General Aulus Plautius in A.D. 45.

Gladys (took name, Claudia, adopted by Emp. Claudius): daughter of Caradoc; married Rufus Pudens (aide to Plautius and son of Senator Pudens); mentioned in Romans 16:13.

Linus: son of Caradoc; invested as bishop of Rome in A.D. 66 by Paul; mentioned in II Timothy 4:21.

Cyllinus: son of Caradoc; ruled Cambria from A.D. 52 during Caradoc's incarceration in Rome.

Cynon: son of Caradoc.

Coel (King Cole): son of Cyllinus; first king of all Britain.

Helen (Helena): daughter of Coel; married Constantius Chlorus, Roman emperor of Britain, Gaul and Spain.

Constantine: son of Helena and Constantius; first Christian Roman Emperor.

Selected Bibliography and Sources Consulted

I. Relevant Apocrypha

Account of Joseph of Arimathea
Acts of Pastor and Timotheus (by Hermas of Rome)
Acts of Pilate
Acts of Thaddaeus
Acts of Thomas
Coptic Narratives
Descent into Hell
Dialogue of the Savior
Doctrine of Addai
Gospel of Nicodemus
Gospel of Peter
Gospel of Philip
Gospel of Thomas
Letters of Christ and Abgarus
Letters of Pilate to Claudius
Narrative of Joseph of Arimathea
Narrative of Pseudo-Melito
Pistis Sophia
Protevangelium of James
Story of Joseph of Arimathea
Syriac Narratives
The Shepherd (by Hermas of Rome)

II. Collections and Evaluations of Apocrypha

R.O. Ballou, ed., *The Other Jesus,* Doubleday, N.Y., 1972.

M. Burrows, ed., *Dead Sea Scrolls,* Viking, N.Y., 1955.

R. Cameron, ed., *The Other Gospels,* Westminister Pr., Phila., 1982.

D.R. Cartlidge and D. L. Dungan, eds., *Documents for Study of the Gospels,* Fortress Press, Philadelphia, 1980.

J.H. Charlesworth, ed., *New Testament Apocrypha and Pseudepigrapha,* Scarecrow, Metuchen, 1987.

J.D. Crosson, ed., *Four Other Gospels,* Winston-Seabury, Minneapolis, 1985.

T.H. Gaster, ed., *Dead Sea Scriptures,* Doubleday/Anchor, N.Y., 1956.

Health Research, *Gospel of the Holy Twelve,* Mokelumne Hill, CA., 1974.

G. Howard, ed., *The Teaching of Addai,* Scholars Press, Chico, CA., 1981.

W. Hone, ed., *Lost Books of the Bible,* Crown Pub., N.Y., 1926, 1979.

M.R. James, ed., *Apocryphal New Testament,* Clarendon Press, Oxford, England, 1924, 1972.

J.M. Robinson, ed., *Nag Hammadi Library,* Harper & Row, N.Y., 1977.

C.T. Tischendorf, ed., *Evangelia Apocrypha,* Lipsiae, Avenarius et Mendelssohn, 1953.

III. Biblical

W. Barclay, *The Master's Men,* SCM Press, London, 1960.

C. Baronius, *Annales Ecclesiastici,* 1596.

S.G.F. Brandon, *Fall of Jerusalem and the Christian Church,* SPCK, London, 1981.

S.G.F. Brandon, *The Trial of Jesus of Nazareth,* Stein & Day, N.Y., 1979.

S.G.F. Brandon, *Jesus and the Zealots,* University Press, Manchester, England, 1967.

R.E. Brown, *Community of the Beloved Disciple,* Paulist Press, Mahwah, N. J., 1979.

R.E. Brown, *Churches the Apostles Left Behind,* Paulist, Mahwah, 1984.

R.E. Brown, *Birth of the Messiah,* Doubleday/Image, New York, 1977.

R.E. Brown and J.P. Meier, *Antioch and Rome,* Paulist, Mahwah, 1983.

J.H. Charlesworth, *Jesus Within Judaism,* Doubleday, New York, 1988.

G. Cornfeld, ed., *The Historical Jesus,* Macmillan, New York, 1982.

J.D. Douglas and M.C. Tenney, eds., *New International Dictionary of the Bible,* Zondervan, Grand Rapids, 1987.

R. Errico, *Let There Be Light* (1985), and *Treasures from the Language of Jesus* (1987), DeVorss, Marina del Rey.

Eusebius, *The History of the Church,* Penguin, Baltimore, 1965.

H. Falk, *Jesus the Pharisee,* Paulist Press, Mahwah, 1985.

R. Findlay, *Turn Again,* CFPSS, London, 1979.

J. Finegan, *Handbook of Biblical Chronology,* Princeton Univ. Press, Princeton, 1964.

J. Gaer, *Lore of the New Testament,* Little-Brown, Boston, 1952.

R.M. Grant, *A Historical Introduction to the New Testament,* Collins, London, 1963.

G.R. Habermas, *Ancient Evidence for the Life of Jesus,* Nelson, N.Y., 1984.

H.W. Hoehner, *Chronological Aspects of the Life of Christ,* Zondervan., Grand Rapids, 1977.

F.G. Holweck, ed., *A Biographical Dictionary of the Saints,* Gale Research, Detroit, 1969.

A. Jones, ed., *Jerusalem Bible* (editorial notes), Doubleday, N.Y., 1966.

H. Koester, *History and Literature of Early Christianity*, Vol. 2, Fortress, Philadelphia, 1982.

D.I. Lanslots, *The Primitive Church,* Tan Books, Rockford, Ill., 1926/80.

P.L. Maier, *First Christmas,* Harper & Row, N.Y., 1971.

P. L. Maier, *First Easter,* Harper & Row, N.Y., 1973.

W. S. McBirnie, *Search for the Twelve* Apostles, Tyndale, Wheaton, 1983.

A. Roberts and J. Donaldson, eds., *Ante-Nicene Fathers* (Writings of), Vol. VIII, Eerdmans, Grand Rapids, 1951.

J.A.T. Robinson, *The Priority of John.* Meyer-Stone, Oak Park, Ill. 1985.

J.A.T. Robinson, *Redating the New Testament,* Westminister Press, Philadelphia, 1976.

L. Roddy and C. E. Sellier, Jr., *In Search of Historic Jesus,* Bantam, N.Y., 1979.

C. B. Ruffin, *The Twelve,* Our Sunday Visitor, Huntington, Ind., 1984.

R. Schnackenburg, *The Gospel According to St. John,* Vol. 3, Crossroad, N.Y., 1982.

L.D. Weatherhead, *The Manner of the Resurrection,* Abingdon, N.Y., 1969.

IV. SHROUD OF JESUS AND EDESSA

P. Barbet, *A Doctor at Calvary,* Doubleday/Image, N.Y., 1950, 1963.

N. Currer-Briggs, *The Shroud and the Grail,* Weidenfeld & Nicholson, London, 1987.

P. Jennings, ed., *Face to Face with the Turin Shroud,* Mahew-McCrimmon, London, 1978.

J. Marino, *Jewish Burial Customs,* St. Louis Priory, St. Louis, 1987.

R. Morgan, *Holy Shroud and Earliest Paintings of Christ,* Runciman Press, Manly, N.S.W., Australia, 1986.

G. Ricci, *The Holy Shroud,* Roman Center for Shroud Studies, 1981.

J.B. Segal, Edessa, *The Blessed City,* Clarendon Pr., Oxford, 1970.

J.B. Segal, *Edessa and Harran,* Univ. of London Press, 1963.

K.E. Stevenson and G.R. Habermas, *Verdict on the* Shroud, Servant Publications, Ann Arbor, 1981.

F.C. Tribbe, *Portrait of Jesus?* Stein & Day, 1983.

I. Wilson, *The Shroud of Turin,* Doubleday, N.Y., 1978.

V. ENGLAND

G. Ashe, *Avalonian Quest,* Methuen, London, 1982.

E.R. Capt, *Traditions of Glastonbury,* Artisan, Thousand Oak, CA, 1983.

E. R. Capt, ed., *The Sonnini Manuscript,* Artisan Sales, Thousand Oaks, Calif.

E.R. Capt, *King Solomon's Temple,* Artisan Sales, Thousand Oaks, CA., 1979.

E.R. Capt, *Missing Links Discovered in Assyrian Tablets,* Artisan Sales, Thousand Oaks, Calif., 1985.

J.P. Carley, ed., *Chronicle of Glastonbury Abbey,* Boydell Press, Woodbridge, England, 1985.

H.H. Carter, ed., *Portuguese Book of Joseph of Arimathea,* Univ. of North Carolina Press, Chapel Hill, N.C., 1967.

B. & J. Coles, *Sweet Track to Glastonbury,* Thames & Hudson, London, 1986.

R.G. Collingwood and J.M.L. Myres, *Roman Britain and the English Settlements,,* Oxford Univ. Press, 1937.

P. E. Corbett, *Why Britain?* RJ Press, Newbury, England, 1984.

G. Cornfeld, ed., *The Historic Jesus,* Macmillan, N.Y., 1982.

H.P. deCressy, *Church History of Brittany,* 16th c.

C.C. Dobson, *Did Our Lord Visit Britain As They Say in Cornwall and Somerset,* Avalon Press, Glastonbury, 1949.

D.R. Dudley and G. Webster, eds., *Roman Conquest of Britain,* Dufour Editions, Chester Springs, Penna., 1965.

I.H. Elder, *Joseph of Arimathea,* Real Israel Press, Glastonbury, 1982.

I. H. Elder, *Cult, Druid and Culdee,* Covenant Pubs., London, 1973.

M.G. Finlay, *Joseph of Arimathea and the Grail,* Columbia Univ., N.Y., 1950.

S. Frere, *Britannia—History of Roman Britain,* Harvard Univ. Press, Cambridge, Mass., 1967.

P.S. Fry, *Roman Britain,* David & Charles, London, 1984.

Guide to Glastonbury, Isle of Avalon, Avalon Press, Glastonbury, 1954.

R. Gibbs, *The Legendary XII Hides of Glastonbury,* Llanerch Ent., Felinfach, Wales, 1988.

N.L. Goodrich, *King Arthur,* F. Watts, New York, 1986.

G.F. Jowett, *Drama of the Lost Disciples,* Covenant Pub., London, 1975.

L.S. Lewis, *St. Joseph of Arimathea at Glastonbury,* J. Clarke, Cambridge, England, 1922, 1982.

R.W. Morgan, *St. Paul in Britain,* Covenant Pubs., London, 1960, 1980.

J.A. Robinson, *On the Antiquity of Glastonbury,* Oxford U. Pr., 1921.

J.A. Robinson, *Two Glastonbury Legends,* Cambridge Univ. Press, 1926.

O.L. Reiser, *This Holyest Erthe,* Perennial Books, London, 1974.

H.H. Scullard, *Roman Britain,* Thames & Hudson, London, 1979.

J. Sharkey, *Celtic Mysteries,* Avon, New York, 1975.

H.W. Stough, *Dedicated Disciples,* Artisan, Thousand Oaks, Calif. 1987.

G. Taylor, *The Early Church,* Covenant Pub., London, 1987.

G. Taylor, *The Hidden Centuries,* Covenant, London, 1969.

J.W. Taylor, *The Coming of the Saints,* Methuen, London, 1923.

R.F. Treharne, *The Glastonbury Legends,* Sphere/Abacus, London, 1967/75.

A. Watkin, *Story of Glastonbury,* Catholic Truth Soc., Bristol, Eng., 1982.

G. Webster, *Rome Against Caractacus,* Dorset Press, N.Y., 1985.

VI. GENERAL BACKGROUND

M. Avi-Yonah, *Holy Land from Persian to Arab Conquest,* Baker, Gr. Rapids, 1977.

E.J. Bickerman, *The Jews in the Greek Age,* Harvard Univ. Press, 1988.

F.F. Bruce, ed., *Jesus and Paul—Places They Knew,* Ark Pub., London, 1981

A. Butler, ed., *Lives of the Saints,* Christian Classics, Westminister, Maryland, 1956.

L. Casson, *Ships and Seamanship in the Ancient World,* Princeton Univ. Press, Princeton, 1971.

Columbia Encyclopedia, Third Edition, Columbia Univ. Press, N.Y., 1963.

Dictionary of National Biography, Vol. III, Oxford U. Pr., Oxford, 1917.

D. DuMaurier, *Vanishing Cornwall,* Penguin , Middlesex, England, 1984.

Everyday Life in Bible Times, National Geographic Society, Washington, D.C., 1967.

I.M. Franck and D.M. Brownstone, *To the Ends of the Earth: The Great Travel Routes of Human History,* Facts on File Publications, New York, 1984.

Harper's Bible Commentary, Harper & Row, New York, 1988.

W.H. MacLeish, *The Gulf Stream: Encounters with the Blue God,* Houghton Mifflin, Boston, 1989.

M. Maedagen, *City of Constantinople,* Praeger, New York, 1968.

P.L. Maier, *Josephus—The Essential Writings,* Kregel, Gr. Rapids, 1988.

Packer/Tenney/White, *The World of the New Testament,* Nelson, N.Y., 1982.

R.D. Penhallurick, *Tin in Antiquity,* Inst. of Metals, London, 1986.

L. Stephen and S. Lee, eds., *Dictionary of National Biography,* Vol. III, Oxford University Press, 1917, 1973.

Suetonius, *Lives of the Twelve Caesars,* Modern Library, N.Y., 1931.

Tacitus, *Complete Works of Tacitus,* Random House, N.Y., 1942.

H.T. Thurston, ed., *Lives of the Saints,* Kennedy Pubs., N.Y., 1931.

B. Tuchman, *Bible and Sword,* N.Y.U. Press, 1956; Ballantine, 1984.

Y. Yadin, *Tefillin from Qumran,* Hebrew University, Jerusalem, 1969.

VII. FROM PERIODICALS

N. Avigad, V. Tzaferis and N. Haas, "Excavations in Jerusalem, 1969/70," *Israel Exploration Journal,* 20/1 & 21 1970.

R.E. Brown, "The Burial of Jesus (Mark 15:42-47)," pp. 235-245, *Catholic Biblical Quarterly,* Vol. 50, April 1988.

R. Bucklin, "Medical Aspects of the Crucifixion," *Linacre Quarterly,* London, February 1958.

L. Cooper, "The Old French Life of St. Alexis and the Shroud of Turin," pp. 1 17, *Modern Philology,* August 1986.

F. L. Filas, "The Dating of the Shroud from Coins of Pontius Pilate," Loyola University (occasional papers), Chicago, 1980.

V.P. Furnish, "Corinth in Paul's Time—What Can Archaeology Tell Us?" *Biblical Archaeology Review,* XV-3, May/June 1988.

N. Glueck, "Ezion-geber," pp. 70-87, *Biblical Archaeologist,* Vol. XXVIII, 3, 1965.

T.A.D. Lawton, "A Buried Treasure in the Gospels—Joseph of Arimathea," pp. 93-101, *The Evangelical Quarterly* (Br.), 39/2, Apr/Jun 1967.

E. Netzer, "Jewish Rebels Dig Strategic Tunnel System," *Biblical Archaeology Review,* XV-4, Jul/Aug 1988.

E.L. Nitowski, "The Tomb of Christ from Archaeological Sources," *Shroud Spectrum International,* No. 17, 1985.

J.M. O'Connor, "On the Road and on the Sea with St. Paul," pp. 38-47, *Bible Review,* Summer 1985, Washington, D.C.

B. Rothenberg, "Ancient Copper Industries in the Western Arabah," pp. 5-71, *Palestine Exploration Quarterly,* Jan/Jun 1962.

v.J. Schreiber, "Die Bestattung Jesu durch Josef von Arimathea," pp. 141-177; von Dieter Luhrmann, "Fragments of an Apocryphal Gospel re Joseph of Arimathea," pp. 216-226: *Zeitschrift fur die Neutestamentliche Wissenschaft,* 72 Band 1981, Heft 3/4.

M. Scrogin, "Jesus a Feminist?" *Messenger,* February 1979.

J.S. Setzer, "Did Lazarus Write the Gospel of John?" *Spiritual Frontiers,* XII-1, 1980.

H. Shanks, "Nelson Glueck and King Solomon," pp. 1-16, *Biblical Archaeology Review,* 1/1, March 1975.

H. Thurston, "The English Legend of St. Joseph of Arimathea," pp. 43-54, *Month Magazine* (Br.), July 1931.

F.C. Tribbe, "Enigmas of the Shroud of Turin," pp. 39-49, SINDON No. 33, Dec. 1984, Centro Internazionalle della Sindone, Turin.

F.C. Tribbe, "The Shroud of Turin, Mystical Visions and Retrocognition," pp. 43-51, SINDON No. 34, December 1985, Centro Internazionalle della Sindone, Turin, Italy.

F.C. Tribbe, "Glastonbury—Christianity's Stepping-Stone to Rome?" *Glastonbury Treasures,* Stonehenge Viewpoint, 1989, Santa Barbara, California.

F.C. Tribbe, "Has Science Judged the Shroud of Turin to Be a Fake?" *Journal of Religion and Psychical Research,* XI-2, April 1989.

A. Wall, "Calendar of Coligny of the Celts," pp. 3-14, *Horus Magazine,* III-1, Winter 1987.

FRANK C. TRIBBE is an attorney, retired from U.S. Government service, living in the Shenandoah Valley of Virginia, where he is writer, editor and lecturer on the subjects of consciousness, spirituality, Bible research, the paranormal, the Shroud of Turin, and the Holy Grail. Since 1976 he has been Editor of *Spiritual Frontiers,* the journal of Spiritual Frontiers Fellowship. He is author of *Creative Meditation* (1975), *Portrait of Jesus?* (1983), and *Denny and the Mysterious Shroud* (1998). He was the reviser/editor of *The Ashby Guidebook for Study of the Paranormal* (1986), editor of *Speculations on the Nature of God* (1986) and *An Echo in Search of a Mountain* (1995), and compiler/editor of *An Arthur Ford Anthology* (1998). He has contributed chapters to 14 anthologies, and has written scores of articles and reviews for periodicals worldwide.

Watch for two sequels to Joseph's account:

I, Linus, Bishop of Rome

Linus was consecrated as first Bishop of Rome by Saint Paul, shortly after the death of Saint Peter.

I, Aggai X: The Story of the Face of Edessa

Aggai was Keeper of the King's Treasury when the "Face" was "found" in A.D. 525, after being "lost" for 468 years. With the enthusiastic support of Emperor Justinian, copies of the Face were made and placed on display at numerous churches and Christian shrines of the Roman Empire, including three in Saint Catherine's Monastery, Sinai.